# False GOD

C.W. FARNSWORTH

# The Kensingtons

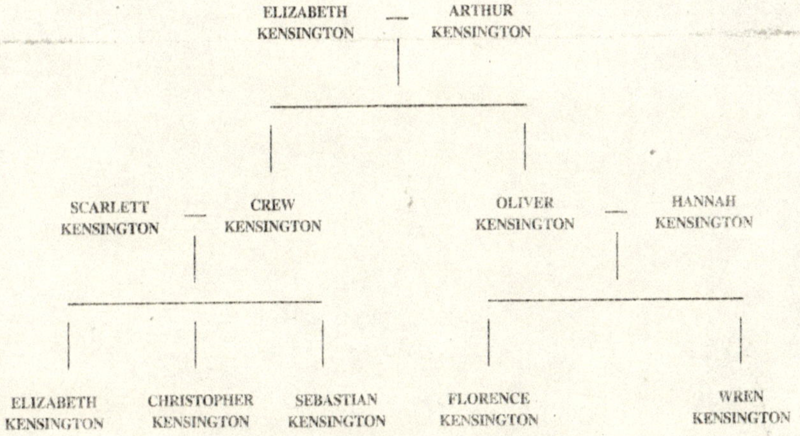

# Playlist

**National Anthem** | Lana del Ray

**England** | The National

**so american** | Olivia Rodrigo

**you should see me in a crown** | Billie Eilish

**Dancing in the Moonlight** | King Harvest

**Accidentally in Love** | Counting Crows

**This Year's Love** | David Gray

**The Bolter** | Taylor Swift

**Viva la Vida** | Coldplay

**Kings & Queens** | Ava Max

**Big Jet Plane** | Angus & Julia Stone

**Supercut** | Lorde

# CHAPTER 1

## Lili

"**B**eautiful."

The low voice is unfamiliar—syllables crisp rather than drawled—but the sentiment is identical to the one I've been hearing all afternoon. A few *stunning*s, a couple of *gorgeous*es, and one *hot as fuck*—from my friend Daphne—but most men stuck with the same compliment.

I suck in a deep breath of air that tastes like rich leather and sweet hay, hoping to inhale some patience along with the oxygen expanding my lungs.

"I'm flattered," I say, continuing to gently stroke Lexington's neck.

Five minutes. I wanted *five minutes* away from the attention. It wasn't supposed to follow me into the barn. But I should really know better after twenty-four years of being a Kensington.

When you're born into one of the richest families in the world,

attention follows you *everywhere*. Never-ending interest is as inescapable as your own shadow.

"I was referring to the horse," is the droll reply.

That answer, paired with the realization that the precise enunciation I heard was with a British accent, is enough to make my hand slow. I pet Lexington ten more times, counting each stroke, then glance to the left.

"The horse is a gelding," I inform the stranger who's appeared beside me.

The eyebrow I can see curves into a textbook display of polite disagreement. An indulgent, silent, exaggerated, *So?*

There's an answering tug of intrigue low in my stomach.

"Males can't be beautiful?" he asks.

*You are*, is my first absurd and annoying thought.

His gaze is on Lexington—like he's trying to emphasize how vapid I am; how, obviously, his attention is focused elsewhere—so my eyes unashamedly linger on the limited view his profile offers.

He's tall—well over six feet. Taller than me by several inches, even including the added height from the impractically high stilettos I'm wearing in a barn.

I try not to look past his height. But other details trickle in. Light-brown hair. Bone structure befitting a Greek god. Tailored navy suit.

"I thought men preferred to be called handsome," I respond.

"Based on what?" he questions. Still looking at the horse, not at me.

Annoyance from the interruption and embarrassment from the misunderstanding have faded. Now, I'm kind of … offended, I guess, that he still hasn't bothered to glance my way. Casual disregard isn't how people act around me.

"You obviously haven't complimented many men," I say.

"None with small egos, it seems."

A snort echoes along the empty concrete hallway. It takes a few seconds, the reverberation already fading, for me to realize that sound of amusement came from me.

I clear my throat, attempting to regain some composure. His tone was calm and matter-of-fact. Far from challenging. But it feels like we're weighing words and keeping score. Like he just gained a point by making me laugh, and now, I need to level the uneven tally.

"Is he yours?" the stranger asks, nodding toward the horse.

I shake my head, then remember he's *still* not looking this way.

My eyes focus on Lexington as well, and I reach out to stroke his smooth neck once more. Thick muscles ripple beneath my fingertips as the gray gelding bobs his head, appreciating the attention in the quiet barn. Most of the grooms and riders are busy with the polo match taking place.

"No."

He could've been.

"Are you playing today?"

My gaze snaps back to the stranger's carved profile as soon as the unexpected question registers.

Women don't play in the polo matches at the club. They stand on the sidelines, sipping fancy cocktails and swapping gossip about who is having affairs or hiding a drug addiction.

Societally speaking, Atlantic Crest Country Club hasn't progressed very far past 1923—the year it was established. Its members are still snobby. Also sexist.

"I'm not dressed for it," I reply, because the words *women don't play polo here* won't leave my mouth.

I've played here with my brothers and friends. But only casually, never during a formal match.

*Finally*, he looks at me.

I've been waiting for it. Anticipating the moment when our eyes would connect since the second he spoke.

And I thought reality would be underwhelming. That any allure would steadily disappear the longer I talked to him. But there's an instant reaction—the strike of a match or a flash of lightning—when our gazes collide.

I saw enough of his profile to tell that he's attractive. *Notably* attractive. His face not just symmetrical, but also striking. Features that are unforgettable, even if you tried to forget.

His blatant beauty is a poor explanation for why I'm staring at him though. It's something more than superficial.

The tug of a tide.

The attraction of a magnet.

The temptation of the unknown.

All formidable forces.

"No, you're not."

His appraisal of my outfit only lasts a few seconds. Yet, in the short time his gaze dips down, it manages to touch every inch of my skin. Heat floods my cheeks and spreads, producing warmth the industrial fans spinning overhead can't combat.

There's nothing in his expression that conveys what he thinks of my blue dress beyond him agreeing it's inappropriate riding attire. It's brand-new, a design of Mom's that won't be released until next year. A waterfall of indigo that looks pretty damn good on me, according to the mirror in my grandparents' guest room and to everyone else I've talked to today.

"I'm Charlie." He holds a hand out, the formal gesture and his fancy accent a strange contrast to the casual tone and lack of a last name.

The waiting list for a membership at Atlantic Crest stretches decades. The Hamptons' most exclusive country club caters to the rich and powerful. To step foot on this property, you have to be well connected, meaning it's rare to see an unfamiliar face.

Maybe that's why I'm still staring.

I bite the inside of my cheek once, trying to collect my wandering thoughts.

"I'm Lili."

My last name usually gets mentioned when I meet strangers.

And most people don't hide envy or awe well—two common receptions to hearing *Kensington.*

But I can't tell if Charlie knows who I am—what he thinks of me *at all*—and it's a cheap thrill. A small mystery in the sea of flattery I've been drowning in all afternoon.

"Lili," he repeats.

My childhood nickname sounds much more sophisticated when spoken with a British accent. I could listen to Charlie read a cookbook and find it enthralling.

I nod once, simply for something to do that's not fidgeting with my bracelets or playing with my hair. Now that he's looking at me—*staring* really—I'm starting to wish he were still focused on Lexington. Charlie's undivided attention is the equivalent of standing solo under a spotlight.

"Pretty name," he adds.

"Wait until you hear the horse's," is out of my mouth before I can decide if that's something I should actually say out loud.

I'd like Charlie to forget I interpreted his compliment as meant for me, not remind him about it.

Victory replaces regret when my glib comment coaxes a small smile out of his neutral expression. Based on the few minutes I've known him, Charlie doesn't express much amusement easily. It's the first smile he's shared with me.

His palm is still extended toward me, waiting.

I reach for it slowly, nervous about a simple handshake for some ridiculous reason. There's a foreign flap of butterflies near where the tug appeared—another silent, strange response that makes me worry my palms might be sweating because of something other than today's tropical heat.

His hand eclipses mine easily, the skin warm and calloused. Capable.

"Lexington is not what I'd name a horse," he tells me.

"How do you know his name?"

As soon as I voice the question, it occurs to me he's probably a friend of Cal's. The realization that he might know my ex is more disappointing than it should be. It ruins the reverie of us being complete strangers.

Charlie tilts his head to the left, his eyes remaining on mine the whole time. They're a unique combination of hazel, the brown a smaller circle in the iris, almost swallowed by the surrounding green. "It's on the stall door."

"Oh." I force a laugh, hoping the mixture of embarrassment and relief sounds less awkward to him than it does to me. "Right."

We're still holding hands. In a business sense, *not* a romantic one. But it feels oddly intimate. Not professional at all.

My phone rings.

I startle at the sudden sound, shocked that Charlie distracted me thoroughly enough to forget this call was the whole reason I'd left the tent and stopped to pet the Winstons' polo pony.

"I should, uh, take this."

"Of course." His hand releases mine. "Nice to meet you, Lili."

Charlie is in motion before I can muster a response, continuing down the stable aisle, then turning right. Disappearing as quickly as he appeared.

I give Lexington one final pat before continuing in the opposite direction, pulling my phone out of my purse and answering Chloe Beaumont's call with a cheery "Hi!"

"You're in the Hamptons?" my best friend asks, not bothering with a traditional greeting.

We set up these weekly calls when Chloe moved to London two years ago to keep in touch despite the distance. Although we haven't missed a single one, they're often short. And after two decades of friendship, we bypassed small talk a long time ago.

"Stalking is illegal, you know."

Chloe laughs, and it's an immediate hit of nostalgia. "I was checking Theo's location. Just happened to see yours."

"Was he at The Black Dog?"

She laughs again, then sighs. "Worse. Work."

"You're the one who agreed to marry a lawyer."

"*Barrister*, Lili. Did you avoid Atlantic Crest?"

I carefully sidestep a pile of abandoned leg wraps in the aisle. "I'm in the polo barn."

Chloe groans, sharing the same low opinion about the stiff snobbishness of this place. "*Why?*"

I sigh. "Grandfather."

My parents own a house on Meadow Lane, but I hardly ever stay there. Whenever we're in the Hamptons, my grandparents insist on hosting us at their estate. And my grandfather always manages to include at least one trip to Atlantic Crest during these visits.

Kit and Bash delayed their arrival date until tomorrow—a decision I plan to cuss my brothers out for when they do finally show up. They know I hate coming to the club.

I wasn't a fan of this place when Cal and I were dating, but it's even less appealing since we broke up. At least I know he's not here today, or Lexington would be out on the field instead of standing in his stall.

"Did you have a paloma? How many marriage proposals …" Chloe's voice trails awkwardly, followed by a cough that our friendship of twenty years tells me is fake.

"They're overdoing it on the grapefruit juice this year," I tell her. "It's a true travesty."

She huffs a laugh. "I'm trying to be sensitive, Lili."

"Don't be. I'm fine."

A pause.

"Is Cal there?"

"No. Even if he were, I'd still be fine. And stop avoiding talking about marriage around me. He never proposed."

Another pause.

"He would have."

I know Chloe's right, so I don't bother arguing.

"How's engaged life?" I ask instead.

Another pause as Chloe attempts to gauge my true feelings about the topic from over three thousand miles away.

"Wow. That bad?" I tease.

"*No.* It's good." I can hear the smile in her voice as she adds, "It's really good."

A pang hits right in the center of my chest. Not the excited thrill I felt around Charlie. A what-if. A second-guess. A wondering if I chose wrong.

"Good."

Chloe moved to England to attend the London Academy of Music and Dramatic Art. Her program ended in the spring, but she's staying in London with her new fiancé, Theo. Their wedding is set for next July.

Honestly, I'm more bummed about Chloe's temporary relocation becoming a permanent move than I am about recovering from a breakup while she's celebrating her engagement.

"How is the Davis project going?" Chloe asks.

"It's fine. I'll send some photos of the topiary. And before you ask, no, I still haven't seen Christian. Katie said that he's away on location for a new film."

"What film?" Chloe questions eagerly. "The new Martinez action thriller?"

Ever since Chloe learned that the wife of one of her favorite Hollywood actors had hired me to redesign the grounds of their mansion in Montecito, she's been badgering me for more details. The only reason I took the project in the first place was that relocating for a few months sounded like a good idea after ending a two-year relationship. A chance to recalibrate and refresh. To swap bustle and blacktop for sprawl and sunshine. Aunt Hannah's brother, Eddie, taught me how to surf, and I had weekly dinners with my parents. All great distractions, until I returned to New York.

"I don't know. I didn't ask."

Chloe groans in exasperation.

She's so dramatic. Theater is definitely her calling.

"What were you going to do?" I ask. "Show up on set in a trench coat? He's married. You're engaged."

"It's about *feeding the fantasy*, Lili. Remember crushes? A vivid imagination is healthy. Just because it's unlikely I'll ever meet Christian Davis doesn't mean I can't think about touching his abs between takes in Belarus—or wherever the hell he's shooting."

I laugh, shaking my head even though she can't see me. "If it comes up again, I'll ask, okay?"

"*Thank you.*"

We're both silent, our standard few minutes of chitchat almost up. It's dinnertime there. And I've stood in the polo tent most of the afternoon. I should go find my grandfather and hopefully talk him into heading home.

Instead of saying I'll talk to her next week, I blurt, "I met a guy."

"What?" All the dreaminess from discussing her celebrity crush has disappeared from Chloe's voice. She sounds alert. Annoyed. "*How* did you not lead with that, Lili?"

"It wasn't a big deal." I already feel foolish for bringing it up. But a little giddy, too, my palm still tingling from touching Charlie's. "We only talked for a couple of minutes."

"You saying you met a guy is a *huge* deal. Who is he?"

"I don't know really. I'd never seen him before."

"You'd *never* seen him before?" Surprise saturates Chloe's tone. She's as familiar with the recurring guest list at these sorts of events as I am. I don't think Atlantic Crest has admitted any new members since the '90s.

"Never," I confirm.

"Huh. What's his name?"

"Charlie."

"Charlie …"

"I don't know his last name."

"Is he hot?" Chloe's question is tentative.

It's been a long time since we discussed a guy who wasn't Cal. I'm sure it's as weird for her as it is for me.

"No, he's balding and middle-aged," I drawl. "Yes, he's hot!"

*Hot* is a bland adjective to describe Charlie though. It doesn't account for how hard it was for me to think when he was looking at me. For his overwhelming presence and overbearing attitude.

And I'm not an easy person to impress. I've met presidents. Movie stars. Famous athletes.

"What does he look like?" Chloe asks.

I reach the end of the stable's stone aisle, staring out at the fairway of the golf course. Lush green stretches as far as the eye can see, chlorophyll brilliant and bright, thanks to the scorching sun.

"Brown hair. Hazel eyes. He's really tall."

"He does sound hot," Chloe agrees.

*He looks nothing like Cal*, is what I'm sure she's thinking.

Cal is a golden boy in every sense of the phrase. Tan skin. Blond hair. Blue eyes. Like a surfer who just happened to grow up on the Upper East Side.

"Go talk to him again," Chloe suggests.

"Yeah?"

It sounds like Chloe exhales before saying, "Yeah."

"Okay." I sigh too. "Thanks."

"Text me after, tell me how it goes."

I half smile, appreciating the support more than the nudge. Now, I'll have to talk to him or else text her *Nothing happened*. Chloe knows I'm too competitive to admit that kind of defeat.

"I will. Love you, Chlo."

"Love you too. Drink a paloma for me."

My smile turns into a full one before I hang up, staring out at the mowed expanse before me.

It's so open. So empty, aside from the distant dots of a golfer or caddie.

Endless possibilities.

The sketch forms in my mind as I locate the perfect spot for a trio of fountains, surrounded by a maze of walkways. Trellises and a central path, lined with oak trees and lavender.

If that garden actually existed, I wouldn't dread coming here so much. I'd add a couple of benches and visit just to listen to birds chirp and horses neigh. A little oasis, so different from the constant activity of the city. There's nowhere you can go in Manhattan and hear silence.

I enjoy the quiet for a few more minutes, then turn and head back toward the tent.

# CHAPTER 2
## Charlie

Ellis spots me about five seconds after I step into the lobby. The chilled air is an immediate relief from the August heat outside. Today's temperature is high, even by summer's standards. And made more stifling by the attention that's followed me around ever since I arrived an hour ago. Scrutiny that doubled as soon as I opened my mouth and confirmed I'm a foreigner.

My cousin herds me into one corner, past the grand piano and to the left of one of the stone archways. Both eyebrows lift in a silent question that he voices a couple of seconds later. "Where'd you go?"

"Took a walk."

"You missed meeting the Howards. And Violet DuPont. She's the redhead I was telling you about earlier."

I nod, barely listening to Ellis. I'm too busy scanning the small groups gathered in the mahogany-paneled lobby for a head of dark hair and a blue dress. It's more crowded in here than it was when I

left, likely because the polo match just ended.

"Ava Wilson practically *swooned* when I told her you're a duke." Ellis grins.

If you ask my cousin, aristocracy is one big joke. He'd probably set a new record for getting thrown out of the royal box at Wimbledon.

I exhale, my sweep of the room complete and no sign of Lili. It's probably for the best. I'm acting like my pussy-obsessed twenty-one-year-old cousin. Like a former version of myself I can no longer afford to be.

Ellis sees my new title as amusing and maybe attractive. He grew up in the States. He has no clue what weight comes along with the history and privileges of being the eighth Duke of Manchester. No idea that losing my father was equivalent to having the bottom of my life fall out and that subsequently learning the truth about my family's finances was like being spun around in endless circles and then told to walk straight.

It's bloody exhausting—the crushing responsibility and the mounting stress. I'm beginning to better understand why my father attempted to drink himself to death rather than deal with any of it.

A grim smile twists my lips. At least my—dark—sense of humor is intact.

Ellis is oblivious. Grinning at me expectantly, waiting for me to comment on a woman I remember nothing about.

My cousin misinterpreted me asking him to introduce me around my stepfather Derek's fancy country club as my needing assistance with finding a female to shag.

"I don't care," I state.

His smile doesn't dim. "They'll both be back—I guarantee it. I had no idea the whole duke thing would be such a hit. One hell of a pickup line, seriously. Is there a title for a duke's cousin? Like squire or something? Think I've heard that one before. Maybe I could use that."

I sigh, glancing around for investor prospects.

"Oh! Some guys I golf with said that Elizabeth Kensington is here. I've been trying to—"

I've had enough of Ellis's commentary. "I'm not here to stroke the ego of a vapid heiress who has nothing to do except wonder about how much of daddy's money she can spend today. You said *important* people would be here, Ellis. That's the only reason I came."

God, do I sound bloody bitter.

I'm learning the hard way it's a lot more difficult to have had something and lost it than to have never experienced it. I wish I could go back in time and be ignorant again. Or jump ahead to some solution. Not be stuck in this purgatory of not knowing what the next fucking move should be. Of having nothing except an empty title, plus an aging grandmother and a younger sister relying on me to fix everything.

I couldn't have bought my entry today. The only reason I made it past the guarded gate of Atlantic Crest Country Club was because my mother married a man twice her age, five times as wealthy, and far too kindhearted for her lecherous tendencies. He's allowed my aunt and her two grown kids—Joanna and Ellis—to live in his Hamptons home since May.

Ellis appears unfazed by my irritated outburst, taking another swig from the glass he's holding as he surveys the crowded room.

He has no clue how precarious of a position I'm in. I doubt he'd care, even if he did know about the massive pile of debt my father left behind. His life is unaffected by my father's decisions, and my mother's recent choices allow him to golf and flirt all day.

"You sound like you really need a drink, man," Ellis tells me, then takes another sip.

I do. But this isn't the time or place.

"What I *need* is for you to introduce me around to some *men* I can make *business connections* with." I enunciate all the important words, hoping it'll finally get through to him. "I don't need or want your help getting laid."

Ellis heaves a sigh. I have no idea what *he's* irritated about. "Yeah, yeah. Come on."

He leads me toward a middle-aged man standing next to an oil painting of a majestic stallion. The man is typing on his phone. Unless he's texting a mistress, his lack of attention is promising. Businessmen who are more focused on checking emails than enjoying the drinks and appetizers being circulated around are the type of investors I'm looking for. Ones who study balance sheets and business plans rather than anatomy and pathology.

"Mr. Cushing!" Ellis calls out as we approach.

The man glances up from his device, recognition evident in his expression as soon as he spots Ellis.

At least Ellis wasn't exaggerating about how well connected he is here. Since his mother moved their family into Derek's summer place, Atlantic Crest Country Club is where he's spent most of his time in the Hamptons.

I paste a polite smile on my face as Ellis introduces me to John Cushing, who owns a technology software company. I barely understand half of what he explains about his business, but that isn't the point. Moguls of more than a dozen industries are in this room. Introductions to Americans with deep pockets and important connections can only benefit me, the broke Englishman. I have to start somewhere.

So, I make obligatory small talk. Listen to Mr. Cushing's explanation of nanotechnology until a brisk, "John, good to see you," interrupts.

Conversation halts as a silver-haired man approaches. Not just ours, but the chatter of several surrounding groups fades as their attention swings this way.

The older man is walking with a cane. It thumps almost ominously as he nears, the steady thud of the varnished wooden stick against gleaming floorboards audible over the soft music trickling out of the piano in the corner.

"Hello, Hanson," John replies. I see his shoulders straighten.

Next to me, Ellis's posture also noticeably improves. "Good afternoon, Mr. Ellsworth."

Since we arrived, Ellis has treated everyone he introduced me to with the same friendly politeness. Excluding the women he flirted with shamelessly. He's looking at the man in front of us with a respect that's new.

Mr. Ellsworth studies my cousin for a few seconds. "Ellis, is it?"

Ellis inflates with importance. "Yes, sir."

The man's attention lands on me next. He holds out a hand. "Hello. I'm Hanson Ellsworth."

"Charles Marlborough," I respond, shaking his hand. His grip is firmer than I would have expected for a man his age.

"Charlie is my cousin. He's the Duke of Manchester."

Hanson's expression doesn't change in response to Ellis's boast. But he surprises me by saying, "I was very sorry to hear about James's passing. My condolences."

"Thank you," I reply, stiffening some. I wasn't anticipating any sympathies this far from home. "I wasn't aware you knew my father."

"Not well. Our paths crossed a few times when I was doing business in London."

Hanson doesn't elaborate any further, making me think he shares the same low opinion of James Marlborough that most people have. My father agreed with Machiavelli on fear versus love.

Hanson is still studying me, head tilted slightly, like he's an art critic assessing a painting. "What brings you to—Elizabeth!" He cuts himself off mid-sentence, his attention totally focused on something—someone—behind me.

I resist the urge to look over my shoulder at who caught his interest.

"Hi, Grandfather."

A woman nears our circle. And with a start, I realize I recognize her.

It's Lili, the one person I genuinely enjoyed talking to since I arrived an hour ago. Her strides are smooth and confident in the high heels she's wearing. I thought maybe she was hiding in the barn for an escape, like I was. But she appears as effortlessly poised in the crowded lobby as she did while standing alone in the stable.

I'm not the only one watching her walk. Ellis's eyes are glued to her endless legs. Lots of heads are turned this way, many more than when Hanson interrupted.

I've never heard the name Ellsworth before, so I make a mental note to look the family up later. Tell myself it has to do with Hanson's worth as a possible investor and nothing to do with his granddaughter.

"Where have you been?" Hanson asks when Lili reaches us.

"Polo tent," she replies breezily. She glances at John. "Hello, Mr. Cushing."

"Wonderful to see you, Elizabeth." John greets her more warmly than he did Hanson, which I find interesting.

"I'm Ellis." Ellis smiles wide as he introduces himself. "We met by the tennis courts, Fourth of July weekend."

I suppress a snort.

"Nice to see you," Lili replies smoothly, giving no indication of whether or not she remembers Ellis. She glances at me last. "Who's your friend?"

At first, I think she's kidding. We met less than fifteen minutes ago, and it wasn't just an exchange of cursory pleasantries. Full sentences were shared.

But there's no sign of teasing in her neutral expression. No spark of recognition.

For a few unsure seconds, it makes me question my own sanity.

I hesitate. My options are either to remind her we *just* met and had an entire conversation—pathetic and possibly rude, depending on how I phrase it—or to follow her lead on pretending this is a first encounter.

I hold out a hand. "Charles Marlborough."

She doesn't stall the way she did before. Lili grabs my offered palm, shakes it once, then immediately relaxes her grip.

I don't let go right away, and there's a flash of some stronger emotion that erases her passivity for a few seconds. It's gone before I can determine what the change is, her hand disappearing from my hold with a quick yank. Her fingers fidget against the blue fabric of her dress as they fall to her side, like she's fighting the urge to wipe away any trace of my touch.

Lili clears her throat. "Elizabeth Kensington."

Kensington.

She's a *Kensington*. Her first name isn't Lili, and her last name isn't Ellsworth. She's Elizabeth Kensington—the woman Ellis was talking about earlier. Part of the famous American family with a net worth so staggering that no one is sure what the exact number is. Lots of zeroes that add up to hundreds of billions. Name an industry and they own stock in it.

"Nice to meet you," I manage to say through my shock.

Lili nods once, then glances at her grandfather. "I'll be in the car."

"I'll be right there, darling," Hanson responds.

Lili heads for the imposing double doors that mark the main entrance, pausing briefly to say something to a blonde woman before continuing outside.

"Family comes first, gentlemen," Hanson says before beckoning a uniformed employee over and murmuring something that has the man nodding. "Enjoy the rest of your afternoon."

He strolls away without a more formal farewell, which appears to be a family trait.

Hanson's abrupt dismissal bothers me a hell of a lot less than Elizabeth Kensington's did.

# CHAPTER 3
## *Charlie*



The skyscraper that houses Kensington Consolidated's corporate headquarters is massive. From my vantage point on the sidewalk, it appears to be a physical embodiment of its name, flat roof brushing against the bottom of gray clouds that hover angry and dark overhead. Thunder rumbles ominously in the distance.

Lack of sunlight does little to temper today's heat. The beginning of July doesn't suggest any end to the heat in sight. The summer air is humid and sticky, more dampness soaking the starched layers of my suit, the longer I stand on the sidewalk.

I don't *want* to walk inside.

I'm too proud. Too similar to my father.

I'm also rapidly running out of other options. Selling off a couple

of smaller properties and making minimum payments were enough to limp through this past year without filing for bankruptcy. But not a long-term solution. Interest is continuing to pile up. Off-loading a few assets didn't draw much attention, but selling more will create speculation.

No one except me, my grandmother, and my father's barristers know about the disastrous state of the family's finances.

No one's started asking questions. Yet.

A steady drizzle starts to fall, followed by a loud clap of thunder that suggests the storm is just beginning. If I don't move soon, I'll walk inside soaked.

I don't care. The stormy weather is oddly soothing. It reminds me of home. Reminds me why I'm here.

*Fuck you, James.*

The angry words echo in my head for a minute. I never called him anything except Papa to his face. Using his Christian name creates a little distance—space that feels necessary right now.

My relationship with my father was complicated while he was alive.

Following his death, it's never been worse.

I'm so *furious* with him, wondering how he could have done this to me. To my sister Blythe. To Granny. Did he think he could fix it before anyone found out? Did he think getting pissed at a local pub and driving into a tree would be any sort of solution? Did he realize, when he lost control of the car, who would have to deal with the aftermath of his mistakes?

I'll never know the answers to any of those questions, and that only adds to my anger.

I square my shoulders as I head for one of the revolving doors beneath the large silver letters that spell out *Kensington Consolidated.*

For a few seconds, my mind drifts to the only Kensington I've met in person. As far as I know, Elizabeth has no involvement in her family's company. The current CEO is her uncle, Oliver Kensington.

I'm supposed to attend a polo match at Atlantic Crest Country Club tomorrow, and I can't help but wonder if Elizabeth—or Lili, as she's imprinted in my mind as—will be there again. And if she is, which version will I face—the enigmatic, intriguing stranger I met in the barn or the cool, reserved heiress who pretended not to know me?

Every time she's crossed my mind in the past year, I've told myself that bizarre transformation is the only reason she's of recurring interest. Seeing her in person again will simply solve a mystery I shouldn't have been puzzling over in the first place.

The young woman working at the front desk glances up with a prepared smile as I approach the massive block of marble she's seated behind. She brushes the bangs out of her eyes, and I read the interest there immediately. She taps a capped pen against her chin, smirking a little as my gaze dips to her tits. The silk fabric of her blouse is so snug that I can see the outline of her bra.

Maybe I'll ask for her number on my way out of here. I'm supposed to have dinner with my mum, Derek, and Ellis before we head to the Hamptons tomorrow, and I could use something to look forward to after. If last night's meal was any indication, it's going to be another awkward evening.

"Charles Marlborough here to see Asher Cotes," I tell the pretty receptionist.

"Of course, Mr. Marlborough." Her smile is still flirty, but her tone is cool and professional. "Can I please see some identification?"

I tug my leather wallet out of my pocket, extract my driving license, and slide it across the counter. My signet ring clinks against the marble, and she eyes it with interest.

"Thank you. I have your visitor's badge right here." She slides a square of plastic my way, along with my license. "Please return it on your way out."

I nod, clipping the badge to the damp lapel of my suit.

"Mr. Cotes's office is on the fifty-fifth floor."

I nod again, nerves constricting my throat and making it difficult to speak. Months of preparation for this meeting, and I'm bleeding confidence by the second.

*Fuck you, James,* I think again, then start toward the lifts.

A group of three older men steps off, one eyeing my dress shoes disdainfully. They're saturated with water, just like the rest of me, squeaking against the shiny floor. The haughtiness vanishes when he scrutinizes closer, noticing my tailored suit and expensive watch.

The shift should be reassuring; it only irritates me more.

I look like I belong here—minus my sogginess—but I don't. Everything about me is false. I'm a fraud, leveraging my title, along with the wealth and connections associated with it, to enter places I shouldn't be allowed anymore.

The ascent to the fifty-fifth floor feels like it takes an eternity even though the lift doesn't stop once. Silver doors part to reveal a more welcoming atmosphere than the sterile lobby downstairs. There's a waiting area with potted plants scattered throughout. Another female receptionist—older, closer to my mum's age— is seated beneath more metal letters that spell out *Kensington Consolidated*.

They sure do like to stamp that name all over this place.

The receptionist's gaze lifts from the computer screen to home in on the visitor's badge I'm wearing. "Good afternoon, Mr. Marlborough. Mr. Cotes is expecting you. His office is at the end of the hall—5523." She gestures to the left.

"Thank you," I tell her, impressed by the efficiency, then continue walking.

The carpeted hallway is wide, lined by large glass offices. Some doors are shut with walls frosted for privacy. Some are open with unoccupied desks and framed windows, boasting impressive views of downtown Manhattan.

This must be the executive floor. There's no sign of any cubicles. Just sleek offices, most with a private secretary stationed outside.

Asher's secretary is another attractive young woman. She glances up at the sound of my footsteps, tightening her grip on the chunky cardigan she's swaddled in. Compared to outside's temperature, it does feel like the Arctic in here.

"Mr. Marlborough, I assume?" she questions, glancing at my badge.

"Yes." My voice shares the same consistency as gravel. I clear my throat once, wishing I had some water. Between the blasting air-conditioning and my expanding nerves, my mouth feels drier than a desert.

The secretary's eyes widen when she hears the trace of my accent, but she doesn't say anything else before pressing a button on her desk. "Asher, Charles Marlborough is here."

A few seconds later, a deep voice responds. "Send him in, Indy."

Indy offers me another polite smile, then nods toward the door.

Asher's office isn't constructed from the same glass I just walked past. It's a coveted corner spot, the walls a cream-colored plaster and the dark wood door completely solid.

The brightness inside is more brilliant than I was expecting based on the office's solid exterior. Floor-to-ceiling windows span two sides, the glass entirely unblemished. If not for the rain sliding down, it'd appear invisible. Looking out is the same vertigo as standing at the edge of a cliff.

Asher Cotes is seated behind a mahogany desk. He stands when I enter his office, smiling and buttoning his jacket before approaching with a hand outstretched. "I'm Asher Cotes. Pleasure to meet you."

I shake his hand firmly, some anxiety draining away now that I'm here and close to getting this over with. "Charles Marlborough. Nice to meet you."

Asher gestures toward one of the chairs facing his desk. "Have a seat."

I sink down into the one closer to the bookcase, taking a moment to appreciate the view out the window. New York has a certain appeal, I guess.

"Can I get you anything to drink?" he asks, opening a cabinet door to reveal a shiny mini fridge. "I've got water or"—he glances at the bar cart by the bookcase—"scotch."

"Water would be splendid. Thank you."

"You got it." Asher hands me a chilled glass bottle, takes one for himself, then returns to his chair. He leans back, entirely relaxed. "What team do you support?"

"Team?" I ask blankly.

"I know you Brits take your socc—I mean, football very seriously. Was just wondering which team you support."

"Oh." I relax, too, twisting the top off the water. "Aston Villa."

Asher's enthusiastic nod tells me he knows nothing about Premier League. "I'll have to check out a game sometime."

"You should," I say, forcibly blocking out the memories I have of attending matches. Most feature my father.

He's the reason I'm a Villan—because I believed him when he told me they were the team to support. Just like I believed him when he told me the dukedom I would one day inherit was a thriving legacy.

My fingers tighten around the handle of my briefcase before I open it. There's a reason I put off this moment for as long as I could. Once I set securing an investor into motion, it'll be done. I'll be losing something I can never get back.

But if I don't let *something* go, I'll lose *everything*. And I won't be the only one.

So, I pull out the folder stuffed with packets of paper and set it on Asher's desk. "Here's the offer."

The corners of Asher's eyes crinkle as he reaches for the folder. "You're not going to ask me about the Jets?"

I give him a blank look.

He chuckles. "Never mind."

My knee wants to bounce anxiously as Asher flips through the papers. I don't have my own copy, but I don't need one. I've spent the past several weeks poring over the documents with barristers, discussing which properties and terms to offer. I have the contents memorized.

My father was one of the best-connected men in England. There was a long list of people I could have called for advice or assistance on divesting shares. But a large percentage of those are shrewd businessmen who would have had their own interests. And the others … the center of my father's inner circle? It would have killed him all over again, having his weaknesses exposed to the men he'd respected most.

I shouldn't care. I'm trying not to care. He's gone, and he'll never know what choices I've made with the limited options he left me.

I can't shake the compulsion to consider his opinion though. Habit, partially. Pride is another piece. And also … I was raised to be the eighth Duke of Manchester. Now, I *am* the eighth Duke of Manchester. Just because it happened in a different way than I'd ever anticipated doesn't mean I didn't know it was coming one day. Doesn't make the dukedom any less my responsibility.

Asher's nod is approving as he closes the folder. "Impressive pitch."

I nod back, keeping my posture relaxed. It's in my interest for Asher to consider me confident, not desperate. Experienced, not unsure. Hopefully, my father's proclivity for selling stretched truths as facts was genetic.

And it *is* a good pitch. I'm offering Kensington Consolidated forty-nine percent of two five-star hotels near Covent Garden and in Belgravia. The historic buildings are worth tens of millions of pounds each, never mind the sterling reputation of the luxury businesses that were established over a century ago. I'm asking for a fair price and offering an opportunity that's rarer than once in a generation.

Dozens of companies would beg for this offer. But I came here first because Kensington Consolidated is known as being the best. They have deep pockets and endless resources and a shockingly low number of lawsuits for its size. If I *have* to sell—which I do—they're the best option.

Asher sits up straight, setting the folder on his desk. "I'll bring this to the board. Be in touch as soon as possible."

"Sounds good." My tone is as straightforward as his.

I'm grateful to Asher for taking this meeting. My surname carries a lot of weight back home. Not so much here. And I'm relieved it wasn't an outright rejection. But also disappointed.

I knew an immediate answer was unlikely. Asher might be high up in the company, but he's not at the top. Of course there's a process that has to take place.

I'm so tired of waiting though. Each day, the weight I'm carrying feels heavier.

I follow Asher out of his office, into the hallway that's just as empty as when I arrived. Asher's secretary is talking quietly on the phone, but otherwise, it's so silent that I think I can hear the rain pattering outside.

"Holiday weekend upcoming," Asher explains, noticing my perusal. "Lots of folks already took off."

I nod, my high opinion of Asher improving even more. I don't know if he had other meetings today or if ours was the only one, but I'm impressed he was willing to come in on a day when he knew most of his colleagues—his *subordinates*—would be on vacation.

"Hopefully, you'll have a chance to get away too," I tell him.

Asher grins. "Headed to Nantucket with the family tomorrow. How about you? Any plans for the Fourth?" His smile holds for a couple of seconds, then dims. Twists into a grimace. "It's just occurring to me that might be a holiday you don't celebrate."

My chuckle is genuine. Which has been rare for the past fourteen months. "I'll be in the Hamptons."

"Oh, really? You should—" Asher cuts himself off, his attention behind me. A broad grin stretches across his face. "No way!"

I turn to see a brunette, middle-aged woman walking down the hallway toward us. She's statuesque and stunning, her dark hair pulled back in a neat chignon and her elegant dress impeccably tailored. I'm certain we've never met before, but something about her appearance strikes me as vaguely familiar.

When she reaches us, Asher picks her up and twirls her around in one of the more undignified displays I've witnessed in a professional setting.

"What are you doing here?" he exclaims. "Crew said you guys wouldn't arrive until tomorrow!"

The woman smirks, smoothing the wrinkles Asher added to her dress. "He follows my schedule."

Asher nods like that response makes total sense. Then glances at me. "Charles, this is Scarlett. Scarlett, this is Charles." He puffs his chest up with theatrical significance. "We were just discussing some important business."

"Really?" Scarlett drawls. Her voice has the teasing, exaggerated lilt of an older sibling talking to a younger one.

"Really," Asher confirms, still grinning widely.

Pieces are slowly clicking together in my mind. This must be Scarlett Kensington, also known as …

"Mom, they were out of—"

Lili stops speaking as soon as she sees me, a bottle of sparkling water clutched in one hand.

Immediately, I realize why Scarlett looked so familiar. She's an older version of the woman I met in a stable—and then a wood-paneled lobby—last summer.

The woman who's suddenly standing right in front of me.

"Whatever we're out of, ask Indy," Asher says, interrupting the silence that feels glaring but has probably only lasted a few seconds. "Or I can take a look. I was just wrapping up a meeting."

Without glancing over, I can tell he's still smiling. Emanating a friendliness that's much warmer than obligatory.

Kensington Consolidated must employ hundreds of people. Maybe thousands. Even considering Asher's prominent position in the company, I didn't expect that he knew the family personally, much less that I'd run into any Kensingtons during this short visit.

"We didn't mean to interrupt," Scarlett says.

"No interruption," Asher replies.

My gaze remains on Lili as they talk. I'm still processing her unexpected appearance. That she's suddenly … here. *Fuck.* My memory didn't do justice to how bloody gorgeous she is.

She's staring back, blue eyes sucking me in like a siren seducing a sailor lost at sea.

"… glad I could introduce you to—"

I'm still distracted, but I register enough of what Asher said to realize he's trying to introduce me to Lili as well. "We've actually—"

"Elizabeth Kensington." Lili holds a hand out, a polite smile I can't see through pinned on her face as she interrupts me with the same cool confidence I've encountered before.

Annoyance flares in response, hot and bright and stifling. I have to work hard to keep the flood of irritation off my face, not wanting to give her the satisfaction of seeing it in my expression.

Lili's fingers are cool as they wrap around mine, her nails painted an icy shade that matches her eyes, which don't drop from mine. Unflinching blue irises reveal nothing, like the calm surface of a mountain lake.

This woman must play a lot of poker. And if she doesn't, it's a missed opportunity to add to her sizable fortune. I have absolutely no idea what she's thinking. That only adds to my aggravation because I'm usually excellent at reading people.

"Nice to meet you," I grit out.

Pretty sure that was my same response the last time she reintroduced herself to me.

One of her eyebrows lifts. "And you are ..."

I'm silent.

A flash of amusement appears on her face, but it's gone from her expression before I can blink twice. I'm not sure if she's entertained by my muteness or if she's messing with me.

*Am I that bloody forgettable?*

A question I'm certain Elizabeth Kensington wouldn't have a complimentary answer to. This is the third time we've met, and she's acted like each one was a first encounter.

A wrinkle forms on her forehead, the longer I hesitate. What *she's* frustrated by, I have no clue.

"Charles Marlborough," I say, wondering if Lili is experiencing the same flash of déjà vu when I introduce myself to her ... again.

It's been almost a year. There's a good chance that she *has* forgotten that we've met before.

The possibility does nothing to improve my declining mood.

We stare at each other for a few more seconds. Lili looks away first. I shake my head once, refocusing on why I'm really here.

I turn to Asher. "Thanks again, Asher."

"Of course, Charles. We'll talk soon."

Asher and I shake hands one final time. I say a generic goodbye to the Kensingtons, avoiding looking directly at Lili. I'm irrationally irritated with her, to the point that I have no confident control over my voice. Vexed with myself, too, for not foreseeing she'd pretend not to know me after how our last conversation went. Confused why I give a shit either way.

When I turn in the visitor's badge at the desk downstairs, the only thing I say to the woman working is, "Have a good rest of your day."

# CHAPTER 4

## *Lili*

I stare after Charles Marlborough's retreating back, an unpleasant prickling sensation starting in my stomach and crawling around until the pins and needles spread to my extremities.

*What was he doing here?*

I want to kick off my heels, sprint down the hallway, corner him by the elevators, and ask. The *audacity*, to insult me and then show up at my family's company.

I haven't seen him in a year. Eleven months, to be exact, and I'm annoyed that I can be so accurate. That I even remember it was an August afternoon when we first met and that I was wearing a blue dress, and he had on a navy suit.

Gossip about Britain's youngest duke visiting the Hamptons made quick rounds around Atlantic Crest Country Club. By sunset, it'd spread about the entire peninsula, becoming the favorite topic at the cocktail party I attended with my grandparents that evening.

While I thought, *Who cares that he's a duke?*

*Everyone* cared, even though I'd thought any love affair with aristocracy ended around the start of the American Revolution.

"Lili? Lili!"

I blink rapidly, refocusing on Asher. "Sorry. I was thinking about … work."

Asher smiles, then glances at Mom. "Apple sure fell far from you and Crew," he tells her.

My gaze travels to the windows that boast an impressive view of Manhattan. If I had a dollar for every time someone compared me to my parents, I'd be … richer than I already am.

I'm not just *a* Kensington. I'm the oldest child and only daughter of Crew and Scarlett Kensington. In addition to coming from wealthy, well-connected families, my parents happen to be the most powerful, driven, and successful people I've ever met. They turned two kingdoms into a dominant empire, and that's a lot of legacy to live up to. Unless I cure cancer or broker world peace, the bar is pretty unachievable. And considering I flunked junior-year Biology and more people would categorize me as an instigator than a neutral party, neither of those achievements is likely to ever happen.

"I was asking if I could have Indy get you anything," Asher says.

"Oh, no. I'm fine, thanks." I give Asher's secretary a warm smile, which she returns, then hand Mom the glass bottle of sparkling water I just grabbed for her.

"I wanted a latte, but this is better for me anyway," Mom explains.

Asher's forehead furrows. "The machine should be—"

"What was Charles Marlborough doing here?" I blurt.

The espresso machine in the executive lounge is working fine.

But I've seen Mom chug two coffees since she and Dad landed a few hours ago, and I'm positive her flawless makeup is hiding dark circles. She needs to stop tackling marathon days like they're sprints and slow down a little.

Also, I've wanted to say that since the second I spotted Charlie. But I wasn't going to give him the satisfaction of asking in front of him, which was one of the reasons I pretended not to know him. Again.

"We were discussing an investment opportunity in London," Asher says, which essentially tells me nothing. He moves on before I can question him further—*What's the investment opportunity? Are you going to pursue it?*—entirely oblivious to my burning curiosity. "Are you ladies stopping by Oliver's office? I have a file to drop off to him."

"We are," Mom replies. "I wanted to invite him and Hannah to dinner tonight, and I was hoping you and Sophie could join us too."

Asher sighs. "We'd love to, but Millie has her agility class tonight. I told Soph we're switching back to Saturday mornings as soon as this session ends. But Beckett's been talking about it all week."

"Sounds fun," Mom says, fighting a smile.

Every time we catch up with Asher and his family, they've started some new activity. Last visit, it was pottery classes. They've since moved on to training their Shetland Sheepdog apparently.

"Oh, yeah. We're starting competitions in the fall. If any coincide while you're here on a visit, I'll let Crew know."

"Please do. And we'll miss you guys tonight, but I get it." Mom glances at me. "My kids are all too busy to come as well."

I roll my eyes. "This dinner has been planned for weeks, Mom. I was going to come over *tomorrow* night, when you were supposed to arrive. And I already rearranged my afternoon to pick you and Dad up from the airport, which Bash and Kit did *not* do."

Mom heaves a long-suffering sigh. "It doesn't get easier as they get older, Asher."

My godfather grins. "Yeah, I noticed. And you should have known that. Remember what you and Crew were like at twenty-five? Because *I* sure do."

Asher mutters something else under his breath. All I catch is *rock climbing.*

"Where is Crew, by the way?" he asks at a normal volume.

"He had to jump on a conference call," Mom answers.

"Of course he did." Asher is as familiar with my parents' workaholic tendencies as I am.

The phone next to Indy begins ringing. She answers with a polite, "Asher Cotes's office, Indy speaking. How may I help you?" She listens to the response for a minute, then hits a button on the phone and looks at Asher. "Lucas Donovan is on the line. What should I tell him?"

"Tell him I'm available," Asher decides. "I'll meet you two in Oliver's office. This shouldn't take long."

Without waiting for a response, he heads back into his office and closes the door.

I follow Mom down the carpeted hallway in what I assume is the direction of my uncle's office. I don't know the floor layout very well. The few times I've been here has always been with one or both of my parents or my grandfather.

I'm trailing after Mom aimlessly, trusting her to guide us the right way, so it takes me a few extra steps to realize she's stopped. I backtrack, glancing between Mom and the empty office she's staring at.

A few steps and a few seconds of peering at the plaque affixed next to the door tell me it reads *Christopher Kensington.*

An unpleasant combination of dread and surprise settles in my stomach. I've known Kit was going to work here for years. Assumed he would for decades. *Seeing* it is something else.

"Prime location," I comment.

You don't have to know the layout of this floor to tell that.

"This was your dad's office."

When I look over, Mom's smile is soft and sentimental. She heads inside.

After a beat of hesitation, I do too. "Corner on the executive floor. Perfect for an entry-level twenty-two-year-old employee."

"Elizabeth," she chides gently, continuing to scan around the large office.

I look, too, minus the nostalgia Mom is clearly experiencing. My dad left Kensington Consolidated when I was a toddler. My recollections of his office are all of the sleek, glass-front structure that has a prime view of the Hollywood sign. Not this space—with its paneled walls, custom bookshelves, and leather chairs.

But I can picture him here. I actually think it fits Dad better than his current office does. Maybe because he's a native New Yorker, and this office—this city—has an aura of established history I've never experienced on LA's freeways or palm tree–lined shores.

I wonder if Kit has seen this yet. He isn't supposed to start working until the end of August, so probably not.

"Looks like he'll have an assistant," I state, gesturing to the desk stationed outside.

Mom hums an agreement, running her fingers along the spines on the shelves. She's lost in memories I don't have of this place.

And all I can think about is how this might have been *my* office.

Not that I *wanted* to work here necessarily. I just wanted it to be an option. To know that I chose against it, but could have chosen it.

Mom glances out the window, then walks back toward the doorway. "Sorry. Got distracted. Let's go."

We continue down the hallway. Most of the offices we pass are currently unoccupied. Personalized, with diplomas on the walls and unsorted papers stacked on the desk, but with empty chairs. Saturday is the Fourth of July, and a good portion of the people on this floor have relocated to their summer homes ahead of the holiday weekend.

There are two types of powerful people in this world, I've discovered. Those who inherit status and enjoy it—lift their foot off the gas, lean back, and coast. Or those who earn success and use it as fuel to strive for more—dig deeper and press harder, searching for the next opportunity.

Most of my friends, acquaintances, classmates, exes are powerful people who fall into the first category. It doesn't mean they're not thoughtful or kind. It means they're content, not hungry.

I'm related to a lot of powerful people who define the second category. My grandfathers, my uncle, my parents. There's a reason the Kensington name is worth hundreds of billions, and it has nothing to do with luck. It's common knowledge that my family *works* rather than simply collects sizable paychecks.

My parents were there for me, growing up. I have memories of my dad driving me to swim practice and my mom baking cakes for my birthday parties. But they also worked full-time. We had nannies. Chefs who cooked dinner most nights. Drivers who shuttled us to and from school most days. Family vacations were a regular occurrence, but they weren't frequent. Mom and Dad didn't let parenthood derail their careers or diminish their determination.

I have it too—that drive. There was a time when I was worried I didn't, back when I was struggling in school and with a handicap no one else in my family had. At some point, I realized that struggle was proof of ambition. If you're not trying to get somewhere, you don't worry about being behind.

Mom says hello to the few secretaries working as we pass them, and they all greet her by name.

She's probably the most recognizable Kensington, thanks to the magazine covers and full-sized advertisements common in the fashion industry. Mom owns one of those magazines, *Haute*, and her fashion line, rouge, is featured everywhere. Dad wanted to use the photo of me and my brothers posing in front of her umpteenth Times Square billboard for our family holiday card last December.

Since I look a lot like her, I'm pretty recognizable too. I inherited my dad's eyes and his height, but my hair and my face are basically a carbon copy of my mom's.

Uncle Oliver's assistant is on the phone. She waves us past, mouthing, *He's expecting you.*

"You told Uncle Oliver the right arrival date?" I ask.

Mom laughs. "Your father talked to him this morning. I tried to call you, too, but you didn't answer."

"It was seven a.m. here," I grumble.

Uncle Oliver stands as soon as we walk into his office, tossing a pen onto the desk and walking this way, wearing a wide smile.

"So good to see you," Oliver tells Mom, giving her a hug first.

I glance around. There's a new portrait hanging since I was last in here—Uncle Oliver with his wife, Hannah, and their two daughters. A new couch nestled in the attached sitting area. A presentation projected on-screen in the private conference room from a meeting that must have just happened.

"Lili. Nice of you to stop by for a visit." My uncle's smile is wry.

I smile back as I give my uncle a hug. My lack of interest in the family company is well known. Or lack of involvement, I guess. That makes my trips here rare.

"In my defense, I've been mostly living in Chicago."

"I know; I know. You're a busy bee. Hannah is headed there in September for a conference. I'm going to try to tag along so I can see Claremont Park in person."

"You don't have to do that," I mutter, embarrassed.

"I want to." The corners of Oliver's eyes crinkle as he squeezes my shoulder. "We're very proud of you."

I clear my throat. "Thanks. It wasn't that big of a deal."

Mom and Oliver exchange an amused look.

"She takes compliments like a Kensington," Oliver says.

"She does," Mom agrees. "And the park is incredible, by the way. Well worth a visit."

She and Dad came to the official opening ceremony of my most recent project a couple of weeks ago.

"I have no doubt," Oliver replies. "Can I get you ladies anything to eat or drink?"

Mom holds her water up. "I'm all set. But speaking of eating and drinking, I was hoping you and Hannah were free for dinner tonight."

"We'll be there," Oliver replies, pulling his phone out of his pocket. "I'll text Hannah right now. Can we bring anything?"

"Just yourselves."

"Okay. But we're going to bring *something*, so any preferences?"

Mom laughs. "Wine."

"Got it." He types something. "Hannah said she'll be home by six."

"Perfect. Come over whenever."

"Is it just the four of us?"

"Yes. My kids all have plans, and Asher and Sophie are busy."

"Bowling league?" Oliver guesses.

"Dog agility class."

Oliver smirks, then shakes his head.

"We passed … Kit's office," Mom says.

Oliver sobers, slipping his phone away and then straightening his tie. "It felt right."

I look out the windows. It's still raining, tiny rivers streaking the glass and blurring the view.

"It'll mean a lot to him," Mom tells Oliver. "To *both* of them."

The office door opens again.

Asher appears, a folder in one hand, which he holds out to Oliver. "Take a look at this when you have a chance. Let me know your thoughts."

Oliver nods, walking over to his desk and setting it down.

"How much longer are you ladies gracing us with your presence?" Asher asks.

Mom checks her watch. "Not long. I promised Celeste I'd stop by *Haute*'s office to sign off on a couple of things in person. And give Lili a chance to raid the closet before her big Europe trip." She smiles at me.

"I didn't hear you were headed to Europe this summer, Lili," Asher says.

I nod. "My best friend is getting married in Wales next week. Her fiancé is British."

"*Married*. Wow. When did you get old enough to have friends who are old enough to get married?" Oliver asks, shaking his head.

"You're telling me," Mom says. "I'll see you tonight." She looks at Oliver. "And you and Sophie soon," she says to Asher.

"Definitely," Asher confirms. "She'll be ecstatic you're in town."

We say goodbye to Oliver and Asher, then head toward the elevators.

Mom's staring at *Kensington Consolidated*, affixed to the wall in silver letters between the two banks. I don't even have to look to know what it says.

"Is it weird for you, being back here?" I ask.

My family split time between coasts because of her job, not Dad's. But I know Dad worked here at one point, and it made enough of an impression on Mom that she remembers his office two decades later.

"A little," she replies, still looking thoughtful.

"Because Dad stopped working here or because Kit is about to?"

"Both."

We step into the elevator.

"Both," she repeats as the doors slide shut.

# CHAPTER 5
## *Charlie*

A dive bar.

Ellis sent me the address for a dive bar.

I scoff, standing on another grimy city sidewalk and seriously debating entering the building in front of me. I should have looked up what the address was before braving New York traffic and driving here. But I didn't because I was busy replaying the meeting at Kensington Consolidated and marveling over Elizabeth Kensington's stubbornness.

She remembers me, right? I'd introduced myself to her *twice* before.

Most people I meet already know who I am. Introducing myself is just a formality. And Lili does not strike me as shy or forgetful.

And what was she doing there? *Does* she work at Kensington Consolidated?

I grimace, imagining her sitting in a conference room, picking

apart the proposal I spent two months working on, exuding the cool indifference that appears to be her trademark.

Then, I shove through the flimsy door, deciding a distraction outweighs the concern of potentially contracting tetanus in this place.

The interior of the bar is as unkempt as the outside suggests. It's a small space, and it feels even tinier because of the significant amount of *stuff* littering every surface. The shelves behind the bar top are shoved so full of liquor bottles; most of the dusty glass cylinders look in danger of crashing to the dirty floor. It's impossible to tell what color the walls were originally because they're entirely covered by stickers and posters and sketches and crooked frames and sports pennants. There are mismatched stools lining the length of the scarred wooden counter and several booths in the very back.

Ellis is slumped in the middle one.

I head for him, nodding a greeting back to the grizzled bartender, the bottoms of my shoes sticking with each step.

*How* did Ellis find this place? And *what* is he doing here at—I check the Patek Philippe watch my father gave me for my eighteenth birthday—three p.m.?

"Hey!" He grins crookedly as I slide into the bench opposite him. "Was wondering what was taking you so long. Did you get lost?"

Without waiting for an answer, he downs one of the shots sitting in front of him. Tequila, I think, although there are so many competing smells in this place that it's hard to tell for certain.

"Traffic."

Ellis nods. "That's why I bike everywhere."

"I thought biking was your job?"

Last night, he said he worked for one of those food-delivery apps.

"Yeah. That too." He pushes one of the full shot glasses toward me.

"I'm good," I say.

He squints at me. "Are you an alcoholic?"

"Because I won't do a tequila shot in the middle of the afternoon?" I shake my head. "No, I'm not an alcoholic."

But I did develop a bad habit of escaping into a bottle for a few weeks after my dad died, and I'm determined to stop letting my anger at him keep me from acting like the man—the fucking duke—I was raised to be. Getting drunk in a dingy bar that smells faintly of piss with my underachieving cousin is not how I'll be spending the remainder of my afternoon. Plus, based on the number of empty glasses, he's going to need to lean on a shoulder to walk out of here. And probably a ride home for him and his bike.

"Thought you could use a drink after last night." Ellis downs the shot he offered to me.

I wince like I'm the one who just swallowed it.

Dinner last night with my mum, my stepfather, and Ellis—who no longer lives *with* them, but still lives in the city—was awkward. About as uncomfortable as my last visit. If not for the business opportunities New York offers, I doubt I would have made the trip back this summer.

But then there's still the confused ten-year-old in me, searching for answers as to why my mum left us. My dad, I get. Their marriage was an unmitigated disaster. Abandoning me and Blythe? That I do *not* get.

An unforgivable choice maybe. But I'm already dealing with

enough bloody resentment toward a parent, and I needed to come to New York for my meeting with Asher Cotes. So, I flew into JFK, rented a car, and showed up at my mum's husband's house for dinner. Ellis joining us for a free meal—that's not speculation, as he announced it when he arrived—cut the tension a little. Not that much though.

I left their home early this morning and haven't been back since. I'm supposed to meet them for dinner in four hours. Ellis was invited, too, but I'm doubtful he'll be in shape for it based on his current appearance.

"So …" I glance around, trying to come up with something to say.

I don't know Ellis well. The first time I met him—met *any* of my mum's family—was at her wedding to Derek two years ago. Georgia's close to her sister, apparently. Her parents weren't there, and I have no idea where they are. There are a lot of other questions I'd ask my mother before inquiring about my grandparents' whereabouts.

"What are you doing here?"

"My dad's an asshole and a liar," Ellis replies conversationally.

"Oh."

*Bloody hell.* I'm the last person who should be sharing advice on paternal relationships.

I loosen my tie and relax in the booth a little, eyeing the one remaining shot wistfully. I might need some alcohol to make it through this conversation. "Are you two close?"

Ellis has never mentioned his father to me. The topic never came up last summer either, when he, his sister, and his mum were all living at Derek's Hamptons house.

"No. Dad's a surfer. He and Mom met in Hawaii. He was there for a championship." Ellis is talking even slower than usual, probably thanks to the alcohol in his system. "Still travels all over the world for them. Sometimes, he'll send me and Jo postcards. Chile, Portugal, Indonesia, Mexico. He sleeps on the beaches usually. Says it helps him commune with the waves."

I reach for the shot and suck it down in one gulp. It's shit liquor, not smooth at all, but better than nothing.

Ellis's face lights up like us drinking together has turned around his whole damn day. "Good, right? They're out of limes, but I think tequila tastes fine on its own."

I'd disagree, but I nod. "You surf?"

"Not well." His posture slumps more. "Dad's been saying we're going to do a trip to South Africa together for years. For my twenty-first, which was *last* summer. He promised it would be this year instead. At the end of August so we could catch the Roaring Forties." Ellis sighs. "He called me this morning, saying he had to cancel. Guess I should be grateful he remembered we had a plan at all. He usually doesn't."

"That's really shitty, Ellis. I'm sorry."

"He doesn't need to be a damn duke, you know? I just want a dad who wants to spend time with me sometimes."

I sympathize more than he knows. "My dad being a duke just meant he wanted to shape me into a duke. That was all we talked about when we spent time together. He might have been around, but he always had an agenda."

Ellis perks up again. "Maybe *we* should go to South Africa!"

My mobile buzzes in my pocket. I pull it out and see *Blythe* flashing across the screen.

"One sec," I tell Ellis. "I need to answer this." I slide out of the booth. "Order some water, okay? No more shots."

He shoots me a shit-eating grin that makes me think I just ensured more shots will be on the table when I return.

I sigh, then head outside. The rain has stopped, and nothing looks cleaner. Now, the sidewalk is dirty *and* wet.

"Everything okay?" I ask, watching water drip off the piled trash bags on the curb.

"My card isn't working," my little sister informs me.

At least, I *think* that's what she says. There's lots of commotion in the background on her end. Loud music and louder voices.

"What?"

"My card isn't working!" Blythe shouts.

*Shit.*

I pinch the bridge of my nose. "Which one?"

"The one I use to pay, Charlie."

I exhale. "What bloody color is it, Blythe?"

"Hang on."

Her voice fades, all the background noise remaining at the same ear-splitting level.

I think, *Fuck you, James*, for a third time today, but there's no accompanying flash of anger. I'm drained, unable to summon even a small twinge of irritation right now.

I hear Blythe's voice again, but it's muffled. "No, it's my brother," she says.

"*Ooh*," another female voice trills. "Ask him if he's looking for a duchess."

I roll my eyes.

"He's not," Blythe replies flatly. "Go wait with Zara. I'll be right there."

A few seconds later, her voice is back at a normal volume.

"Silver card," she informs me.

"Use the blue one."

"Oh. Okay. Thanks!" Now that her problem is solved, she sounds perky and cheerful. "Bye!"

"Wait." I rub at my forehead. "Where are you?"

"Budapest."

"I thought you were staying in London this week."

Because she *told* me she was staying in London this week.

"I was. But then Zara suggested a trip, so here we are. I gotta go, Charlie. We're headed to another club."

*Another* club? It's only nine p.m. there.

Ellis might be inside, ordering more tequila shots, but that's something Blythe would *definitely* do. The shorter the leash, the harder she pulls, just to prove she can. The only person she ever listened to was our father. Not only is he gone, but she's also grieving him. I'm trying to be there for her and also give her space. I'm not sure I'm succeeding at either.

"I'll be home on Monday," I tell her.

"Okay. Have fun with *Georgia*."

I exhale. "I told you this was a business trip, Blythe. But since I was here, I thought—"

"Whatever, Charlie. Don't explain. I don't care."

Another sigh. "Be safe, Blythe."

"I will; I will," she assures me. Then hesitates. "I love you."

"I love you too," I tell her.

The silence after she hangs up is startling, my eardrum still ringing, like I was standing in that club too.

I drag a palm down my face, adding *call the bank* to my long to-do list.

When I get back to the booth, Ellis is fast asleep on top of the scratched table.

# CHAPTER 6

## *Lili*

Low chatter echoes off the tiled walls of Number 34 as I squeeze past a laughing group of college girls and skirt around a middle-aged couple standing along the stools that line the far end of the bar top.

"Good evening," the maître d' greets politely. "Do you have a reservation?"

I nod, pulling my hair over one shoulder and then smoothing the front of the silk jumpsuit I'm wearing. "Under Martin, I believe. For … seven?"

As far as I know, everyone except Chloe is coming tonight.

The woman scans the screen in front of her. "Ah, yes. Here we are. It'll just be a couple of minutes, Miss Martin."

I don't bother to correct her. "Okay. Thank you."

I head for an opening along the bar to order a drink to sip on while I wait for my friends to show up.

Number 34 only opened a few months ago, and it's quickly become one of the most popular restaurants in the city. Bridget snagged a reservation through the chef she's dating, who knows the owners.

The bartender recommends one of the seasonal specialties—a rosemary mezcal fizz. The cocktail is delicious, smoky and citrusy. The perfect distraction from my pinched toes and my friends' tardiness.

"Club soda with lime, please."

I glance over so fast that my neck cracks, telling myself it's because carbonated water isn't a common order at a bar. My interest has nothing to do with how the request was spoken in a British accent.

The commotion of voices and activity around me fades away as I look at him. Along with any flimsy excuses about why I'm suddenly intrigued by who's standing next to me.

"Hi." Charlie sticks out a broad palm. "I'm Charles Marlborough."

I take a sip from my drink to hide the grin trying to appear. "I know," I say, relieved when my voice comes out sounding indifferent. "We met this afternoon."

It's a struggle not to laugh, watching irritation and incredulity war on Charlie's face. And it's a shame they don't make him look any less attractive.

His hand lifts to run through his cropped hair as he nods his thanks at the bartender who's already procured his drink. "I know," he mutters. "*Now*, you know who I am."

Again, I have to work hard not to express any amusement.

Again, I have to remind myself any charm or politeness is a

pretty facade.

It's been eleven months since I snuck in the side door of Atlantic Crest Country Club, spotted Charlie standing by the piano, and reached the stone archway just in time to hear my name mentioned, followed by, "I'm not here to stroke the ego of a vapid heiress who has nothing to do except wonder about how much of daddy's money she can spend today."

Yeah, I memorized what he'd said.

I know what's whispered behind my back. Know that my life is easy in comparison to so many people's.

The envy-inciting amount of money my family has can buy just about anything.

Anything … except love.

I always have to second-guess intentions. To wonder if guys are interested in me or the money. To consider that men want to be in my bed *and* my bank account.

With a few harsh words, Charles Marlborough dredged up all those insecurities. The insult cut deeper because I'd actually enjoyed talking to him before I overheard him belittling me. And even more inflaming? He's a fucking *duke*. A simple Google search revealed he'd attended Eton and Oxford. He's from the same privileged world I am, just located on the other side of the Atlantic, and I bet *his* daddy paid for more than his fancy degrees. Yet he was judging *me*, as if I'd had any control over who my parents were.

"I heard you're a duke."

His gaze returns to mine. There's a twinge in my chest when our eyes connect, like the pluck of a guitar string, that reverberates throughout my body.

"Yes."

That's all he says, and I can't tell if he's surprised or pleased that I brought his title up.

"How … historical." I make *historical* sound like a slight, and I know it registers.

Rather than annoyed, Charlie appears amused by my choice of adjective. "Mmhmm," he replies, then takes a sip of his club soda.

"What are you doing here?" I ask, increasingly irritated by his lack of reaction.

I want him to argue with me. Make another demeaning comment—this time to my face. It feels like the upper hand is slipping now that I've dropped our little game of repeating introductions. Which I didn't mean to make a recurring instance. I was pissed at him the second time we met. And earlier, I was so shocked to see Charlie standing outside Asher's office that obliviousness was my first instinct.

"This restaurant? Or this city?"

"Either. Both."

"Same answer really. I'm visiting my mother."

I blink at him. "Your mother."

He makes another one of those maddening *mmhmm* sounds.

"Your mother is American?"

Charlie holds my gaze. "Yes."

"So, you spent time in the US, growing up?"

"I did not."

Still with the unwavering eye contact. I'm sweating.

"Oh." I'm bumping up against the boundaries of politeness, swallowing more questions and trying to extinguish a curiosity I shouldn't possess in the first place.

"I didn't realize you worked at Kensington Consolidated,"

Charlie states.

"I don't," I say, rubbing a finger against the condensation collected on the side of the glass. "Mom and I just stopped by the offices for a visit."

"Asher seems very close with your family."

My eyes narrow. Charlie sounds … disgruntled about that. Like that familiarity makes him like Asher less.

"Asher is best friends with my dad," I inform him. "He's my godfather."

"I see."

I'm not sure *what* he sees. Does he think his fancy dukedom is too good for my family?

"The company is called *Kensington* Consolidated, Charles. You couldn't have missed that when you walked into the building."

His head tilts to the left. Two women squeeze past us, both blatantly checking him out, and his gaze never wavers. "What do you do?"

I feel the lines form on my forehead. "What do you mean?"

"You said you don't work at *Kensington* Consolidated." He emphasizes my last name obnoxiously. "What *do* you do, Elizabeth?"

I flick my hair over one shoulder, flashing him my most seductive smile. "Don't you know how much money I have? Why would I bother working?"

Charlie doesn't react to my sarcastic tone, just keeps staring at me. His attention is consuming. It's sucking away everything around me, like I'm on a plane and a door was opened thousands of feet up in the air. My surroundings are a blur of moving objects, the only focal point his unwavering gaze.

I'm treading dangerously close to the comment he made about

me. The one I should have brushed off instead of allowed to soak in. His opinion shouldn't matter to me. Not that day. Not now.

He shakes his head, then glances at the door as the silence between us stretches. A silent dismissal that almost seems disappointed.

I exhale, belatedly realizing it was overdue. At some point since he appeared, my breathing became irregular. "I'm a landscape architect, okay?"

Those damn eyes are right back on me. "A landscape architect," Charlie repeats slowly. He rests a forearm on the quartz counter. The motion means he's a little closer. Close enough for me to learn that he smells like laundry detergent and a hint of something spicy. "What does that mean?"

"It means I design outdoor spaces. Parks, gardens, places like that."

By now, I've heard it all. Calling my job an "interesting hobby." A comment about how lovely "playing with plants" sounds. Wondering if I'm available to put in a vegetable garden at a summer house.

Charlie says none of that. He asks, "Is that what you want to be doing?"

I consider the question for a few seconds, the new name plaque outside my dad's old office flashing in my brain brighter than a neon light. "Yes."

He picks up his glass. "Then, good for you."

"What about you? What does a *duke* do? Aside from hosting jousting matches and visiting foreign kingdoms, of course."

Charlie smirks at my sarcasm. "He does whatever he bloody hell wants."

There's a hollowness to the bravado. Something that suggests there's more constriction than he's letting on.

"Is that what you want to be doing?"

As soon as I echo his question, Charlie's smile slides off his face.

"Lili!" Arms wrap around my side a split second before the scents of jasmine and vanilla hit me. Francesca's worn the same perfume since middle school, the sweet, floral smell a nostalgic reminder of sleepovers and shared vacations and secret crushes.

I turn to hug Fran back properly. It's been six weeks since I last saw her.

Fran is the free spirit of our friend group. She bounces between jobs. Swaps out hobbies. Flips through guys. Spends her family's money liberally and could care less if anyone judges her lack of direction.

Honestly, I'm envious of her carefree attitude.

She wouldn't care if Charles Marlborough called her a vapid heiress.

"How was Greece?" I ask Fran as soon as we separate.

Fran beams, her skin tan and glowing. She looks refreshed and relaxed, exactly like she spent the past month and a half sunning herself on a beach. "Amazing," she gushes. "I wish you'd come."

"Next time," I promise. "Now that the Claremont job is finished."

My largest project to date wrapped up a week ago. Eight months of tireless work—from the initial site analysis and planning to the final flourishing park.

"Yay! I want to see pictures." Fran glances to my left, then does a double take. Unleashes a coy smile. "Who's this?"

If we hadn't been in different time zones for what Fran would dramatically deem "an eternity," there's no way it would have taken her so long to notice Charlie. *I'm* taken aback by his attractiveness all over again as I follow Fran's interested gaze to where he's standing a few feet away.

Charlie removes his right hand from his glass and holds it out. "Charles Marlborough."

"It's wonderful to meet you, Charles Marlborough." Fran glances at me, interest visible on her face. "How do you two know each other?"

"We don't," I state.

"We just met earlier," Charlie confirms. "At *Kensington* Consolidated."

I have to press my lips together to keep from scowling. Because I'm 90 percent certain he remembers talking to me in the stable at Atlantic Crest last summer, and now, I can't ask him about it.

And because his attention is so stifling, it's really noticeable when it shifts to someone else.

"Do you work there?" Fran asks. Someone shuffles by, and she uses it as an excuse to take a step closer.

Charlie doesn't shift away as he answers, "No. It was just a business meeting. Discussing some potential ventures."

"Sounds boring," Fran comments.

Charlie smiles, but doesn't disagree or agree.

"I see Bridget," I say, seizing the lull in conversation. "Should we go see if our table is ready?"

"I'll be right there," Fran replies. "Just going to order a drink while I'm over here."

Her eyes are on Charlie, not the bartender.

I want to warn her away. To tell her that Charlie is just a

handsome vessel for lots of hypocritical contempt.

But Fran is smart and capable. People underestimate her. *Charlie* will underestimate her, and she can take care of herself. Find out the truth about him for herself.

"Okay," I respond. Then glance at Charlie, attempting to ignore the way my entire body reacts to his steady stare refocused on me. "Nice to see you, Charles." My voice is stiff and formal.

"You too, Elizabeth." His tone sounds just as rigid. Maybe more so, thanks to his posh accent.

I grab my glass and head toward Bridget. She spots me halfway and waves, weaving her way around tables to give me a big hug in the center of the room.

The Claremont Park project was based in Chicago, requiring me to spend most of the past year outside the city. The last time we got together as a group was a weekend back in March, for Tripp's birthday.

He's walking in the front door now, Hugo and Jasper right behind him. I'm expecting Cal to appear next, but the door shuts behind Jasper and doesn't reopen.

The maître d' approaches at the same time the boys reach us, obviously eager to seat our larger group.

Tripp, in particular, is incapable of much reserve. He says and does whatever he wants. Sometimes, it's nice, like when he punched Cooper Thomas for proposing I pay for our junior-prom limo. Sometimes, it's exhausting, like how he still asks if I'm going to give Cal a second chance.

Tripp picks Bridget up and twirls her around. She laughs and pounds her fists against his back—with no effect. He spins her three times before setting her back down beside the wide-eyed maître d'.

He reaches for me next, and I shake my head.

"Don't you dare."

His laugh is a deep, easy rumble, which is another reminder of childhood.

Tripp swallows me up into a giant hug—some of my drink sloshes out of the glass and onto my wrist—and then he manages to muss my hair once before I swat his hand away. "Good to see you, Lili."

I roll my eyes. "You too, Tripp."

"Your table is all ready." Once again, the maître d' tries to move us along.

To be fair, people are staring. Because they recognize some of us or because we're a noisy group—who knows?

Hugo and Jasper both give me side hugs on our way to the table.

It's seated for six, not seven, and I heave out a sigh as I sink down next to Bridget. I try to keep my tone light as I wonder aloud, "Cal isn't coming?"

Tripp studies me from his spot across the table. "No. He's already in the Hamptons with Violet."

"Oh." I'm relieved, and it sneaks into my voice.

Tripp frowns. "You're supposed to care he's dating someone else, Lili."

I reach for a piece of sourdough and slather it with salted honey butter. "We broke up over a year ago, Tripp. I'm happy for him."

"Don't mention that to Cal," Hugo mumbles next to me.

I sigh. "Look, I know it's awkward, guys. Nothing I can do about it."

"Nothing *you* can do about it," Bridget pipes in with. "But *these two* could stop delivering messages, trying to make you feel guilty."

She glares at Hugo first, then Tripp. "She's your friend too, guys."

I reach for my glass, hoping a healthy sip will clear the apprehension crawling up my throat.

Since we broke up, I've only seen Cal twice. Once at a Labor Day party in the Hamptons, which was where I found out he was moving to London to start a master's in economics. And then at his family's Christmas party seven months ago, when he came home for the holidays. Both were uncomfortable, stilted interactions with lots of prying eyes on us. I was hoping tonight—a casual dinner with our closest friends—we could finally make some progress toward returning things to normal.

I'm also glad he didn't come, which I feel guilty about.

"Is that Charles Marlborough Fran is talking to?" Jasper suddenly asks, his gaze on the bar.

Everyone looks. Everyone except me. I'm focused on Jasper.

"You know him?" I say, surprised.

We've gone to school together since preschool, so we tend to know all the same people.

"Of him," Jasper answers.

Maddeningly, that's all he says. Forcing me to press and ask, "What have you heard?"

Jasper shrugs. "The Marlboroughs are a big deal in England. Charles just inherited everything after his dad died."

My eyes dart to where Charlie and Fran are standing. From this angle, all I can see of Charlie is the back of his head and his right shoulder.

"When did his dad die?"

"Last year, I think."

"What happened?"

"I don't remember. Tripp, you remember?"

"Nope," Tripp replies. "Dad met him at Atlantic Crest last summer though. Said he's the youngest duke in centuries or something like that. Brits care a lot about that shit, apparently."

"He's a *duke*?" Bridget asks, craning her neck to get a better look.

Hugo snorts. "What difference does that make?"

"Every girl wants the fairy tale, man," Tripp says.

Then, he glances at me, and I know what he's thinking.

I flushed the fairy tale away, and no one is really sure why.

I swallow some water, then rub at the embossed letters on the cover of my unopened menu. "We can take the jet next week."

Excited chatter erupts around me, following the announcement.

My uncle Oliver was originally supposed to borrow my parents' jet for a meeting with developers in Singapore next week, but the dates were changed. Which freed it up for Chloe's wedding. She's getting married in Wales next weekend. We're flying there on Monday, then spending the week after the wedding celebrating at her family's villa in Saint-Tropez. If not for the approaching awkwardness with Cal, I'd be looking forward to it unreservedly.

Many of my friends from college come from more modest backgrounds, but Bridget, Fran, Hugo, Jasper, Tripp—and Cal—are all outrageously wealthy. Just not Kensington wealthy. None of them have access to a private jet.

There's no break in the eager discussion of next week's plans until Fran joins us at the table.

She slides into the last open seat with a dramatic huff that captures everyone's attention. "Well, that was a waste of time."

"What do you mean?" I respond first, far more interested than I should be.

Fran reaches for a slice of bread. "He's taken."

The stab of disappointment is unexpected and uncomfortable. "Oh."

"*Really?*" Jasper sounds highly skeptical.

"That's what he said. I asked if he wanted to join us for a drink, and he said he was meeting his family for dinner."

I glance at where Charlie was standing. He's still in the same spot, now talking to a white-haired man, a middle-aged woman with blonde hair, and the same guy he told I was a vapid heiress.

"So, I suggested we get a drink later," Fran continues. "And he said he wasn't available." She sighs. "I swear, all the hot ones are taken."

"Excuse me?" Hugo says.

Tripp and Jasper appear equally offended.

All three of them are single.

Fran flicks a few careless fingers in Hugo's direction. "You don't count. I'm not going to fuck you. We all saw how that worked out for …" She glances at me. "Sorry."

"It's fine," I say, filling the uncomfortable pause with a hasty gulp of my mezcal drink.

Now, I'm extra glad Cal didn't come.

"Holy fuck," Bridget says, scrolling on her phone. "He *is* hot."

"I know." Fran sounds mournful. "We're going to have to hit Proof after this to restore my ego."

Tripp leans to see the screen of Bridget's phone. Snorts. "Yeah. No way he's not single."

"What do you mean?" Fran is trying to look at the screen now, too, and I have to fight the urge to crane my neck as well.

"Guy who's gotten around *that* much—and these are just the

women he's been photographed with? He's either gay and in the closet or single. No way he's in a committed relationship."

"He's not gay," I blurt.

Everyone's looking at me now.

"How do you know?" Bridget asks, lifting one eyebrow.

"I just do. Talking to him, there's … rizz." I don't know how better to describe the buzzing sensation I experience around Charlie.

"I agree," Fran pipes in with. "He's definitely straight."

"So, it was you," Hugo concludes. "You probably came off as too high maintenance again."

Fran tosses a chunk of sourdough at him.

Hugo catches the bread and takes a huge bite, grinning around it. "Nice throw."

The waitress appears to take our order.

I continue rubbing the raised lines on the front of the menu, the bread, water, and mezcal in my stomach churning around unpleasantly. Mom wanted to stop by rouge's offices after we left *Haute*, and I barely had time to change before rushing here.

Bridget leans into me. "Chase said the salmon and the steak are the best entrées."

"I'm thinking oysters and charcuterie for appetizers?" Tripp suggests.

"Can we do rosé for the table?" Fran asks. "I want something summery."

"Just pick," Hugo says. "I'm good with whatever." He passes his menu to the waitress. "You all set, Lili?"

I hand the waitress my menu. "Yep. I'm good with whatever too."

# CHAPTER 7

## Charlie

I'm standing on the patio beside an oversize potted plant, talking to John Cushing, when I see her.

Despite his tendency to use phrases like *quantum mechanics* and discuss properties of matter, I enjoy speaking with John. Respect his dedication to learning about the industry he's involved in rather than just signing checks. And when I reintroduced myself, I was also impressed he'd remembered our conversation last summer.

But focusing on understanding the jargon John is using becomes impossible once the Kensingtons arrive.

They're part of a large group, eleven in total. Hanson Ellsworth walks in front, conversing with a dark-haired, middle-aged man. Two women—one who appears close to Hanson's age (his wife, I assume) and the other a blonde who looks a couple of decades younger—are behind them. Scarlett and Lili are next, followed by another man who bears a striking resemblance to the adult Hanson

is conversing with. A younger generation trails last, their ages ranging from teenager to early twenties and their expressions varying from resigned to polite.

Lili's wearing sunglasses and a hat today, so I can't tell where the woman who took three tries to remember me is looking as she talks to her mother.

Georgia guilted me into coming today, complaining we hadn't gotten to spend enough time together during my short visit. Tomorrow is the Fourth of July, and I'm flying back to London the following day.

Since my mother is the least maternal woman I've ever met, I'm suspicious her insistence on my attendance had more to do with how she wanted to show me off at Derek's country club than any quality time.

Unlike my sister, I've rarely held our mother's lack of affection against her. She was barely older than Blythe when she married our father—a cold man ten years her senior. And Georgia thrives under attention. She needs to be flattered and admired and coddled to keep from wilting like a neglected flower. She married my father for his title and his money and couldn't have been more miserable.

I have sympathy for her. More since my father died and I learned how privilege could double as a prison. She kept up appearances for twelve years, trying to supplement the lack of praise from my father with parties and maybe even motherhood. We moved from a London flat to Newcastle Hall—my family's ancestral seat—just before my tenth birthday. A grand manor, surrounded by twenty thousand acres of gardens, farmland, and woodland.

After we moved, my mother locked herself in her wing of the house for two months. One day, she left and never looked back.

Watching her smile and laugh, flitting between the groups clustered on the patio like a true social butterfly, I'm glad she escaped. But I understand Blythe's resentment, too, better than anyone. Blythe was only five when our mom fled. Her strongest memory is of Georgia's absence.

John excuses himself to grab a fresh drink, and my mother seizes the opportunity to call me over to where she's standing.

"This is my son, Charles," my mom explains to yet another female friend, gesturing in my direction as I approach. Beaming at me like we're best friends or two members of one big, happy family.

I'm sympathetic, but I share Blythe's resentment toward Georgia too. Today especially, when it feels like she's taking advantage of my presence and using it as a prop. I had to make this trip to New York, and seeing my mother while I was here felt … necessary. A way to prove I was unaffected by her abandonment or that I was different from my unforgiving father. Coming to the city and avoiding her felt juvenile. Right now, I can't decide if that was the correct decision.

"Pleasure to meet you," I say politely.

The woman fans a hand toward her face, which is mostly blocked by the broad brim of her hat. "My goodness. What a lovely accent!"

I force my friendly expression to remain fixed in place, relieved when their conversation moves on from me to discussing a party tomorrow.

I tune out their chatter as they talk animatedly, surveying the crowd on the patio instead. My wandering gaze lands on Lili. She's seated at one of the circular glass tables toward the opposite end of the patio, talking to a blond man. His back is to me, one of his shoulders and the umbrella stand blocking Lili's face.

"Charles. *Charles.*"

My mom's bright smile has dimmed. It's drawn tighter, webs of wrinkles no injection could combat cracking her enthusiastic expression.

"Yes?" I keep my tone pleasant, but there are traces of exasperation close to the surface.

I'm awfully tired of playing parts. Since I inherited the title, I've been the impervious duke. Now, I'm also stuck with acting like the dutiful son.

"Katherine was asking if you've enjoyed your visit—"

A loud shout of "Hannah!" cuts Georgia off.

The blonde woman who arrived with the Kensingtons pauses a couple of feet away, aiming a polite smile at my mother's friend.

"Hello, Katherine," the woman—Hannah—greets.

"I didn't know you would be here this weekend."

"It was last minute," Hannah explains. "Oliver had a work trip get canceled, so we decided to come for the holiday weekend. Didn't want to miss the Red, White, and Blue party."

"*Of course* not." Katherine rapidly nods in agreement. "Is the whole family here?"

"Yes," Hannah confirms. Then glances at my mother and holds out a hand—a gesture that makes Georgia immediately perk up. Whoever this woman is, she's a person my mother cares about impressing. "I'm Hannah Kensington. It's nice to meet you."

My drifting attention moors as soon as Hannah's last name registers. I should have assumed she was a Kensington based on who all she arrived with. She must be married to Oliver Kensington, Lili's uncle and the current CEO of Kensington Consolidated.

"Georgia Marlborough-Barclay," my mom replies sweetly.

I've never asked why she kept my father's last name after their divorce and following her second marriage. Mostly because I'd like to think it was Georgia's way of not turning her back on me and Blythe entirely, not that the Marlborough name carries weight in certain circles.

"And this is my son, Charles Marlborough."

I shake Hannah's hand as Georgia introduces me, wondering if I'm imagining the way Lili's aunt pays closer attention to me than she did to Katherine or my mother. Maybe Asher Cotes mentioned my name. The way Lili made it sound at the restaurant last night, he's practically part of the Kensington family.

"Nice to meet you, Charles," Hannah says.

"You too," I respond.

Hannah gets called over to another group of women a minute later. I spot Ellis and excuse myself as well, strolling over to where he's slouched next to the bar.

"Wassup, Duke?" my cousin greets me with a tilt of his full glass and a familiar smirk—I'm not sure if it's familiar because he's drunk or because we've spent more time together the past few days than in our entire lives combined.

"Not much."

I order a water from the bartender, ignoring Ellis's exaggerated eye roll.

"Doubt that'll help," he mutters.

It's a little cooler by the bar, the green-and-white-striped awning shading the twenty or so feet of patio closest to the building. I sip my water and stare straight ahead, past the patio. Tennis courts are visible to the left, and the polo field is located on the right. Beyond all the manicured grass, the vivid blue of the ocean fades gradually into the sky's lighter horizon.

"Are you gentlemen enjoying yourselves?"

I stiffen involuntarily as soon as I hear Derek's voice. Georgia's husband—technically my stepfather—has never been anything except perfectly pleasant toward me. He's jovial yet quiet, usually nodding along agreeably to whatever my mother says. I don't know what Georgia has shared with Derek about her past, how she explained my existence or our estrangement. All I know is, it's strange, seeing my mother with a man who's not my father. He's a reminder I'm not as over the past as I'd like to be.

"Course," Ellis answers. "I fucking love this place."

Derek appears unfazed by my cousin's profanity. Or just very used to it. Ellis seems to spend a lot of time with him and Georgia. His mother moved to Philadelphia, and his sister goes to college somewhere in the South. And, as I learned a few days ago, his dad isn't around.

Expectantly, Derek looks at me next.

My grip tightens on the condensation-covered glass I'm holding. "It's very nice," I tell him. Then add, "Thank you for the invitation," because Derek's attention is still aimed at me and my father drilled what he deemed *gentlemanly* conduct into me.

This might be the one instance he would have made an exception for though.

"No invitation necessary," is Derek's response. "You're family."

The sentiment is … thoughtful, I suppose. Generous even. But his matter-of-fact delivery is almost comedic. The people I consider family are all on the other side of the ocean I was just staring at.

Thankfully, Derek gets drawn into a different conversation before I have to conjure a reply.

"You doing all right?" I ask Ellis, who's plowing through the contents of his glass. It's half full now.

"Fucking fantastic." Ellis nods to the left. "Open bar. And hot, rich girls everywhere."

He flashes a smile at a redhead passing by. She giggles and flips her hair.

I roll my eyes, but my cousin is still focused on the redhead and misses it.

"I meant with your dad."

Ellis sobers a little, stuffing his free hand into the pocket of his trousers. "I'm fine."

"Is that what you told him? Maybe he doesn't realize you're upset—that the trip is important to you."

"He called. I didn't answer. We'll talk … eventually."

"Don't assume there will be an eventually," I advise. "Life is bloody short."

Ellis says nothing in response, but I catch a couple of rapid swallows out of the corner of my eye and know he heard me.

I return to surveying the crowd. Lili is still talking to the same blond guy, and that bugs me for some reason I choose not to analyze. But I do decide to test Ellis's brag of knowing everyone here.

"Who's the bloke talking to Elizabeth Kensington?" I ask.

He glances in their direction. "Callahan Winston."

I don't recognize the name, but that's true of most people here. I barely follow British society, let alone who's deemed relevant in New York.

"Have you met him before?"

"Nah. Just seen him around. He spends a lot of time here."

I let the topic drop as Georgia approaches. This is the first time I've seen her alone. Since we arrived, there has been an endless stream of people she simply had to catch up with.

She requests a paloma from the bartender, then smiles at me and Ellis standing together. "I have to take a photo for Arizona. Our two boys, all grown up."

Ellis makes an amused sound in the back of his throat, but he indulges my mother, taking a step closer to me and slinging his left arm over my shoulders. We pose for a few seconds as she takes what seems like dozens of photos to share with my aunt.

"Perfect," she proclaims. "Something to remember your visit by, Charles, until next summer."

I'm bothered by Georgia's assumption that I'll be the one visiting her—again. "We can *remember my visit* when you come to Newcastle Hall."

The smile evaporates right off my mother's face. "Oh." Her laugh is light and breathy and fake. "I'm not sure that'll work out."

"Why not?"

Ellis starts tapping his finger against the side of his glass. *Tap, tap, tap*. Counting each second as Georgia searches for an excuse.

"I'm really not keen on flying," she tells me. "So many awful accidents these days."

"You and Derek flew to Hawaii for your honeymoon."

"Yes, well … that was for a special occasion."

"And seeing your daughter for the first time in *sixteen years* isn't one?"

"*Charles.*" Georgia's glancing around rapidly now, no longer thrilled about being amid people whose opinions she cares about. "Please don't make a scene."

I press my lips together as she scolds me like a misbehaving child. Disciplines me the way she *did* when I was a misbehaving child.

Unlike Blythe, I have memories of our mother *being* a mother, and I'm not sure if my sister or I got the worst deal. You can miss something you never had, but I think you miss what you had and lost more.

Ellis is no longer tapping his glass, but he's shifting his weight between his feet uncomfortably. He might act carefree and cavalier most of the time, but he's not oblivious to the fact that my family's dynamic is as messed up as his—if not more than.

I walk away from the bar before I can say anything I might regret. As I'm waiting in line at the buffet, a couple, who introduces themselves as Olivia and Andrew Spencer, strikes up a conversation with me. John Cushing reappears and includes me in a discussion with several of his business associates. And then Ellis waves me over to the far edge of the patio. I hand my empty plate off to a uniformed waiter, then head in his direction.

There's no sign of Georgia, but a young guy, who looks to be a similar age to Ellis, is standing next to my cousin.

"Polo match is starting soon," Ellis tells me. "We're headed over there, if you want to come?"

"Sure," I reply.

I've never attended a polo match I wasn't playing in before, but a change of scenery sounds nice.

"This is Bash Kensington," Ellis says, nodding to the bloke beside him as we head toward the field.

*Lili's brother.*

It's disconcerting how I diminish the famously wealthy family down to their association with her. Asher Cotes—a potential investor—is her godfather. Oliver Kensington—CEO of the company I'm hoping to work with—is her uncle. And now, I'm searching for facial similarities in a stranger she's related to.

"Charlie. Nice to meet you."

"Yeah, you too," Bash responds. "Ellis talks about you a lot."

A funny prickle appears in the back of my throat. I avoid looking at my cousin as I clear it. "How do you two know each other?"

"Golf mostly," Bash answers. "Not my best game, but not much else to do around here."

"Not your best game?" Ellis repeats. "You shot eighty-three the last time we played."

Bash shrugs modestly. For all their privilege, the Kensingtons I've met seem surprisingly grounded.

We reach the edge of the polo field. Spectators and players are already gathering, several horses standing on the grass as riders make final adjustments to their tacks.

"This isn't a professional match," Bash tells me. "Just a meetup between members."

"These games are more entertaining," Ellis adds.

They continue toward the white tents set up on the sidelines. I step over the short picket fence surrounding the field and head toward the blond man Lili was talking to earlier.

"Handsome horse," I say, stopping a few feet away.

Callahan Winston turns, an easy smile spreading across his face. "Thanks, man."

I dislike him instantly, and it definitely has something to do with how I recognize his horse as the same gelding Lili was stroking last summer.

"How much would you want for him?"

There's no way I'd ship a horse I don't have time to ride back to

Newcastle Hall, even if I still had frivolous spending money. But Callahan doesn't know that, and I have some strange impulse to make certain he considers me as rich as everyone else here.

He shakes his head, still smiling. "Lexington isn't for sale. Had this guy since college." Callahan notches the girth, then lets the saddle flap fall with a smack of leather and grabs the reins. He sticks a palm out. "I'm Cal Winston."

"Charles Marlborough." I shake his hand more firmly than is really necessary.

Cal's eyes widen, but I don't think he's reacting to my tight grip. Sure enough, "I was wondering, with the accent and all. You're the duke everyone's talking about."

"I am."

"Figured you'd be … older. No offense. Duke just sounds ancient to me."

"We come in all ages," I respond, not mentioning that I'm the youngest in centuries.

"How many dukes does England have?"

"Thirty-four," I answer.

A horse with a mounted rider approaches. I squint upward, the sun's glare making it impossible to distinguish any details.

But I have no problem recognizing the voice that says, "You forgot his martingale, Cal."

"What are you doing, Lili?" Cal asks.

"Exactly what it looks like," she replies. "The Carmichael twins didn't show up, so I volunteered." Lili nudges her mount forward without acknowledging me at all, transitioning to a trot.

Cal mutters something beneath his breath.

"Is she a bad rider?" I ask, already knowing the answer. She's handling the horse expertly.

"No," Cal says grudgingly. "She's just … she's making a scene. Women don't play in the charity matches. Or any matches at the club. It's just … not done."

*So?* I want to ask.

Maybe it's a side effect of growing up with an über-independent sister, but I've always been sensitive to small-minded views of gender norms. For all of his convictions about societal roles and obligations, my father never allowed Blythe to believe she was inferior to a man in any way.

"Tripp!" Cal calls to a guy lounging on the sideline. "We need an extra."

Tripp raises the glass he's holding. "Fuck no. I'm relaxing," he calls back, prompting scattered laughter.

"I'll play," I say impulsively.

Cal's gaze returns to me. "Really?"

"As long as you've got gear and a horse."

"Yeah. Yeah," he repeats, warming to the idea. "Hey, Ezra."

A passing groom pauses. "What's up?"

"Can you show Charles here to the locker room, saddle up one of the club's polo ponies, and"—he glances at the rider now cantering in circles—"bring me a martingale for Lexington?"

"Sure thing," Ezra replies, then nods at me. "This way, man."

Twenty minutes later, I'm back on the field, atop a chestnut mare named Amarillo. In addition to a borrowed horse and clothes, I was lent a helmet, knee guards, and a polo stick. All brand-new, top-of-the-line equipment.

The look on Lili Kensington's face when I ride up beside her is one I never want to forget. The color of my borrowed shirt doesn't match hers, which is fine with me. I'd rather play on opposing sides.

"What the hell are you doing?" she hisses at me.

"Exactly what it looks like," I reply, parroting the line she gave Cal earlier.

I can hear her teeth grinding as she eyes the *3* on my navy shirt. Her green one has a *2* on it.

I nudge Amarillo forward, adjusting to her rocking gait. My feelings toward riding are complicated. Most memories feature my father. Atop a horse is where I feel his presence most keenly, expecting to glance over and see him riding alongside me.

The two teams line up, and then one of the mounted umpires tosses the ball down the middle. I tune out the commentary on the loudspeaker as Amarillo canters forward, focused on the green shirt with possession of the ball. I can't tell if he's someone I've been introduced to, and I don't care. Amarillo pulls up even to his horse, and I prepare to ride him off.

It's been several years since I last played polo, but my muscles remember exactly what to do. The game is a welcome distraction from … everything.

Whoever the green shirt is, he doesn't put up much of a fight. Less than a minute into the chukka, I score the first point.

I look at Lili as soon as the ball rolls through the goalposts. In time to see the annoyance flash across her perfect features.

It's immensely satisfying. On the surface, all of our conversations have been completely civil. But there's always been something simmering beneath, and it makes me feel a little saner to see that it's not just in my head. To learn that she's affected too.

The umpire throws the ball again. I scan the field for an opening, now headed in the opposite direction. Amarillo's hooves hammer against the lush grass, probably carving a few divots that spectators will get to stomp later. My grip on the mallet tightens as I drop the stick. My muscles tense as I prepare to swing.

Another mallet appears seconds before I make contact with the ball, hooking the end so I miss the angle. I know it's her before I read the *2*. I have to yank the right rein to swerve back toward active play. Amarillo responds immediately, but it's not fast enough. Cal has possession, the *1* on the back of his shirt stretching tight as he bends over Lexington's withers.

I'm no longer distracted by Lili. I'm hell-bent on beating her.

An hour and a half later, the match ends. The navy jersey I'm wearing is sticky with sweat. White froth drips from Amarillo's mouth, her brown coat dark with sweat and her sides heaving against the stirrups.

I dismount, unbuckling the girth and tossing the leather strap over the saddle's seat before one of the grooms approaches to take the reins. I pat the mare's shoulder one last time, then pull my helmet off and run a hand through my damp, flattened hair.

There's a brief awards ceremony.

When I approach Lili afterward—holding my shiny little trophy because I'm a bit of a wanker like that—she's talking to the guy in the green *2* jersey, who I scored against at the start. He doesn't seem to be holding a grudge, flashing me a wide grin as I near. As soon as Lili sees me, a scowl appears.

"I'm Charles. Just wanted to say, good match."

I hold out a hand to the guy, and his smile widens.

"Conrad Randolph. You're one hell of a player."

Lili's glower remains.

"Thanks."

Conrad glances at Lili. "Have you met Eliza—"

"We've met," I interrupt before Lili can say a word.

The naked disdain on her face makes me think she'd claim we'd never met once again if given the opportunity.

It's entertaining—and confusing.

Our conversation at the restaurant last night was *almost* friendly, and I was perfectly polite to her flirty friend. I can't come up with any reason for her frostiness, unless she's that sore of a loser.

Conrad shifts his weight between his boots, clueing in to some of the tension hovering in the hot air. "I'd never seen you play before, Elizabeth. You're as good as Cal is."

Lili barely reacts to the compliment. She stares straight at me as she says, "Thanks. *Some* people think I'm just a vapid heiress whose only skill is spending daddy's money. You know, *unimportant.*"

Conrad frowns. "I'm sure that's not true. You're, uh—" He looks uncomfortable and confused, fumbling for something polite to say.

Me? I'm frozen, an icy realization trickling down my spine.

*She heard.*

She heard what I said to Ellis about her last summer. I'm not sure how, but she did.

Except I wasn't talking about *her*. I was talking about the women who'd been circling me earlier that afternoon. The ones who'd perked up when they heard my title and contributed little to the conversations except blatant flirting. I had no idea I'd met Elizabeth Kensington when I went off on Ellis.

Somehow, I'm certain Lili won't consider that much of an apology.

"Remarkable," Conrad concludes, finally finishing his sentence.

I clear my throat. "Elizabeth, I—"

"Have a *wonderful* afternoon, Conrad," Lili says, then turns and walks away.

I no longer feel victorious.

# CHAPTER 8

## *Lili*

An impressive spread of patriotic-colored food is on display when I walk into the dining room for breakfast on the morning of July 4.

Cinnamon rolls with white frosting. Blueberry coffee cake. Raspberry muffins. Waffles piled with strawberries and blackberries. Vanilla yogurt. Slices of watermelon. Crepes topped with whipped cream.

My grandmother's favorite holiday is the Fourth of July, and she celebrates it to the fullest extent. Breakfast is just the opening act for a full day of activities.

First up, the parade in town. Followed by the family tennis tournament. Then lunch at the yacht club. Finally, the grand finale—the Red, White, and Blue party that predates my existence and is tonight's most exclusive invitation.

The chairs surrounding the table are empty, except for one.

"Where's Mom?" I ask, taking the upholstered chair next to Dad and grabbing a muffin from the pile on the lobster-patterned plate. They're still warm, steam curling from the tops.

"Good morning to you too, dearest daughter." His eyes stay on the newspaper he's scanning.

I roll mine as I reach for the carafe of coffee. "Good morning, favorite father. Where's Mom?"

"Still sleeping," he replies, flipping a page.

"Really?"

Mom's normally an early riser.

Dad folds the paper and tosses it onto the table. "Well, first, she got up at three a.m. for a two-hour conference call with Milan and Paris. *Then*, she came back to bed and is still sleeping."

That sounds about right.

"She works too hard," I say.

"Agreed. But she promised she'd take the rest of the day off, even though 'it's not a holiday anywhere else.'"

"Gigi will be happy to hear it."

Neither of my grandparents is very supportive of my mom's jobs, but my grandmother is especially dismissive. It's one of several reasons I've never been close with Mom's parents. They're both hyperaware of appearances and perception—a prime example being Gigi's worry that Mom working will make people think she's not as rich as she is. And it's also why my grandmother insists my brothers and I call her Gigi since that sounds "chicer" than Grandmother.

I wonder, not for the first time, if my dad's mom would have cared what her grandchildren called her. I know very little about the original Elizabeth Kensington, aside from that I inherited her name. She died when my dad was five. One of my earliest memories is asking my father why I only had one grandmother. I don't remember his exact response, but I do remember the haunted look on his face.

I never asked again.

"Did you and Mom decide how long you're staying?" I ask.

Dad's forehead wrinkles as he helps himself to some waffles. "Not for certain," he replies, which is a bizarrely vague answer from the man who plans his calendar months in advance.

Both of my parents do. It was a necessity as they juggled two high-powered careers and three kids. Even now that Bash is in college, neither of my parents shows any sign of slowing down.

"Will you still be here when I get back from Chloe's wedding?"

"Yes."

The concrete response should reassure me. But there's a distant patter of uncertainty that sticks in the back of my head. I won't be back from Chloe's wedding for two weeks. That's a lot longer than my parents typically stay in one place. They jet between meetings and movie premieres and fashion shows and galas and conferences and shoots.

Before I can press my dad for more details, Mom sails into the dining room, wearing a white sundress and her signature red lipstick.

"Morning!" she greets cheerily, squeezing my shoulder as she passes by the back of my chair before kissing Dad on the cheek.

He pulls her in for a real one.

I mime vomiting into my coffee cup. Unfortunately, Mom and Dad are too busy making out to appreciate my acting skills, and my brothers aren't here to share commiserative looks with. They're probably still both hungover and asleep.

Kit and Bash went out last night after we got back from Atlantic

Crest while I was hunkered down in my bedroom, reviewing potential projects. I purposefully timed the Claremont Park project so that I could take most of July off around Chloe's wedding. But I've never *not* had a next project lined up, and the lack of future direction is making me anxious. When I'm busier, it's easier to shut up the self-doubt.

"You turned in early last night, Lili," Mom says, taking the seat on Dad's other side. "Everything okay?"

"Mmhmm. I was just tired."

"Must have been the polo," Dad comments.

Since my impulsive decision to participate in yesterday's polo match, I've endured no shortage of commentary from my family. Taunts from my brothers about losing. Worry from my dad about the number of fouls during the game. Thinly veiled disappointment from my grandmother about my "unladylike" behavior.

Sometimes, I'm not sure how Gigi and my mom are related. But I'm very grateful I was raised by Scarlett Kensington instead of Josephine Ellsworth. My mom's the only one who acted like me playing was completely normal while everyone else was staring and whispering.

Kit appears in the dining room a few minutes later, yawning, decked out in American flag board shorts and nothing else. Barefoot and sporting bedhead, looking like he just rolled out of bed and is headed straight to the beach.

Mom takes one look, then says, "Christopher. Shirt. Now."

Kit casts a longing look at the spread of food, then drags a palm down his face. "It's the Fourth, Mom," he whines, looking to Dad for backup.

"No shirt, no service," Dad tells him. "Listen to your mother."

Kit groans, then walks back out of the dining room.

"If only Josephine were here," Dad muses.

Mom gives him a side-glance. "Yeah? You're in the mood for a lecture on how we're raising our kids?"

"There wouldn't be any lectures if we were staying in our own house."

"Don't start, Sport." Mom grabs the carafe and pours some coffee.

My dad is civil with Gigi and Grandfather, but I wouldn't call them close. I suspect it has a lot to do with their disparaging attitude toward Mom's work, but I've never directly asked.

"Leah sent an email this morning," Mom tells me. "The dresses just arrived at Carys Park."

My mom's fashion label, rouge, designed the bridesmaid dresses for me, Bridget, Fran, and Gwen—Chloe's older sister—to wear to Chloe's wedding.

"I'll let Chloe know. Thanks, Mom."

"Of course," she replies. "I want to see lots of photos."

"You will," I assure her. "Chloe's handing out disposable cameras to all the wedding guests."

Bash wanders into the dining room. He has a shirt on at least, but it's a wrinkled one that he's wearing with basketball shorts.

"You never texted last night," Mom scolds as he sits down across from us.

Bash yawns before apologizing. "Sorry."

"You were with Kit?"

My youngest brother glances around the chairs before answering, "Yep."

*Bullshit.*

I take a dainty sip of coffee, glancing between Mom's narrowed eyes and Bash's bleary ones. My parents were equally strict with all three of us, but Bash is the last one partially living at home. He has two years left at Dartmouth.

Dad intervenes. "If you're out past midnight, your mother and I expect a text. Understood, Sebastian?"

"Uh-huh," Bash says as he reaches for a cinnamon roll.

He's always been the smartest out of the three of us. Unlike me, who hated school because of my dyslexia, and Kit, who was more interested in being the life of the party than getting straight As, Bash's the sort of student teachers see as a future judge or surgeon. He's more easygoing too. Kit or I would have argued for a one a.m. curfew.

Gigi enters the dining room next. Everything about her appearance is pristine, and her expression is as animated as I expected on this date.

She and Mom might not act a lot alike, but they look it. Meaning I resemble Gigi too, aside from the blue eyes Mom once confided are her favorite feature of Dad's.

My grandmother smiles approvingly at my outfit. Her smile drops a little when she spots a slouched Bash, then another centimeter when Kit returns to the room. He pulled on a white T-shirt, but he's still barefoot with messy hair.

"I'm not sure when breakfast became so … casual," Gigi remarks.

"They'll change before we leave for the parade," Mom tells her.

Kit opens his mouth—to protest, I'm positive—but Dad shuts him up with a hard look.

"What time are you expecting Oliver and his family to arrive?"

Gigi asks Dad.

He checks his watch. "They should be here in twenty minutes, Josephine."

Gigi and Grandfather's house is plenty large enough to host Uncle Oliver, Aunt Hannah, and my two cousins, but they're staying at my parents' house instead. A house I suspect Dad bought to avoid staying here, but Gigi always insists we keep them company to make up for "all the time spent on the West Coast."

"Where's Dad?" my mom asks her.

Gigi sighs. "He took an early tee time. He promised he'd be back by …" She glances at the clock above the mantel. "Now."

My parents exchange a loaded look. Mom appears exasperated. Dad amused.

Gigi takes a seat at the table and fills a crystal bowl with yogurt and berries. A maid delivers a steaming cup of tea in front of her as she writes in the leather portfolio that was tucked under her arm. Her penmanship is the type of precise cursive that looks like it was drawn by a machine, the perfect loops evident from across the table. Her to-do list for today, I'm guessing. The Red, White, and Blue party is not a small event. In years past, the guest list was around a thousand.

For a few minutes, the only sound in the room is the clink of silver against china. Breakfast with my parents and brothers is normally a much noisier affair, but we're mostly on our best behavior here.

Gigi closes the portfolio a moment later, taking a careful taste of her hot tea. "I hope you'll refrain from any unrefined activities today, Elizabeth."

My mom's parents have always called me by my full name. My

dad's father is the only one of my grandparents who calls me Lili.

"I just felt like doing something different," I say, grabbing another muffin.

Playing yesterday felt like a golden opportunity to corrupt conventionality a little. Most of Atlantic Crest's members probably think I'm a "vapid heiress." At least I showed them I'm also proficient with a mallet. That I'm more than my last name and my looks.

"Events at Atlantic Crest aren't meant for making bold statements, darling."

There's a cacophony of responses to that statement.

"Who cares? She's a fucking Kensington." Kit.

"If polo is *unrefined*, why do they play it at the club?" Bash.

"Lili played well." Dad.

"Perhaps we should stop going to events at Atlantic Crest then." Mom.

My family members all leap to my defense, and their support coalesces into a warm glow in my chest. Kensingtons are allowed to give each other shit, but no one else is.

Gigi dabs at her mouth delicately. I know her expressions well enough to tell that she's regretting mentioning yesterday.

My grandfather's booming voice alleviates some of the tension in the room. Even in his seventies, Hanson Ellsworth has the kind of presence that can't be ignored. He's had two heart attacks, and he sometimes walks with a cane, but his mind is as sharp as ever. He sold Ellsworth Enterprises eight years ago and has spent most days since golfing and telling other people how to run their businesses. The only two people I've never heard him dole out advice to are Mom and Dad. He draws better boundaries than Gigi does—barely.

"You're late, Hanson." Gigi gives the mantel clock a pointed look.

"Apologies, Josephine." Grandfather takes one of the few remaining seats—the head of the table, of course—then surveys us all with a proud smile. "Busy morning. Had a hard time getting away."

"Great breakfast, Gigi," Bash says, grabbing a waffle.

We all murmur our agreement, even Grandfather, who hasn't touched a thing on the table.

Gigi beams. "Thank you, Sebastian."

I swear he milks being the baby of the family every chance he gets. Mom's an only child, so the three of us are Gigi's only grandchildren.

"I invited a few more guests, Josephine," Grandfather declares.

We all glance at Gigi, whose lips are tightly pursed.

"You did what?"

"I was playing golf with William Waldorf, and he invited Derek Barclay to join us. Tonight's festivities came up, and it would have been rude not to extend an invitation."

Gigi huffs dramatically, then reaches for her portfolio and makes a note.

Grandfather sighs. "You ordered enough food for the entire East Coast. A few more people won't be much of an imposition."

My family is entirely silent. This is Gigi's day. And her Red, White, and Blue party is the event she prioritizes over everything else. Everyone—most of all Grandfather—knows she doesn't take well to last-minute changes made without her explicit authorization.

"*A few more?* How many people did you invite, Hanson?" With each word, Gigi's tone climbs closer to shrill.

Another heavy sigh from Grandfather.

For the most part, he and Gigi have a symbiotic relationship. He has his priorities, and she has hers. This overlap is equivalent to her showing up on the fairway and telling him which club to choose.

"He said his wife would be coming. And that his stepson is visiting from England and would likely join them."

"The duke?" Bash asks.

A cold weight drops in my stomach. *Fuck no.*

"Elizabeth!" Gigi exclaims. "What unbecoming language."

That loud exclamation that was supposed to stay in my head? Turns out, I said it aloud.

"Sorry, Gigi," I mutter.

Bash's staring at me. So is everyone else. "You know Charles?"

"*You* know Charles?"

"I met him yesterday at the club," Bash tells me. "Seems like a cool guy. Only knew he was a duke because his cousin talks about it."

"How well acquainted are you with this aristocrat?" Gigi asks me, tilting her head to the side. Her neat chignon doesn't so much as wobble with the movement.

"Could we not discuss Lili's se—I mean, love life while I'm eating?" Kit drawls.

"*Christopher,*" Mom chides.

Following her disciplining, I don't miss the flash of curiosity on her face. I told Mom I broke up with Lawrence—the lawyer I was dating in Chicago—but haven't mentioned anyone since. Because there's no one *to* mention.

"I'm not acquainted—I hardly know him. Not even hardly. I don't know him." The truth comes out more defensive than emphatic.

"He ghosted you, huh?"

"*Christopher.*" Dad this time.

"He did not." I glare at my brother.

It should have occurred to me that Charlie might wind up at my grandparents' party tonight. In the past two days, we've ended up in the same place three times. There was no advance warning at Kensington Consolidated or Number 34 or Atlantic Crest though. And those encounters were all prior to me informing Charlie I'd overheard him insulting me last summer.

I saw the look on Charlie's face before I walked away yesterday—he got the message loud and clear. Rather than my feeling triumphant, the thought of seeing him later fills me with trepidation. Any outcome is far from ideal. Either he addresses what happened and I lose the armor of categorizing him as a smug snob, or he ignores it and I'll have to act the part of polite hostess while watching everyone else fawn over him.

None of it should matter. After tonight, there's a good chance I'll never seen him again. According to Fran, he's in a relationship— *poor girl.*

But I'm still bothered.

"If you don't know him, why don't you like him?"

I glower at Bash, who's decided to battle Kit for the title of Most Annoying Brother this morning. "I find him … pretentious."

*And rude and condescending and entitled and haughty and …* *fascinating.*

"Well, he *is* a duke," Gigi says, as if that's a reasonable excuse for any character flaw.

Two servers enter the dining room with fresh plates of food.

Once they return to the kitchen, Gigi launches into today's schedule.

I try to pay attention, but mostly focus on my plate.

Hundreds of people will be attending the patriotic party tonight.

If I decide to, I'll be able to avoid Charlie entirely.

# CHAPTER 9

## *Lili*

I'm halfway down the stairs when the front door opens and Charles Marlborough strolls into the entryway. My foot fumbles on a step, the point of the heel slipping to the left. I tighten my grip on the railing as I swear under my breath.

A thousand guests and another hundred staff are at this event, and we're the only two people in the soaring entryway.

I can't go back upstairs without him seeing me. I can't continue downstairs without him seeing me. I'm screwed either way.

My chin lifts, and I avoid Charlie's eyes as I carefully descend the rest of the curved staircase. The last thing this moment needs is me falling flat on my face.

I don't need to look at him. I already memorized his appearance—the shade of his suit and the variety of flowers in the beautiful bouquet he's holding. He abided by the patriotic dress code, wearing a blue suit and a crisp white button-down. No tie.

Two buttons undone to show off the twin curves of his collarbone and tease at the tan skin of his chest.

Fuck him for being so good-looking.

I'm regretting my choice of red dress. Together, we look … coordinated. Complete.

I reach the marble floor, forced to face him.

He speaks first, shattering the deafening silence. "Elizabeth."

"Charles."

His gaze doesn't stray away from my face, ignoring the low neckline of my dress and the opulent furnishings of my grandparents' summer home.

"You're supposed to head straight into the backyard," I inform him haughtily. "Not come inside."

The sole job of five of the hundred employees my grandmother has working this event is to direct foot traffic from the parking area straight toward the patio and tent.

"I asked to put these in water." Charlie lifts the flowers a couple of inches. "Figured they would wilt fast in this heat."

They would. It's blazing hot out. I'm dreading leaving the air-conditioning to go mingle by the pool, barely recovered from the tennis match earlier. I had to shower twice to feel like I was sweat-free.

A vent blasts the sweet perfume of the bouquet straight into my face, mixed with the intoxicating aroma of whatever musky aftershave or cologne Charlie wears. Some scent that makes me want to inhale deeper.

I hold a hand out, wiggling my fingers impatiently. "I'll take care of it."

"I don't mind."

"Well, *I* do," I snap.

He studies me for a few seconds, then takes one step closer.

I fight the strong urge to step back and maintain the same amount of distance between us.

"Elizabeth, I—"

"You must be Charles Marlborough." Kit is buttoning his jacket as he jogs down the staircase.

I stiffen, shooting my brother a warning look as he approaches us.

One he pays no attention to. "I'm Kit Kensington. Heard a lot about you."

I tense even more.

Surprisingly, so does Charlie. Out of the corner of my eye, I catch a jump in the firm muscles of his jaw.

"Nice to meet you, Kit."

They shake hands.

"You played well yesterday," Kit comments.

The praise isn't aimed at me. He might have joined my defense against Gigi at breakfast, but my brother is otherwise uninterested in complimenting me. And I'm annoyed he's interested in complimenting Charlie.

"You fell off the horse last time you played," I remind my brother.

"I don't see what that has to do with anything," Kit retorts. "Come on, Charles. I'll introduce you around."

I have to work at hiding my shock. Kit makes friends easily, but I didn't expect him to embrace Charlie so quickly.

What is it with this guy becoming buddy-buddy with my brothers?

Charlie doesn't follow Kit right away. He holds out the flowers. "These are for you," he says quietly.

Damn his crisp accent. It's consuming, just like his unflinching gaze and intoxicating smell. It takes me a few seconds to remember, one, I'm mad at him; two, my plan was to avoid him; and, three, he's not single. This bouquet is just a half-assed apology for what he now knows I heard him say about me last summer. Remorse minus admittance.

I force out a "Thank you." The relief that my voice sounds normal is smothered by the swarm of butterflies that appears when his thumb brushes my knuckles during the transfer of flowers.

"You're welcome."

"Come on, Charles. Lili likes to make a grand entrance. Alone." Kit's no longer trying to annoy me. He's just impatient.

Charlie is fighting a smile. The sight of him struggling against amusement—even at my expense—does something strange to my insides. My chest squeezes tight, and my stomach spins as he heads toward the wall of French doors that open out onto the patio surrounding the pool.

"Guy brought you flowers. What an *asshole*," Kit whispers.

I flip him off.

Kit chuckles, then saunters after Charlie.

I stop in the butler's pantry to find a crystal vase for the flowers. A petty urge has me considering letting them wither, but it's not like I can toss the shriveled blooms in Charlie's face. Not without causing a scene and giving my grandmother a conniption at least. So, I snip the ends and make sure the water is lukewarm before setting the vase in a patch of sunlight on the marble counter.

There's no sign of Kit or Charlie when I walk onto the patio. My brothers tend to be the ringleaders of a less formal party amid my grandmother's annual bash. When I was younger, I'd participate, but expectations are different now. Ones Kit has always had an easier time ignoring. The only reason he spent any time by the pool last year was because my college roommate was visiting and Kit had a massive crush on her.

This year, most of my friends are missing. We're leaving for Chloe's wedding tomorrow, so Bridget, Fran, and Jasper all opted to stay in the city for the holiday weekend.

Tripp and Hugo are standing by the buffet table, talking to a bunch of other guys I recognize. I head in the opposite direction, toward one of the bars that's been set up throughout the yard. I've been outside for less than a minute, and I can already feel sweat prickling the back of my neck and small of my back.

Aunt Hannah is accepting a glass of wine from the bartender. She's changed since this afternoon, now wearing one of Mom's designs—a blue-and-white-patterned sundress—and her fingernails are painted bright crimson. Gigi would approve.

She glances over as I approach. Smiles. "Nice dress."

I smile back. "You too."

"I knew it was a Scarlett original from the color alone."

I order a ranch water from the bartender. Simple and refreshing sound perfect right now.

"Have you seen Wren or Rory?" Hannah asks me.

"No," I reply. "I delayed leaving the air-conditioning for as long as I could. Barely been out here for five minutes."

My aunt grimaces, tucking a piece of blonde hair behind her ear. "We're in a bit of a parenting rough patch. Oliver caught Wren sneaking in last night. He's having a hard time accepting his little girl is seventeen."

That explains Wren's scowl at the parade. When I asked her what was wrong, she told me she had a headache.

"Guess he didn't have to worry about that with Rory," I say.

Hannah and Oliver's older daughter is a carbon copy of my uncle. Serious, meticulous, and rule-abiding. She was the one who always tattled on pranks we played as kids.

"Not so much." Hannah sighs. "How did your parents handle it?"

I smirk. "Handle what?"

She raises one eyebrow. "You're telling me you never snuck out, Lili?"

"I'm saying I never got *caught* sneaking out."

Hannah laughs, then shakes her head. "Great. We'll suggest she be more quiet next time."

I laugh too, then sober. "The harder you try to slow it down, the faster she'll try to grow up."

My aunt smiles, but it's a bittersweet one. "I know. I was seventeen once too, you know."

I take my drink from the bartender and tap my glass against Hannah's. "Cheers. Also, you could try changing the alarm code. That'll slow her down at least."

Hannah's face lights up. "The alarm code! That's brilliant." She immediately pulls her phone out of her clutch, presumably to text Oliver. "I've heard rave reviews about the Claremont project, by the way. Very impressive, Lili," she tells me as she types.

"Thanks," I reply before taking a sip of my cold drink. Tart fizziness hits my tongue, followed by the smoky aftertaste of tequila.

When it comes to work, I value my aunt's opinion over anyone's.

She works for one of the city's top architecture firms.

When I was floundering during college, hating all my classes and trying to figure out what I wanted to do for the rest of my life, she offered me an internship at her firm. My first assignment involved a museum in Boston. The design of the indoor space was interesting, but I was fascinated by the work done by the landscape architect. The building was there—needing extensive renovation and improvements, but framed and standing. The surrounding gardens morphed from dirt that had been packed flat by an endless stream of construction vehicles delivering materials. That challenge—creating something from nothing or shaping wild beauty into purposeful design—was what appealed to me the most. I abandoned my public relations major at Yale, transferred to Cornell, and packed the following summer with extra credits so I could graduate on time. I passed the Landscape Architect Registration Examination on my first try—by far the best I'd ever performed on any academic assessment—and have no regrets about my career choice.

It's just not what people expect from a Kensington. My mom is editor in chief of an incredibly successful magazine in addition to her luxury fashion label that's expanded into skin care and beauty. My dad runs a production company in LA, which has won so many Oscars that I've lost count. Kit is about to start working at Kensington Consolidated, which is considered a titan among powerful, wealthy corporations. Bash is going to graduate summa cum laude. And then there's me, the glorified gardener.

No matter how much support I receive from my family—and I do; even Kit would never make a disparaging comment about my job—it's hard not to feel like I'm the solitary outlier in a series of success stories.

"Are you still working on the nature preserve in Queens?" I ask Hannah.

She nods. "But we're in a holding pattern, waiting for the construction company to come through with permits, so I'm taking on a couple of smaller projects in the meantime."

"Hi, Lili."

My stomach twists unpleasantly as I glance away from my aunt. Cal is standing a few feet away, his hand resting on Violet DuPont's lower back.

We talked for a while at Atlantic Crest yesterday. About Chloe's upcoming wedding and Claremont Park and how his master's is going. The sort of superficial catchup that did little to alleviate the awkwardness that was heavy in the hot air.

"Hey, Cal," I reply. My grip tightens on my glass as I wish I'd swallowed more tequila before he appeared.

"I should go check on the girls," Hannah says. "Excuse me."

Before walking away, my aunt shoots me a small, encouraging smile. She knows about my history with Cal, just like everyone else here. Over Violet's shoulder, I can see Gigi looking this way. She approved of my decision to date Cal. Disapproved of my decision to break up with him, which is the recurrent reaction.

"Nice to see you, Violet," I add.

"You too." Violet fiddles with a gold bracelet on her wrist, a forced smile on her face.

Cal and I went to school with Violet up until ninth grade, when she left New York to attend a private boarding school in Connecticut. I've seen her a handful of times since, but I don't think we've actually spoken in over a decade. That's not why this is so uncomfortable though.

Violet's beautiful, her auburn hair carefully curled and her dress the same shade of blue as the clear sky above. I hope Cal truly likes her, but the way he hasn't broken eye contact with me since they appeared makes me think she's a pawn in the game I quit playing.

"Did you guys make it to the parade this morning?" I ask.

Not my best attempt at small talk, but better than standing in uncomfortable silence.

"We were planning on it, but it was so hot …" Violet's voice trails off as she glances at Cal. "Cal suggested we skip it this year."

"Good call," I say. "It was pretty unpleasant out." Still is actually.

"Did you guys still have your tennis match?"

I make sure all the warmth in my expression has drained away before looking at Cal. "Yes, we did."

He participated in the family tournament the two years we were dating. A few times before, back when we had been just friends. I can't tell if he's reminiscing about our relationship or our friendship, which bothers me. I'm only interested in resuscitating one of them.

"Cal's been telling me about the plans for Chloe's wedding," Violet comments. "It sounds like it'll be an amazing trip. I'm sad I have to miss it."

"Oh. I assumed you …"

Violet sighs, then shakes her head. "I can't take the time off work."

I was banking on her being Cal's date to the wedding. I even told Tripp to make sure that Cal knew Violet was welcome on the jet tomorrow, and he said *nothing* to me about Cal's girlfriend not coming with us.

I take a sip of my drink, tempted to drain the whole glass. "Where do you work, Violet?"

"At Maxwell & Lewis," she answers.

I've heard of it. It's a popular interior design firm in Manhattan.

"Vi really spiffed up my parents' place," Cal says.

"That's great," I say, trying to come up with some excuse to go … anywhere else. Getting stuck in a conversation with my ex and his new girlfriend is not an ideal start to the evening.

"Hell of a party, Kensington."

I relax as soon as I hear Tripp's booming voice, even more when he tugs me into his side for a hug.

Hugo is right behind him, followed by Malcolm Crane. I've never liked Malcolm very much, mostly because he makes a point to flirt shamelessly every time we interact. My aversion is nothing compared to my dad's though. He hates the Crane family for some reason.

Malcolm won't flirt with me now. Not in front of Cal. Most of the guys I grew up with still consider me "his." It *almost* makes me want to ask Malcolm to get me another drink.

"I can't take any credit," I tell Tripp. "This is all Gigi."

"You're here, Lili. That's why half these people showed up."

I roll my eyes. Tripp is exaggerating. But there's a kernel of truth to it. I'm Crew and Scarlett Kensington's oldest child and only daughter. Just because I chose not to get involved in any of my family's businesses, people still care about what I do. Where I go. What I say.

Because I might not have any part in my family's businesses right now, but I'm set to inherit a massive stake in all of them.

I'm distracted by a waving Madeline Spencer. We attended the same private schools but didn't become close friends until I transferred to Cornell.

"There's Maddie," I say. "I'll see you guys later."

I walk away carefully, as the grass and flagstone patio are challenging surfaces to navigate while wearing heels.

Catching up with Maddie gets interrupted after about fifteen minutes by a friend of Gigi's. That leads into two hours of nonstop conversation. I finally excuse myself to use the bathroom, opting to head inside rather than use the pool house one.

My stomach growls as I pass the kitchen and walk down the hall—a reminder that all I've eaten since lunch at the yacht club was a few canapés. Clangs echo behind me as the catering staff prepares the upcoming courses.

My heels click against tiles as I walk into the closest bathroom. My dark brown hair and vibrant red dress are vivid splashes of color in the reflection of the massive mirror above the twin sinks. Everything in here—porcelain and marble and Egyptian cotton—is white. I pee, wash my hands, then attempt to smooth the frizz that's appeared along my hairline.

Humidity: 1. Hair spray: 0.

I debate going upstairs to grab a lipstick out of my room, but decide against it. It's completely dark out, so the fireworks are set to start soon. I'll grab some food, then head down to the beach to watch them.

When I'm halfway down the hallway that connects to the front entryway, a tall figure approaches from the opposite direction. My heartbeat stutters, then accelerates, when I recognize Charlie Marlborough. I spotted him once, about an hour ago, talking with two friends of my grandfather's, but we haven't spoken since he arrived.

*His* hair is perfect. So is the rest of his immaculate appearance. I can't even spot a wrinkle in his suit.

I raise my chin when he reaches me, determined to hold eye contact. "What's your excuse for trespassing this time?"

"Trespassing?" His left eyebrow lifts. I feel the movement as a spasm in my stomach, same as the first time we met. "I know you wouldn't have invited me, Kensington, but I *was* invited."

"Not inside. There are four bathrooms in the pool house for *guests*."

Anyone else, and I wouldn't give a shit. But combat has become my default setting around Charlie. He's never tried to flatter or impress me the way most men do. And I'm … honestly, I'm not sure how else to act around him.

"I'm not looking for the loo," he tells me. "I was looking for you."

My next step makes me totter in my heels, off-balance for reasons that have everything to do with him. "I actually need to—"

A warm hand wraps around my left bicep, halting me in place. My world narrows to nothing but that confident touch. I'm instantly aware of everything about it. The strength in his grip. The searing warmth of his skin. The rough calluses on his palm.

"The only thing you need to do is listen to me."

The words drip with arrogance. I'm sure he's accustomed to always being indulged.

"Like hell I—"

Again, he interrupts. "I'm sorry." That mostly green gaze drills into me, fierce and persistent.

It's impossible to ignore the sincerity in his voice, yet I try very hard to.

"What I said last summer …" He grimaces. "Well, it goes without saying, you were never meant to hear that."

"*Wow.* Award for Most Pathetic Apology goes to—"

"I'm not finished." Charlie steps closer, his nearness unnerving me as much as the unwavering eye contact and the way he's still holding my arm. "It was a rubbish thing to say, and I regret ever saying it. I was … upset about things that had nothing to do with anyone there, including you. And speaking of *you*, Elizabeth Kensington, you never told me your surname when we first met. I recognized Kensington when Ellis said it, and I made incorrect assumptions based on …" He clears his throat. "Based on the way other women were acting around me. That's not—I don't think that about you, Lili."

Damn him.

Damn him for apologizing.

Damn him for making me believe him.

Damn him for calling me Lili like he knows me well enough to.

I've met a lot of guys who were incapable of taking accountability for their actions. Who made excuses and shifted blame. It can easily become second nature when you're used to everyone accommodating you. And I would have bet money—lots of money—that Charles Marlborough fell into the category of *entitled man who avoids apologies like a contagious disease.*

"I thought we first met at Kensington Consolidated," I say. "That's what you told Fran."

"You could have corrected me."

I bite the inside of my cheek, attempting to regulate my breathing as he continues staring at me. It's too fast.

I'm too affected.

He's too close.

Close—and getting closer. I'm losing the ability to talk. I forget how to breathe.

I'm frozen, my overwhelmed brain too slow to register *Charlie is kissing me* until we're several seconds into it.

His lips are warm and firm and compelling, suctioning my top one with a persistent skill that speaks to experience. His tongue invades next, brushing mine before tracing the length of my lower lip.

Shivers race down my spine as I palm the plaster behind me, concerned the wall is all that's holding me up. My legs feel numb, all the blood in my body rushing to other places.

Charlie's left hand cups the curve of my cheek, angling my mouth exactly where he wants it. His right hand lands on my waist, the heat of his touch burning through the thin fabric of my dress like there's no barrier between our bodies. One of his legs presses between mine, parting my thighs so that I'm straddling hard muscle.

The friction prompts a blissful surge of pleasure. Tingles erupt and spread. I gasp.

He chuckles against my mouth. And it's that sound—that maddening superiority—that breaks through the hypnotic haze and reminds me why this should not be happening.

I yank my head back and slap him, the smack of skin against skin reverberating down the empty hallway.

My fingers fist around my stinging palm as shock filters through me. I just hit someone. I've *never* hit someone. Never been so consumed by a kiss, either.

I press my lips tight together to keep an apology from spilling out.

Charlie doesn't flinch or grimace. His only reaction is lifting a hand to gingerly poke at the red mark blooming across his cheek.

"What the fuck was that for?" He sounds more entertained than pissed, which makes me scowl.

"You kissed me," I hiss.

He rubs his thumb across his lower lip, then prods the inside of his cheek with his tongue. Winces.

I should feel bad—I do—but I'm also a little proud of my accuracy.

"Well aware," Charlie drawls, still managing to sound condescending. "Seemed like you were enjoying it."

I blush at the accurate statement. His thigh is still wedged between mine—glaring evidence of what just took place. "I'm not a cheater."

His hand drops from his face, bewilderment blanketing his handsome features. "I thought you were single."

"*I* am. *You're* not."

Charlie laughs once. "What?"

"You told Fran you were taken."

The confusion clears from his face. "That seemed politer than mentioning she wasn't the woman I wanted to continue talking to."

"Oh." My cheeks must match my dress. "It didn't occur to you that she might tell me what you said?"

"It did not." Charlie rests one hand on the wall, next to my head. "Does that change anything?"

I bite my bottom lip, the truth spilling out anyway. "Yes."

"Yes?"

I scoff as he stares expectantly. "You want me to say it again?"

"Actually, I do."

"I promise I won't slap you this time, okay?"

One corner of Charlie's mouth lifts. "That's not why I want to hear you say yes to me, Lili." His voice is low and husky.

The tone hits me like a strong dose of a powerful drug. Proof that I really, *really* want to kiss him again.

"Yes," I whisper.

He kisses me.

But it's my tongue that seeks his. My hands that yank his button-down free from his slacks so that I can explore the taut muscles ridging his stomach. My hips that rock forward, grinding against his thigh to chase more delicious friction.

"You're soaking my favorite trousers, Kensington."

"Are you complaining?" I pant the question, too distracted to come up with anything wittier. Lust is coiling tight low in my pelvis, my muscles clenched in anticipation of a release.

Charlie started this, and he'd better let me finish. I've had sex with several guys since Cal and I broke up. None of those encounters were this satisfying, and I haven't even come yet.

He's *barely* touching me. I'm basically getting off on his proximity. Under any other circumstances, I'd be self-conscious. Right now, I'm too consumed to care.

"It was a compliment," Charlie informs me.

I huff a laugh. "Thanks?"

"Of me," he continues. "You must want me bloody bad to be this wet without my fingers or tongue."

I should probably slap him again. Instead, I almost smile. The fact that I'm finding his conceited charm entertaining is a bright red flag.

But he's right. I want him *bloody bad*. Badly enough that my pride has left the premises.

His fingers skim up my left arm, leaving a trail of goosebumps behind. They stop at the strap of my dress, toying with the thin strip of fabric keeping the top up.

Charlie holds my gaze, waiting for me to decide.

Some people think I'm shy. That I act poised and proper in public because I'm not brave enough to be bold.

Really, I'm scared. I was born on a pedestal, automatically elevated. I'm terrified to mess up and embarrass my family. It takes me weeks, months, *years* to fully trust someone. Almost all of my closest friends are people I've known since preschool.

But I barely think before nodding.

For some reason, I trust Charlie. Even though I hardly know him. Even though he's given me reasons I shouldn't.

The top of the dress droops just low enough to expose my left breast.

He stares at my heaving chest for a few seconds before cupping the curve in his palm. I whimper when his deft fingers toy with the nipple, then groan when his hand falls to my waist. The warmth of his touch is replaced by the brush of his suit jacket against my bare breast when he pulls my mouth back to his.

There's something dangerously erotic about imagining what we must look like—me half dressed and humping his leg, Charlie fully covered and in control.

His lips move to my ear. "Show me how wet you can get, Lili."

My muscles tremble, my oncoming release so close that it feels tangible. The edges of my vision shimmer, and my head tilts back as waves of heat wash over me. I ride his thigh as hard as I can, clenching around nothing.

It's incredible and consuming, convulsions continuing to tumble through me, even as the strongest rush fades.

But I want more. I want him inside of me, filling that emptiness.

Charlie steps back before I can suggest we sneak upstairs. Aside from his eyes—which have a feral glint—and the bulge in his pants, he appears unaffected.

"Happy Fourth of July, Elizabeth."

That's all he says before he turns around and walks away.

Leaving me, slumped and breathless and disappointed, wondering what the hell just happened.

# CHAPTER 10

## *Charlie*

Blythe wanders downstairs shortly after noon. It's the first time I've seen my little sister in two weeks. She's spent summer so far traveling with her friends, returning to Newcastle Hall for sporadic weekends, but mostly preferring to stay at the London flat I lived in before becoming the eighth Duke of Manchester.

"Where's breakfast?" Blythe asks, surveying the empty table.

"You mean lunch?"

She makes a face as she sinks into one of the Chippendale dining chairs. Yawns, her brown eyes still bleary with sleep. "Thought you'd sleep in, considering the time difference."

Blythe inspects her fingernails, painted a bright shade of pink, and I know it's the closest she'll come to asking how my trip to New York was.

She flat-out refused to accompany me to the States to visit our

mother, which was the expected response. I get why Blythe doesn't want to see Georgia better than anyone, and it's her decision to make.

But I experience a fresh surge of anger toward Georgia, watching my sister forcibly project disinterest. Blythe shouldn't be the one who has to make an effort with our mother. Neither should I for that matter.

"It was bloody hot. Our cousin Ellis is fairly entertaining." We exchanged numbers last summer, but Ellis never called or messaged. Since I left New York, he's already texted me twice. "I played polo at Georgia's husband's country club."

Blythe doesn't react to the brief recap, continuing to stare at her nails. Eventually, she asks, "Did your team win?"

I smile. "Yes."

She makes an approving hum in the back of her throat.

"How was"—I try to remember where she called me from—"Budapest?"

Blythe perks up, finally making eye contact. "Oh, it was brilliant. And then we went to Sintra. We visited Cabo da Roca and Queluz National Palace." She glances around. "It was about the size of this place."

I snort and shake my head. "I'm sure the Portuguese would appreciate the comparison."

My sister smirks. "They should have built a bigger palace if they wanted to avoid comparisons."

"Are you here this week?" I ask.

"Until Wednesday. I'm going to Saint-Tropez with Zara and Emily."

My stomach churns, the eggs, sausage, and toast I ate for

breakfast threatening to make a reappearance. Part of me—all of me—was hoping I could avoid this conversation until after the sale was finalized.

"I'm selling the villa, Blythe."

A rare instance of my sister being speechless follows.

"What?" she demands. "Why?"

"We hardly use it. It just sits there, and I'm—"

"So?" she interrupts. "*I* use it. Let it sit."

*Do I tell her?* That's been a weekly—sometimes daily—question that's echoed around in my head ever since a roomful of barristers informed me exactly what I'd inherited along with my father's former title.

Blythe has one year of university left, and I don't want to be the one who ruins it for her. I'm all she really has since her independence has never meshed well with Gran's strict nature. For his many faults, our father adored Blythe. Showered her with warm affection I'd thought he was incapable of. She's mourning his death in the same way she grieves our mother's absence, even though she'll never admit to either. Our parents both let her down in different ways, and I never want to do the same.

My hope was to resolve everything without Blythe ever knowing the truth. But until Kensington Consolidated or another investor writes a check, my best option for staying afloat is to sell more assets.

"I need to sell it, Blythe."

"It's Mu—Georgia's." Blythe drops eye contact and starts picking at her nail polish.

"Papa left it to me," I say gently, pretending not to notice her slip of the tongue.

The French villa hasn't been in our family for generations, like most of the properties I own. It was purchased by my father twenty-seven years ago as a wedding gift to my mother. It's where they honeymooned.

I haven't visited it in years, but Blythe goes often. I knew she'd be unhappy about the sale, but it makes no sense to keep it.

"It should have been mine," Blythe mumbles.

I don't disagree. If things were different, I'd give it to her as a graduation gift.

"I need …" I exhale. "I need to sell it, Blythe. There's a lot—*a lot*—that Papa left that I'm trying to learn and catch up on, and I just … it's one less thing to manage. You can still go on Wednesday. It's not going on the market until next week."

I'm traveling to the south of France to sort out the sale—a trip I wasn't looking forward to and am now dreading.

"Why can't you just hire someone to manage everything for you? Then, you can go back to school and—"

"It's my responsibility, Blythe."

"So, my opinion doesn't matter?" she challenges.

"Of course it matters. I just … it doesn't change this decision. I'm sorry."

My sister says nothing, just studies me. For a few seconds, I think she's going to call me out. She knows I sold an office building in Beijing last fall and an apartment complex in Vancouver. Properties I hadn't even known my father had purchased. I'd paid little attention to his business dealings because I didn't think I needed to. Between another sale and her card declining, it's not a massive leap to consider the possibility that we're having money problems.

"Fine. Sell it." Blythe shoves her chair back and stands. "I'll see you later."

"Where are you going?"

"I feel like a pastry from Pain Pain," my sister tells me. "Then, Claire and I are going shopping at Covent Garden."

I sigh. I shouldn't take it personally that Blythe wants to spend time with her friends, but it feels like her haste to leave means my being a good brother is another thing I'm failing at.

"Granny is expecting us for tea at three," I remind her.

"I can't make it."

"Blythe …"

"What? We both know she only wants to see you anyway."

I want to argue, but it's not entirely inaccurate. Changing Blythe's or my grandmother's opinions—and they don't share many to start with—is like attempting to bend iron.

"She loves you."

"And I love her. *Especially* when I'm not being forced to listen to a lecture on my posture or my manners or how fashion is a hobby, not a proper course of study. I'll visit her for tea next week."

"You promise?"

"I promise. I'll see you for dinner." Blythe spins toward the doorway.

"Wait. This is for you." I bend down to retrieve the paper bag on the floor. Set it on the mahogany table and slide it toward my sister. "From Georgia."

Blythe's response is predictable. "I don't want it."

My jaw works as I study her proud stance. Squared shoulders, lifted chin, narrowed eyes. She looks so much like our father. So do I. Blythe has Georgia's brown eyes, but neither of us inherited her blonde hair. We both look like Marlboroughs. Act like

Marlboroughs.

I never saw my father's cracks. Not until he was gone and no longer able to hide them. I'm worried I'm missing Blythe's. That mine are forming under the pressure of holding everything together.

I exhale, trying to keep my composure. It's fucking exhausting, acting as the bridge between two people determined to keep their distance.

Two hours spent in ten stores—that was how long it took to pick out the wrapped handbag sitting on the table. One very similar to the purses spilling out of Blythe's overstuffed closet. One that she would probably love if gifted to her by a friend or an admirer.

But the one thing worse than returning home with a gift my mother didn't want to buy and my sister would never use would have been coming back empty-handed, allowing my mother to completely ignore the existence of her other child.

I nod toward the bag. "Take it."

Maybe she can hear the fissures forming in my voice.

Because Blythe listens for once. She takes the bag and tells me, "I'm glad you're home, Charlie," before leaving the dining room.

My grandmother lives in a townhouse in Knightsbridge that overlooks Hyde Park. For most people, the coveted address and five live-in staff would be a recipe for contentment.

Grace Marlborough is not most people.

For all the privilege in her life, she's also endured more than her fair share of hardship. My grandfather died when I was six. My dad inherited the Duke of Manchester title young, just like I did. She's seen the title pass through three generations in her lifetime.

As I open the metal gate and walk up the short stone path, I pray the tradition ends with me. Assuming I have children and there's anything left of the dukedom to pass on. Otherwise, *everything* will end with me.

Elsie—the woman who's assisted my grandmother for longer than I've been alive—answers the door. She beams when she sees me. "Hullo, Charlie. How are yuh?"

The sound of her Cockney accent hits me with a strong dose of nostalgia. Elsie outlasted all of the nannies Blythe and I had. She's a fond reminder of childhood—the easier, smoother patch of my life between losing my parents. The closest to a surrogate mother I have.

"Good, Elsie." I kiss her weathered cheek, then hand her one of the bunches of flowers I bought from the newspaper stand down the street.

Her smile stretches wider, overtaking her wrinkled cheeks. She's in her early sixties now. "Yuh spoil me. I'm puttin' 'ese in me room." Elsie glances down the stone walkway, one eyebrow, threaded with gray, lifting when she registers Blythe's absence before she shuts the door behind me. "Yuh ain't the strictest bruvah."

I sigh. "I know. Granny in the sunroom?"

"Aye."

I thank Elsie and continue walking down the hallway and past the staircase. The only adornment on the cream-colored wall opposite the stairs is an oil painting of Gran, my father, and my grandfather. It was painted when my father was fifteen. There used to be a similar family portrait hanging in Newcastle Hall, but Papa wiped all evidence of Georgia's existence from the manor as soon as she left. Out of anger or sadness, I'll never know.

My grandmother is perched on the edge of a floral settee in

the sunroom, a spread already laid out—steaming tea, scones, and clotted cream piled high in a glass bowl. My stomach grumbles, still on American time. It's past dinner there, and all I've eaten today was breakfast.

Granny's eyes are sharp and assessing as she appraises me, the flowers I'm holding, and the conspicuous absence of Blythe.

"Hello, Granny."

She accepts the flowers and a kiss on the cheek with a demure smile. I take my usual seat in one of the armchairs opposite her.

"Hello, Charles. Where's your sister?"

It's obvious Blythe isn't here. But of course, she's going to make me say it.

"She couldn't make it."

My grandmother clicks her tongue as she hands the bouquet off to Alfie, her butler. He shoots me a smile before leaving the room.

"You spoil that girl, Charles."

She's not wrong. I've done everything I can to insulate Blythe's world since our father died. Protecting her peace of mind is my main motivation at the moment. The last bit of normalcy in my life.

Instead of that, I say, "You're looking well."

My last visit was a week ago, right before I left for New York, and Granny was coming down with a cold.

A small nod is the only acknowledgment before she asks, "How is Georgia?"

There's little love lost between my grandmother and my mother. Unsurprising, considering how my parents' marriage ended and the years of deterioration leading up to their divorce. Negative feelings toward Georgia might be Blythe and Gran's strongest commonality.

"She's fine," I reply, unwilling to provide my grandmother with any ammunition.

My mother *is* fine. Our relationship isn't.

During my visit to New York, she treated me like I was a trophy to show off, not a son she wanted to reconnect with. I want a confidant. A *parent* to assure me that everything will be okay rather than a grandmother and sister relying on me to restore the life they're accustomed to. Hundreds of staff and employees whose livelihood is entwined with the dukedom.

I fill one of the teacups, then announce, "I'm selling the villa in Saint-Tropez."

"Good. I told James that purchase was a mistake."

Granny's unfazed reaction is as predictable as Blythe's dismayed one was. As far as I know, my grandmother has never visited the property in France. She avoids leaving London at all costs. Unless it's a trip to Newcastle Hall, her outings are purposefully limited to the Chelsea Flower Show, Wimbledon, Royal Ascot, and Christmas pageants at Westminster Abbey. She culls her calendar to accept only the most exclusive invitations.

"You're attending the Hughes wedding this weekend?" she asks.

I take a sip of Earl Grey rather than answering.

Theodore Hughes was a classmate of mine at Oxford. But I received an invitation to his wedding because I'm the Duke of Manchester. It's an occasion sure to be attended by many people I've spent the better part of a year avoiding, so, no, I had no plans to go.

An answer I know Granny won't like.

"*Charles.*" Her tone sharpens, and I brace for the incoming lecture. "The Hugheses are a prominent family. You not attending will raise questions we don't want asked right now."

My jaw works as I take another swallow of tea. Easy for her to say. She doesn't have to deal with the scrutiny reserved for the duke.

But logically, I know Granny is right. I've been … hiding, for lack of a less pathetic word. Mourning my father, grieving the end of life as I knew it, and scrambling to fix my father's mistakes.

I couldn't afford to drop a few thousand quid during a wild night at a nightclub in SoHo any longer. Dropping out of medical school and moving to Newcastle after inheriting the title were somewhat expected, but my abrupt absence from the social scene wasn't.

Finnegan Byrne—better known as Fig—is the only friend who still reaches out regularly. He mentioned the Hughes wedding to me months ago. He was good friends with Theo at university and asked me if I was attending.

I responded with a vague "Maybe," which we both knew meant no.

If I'm recalling right, the wedding's being held at Carys Park in Wales. Only an hour and a half from Newcastle Hall, but an hour and a half farther than I feel like traveling to spout off a bunch of lies.

"Beatrice Campbell will be attending," Granny adds, as if that were an incentive to show up.

I have no issue with Bea. But I also have no desire to get married anytime soon, and that's the reason Gran is bringing Bea up.

In my grandmother's eyes, my father could do no wrong. I think she's still processing that he frittered our family's fortune away.

She let him wait until he was in his early thirties to get married. Approved of his choice of American bride when it couldn't have been very hard to foresee my parents were a poorly suited couple.

Me? Granny has been dropping names of women she considers well-bred and worthy of the Marlborough name since I was still in university. With more frequency in the past year. I'm not just responsible for keeping us out of bankruptcy. It's also up to me to father a son before I die so that the Duke of Manchester title doesn't get passed off to some distant cousin.

No fucking pressure.

"I'll go," I say, knowing that's the only acceptable answer in my grandmother's mind. At the very least, I'll have a chance to catch up with Fig. Hardship—even hidden—has a way of revealing true friends, I've learned.

Granny smiles, satisfied. "Good."

We visit for another hour, and then I leave. It's a forty-five-minute drive back to Newcastle Hall. Unless I encounter bad traffic, I'll have time to go for a ride before dinner with Blythe.

My mobile buzzes in my pocket as I'm walking down the sidewalk toward my parked car. It's a New York number.

"Hello?" I answer.

"Charles, it's Asher Cotes. How are you?"

Foreboding slithers down my spine. I don't know Asher very well, but I got to know his cheery tone during our meeting last week. It's conspicuously absent now.

"I'm good," I lie, struggling to keep the defeat out of my voice. "How are you?"

"Good, good. Unfortunately, I'm calling with some bad news."

My stomach drops in response to the confirmation. "You're not investing."

"Afraid not. The hotels are valuable pieces of real estate, and it's an enticing offer. But we have some internal changes happening at the company—nothing bad and nothing I can share details on—but it means the board has decided to press pause on any new investments during the transition phase."

I release a long breath, hoping Asher can't hear it. "I understand."

"I'm sure it's not what you were hoping to hear. But it's a great opportunity, Charles. Someone else will snap it up."

I hum in what I hope sounds like an agreement, biting my bottom lip until I taste the coppery tang of blood. My voice sounds even as I reply, "No problem. Thanks for letting me know."

"Good luck, Charles. If you're back in New York anytime soon, let me know. Would love to grab a drink, talk some football."

"Will do," I say. "Bye, Asher."

"Bye, Charles."

# CHAPTER 11

## *Lili*

Cal is the last one to climb onto the plane. I'm not sure if his late arrival was a deliberate decision or not. He and Violet had left the party last night around eleven, earlier than most guests.

He looks exhausted, dark circles under his eyes and his normally neatly combed blond hair a ruffled mess. He stops to talk to Jasper, then sprawls out on the couch across from me and Fran. Yawns.

I clear my throat. "Hey."

He nods. "Hey."

"You're late," Fran says from her spot beside me, nudging Cal's foot with hers. "We almost left without you."

Cal grunts, grabbing a navy Yankees cap out of his backpack and covering his unruly hair. He tugs the brim low, then appears to immediately pass out.

We take off fifteen minutes later, the silhouette of New York's

famous skyline shrinking until it's a speck on the ground. The soundtrack for the first hour of the trip is excited chatter—recounts of the Fourth, anticipation of the trip ahead—but then it gradually fades into silence as everyone but me falls asleep.

I stare out the window at the fluffy clouds soaring past, sorting through my chaotic feelings about Chloe's upcoming wedding.

I'm thrilled for her, obviously. I don't resent a single bit of Chloe's happiness. But she's been my closest friend since preschool. The sister I never had. Her moving to a different continent was bad enough. Now, she's shifting to a whole new phase of her life.

And for the first time, I'm not experiencing it at the same time.

I could have.

I risk a glance at Cal, still fast asleep on the couch. His feet hang off the end. I don't regret ending our relationship. But it's impossible not to think about how different this week might look if I hadn't. That decision created a what-if to consider. I'd probably be attending another wedding—my own—later this summer.

My gaze returns to the window. The clouds part for a few seconds, offering a glimpse of the water far, far, *far* below.

The sight soothes me for some reason. A timely reminder that the world is so much bigger than my small problems.

Bridget wakes up an hour later. I've moved to the table at the far end of the plane, wanting to stretch out some and distance myself from Hugo's snores.

"You're not tired?" Bridget asks, taking the seat across from me.

I shake my head. "Got a good night's sleep," I lie.

I did chug a couple of espressos and apply two layers of concealer under my eyes before crawling into the back of the SUV that drove me from the Hamptons to the airport this morning, so I look well rested.

"Red, White, and Blue party must not have been all that exciting this year then."

I take a sip of the sparkling water I grabbed out of the fridge. "Actually, Tripp was right."

Bridget's forehead wrinkles. "Don't let him hear you say that." Without pausing, she adds, "Right about what?"

"Charles Marlborough is single."

"Charles Mar—oh. The *duke*?" She leans forward. "How do you know?"

I raise both eyebrows.

She raises hers right back. "*Details*, Lili."

Heat creeps into my cheeks. "He kissed me last night. So, I slapped him and said I wasn't a cheater. He told me he told Fran he wasn't available … because he was interested in me."

Her eyes widen more with each sentence. "And then?"

"We kissed some more. He said, 'Happy Fourth of July,' and walked off. I went to watch the fireworks, didn't see him for the rest of the night."

Bridget's witnessed plenty of what Gigi would call "unladylike" moments featuring yours truly, but no way am I going to cop to getting off on Charlie's leg while my ex is sleeping fifteen feet away.

"How was it?"

"It was good."

She smirks. "You're bright red, you know."

"It was great," I amend. "But it's never going to happen again."

"Why not?"

"Because he just … left."

Bridget shrugs. "So? He sounds like perfect one-night-stand

material. Treat yourself to a summer fling."

"I'm not looking for a one-night stand or a fling."

"Why not? You want another relationship?"

"No. I—no."

Bridget nods like that's the answer she was expecting. "You didn't blush *once* while talking about that lawyer in Chicago, you know."

I doubt I ever blushed while talking about Cal either. When it comes to relationships, I've always played it safe. I've always been the less invested one.

"He just walked off," I blurt. "So, I'm not going to chase—"

Bridget leans closer. "I think you met a guy who doesn't give a shit that you're *Elizabeth Kensington,* and it's freaking you the fuck out."

She doesn't know the full story. Doesn't know I first met him last summer. Doesn't know the rude comments he made about me. Doesn't know he kissed me after apologizing. Doesn't know I had the best orgasm of my life last night and he'd barely even touched me to achieve it, as he so cockily informed me.

Bridget doesn't know how reckless I feel around him.

My entire life, I've strove for perfection and often fallen short.

Getting into Yale, where my father went for business school, only to transfer and graduate somewhere else.

The Claremont project, which I took because I was afraid to hold out for an opportunity I was more passionate about.

The logical relationship with the loyal guy, which I pulled the plug on.

"It doesn't even matter," I tell Bridget. "I'll probably never see him again."

She stares at me for a few seconds, then laughs. "Doesn't he live in London? The city we're currently, you know, flying to?"

"I don't know where he lives." *In a castle probably.*

Her eyes dance. "You could find out."

"It would be weird … with Cal." I whisper the words, worried about being overheard.

Bridget sighs. "Lili, I love Hugo and Tripp. But they're wrong. You don't owe Cal a damn thing. People break up and move on. You didn't cheat. You have nothing to feel guilty about."

"I don't feel guilty. I'm just trying to be … respectful."

"I get that. But I think it would be good for Cal to see you with someone else. No one mentioned the lawyer guy to him. As far as he knows, you haven't been with anyone else since the split. At a certain point, he's going to think you being respectful is you having second thoughts about calling it quits."

I exhale. "I know."

"*Are* you having second thoughts?"

"No." I play with the cap of my water bottle. "No, I'm not."

"Then, have some fun this week. My vote would be for the hot duke, but Theo probably has lots of single friends with sexy accents."

Charlie has my vote too. But …

"What about Fran? She was inter—"

Bridget scoffs. "Fran's rebound rate rivals a boomerang's. She hooked up with a guy she met at Proof last night. She'll be thrilled for you. And demand lots of details."

I'm out of obstacles. But I know I won't pursue Charlie this trip. I'm too proud to chase after him. There's no way he couldn't tell I was seconds from begging him to fuck me last night, and he walked away for no apparent reason. Left like he'd lost interest. I don't care if Carys Park—Chloe's wedding venue—turns out to be next door to his castle. He had his chance with me, and he fumbled it.

Tripp wakes with a huge yawn and a lot of noise that rouses everyone else, effectively ending my private conversation with Bridget.

We land in London two hours later.

Chloe is waiting on the tarmac of Heathrow's private terminal, waving a huge banner that reads *Bridal Crew* and wearing a wide smile.

I'm first down the stairs, and we start running at the same time. Canvas smacks the side of my face as I throw my arms around my best friend.

"Shit. Sorry." Chloe giggles in my ear, dropping the banner and hugging me back tightly.

I haven't squeezed her since January. She and Theo came to New York for the holidays, leaving shortly after New Year's. Our weekly phone calls have never been an adequate replacement for what used to be shared exercise classes and weekend brunches. Nights spent competing for more phone numbers or bingeing television shows. We're now separated by the six-hour flight I just stepped off of.

Chloe clings to me just as tightly. This is a new chapter for her, and a new chapter can't begin without ending the previous one.

"Stop hogging the bride, Kensington." Tripp elbows me aside to get to Chloe, and then she's passed around the rest of our friends.

I'm relieved when I see the friendly smile she and Cal exchange before hugging.

Everyone might have avoided taking sides in the aftermath of our breakup, but Tripp and Hugo were more sympathetic toward Cal. And Chloe was firmly in my camp. Cal moving to London shortly after our relationship ended was bad timing all around.

"Sweet!" Jasper says, focusing on the shiny black Mercedes van parked on the tarmac behind Chloe. "Riding in style."

"You spoil us, babe," Tripp declares, smacking a loud kiss on Chloe's cheek.

I roll my eyes. "All you guys did when you got on my *plane* was ask where the liquor was."

"I was hungover," Tripp says, an unspoken *duh* hanging off the end of his sentence. "*Obviously*, alcohol was a priority. But thank you, dearest Lili, for saving me from the horrific fate of flying first class with your private jet. Want a kiss too?"

"Pass. Who knows where that mouth has been?"

Cal's snort is louder than Tripp's shouted, "Hey!"

Cal's nap seems to have revived him. There's more color in his cheeks, and he's finger-combed his hair into compliance.

Our luggage gets unloaded from the plane and stacked in the back of the van by the driver—a middle-aged man with salt-and-pepper hair, mostly covered by a linen flat cap, who introduces himself as Blake.

It's hot and humid out, the sky covered by gray clouds that promise rain soon. We climb into the air-conditioned van, one by one. There are four rows of leather seats, so plenty of space for all of us.

Blake begins driving a few minutes later, expertly steering off the tarmac and onto a road that merges into a highway.

As we drive, Chloe fills us in on the plans for the week. Theo isn't able to get away from work until tomorrow, but then he'll join us at Carys Park. I looked up photos of the venue online, and Chloe sent me some videos when they went to sign the contracts.

It's a former country estate with a main manor that was renovated into an upscale hotel. There's also a historic stone chapel, where the ceremony will take place, and a former carriage house that's been expanded and is now an event hall, where the reception is going to be. They're skipping the traditional rehearsal dinner since not many guests are able to stay at the venue. And "to keep attention on the main event."

Chloe has booked high tea and spa treatments at a hotel in London, which the guys groan good-naturedly about. They perk up when Chloe says Theo has arranged a trip to a Formula One track on Friday. We went racing in Monaco for Jasper's twenty-first, and they all still talk about it. They rarely mention how I beat all of them except Tripp.

At some point during the drive, exhaustion catches up with me, and I fall asleep.

# CHAPTER 12
## Charlie

Persistent buzzing pulls my attention away from the flock of sparrows vandalizing the garden. White smears mar the black metal bench shaded beneath the cherry tree; its broad branches weighted with a lot less fruit than this morning.

I turn away from the windows and back toward my father's—now *my*—massive desk. The tooled green leather top is barely visible, the surface of the desk piled high with papers I'm supposed to be sorting through.

My shin slams into one of the walnut drawers as I spin around in the chair. I answer my phone without checking to see who's calling, reaching down to rub at the throbbing spot.

"Hello?"

"Charlie! What's the craic?"

Fig's cheerful voice is a better remedy for the pain than my palm's pointless rubbing. I smile automatically, listening to the lilt of

his thick Irish accent. A soundtrack of easier times—days when my only concern was making it to campus on time and nights when the only decision was which woman to leave the pub with.

"Not much," I reply, picking up a pen and spinning it around one finger. "You?"

"I'm grand. No one's callin' *me* Disappearin' Duke."

I toss the pen toward the highest stack. It bounces off the papers and lands atop one of the curling scrolls woven into the antique rug. "That's rubbish. I'm just busy."

Fig clicks his tongue, his way of saying he doesn't believe me. "Heard yer comin' to Theo's weddin'."

"How did you …" My voice trails off as irritation flares.

The attention my family received used to be flattering. And advantageous. Now, it's bloody annoying. A bright spotlight while I'm trying to fix things in the shadows.

Fig's husky laugh rumbles in my ear. "Yer who everyone's talkin' about, Charlie."

My jaw flexes at the confirmation. I haven't attended a public event since my father's funeral. Granny was right that me hiding away would cause talk. But me showing up is also causing talk, apparently.

"Splendid," I say, knowing Fig will catch the sarcasm.

His family isn't titled, but they're well off, owning a significant share in an Irish brewery. Fig has never experienced the exaggerated societal interest that I have, but he's familiar enough with aristocracy to understand it's there.

"Feel like racin' at Darwen Circuit?" Fig asks. "Take yer mind off yer … busyness?"

I lean back in my father's—*my*—chair, ignoring the leather's squeak of protest. "What the fuck are you talking about, Fig?"

Darwen Circuit is a racing track. Fig and I went to a Formula One event there a couple of summers ago. We talked about going back last summer for the British Grand Prix … and then my life imploded.

"Theo rented it for the day. Right, I'll see you there?"

I glance at the piles of papers. One stack I … started. A dozen untouched. "I can't."

"You feckin' eejit." Fig's accent always gets thicker when he's annoyed. "What else are ye doin'?"

My fingers tap a restless rhythm against my thigh. "Not much," I admit.

Now that Kensington Consolidated rejected the offer, I'm back to researching other potential investors. If I *have* to sell off pieces of my inheritance to a partner, I'm going to at least make sure it's the best deal possible.

"Just give yer name at the door. Theo will have it all sorted."

Fig hangs up in his typical efficient manner before I can reply. Protest. Apologize for being a rubbish friend for the past year.

I leave Newcastle Hall just after lunch, the temptation of an afternoon of escape hard to resist.

The drive to Darwen Circuit takes just over an hour, most of the route roads winding through the familiar countryside with stone walls and patchwork fields. I pass a golf course and a horse farm as I near the racing track, but there's not much else around.

The guard at the gate waves me through after I give my name.

I'm lost in my own head as I follow signs to a parking area and then walk into a cavernous garage space overlooking the track. Stuck with the same swarm of thoughts that has been following me around for what feels like forever. They drone in the background like I'm ensconced inside a beehive.

A largish group—about fifteen people—is gathered ahead, next to a red car.

I crack my knuckles as I approach. I aged sixty years in the last one, transforming into a cranky old man who avoids commotion or crowds. Partly to avoid lying. But also, I just haven't felt like being around many people. At least in New York, no one was offering condolences about my father or asking why I wasn't at Royal Ascot.

Specific queries about topics I don't want to discuss are much more likely in this country.

I spot Theodore Hughes first, leaning against the bumper of the race car. He's sporting a trimmed beard he didn't have at university, but otherwise looks the same as I remember him.

A beaming blonde is saying something to him. They're holding hands, so I surmise she's the woman he's marrying on Saturday. And on the other side of her …

My next step stutters, my brain struggling to compute what my eyes are seeing.

What the *fuck* is Elizabeth Kensington doing here?

Lili glances my way a few seconds later, then does a double take.

Her spine stiffens, her shoulders square, and her chin tilts toward the ceiling.

I've seen her fighting posture before. Today, it's followed by a rush of red to her cheeks, which tells me she hasn't forgotten how our last conversation ended. Plus a purse of her pink lips, which suggests she had no idea I'd be here either.

Bloody hell, she's gorgeous.

I didn't think I'd see her again. Certainly not *here*.

Fig heads straight for me, followed by Theo. We catch up for a few minutes, the rest of the group—minus Lili, who seems to be intentionally looking away—sending curious glances toward our trio until an instructor arrives to give us a safety speech.

"Ye already missed four of 'em," Fig tells me under his breath, clearly impatient to get out on the track.

We all have to sign waivers.

Skimming over the list of warnings, I think of the photos from my father's accident. I looked at the report, even though everyone had told me not to. All that remained of his car was crumpled metal and shattered glass and strips of ripped rubber. Wreckage I've witnessed firsthand.

But I'm not nervous about driving. I'm craving the adrenaline rush. A chance to escape the buzzing and simply react.

Something I've been unable to do for months. The only relief from worry I've experienced was kissing Lili. A reaction so unexpected that I rushed off at the first available opportunity, before I could fully lose control.

I glance at Lili, who's talking with a guy I recognize as Cal Winston. The man he called to during the polo match—Tripp— is here too. So is the woman who hit on me at the restaurant in Manhattan, whose name I can't recall right now.

I scribble my signature on the last page of the waiver.

This feels like another opportunity to prove I'm different from James Marlborough. My father might have lost control—of his car, of his life—but I won't.

We're given suits to change into, the heavy fabric stifling as the sun's unforgiving glare reflects off the blacktop. Four brightly colored cars are parked on the track, covered with sponsor logos. Older models no longer used for professional races.

The girls reach the row of cars first, laughing and posing for photos with the shadow of the huge stadium looming large in the background. Lili wanders toward the yellow McLaren, and I'm walking toward her before I've consciously decided to.

"You going to drive it?"

Lili's shoulders straighten before she turns to face me. She's wearing sunglasses, but I'm 90 percent sure her gaze dips to check me out. Her cheek puckers for a split second, like she's chewing on the inside as she deliberates what to say.

"Have we met before?" she asks sweetly.

I grin, then take another step closer. She tenses even more, but doesn't move away.

"You remembered my name just fine when you were moaning it."

Lili flicks her ponytail off her shoulder. "Right. Good to see you again, *Christian*."

My grin grows. "What are you doing here, *Eleanor*?"

She rolls her eyes at the purposeful mistake. "My best friend is getting married on Saturday."

"Your best friend is marrying Theo Hughes," I realize, glancing at the blonde he was with earlier.

She's staring at me and Lili … same as everyone else. Like they're all at a museum and we're the only painting on the wall.

"You don't even know her name?" Lili scoffs. "What are *you* doing here?"

"I was invited."

"To waste gas by driving around in circles or to the wedding?"

I smirk without meaning to. I'm already losing track of how many times Lili has made me smile during this conversation. "Tell me you didn't fly private here, Kensington."

Her lips stay pressed tightly together.

"I'm attending the wedding too," I tell her.

And this is the first time I've been the least bit enthused about it now that I know she'll be there. But I keep that thought to myself.

"You know Theo?" Lili asks.

I shrug. "Eh."

Her forehead wrinkles. "What does *eh* mean?"

"It means we went to the same pubs in university, and I got invited to his wedding because I'm the Duke of Manchester."

"So … you were college friends?"

I shrug again because I wouldn't really consider us friends, but that sounds sad and suspicious to admit aloud. I don't want Lili asking more questions about why I'd attend the wedding of a guy I hardly know. She doesn't see me as important—because she's American, or because she's from a powerful family and accustomed to influence, or both—and I actually appreciate that she doesn't give a shit about my title.

I glance at the McLaren. "You never answered my question."

Her nose wrinkles. "What question?"

My head tilts to the left. "Are you going to drive it?"

"No."

"You're dressed for it," I remind her.

Lili's full lips part with surprise, and I decide bringing up our first conversation was a mistake. Not only did I reveal how well I remember it, but I'm now focused on her mouth and fantasies of kissing her again. The heat is no longer the only reason this suit is uncomfortable.

"Did you want a photo with this one, Lili?" The blonde—Theo's bride—appears, glancing between the two of us inquisitively.

I should introduce myself. Congratulate her on her upcoming nuptials.

But my eyes refuse to leave Lili. "Hundred quid I win."

Her eyebrows fly so high that I can see them over her sunglasses. "You want to race me?"

"I want to *beat* you," I correct. "Again," I add, just to be a prat.

The blonde makes an amused sound in the back of her throat. I'm assuming it's because she knows the same thing about Lili that I do—she's bloody competitive.

Lili crosses her arms. "A hundred *dollars I* beat *you.*"

More muffled laughter echoes around us.

Elizabeth Kensington is a multibillionaire.

I live on one of the largest estates in England.

Yet we're bartering like broke university students because this wager has nothing to do with money.

She stares me down, and I stare right back, wishing she'd take off the fucking sunglasses so I could see her blue eyes.

"Deal?" Lili holds a hand out, likely wondering why I'm standing silent. "*Your Highness.*" Her voice is teasing. Her expression relaxed.

That amusement fades slowly as my fingers wrap around hers. I squeeze her palm tighter than necessary, reveling in the way her attention remains on me. Absorbing the confusion and the anticipation crackling in the couple of feet separating us.

She doesn't know why I'm doing this. *I* don't know why I'm doing this.

After months of plotting every move, it feels fucking incredible to just *act.*

"The proper address is *Your Grace*, Americana."

"Respect is earned, Redcoat."

Her fucking mouth. I'm dying to fill it with my cock. See what she has to say to me then.

I've never had this visceral of a reaction to a woman before. My interest has always waned over time. It's never grown like this, expanding into insatiable attraction. I blame the foreign feeling for what comes out next.

"I win, I want a date."

Lili looks more stunned than when she first saw me here. "What?"

I'm equally surprised, but I don't let it show. "You heard me."

She visibly swallows. "And what if I win?"

"What do you want?"

Lili's silent for a few seconds as she thinks. "I win, you give a speech at Theo and *Chloe*'s wedding."

My left eye twitches. Public speaking is high on my list of hated activities, and any faith I had in the institution of marriage disappeared around the time of my parents' divorce. There's no way Lili could know those two things about me. What she also doesn't know about me is that there's nothing I wouldn't wager right now. I'm confident I'll win, and I'm ridiculously desperate to spend more time around her, preferably alone.

"Deal," I agree, releasing her hand. Satisfaction courses through me as I pull on my helmet and flip up the visor. "Good luck, Kensington."

I leave Lili standing with her astonished friend, heading toward the blue Lamborghini.

One of the instructors rushes toward me, his mouth puckered

unpleasantly, like he sucked something sour. "Sir, you missed the karts and time in the sidepod—"

"I signed the waiver," I say, tugging the zipper up to my chin.

"I know, sir, but you should really—"

I turn and clap a hand on the man's shoulder. "Look …"

"Milo," he supplies.

"Look, Milo. I'm good. Sit back and enjoy the show, all right?"

Milo frowns like he'd love to argue, casting an uneasy glance toward the group of Americans. He collected the forms, meaning he knows who I am. This is the first time in a while I've been grateful for my title.

He caves, reminding me about the pace car and the ambulance before heading back inside the garage.

I'm about to climb into the Lamborghini when I hear, "… don't get why you're doing this."

I glance over one shoulder. Cal Winston is standing next to Lili's yellow car, blocking her from climbing inside.

My jaw tightens as I register the possessive pose of his lean. None of Lili's other friends are trying to talk her out of racing.

There's too much commotion around for me to catch Lili's response. Hopefully, it's some version of *fuck off.* Whatever she says, it's enough to make Cal back away.

Lili looks in my direction after he walks off, catching me staring. Her sunglasses are gone, her eyes singeing me like blue fire. They cool a few seconds later, flames flickering down to a smolder.

I picture those accident photos again, and this time, there's a stab of panic.

Not for my safety.

For hers.

*Is she up for this?*

She lives in New York, which I learned firsthand is full of terrible drivers. If she has a private jet, she must have a chauffeur in the city.

I goaded Lili into racing because I wanted her attention and couldn't think of any other way to get it. Because I was thinking with my dick instead of my brain.

She sat through the training I missed earlier. But who the fuck knows if she was paying attention during it? She told me she wasn't planning to race.

*Bloody hell.*

I jog toward the yellow car, ignoring the surprised looks from the pit crew preparing to start the race. Lili's helmet is on, the visor up as she studies the controls on the wheel.

She glances up as I approach. I can feel the sweat dripping down my spine.

"Why weren't you going to race?" I ask. Yell more like because it's even louder out on the track now that they're starting all the engines.

Lili blinks. "What?"

"You said you weren't planning to drive. Why not?"

"I-I don't know. This was Theo's thing. I thought I'd be in the stands or something."

"Do you want to race?"

Her forehead wrinkles. "What are you talking about, Charlie? We *are* racing. This was your idea, remember?"

I exhale, trying to expel some of my frustration. "Tell me if you *want* to do this or if you're only doing it because of a stupid bet."

"*Your* stupid bet."

I blow out another long breath. "Lili …"

She props a hand on her hip. "Is this your idea of an intimidation tactic? Because it isn't working."

I yank my helmet off so I can rake a hand through my hair. "I'm being bloody serious!"

"Then, get in your car because I don't want you claiming I had a head start *when* I beat you, *Your Grace*."

Lili knocks her visor down, so I'm staring at my own distorted reflection in the tinted plastic.

I swear under my breath, then turn and walk back to my car.

*Most stubborn woman I've ever met.*

Beatrice Campbell—Granny's favorite for granddaughter-in-law—would have started picking out china patterns if I'd expressed any concern about her safety.

*Bea wouldn't have agreed to race in the first place.*

I climb in the Lamborghini and adjust into the low seat that requires practically lying down, pushing thoughts of Lili far away. I have to trust that she knows what she's doing—that she wouldn't put herself in harm's way, stubborn or not—and focus on not crashing myself.

Everyone's watching—from the chief instructor to the catering crew.

I hang a hand outside the cockpit and spin my index finger around in the air. The roaring engine fires. I rev it three times.

The cars get rolled onto the track, and then the green flag swishes to signal the start.

The clutch has been modified to make it easier for amateurs to use. I switch gears without stalling out and ease on the gas as I approach the first straightaway. Flashing lights on the wheel signal when to shift. Three greens, then a red. I pull on the right paddle.

When the first curve approaches, I hit the brakes hard at the fifty-meter mark. I oversteer, exiting the turn, but manage to correct while easing off the gas some. Once it's straight ahead, I switch gears again and accelerate.

My stomach gets left behind as my head snaps back from the force of the sudden momentum.

Adrenaline spreads through my system, sharpening my senses. It's a rush I've never experienced before, a high I didn't know existed to chase.

I'm flooring the throttle, my body pushed back against the seat by sheer speed. I shift until I'm in sixth gear, going flat out, the surrounding stands flashing by at an alarming rate. The spinning tires eat up the straightaway faster than I would have thought possible as I fly toward another curve. I stand on the brakes, pressing down as hard as I can, then take the turn and start accelerating again.

This is dangerous. Not just the driving. But also the thrill of speed that could so easily become an addiction. The freedom of escaping everything.

I'm ahead, but I push harder.

Three laps.

Four.

Five.

A broad smile spreads across my face when I cross the finish line first at the end of the sixth lap.

Not simply because I won.

But because of *what* I won.

# CHAPTER 13

## *Lili*

There's a knock on the door while I'm deciding on which shade of lipstick to wear.

I pause deliberations between tubes to go answer the door. Charlie said he'd pick me up at eight, and it's only seven forty-five. I was planning to meet him in the lobby, not have him come up to the door, but I wouldn't put it past him to be early and come upstairs to ambush me. Charlie seems to enjoy catching me off guard. Or maybe he's just naturally talented at it.

If there's one thing I've learned about him, it's to expect the unexpected. After a resounding victory—my only consolation was that he beat Tripp and Theo as handily as he did me—Charlie didn't even gloat.

He handed his helmet off to one of the pit crew, told me he'd pick me up at eight, said something to Theo's Irish friend, and then … left. Leaving lots of raised eyebrows and curious glances behind.

When I open the door to my hotel room, there's no sign of Charlie.

Chloe's the one standing in the hallway. She whistles long and low when she sees my outfit.

I fiddle with my Cartier bracelet. "Too much?"

"You said you didn't want to go on this date. That somehow turned into you wanting him to fuck you before you make it to the restaurant?"

I roll my eyes at Chloe's dramatics as I step aside so she can enter. I'm down to twelve minutes to debate between pink and red. "I brought limited options."

This also happens to be the shortest, lowest-cut dress I packed. I want Charlie to get a good look at what he walked away from.

If he's going to manipulate me into going out with him, I'm damn sure going to make him regret that decision.

"And earlier, you told me I couldn't use your wedding tomorrow as an excuse not to go … so I feel like you should have limited input on what I'm allowed to wear."

Chloe flops onto my bed and rests her chin in her hands. "Bridget said you guys kissed at JoJo's party."

I snort, imagining Gigi's reaction to being called JoJo. "Yeah. So?"

"Why didn't *you* tell me?"

"Because it wasn't a big deal."

"Ri-*ght*," she drawls. "That bet seemed super casual."

"It's just a date, Chlo. Actually, I'm not even sure it counts as one since I was coerced into it."

"Coerced?" She snorts. "If you didn't want to go, you wouldn't be going, whether or not I approved of an excuse."

"I'm sorry I didn't tell you about him. If it makes you feel better, I probably would have mentioned it at some point, and I definitely would have said something sooner if I had known he'd be coming to your *wedding*." I give her a pointed look.

"He was on Theo's half of the guest list. I didn't ask for details about every name."

"How well do they know each other?" I ask.

Chloe sits up. "Not that well. Theo said they hung out a few times at university, but that his mom was the one who insisted on inviting him to the wedding."

"His mom? Why?"

She rolls off the bed and strides toward me. "Because the Marlboroughs are a big deal here, Lili. Theo says, even before Charles inherited the title, everyone treated him like a god. Now, he's one of the most powerful men in England. That hotel we went to in London? His family owns it. When it got out he was coming to the wedding, several other schedules mysteriously cleared. Just … be careful."

I raise an eyebrow in the mirror where I was doing my makeup. "You think I can't handle him?"

"I think he's a guy who doesn't get attached."

I spray on some perfume. It's a bottle Mom gives me for my birthday each year, the kind I only use on special occasions. I brought it for Saturday, but one spritz tonight won't hurt. "Do you remember when we talked last August while I was at Atlantic Crest? I told you I'd met a guy named Charlie?"

"The one you couldn't find later, yeah." The pieces click together on Chloe's face. She gasps. "Wait … that was him?"

"Yeah."

"Did he remember you?"

"I think so. I pretended not to know him though."

She laughs. "What? Why?"

"I don't know."

It's not a complete lie. I might have been harboring some residual anger about the insults I'd overheard, but I was mostly just … stunned to see him standing with Asher. And knowing Chloe, if I confided the full truth, I'm sure it would end with her storming downstairs to tell Charlie off. I've forgiven him—mostly—so that'd be totally unnecessary.

A glance at the clock makes my heart speed up double time. Five minutes to eight.

I pick up the red lipstick, slicking a layer across my bottom lip, then my upper one, blotting carefully before dropping the black tube in my Birkin.

I make sure I have my phone and my room key, then blow a kiss to Chloe. "Have a good night."

"You too." Chloe's smile is sly as she follows me out into the hallway.

And into the elevator.

"Please tell me you're not escorting me to the lobby."

Her shrug is sheepish. "Hugo suggested we meet for dinner at eight …"

I groan, resting my head back against the wall as the elevator descends. "Are you *kidding* me?"

They were all there when Charlie announced what time he was picking me up. I should have been more suspicious about their conspicuous lack of nosiness, aside from Chloe showing up at my room, and seen it as a warning sign, but I was too busy—and nervous—getting ready.

My friends' lack of boundaries has never bothered me much before. We're a close-knit crew, and I appreciate knowing they always have my back.

Tonight? Tonight, I would appreciate some subtlety.

"If it helps, I said it was a bad idea."

"Bridget and Fran went along with it?"

Chloe's lips twitch. "Bridget said she wanted to see him in a suit. Fran was, uh, napping."

I sigh as the elevator doors slide open. He'd better be wearing a suit. Otherwise, I'm tragically overdressed. If Charlie'd stuck around the track, I would have asked where we were going on our date. Since he didn't, I went full glam.

Jasper spots me exiting the elevator first, sticking two fingers in his mouth and letting out a loud wolf whistle. Cal, Tripp, Hugo, Fran, and Bridget turn in unison, their expressions ranging from delight (Fran) to disapproval (Cal).

A quick scan of the lobby reveals no sign of Charlie, which is a small relief. I can go wait outside and avoid this entire scene.

"Not cool, guys," I call out, stalking past them. The tap of my heels against the hardwood floor emphasizes my annoyance nicely.

Bridget shouts after me, "You look hot, Lili!"

"Ask him where the fuck he learned to drive like that," is Tripp's contribution.

I hear Chloe hiss, "Could we *not* shout swears in the lobby of my *wedding venue*?" before I step outside.

The sun is just setting, bathing the gravel driveway in golden light. I inhale a deep breath that tastes like honeysuckle, stopping just past the second set of columns. I glance back at the red-brick building, the brilliance of the sunset blinding in the reflection of the windows.

Crunching gravel makes me spin back around. Instead of the town car I'm expecting, the same black Mercedes bus that's shuttled our group around this week is stopping in front of the door I just walked out of. Blake climbs out, giving me a respectful nod, then slides the back door open.

I know what's about to take place before it does: the loud boom of Tripp's baritone announcing his imminent arrival.

Another car is driving up the long, tree-lined driveway. I have a sinking suspicion it means Bridget will get her wish after all. My friends are making the short walk from the stairs to the bus last as long as possible, their attention fixed on the same place mine is.

Butterflies wreak havoc in my stomach as I suddenly become extremely self-conscious. I swap my bag between hands. Tug at the hem of my dress to ensure it's falling straight. Clear my throat. Tuck my hair behind one ear and second-guess my decision to wear it down when I realize he's driving a convertible.

Charlie navigates around the bus easily, then stops right in front of me.

My nerves continue to duplicate as he climbs out of the driver's side, tossing the keys in the air and catching them easily. His attention is all mine. Charlie ignores my gawking friends fifteen feet away, giving me a once-over that makes my thighs clench tight.

He's wearing a suit. I've seen him in a suit before. The first, second, *and* third time we met. At the Red, White, and Blue party.

But none of those times were when he was picking me up on a date.

That makes a difference, if you ask my sweaty palms.

My heart trips over itself as Charlie approaches me, a confident smirk pulling up one corner of his mouth. I have no idea why he changed his end of the bet to a date. One he was certain he'd win.

Charles Marlborough is a heartbreaker. A gorgeous, charming player who's apparently considered a god in this country.

But that's fine. I only want him for one night.

He stops a couple of feet away. "You look good, Lili."

His intense stare makes me feel like a fly stuck in honey. I know I can—will—work my way out of it. But for now, I'm stuck. And I'm okay with that because it tastes sweet.

"I always look good, Charlie."

His smirk transforms into a full grin. "Glad you recovered from your case of amnesia."

I glare at him. "I did. And I remembered I already had plans tonight, so …" My voice trails off as he leans over and procures a bouquet of flowers from the passenger seat.

I think I hear a distant sigh. Probably Bridget, the eternal romantic.

"Couldn't ruin tradition," Charlie tells my surprised expression, holding the bouquet out to me.

I take it reluctantly. They're beautiful, each blossom in full bloom. "You bringing me flowers *once* does not make it a tradition."

"Twice," he corrects, opening the passenger door. "Let's go."

The warning bells Chloe was trying to ring earlier finally chime to life. Not because Charlie's being bossy or demanding—which he's already managed in less than a minute—but because the butterflies are still flapping around. I'm giddy in a way I've never experienced before. On other dates, I always felt comfortable and in control. And it was nice, but not very exciting.

"You don't have a driver?" I ask. Aside from at the track earlier, I can't remember the last time I was in a vehicle that didn't have a professional driver.

Charlie shakes his head. "I like to drive. Promise to keep it under two hundred miles per hour this time."

"How reassuring," I mumble as I climb into the seat.

It's surprisingly soft, the leather supple yet supportive. I don't know enough about cars to tell anything about this one, but Theo—who does know a lot about cars, I learned today—has clear envy on his face as he stares at the green convertible.

I avoid looking at anyone else as Charlie hands me the flowers and then closes the car door.

I finger one of the delicate petals as he rounds the front of the car, lifting one hand in a quick wave, which is the only acknowledgment of our audience. The black bus passes us by a few seconds later, taking my friends to their dinner.

"Where are we going?" I ask once he's settled in the driver's seat.

"You'll see."

His vague response prompts an equal amount of exasperation and excitement.

I've never been on a date where I didn't know where we were going. Cal would always run plans by me ahead of time, knowing I liked to think out my outfits. Lawrence, the lawyer I briefly dated in Chicago, sent me multiple options for me to choose from.

Thinking about my exes is not what I should be doing right now though, even if I'm still not sure a bet makes this an actual date. Charlie gets points for the suit, the flowers, and showing up on time, but for all I know, his vagueness is because he didn't plan anything at all.

I open my handbag and start digging through it, hoping a hair tie is hiding in one of the pockets. Real date or not, I spent way too long on my hair to have the wind turn it into a snarled mess.

"What are you doing?" Charlie asks.

"Looking for a hair tie," I answer.

He leans toward me. I inhale quickly in response to his close proximity, the sudden closeness catching me off guard. Then inhale again because he smells incredible.

He opens the glove box and rummages through some papers, and then his hand emerges with a pink hair tie. "Turn your head toward the window."

I raise an eyebrow.

Charlie raises one right back.

I look away.

His touch is gentle as he pulls my hair over my shoulders and combs through the strands with his fingers before braiding it faster than I could. He snaps the elastic into place, then releases my hair.

I brush the plait before I turn back around, impressed by the neat ridges. "You keep hair ties in your car?" My tone falls far short of casual, which is what I was aiming for.

Rather than reply, he starts the car.

I watch his hand shift deftly. Some of his dominance on the track earlier makes more sense.

"Are you jealous?" he asks once we're rolling down the driveway.

Not as a taunt, more like he's really wondering.

Which makes the fact that I am jealous-*ish* that much worse. It would bother me, if the convertible and the flowers and the perfect braid are all a routine he's trotted out for a long line of women before me. It *is* bothering me.

"Curious," I say. "Is it a British thing?"

Charlie shifts again. We left Carys Park and are speeding along the main paved road.

"It's a little-sister thing," he finally replies. "Blythe always complained about her hair whenever I drove her around. Tried to ride in the bloody boot one time. Drove me bonkers, so I stuck those in there."

A thousand tries, and I never would have guessed that. I assumed—wrongly—that Charlie was an only child based on his brooding superiority. The image of him as a doting big brother is harder to picture.

A reminder I hardly know this man, even if we feel far from strangers.

"Do you have other siblings?" I ask. "Besides Blythe?"

Charlie's knuckles turn white on the steering wheel when I say her name, like maybe he didn't mean to mention it. "No. It's just us two."

*Just us two* has a protective emphasis. Recalling what little else I know about Charlie's family, I realize he's not just talking about siblings. His father is dead. His mother lives in New York. I've seen her from a distance twice—at Number 34 and at Atlantic Crest. But I've never spoken to her.

"Blythe taught you how to braid hair?"

He pauses before answering, "Yes," like it's a difficult question to answer. "Or"—his grip tightens on the wheel again, eyes never wavering from the road—"more like I taught her."

It's another glimpse—a small glimpse—into a side of Charlie I doubt many people get to see.

"She's lucky to have you," I say softly.

Charlie swallows, the most self-conscious I've ever seen him. I don't think he knows *what* to say.

"I would have been more impressed if you'd done a French braid," I add, steering the conversation into lighter territory.

"If you wanted a French braid, you should have agreed to date a Frenchman."

"I didn't *agree* to date you. I lost a bet."

"A bet you'd *agreed* to."

I can't come up with a quick counterpoint, and Charlie chuckles under his breath.

"You couldn't just say *thank you*, could you?"

"Thank you," I say primly.

"You're welcome. Figured it was fair since you put so much bloody effort into your appearance to impress me."

"I'm *not* trying to impress you."

"Whatever you say, love."

I scowl, but it's only to hide my smile.

We're back to bickering. But it also feels like something has shifted between us, and I'm not sure if that's a good or bad thing.

# CHAPTER 14

## *Lili*

"What do you recommend?" I ask, squinting at the menu and then taking a generous gulp of the wine the waitress advised ordering.

Charlie stuck with just water, keeping the grand total of times I've seen him drink alcohol at zero.

"What do you mean?" Charlie replies.

I tap the paper menu. "To eat. What do you recommend eating here?"

"I've never been here before."

"Well, what do British ... people usually eat?"

The corners of Charlie's eyes crinkle. "Food," he deadpans.

I roll my eyes.

*I could tell him.*

The thought surprises me because it's always been a last resort. My group of friends all found out about my dyslexia in elementary

school, when it was impossible to hide. I haven't *told* many people about it. I know it's not my fault, know I should think of it as a challenge, but not a weakness.

I allow myself to feel inferior anyway. Let doubts creep in about my own intelligence whenever reading or writing is involved.

I've found ways to cope with it at work and in most aspects of my daily life. But trusting others with that vulnerability has never gotten easier, so I reserve it for situations when I have to.

Cal is the only guy I've dated who knew about my reading disability, and I wasn't the one who told him. He figured it out because of the teacher's aide who started following me around school when we were seven.

I set my menu down and sip more wine. Glance around.

I'm impressed by Charlie's choice of restaurant. It's not austere or overly formal, but cozy and welcoming. A former bank vault, he told me when we arrived, thick brick walls the only evidence of that former use. Candles cast a soft yellow glow over the open space.

"Why haven't you been here before?" I ask.

He hasn't teased or challenged me once since we arrived, and it has me at a loss for what to say to him.

"I've been meaning to come," he replies. "But it's not that close to Newcastle."

"Newcastle?" I repeat. "Is that a town?"

"It's my family's estate."

"How far is it from here?"

"About an hour and a half."

I nod. "That's not … that far."

My plan for tonight was to annoy Charlie until he regretted his choice of dare. All while looking hot enough that he'd also regret walking away last weekend.

But Chloe was right earlier. If I hadn't wanted to come tonight, I wouldn't have. I hadn't signed a binding contract. Even if I had, my family has a veritable army of attorneys.

I want to be here, with him, and it has me second-guessing every word out of my mouth.

I play with a piece of hair, now loose from the braid Charlie pulled it back in. The pink hair tie is on my wrist, nestled between silver bracelets. I rub at the reminder of that softer moment. I've been attracted to Charlie since the first time I saw him. But that's different from wanting to spend time with someone. To know them.

Charlie tosses his napkin on the table. "I'll be right back."

I watch him cross the restaurant and head down the hallway that I assume leads to the restrooms, and I'm not the only one. I'm not sure if people are staring because he's a gorgeous guy or because he's a duke.

Once Charlie's out of sight, I slouch back in my seat and blow out a long breath.

It seems like he's regretting asking me out, and that doesn't fill me with the sensation of success it was supposed to.

"Can I get you anything else?" Our waitress, Ivy—a young woman with a short blonde bob—stops beside the table, two dirty plates piled in one hand.

She glances at Charlie's empty seat, then back at me with visible sympathy.

My cheeks burn. "We're all set for right now, thanks."

Ivy nods and keeps moving, leaving me to stew alone.

I'm on my last sip of wine when Charlie reappears. I swish the half inch of pinot grigio around in my glass as he approaches the table, searching my mind for something witty to say. Should I joke about being worried he left me here? Or would that sound too close to the truth?

He speaks as soon as he sits down, before I've decided what to say. "I'm having the steak. But the chef recommended the brined cod, if you like fish. Do you like fish?"

I stare at him. "You asked the chef what I should order?"

Charlie reaches for the napkin he left on the table, avoiding my gaze as he spreads the stiff cotton in his lap. "It came up while we were talking."

"You know the chef here?"

He nods. "He was a friend of my father's."

I bite my bottom lip. "I-I'm sorry for your loss," I say awkwardly. "I heard he passed away recently."

Charlie's expression hardens into granite as he nods again. "Thank you."

I take a deep breath, then forge ahead. "Did—did a lot change when he died? I mean, I know you became a duke, but I don't really know what that means."

No response.

"We, um … we don't have to talk about it." I reach for my wineglass, utilizing it like a security blanket as I drain the last bit. "Tripp wants to know where you learned to drive like that."

Charlie still says nothing. He studies me like he's making a decision, and I have no clue what the outcome will be.

"My whole life changed," he finally states. "I lost my father … and I had to become him."

I'm frozen, afraid breathing might be enough for him to change his mind about confiding in me. And at some point—I'm not sure exactly when—I became someone who *really* wanted to know more about Charles Marlborough.

"It's not a job you can turn down," he continues. "It becomes who you are. Your whole identity. All my other plans … they had to change."

"What were your other plans?" I ask.

"I was halfway through medical school when my dad died."

"You were?"

He smiles at the naked surprise in my voice.

I relax some at the sight, relieved to see the seriousness erased.

"That was my dad's reaction too. I played rugby for a while. When I was seventeen, I had to get knee surgery. I couldn't play anymore after that, and … and there was a doctor who got me through the disappointment of finding that out. Guess I got the idea I could do the same for someone else. Make their terrible day a tiny bit better."

I stare at him, at a total loss for what to say. This guy who learned how to braid hair to help his little sister and was on the path to becoming a doctor because of an injury he'd suffered as a teenager … none of it fits with the cocky, calculated aristocrat.

"Wasn't meant to be, I guess." Charlie exhales, settling into his chair a little more.

"I wanted to be a veterinarian when I was little," I tell him. "Made up this fictional vet clinic and everything. I kept a notebook, tracking all my patients. When my dad got home from work, he'd sit with me on the living room rug and ask for updates on every animal. My family still teases me about it sometimes. Whenever anyone we know mentions needing a vet, they suggest my fake clinic. It's *extremely* embarrassing to explain."

He's smiling as he asks, "Why didn't you become a veterinarian?"

"I, uh …" I scramble for an answer that doesn't include dyslexia. Not only because I haven't decided if I want to share that with him, but also because I care—a little—about Charlie's opinion of me, and I'd rather not admit that I decided a career that required another four years of graduate school felt like too much to tackle. "My parents adopted a golden retriever before I was born. They always called Teddy their first child. He had to be euthanized when I was thirteen. That's the only time I've seen both of my parents cry. And after that day, working with animals didn't sound as fun. It was the right—humane—thing to do. But it still sucked."

Charlie nods.

"I also, uh … my family, they're overachievers. My mom and dad—yeah, they both inherited a lot of money, but they work harder than anyone else I know. I was so proud of being Crew and Scarlett Kensington's daughter. Whenever I told someone who my parents were, they looked so impressed. Awed almost. At some point, I guess it occurred to me that I'd have to try to live up to that legacy. I couldn't think of anything that would. Still haven't, honestly."

"You said landscape architecture is what you wanted to do."

I'm taken aback by the realization he remembers what I do for work. "Yeah, it is. I enjoy it. But I know most people think it's silly, and I care about their opinions more than I should."

"I don't think it's silly."

"Would you tell me if you did?" I challenge.

He barely hesitates before answering, "Yes. I only care about two people's opinions."

"Blythe's?" I guess.

Charlie nods. "And my grandmother's."

"Are you ready to order mains?" Ivy reappears, her gaze lingering on Charlie longer than me.

I relax back into my seat. I didn't realize I'd leaned closer to Charlie until right now. He tracks the movement, sharp eyes missing nothing.

"I'm ready, Ivy," I say, glancing at her and then back at Charlie. "Are you?"

He nods. "Ivy, have you ever been to the Sunken Garden near Notting Hill? With the fountain and the—"

"Walking paths?" Ivy nods enthusiastically. "Was there with my mum and my sister-in-law a couple of weekends ago. Beautiful with everything in bloom."

"What would you say if you met the person who designed that garden?"

My stomach swoops as I follow where he's going with this.

When I've confided fears about my inadequacy to friends before, it was met with "Your opinion is the only one that matters," from Bridget or a joking "Tripp doesn't even *have* a job," from Hugo.

But no one has ever tried to *prove* me wrong.

Ivy taps a pen against the notepad she's holding. "Tell them it's bloody brilliant probably."

I've never been to the garden Charlie is talking about. But there's a flicker of warmth in my chest, as if I were single-handedly responsible for its creation, hearing that assessment of a project that sounds similar to the one I just completed from a stranger's perspective.

Maybe someone in Chicago would say the same after visiting Claremont Park.

That's part of my problem, I think. No matter how happy I am with a completed job, it's not something I created for *me*. I want to leave something behind that matters to *other* people, that makes the world a more beautiful place. I'm always too invested to see it objectively, and the opinions I hear are from people who care about preserving my feelings.

Charlie nods as if he knew Ivy's answer before she spoke it.

I wonder what he would have done if she'd called the park a waste of space.

"I'd like the rib eye, please," he requests.

"And I'd like the cod," I say, then hand her my menu. "Thanks."

"Excellent choices. They'll be right out."

Ivy walks away, and the butterflies are back in my stomach. Flapping around and making their presence known.

I feel like I should thank Charlie, but I'm not sure how to vocalize it. So, I take a sip from the wineglass Ivy just refilled, then ask, "Do you bring your dates to restaurants closer to Newcastle?"

"I don't date much," he answers.

"Lack of options?" I make a sympathetic face.

He smirks before leaning forward on his forearms. "What about you? Do you date much?"

"It … varies. I travel a fair amount for work. My last project kept me in Chicago for almost a year. That can make relationships challenging."

"So, you've never been in one?"

"Wow. You're not going to ask what my favorite color is or something first?"

"I don't care what your favorite color is," he replies. "No offense," he tacks on as an afterthought.

I roll my eyes.

Charlie waits expectantly.

I clear my throat. "I've been in a few. One was serious."

"Callahan Winston?"

I nod. He's astute, not that it's much of a surprise. His intelligent gaze reminds me of a hawk's.

"What happened?"

I exhale, rubbing my index finger against the stem of my wineglass. It's thin. Breakable. Fragile in an obvious way. That's how I feel about baring my soul.

Charlie is staring at me steadily, not allowing any opportunity to hide or look away. His blatant lack of boundaries is jarring. Most people treat me with deference.

His unwavering stare makes it clear the only way we'll avoid this subject is if I insist on it—something no one else has done.

I can't decide if I resent or respect him for it.

"We dated for almost two years, right after I moved back to New York for college. I'd started at Yale, then transferred to Cornell when I decided to focus on landscape architecture. Cal had stayed in the city, attending Columbia. We'd grown up together, had the same friends forever, but never really hung out just the two of us before. It *was* like falling. It just … happened, gradual and easy, like it was supposed to all along. And we became that perfect couple everyone assumed was meant to be and would last forever."

Charlie says nothing, waiting for me to finish, his expression completely neutral.

"I gave Cal one of my favorite books, one I thought he'd like, for his twenty-fourth birthday." I swallow, holding Charlie's gaze and praying pity won't appear there. "His parents had rented out a back room at a restaurant. All our friends were there. Anyway, he opened my gift, laughed, and said '*A book*? Babe, you're a billionaire.'"

A muscle in Charlie's jaw twitches, but that's his only reaction.

"He was drunk. We all were. But it stuck in my head. The Winstons were—are—rich. Cal had already gotten a new Rolex and a huge pile of expensive gifts for his birthday. He'd expected me to spend a lot of money on him simply because he knew I had it. It made me second-guess our relationship. Second-guess myself. I'd thought money was something I didn't have to worry about with Cal. I always assumed he wanted *me* … not my net worth." I play with my napkin. "And that probably sounds naive because I've known my whole life what most people think when they hear my last name. That some guys see dollar signs when they look at me. But I'd convinced myself Cal was one of the few who didn't care, and I panicked when I realized that maybe he did. I broke up with him a couple of weeks later."

"Did you tell him why?"

"Not entirely. I said we were moving too fast, which wasn't a lie. Everyone was speculating that he was going to propose soon. Cal was the only guy I'd seriously dated, and I was just starting my career. It wasn't that I knew I *didn't* want to marry him; it was more that I wasn't *sure* if I wanted to marry him. And then, once we broke up, I felt lighter. Freer. I felt terrible for hurting him. Guilty for putting our best friends in the middle of our breakup. But also … I think I'd used him as a life preserver, after moving back to the city and changing majors. He felt familiar and safe, and I needed that security at the time. I realized, when we broke up, I could swim on my own, I guess."

I stop talking abruptly, wondering *why* I'm telling him all this.

Sharing details and thoughts I've never said aloud. It's cathartic, talking to someone who didn't witness any of it firsthand.

Rather than appear bored by my monologue, Charlie's focus is still intent. Like he paid close enough attention that he could recite every word I said back.

"What was the book?"

"Huh?"

"The book you gave your *ex*. What was it?"

My brain is still stalled from the unexpected question. I don't know what I expected Charlie's response to be, but it wasn't that. I'm also hung up on the way he emphasized *ex*.

"Uh, *Middlemarch*."

Charlie smirks.

"What?" I ask, even though I have a good idea why he's amused.

"Your favorite book is set in England."

"I said it was *one* of my favorite books. And so what if it is? It's a compelling portrait of social and political life."

His smile only grows.

"Have you read it?"

He shakes his head.

Ivy reappears, setting our dinner plates down with a silent flourish. "Let me know if you need anything else."

Charlie thanks her before I can.

A simple gesture I rarely see. Most of my social sphere is so used to being catered to that the service is expected. Unremarkable. I would have expected the same from a *duke*, but it's not the first time Charlie's surprised me.

"What about you?" I ask, spearing one of the crispy potatoes that came with my cod.

"What's *one* of my favorite books?"

I roll my eyes. "No. Have *you* ever been in a relationship?"

"No." Charlie's answer is immediate yet sincere.

I tilt my head, more interested in him than my steaming plate, even though the food smells incredible. "Why not?"

"*Why not?*" His small smirk transforms into a full smile. "Coming from the woman who acts personally offended by my company?"

I assume he's referring to the multiple times I pretended not to know him.

"Well, other women seem to find it … tolerable."

The smile stays on Charlie's face. "Tolerable," he muses, rolling the syllables around as he saws through his steak.

For some reason, I think the lilt to his tone means he's thinking about the hallway … incident, which was more than *tolerable*.

"That almost sounded like a compliment, Kensington."

It doesn't bother me when Charlie mentions my last name. That fully registers for the first time.

During our previous conversations, I was already stuck in a perpetual state of annoyance. He says *Kensington* in a way that's almost taunting but also familiar. A tone that reminds me of Dad's, when he calls Mom *Red*. In a way that doesn't feel like he's referring to anything—or anyone—except me.

I shrug. "Not everyone has good taste."

Charlie makes a quiet sound of amusement in the back of his throat. "Mmhmm."

"So?" I press. "What's the reason?"

An explanation feels fair since I bared my heart to him.

He looks bemused—and amused—by my persistence. Then

sobers. "I was a prat," he states baldly.

I lift both eyebrows. I've heard the term before, but it's not part of my vocabulary to the point that I know precisely what he's saying. "Meaning …"

Charlie chuckles under his breath. "You're *so* American."

I know he means it as an insult. But there's the same edge to his voice as when he called me Kensington. A twist that's light. Almost … affectionate.

"We won the war," I jab.

"Claiming personal credit for that, are you?"

I roll my eyes. God, he's good at deflecting. Or maybe I'm just easy to distract. "What does *prat* mean?"

"It means that I drank too much, partied too much, and didn't bother to learn most girls' names, let alone spend enough time around them to end up in a relationship."

He holds my gaze, like he's reading my reaction to that statement.

Most men I know try to hide their vices, not own up to them. I'm oddly unsurprised that Charlie falls into the second category. He doesn't have that type of showy personality. He's the very definition of *old money*. Charlie's privilege is intrinsic. He doesn't need to wear the expensive watch or drive the flashy car. It's written in the ease of his posture at this elegant restaurant. The casual yet complete command of his surroundings that makes it obvious prestige was already earned. That he's a man who gets listened to. Who issues orders rather than follows them.

Important people never have to announce their importance. You can just tell. It's an aura. Particles in the air.

"Are you still a prat?" I ask.

"Not in that sense. I grew up rather than just getting older."

"Because you're a duke now?"

A shadow passes across Charlie's face, like a cloud crossing the sun, as soon as I mention his title. It makes me wish it were possible to pluck the words out of the air and shove them back into my mouth.

"Because I'm all Blythe has left."

"How old is she?"

"Twenty-one. She has a year of university left."

"Twenty-one. Is she a terror?"

He smiles. This one is softer than the smirk I'm used to seeing. Warmer. "She's unpredictable."

"I was *unpredictable* at twenty-one too," I tell him, taking a bite of my cod and nearly moaning out loud. It's one of the best things I've ever tasted, salty and flaky and tender.

Charlie raises one eyebrow. "Only at twenty-one?"

I cut another bite. "What do you think?"

"I think I could handle it."

I think he could too.

# CHAPTER 15

## *Lili*

The rough edges of the ornate metal key, which I pulled out from my Birkin during our charged trip in the elevator, cut into the soft flesh of my palm as I turn to face him. "This is me," I announce.

Charlie glances at the door to my hotel room, and then his attention is right back on me. "Nice room."

"You haven't even seen it."

One corner of his mouth lifts as he rests a hand on the wall next to my head. I have immediate déjà vu, recalling the last time we were in this same position.

He told me during dessert—pistachio tiramisu—that he's staying here rather than driving home to Newcastle tonight and then back here for the wedding tomorrow. Chloe told me Carys Park was fully booked, but I'm not shocked they managed to procure a room for Charlie.

His gaze dips to my lips, the intensity practically a physical sensation against my skin. "Is that your way of inviting me in?"

"No. I'd ask." I pause. "Do you want to come in?"

"Yes."

Such a simple answer, suffused with certainty.

I've spent a lot of time around confident men. Yet Charlie's the only one who's ever managed to make me nervous. His proximity is a drug that makes me feel dizzy and reckless and energized. If he challenged me to something right now, the amount of adrenaline swimming in my system might actually allow me to beat him.

I wasn't certain we'd end up here. My pride still smarts when I picture him strolling away from me, down my grandparents' hallway and out of sight. But I also remember how I felt in the moments before, and I've spent an unhealthy amount of time considering what might have happened if Charlie hadn't left that night.

Bridget was right—his indifference makes him an ideal candidate for a fun night of hot, meaningless sex.

And he's not walking away now. He's staring at me in a way that makes me feel like I'll explode with impatience. Like the amount of desire is too much to contain. Anticipation has been humming through my body, making me feel like I'm brushing against a live wire, ever since we left the restaurant.

"So much for you offering to walk me to my door to be a gentleman."

Charlie huffs a laugh, then twirls a piece of my hair around one finger. He braided it for me again on the car ride back. I undid it during the short journey from his car to upstairs, searching for a distraction from the smothering sexual tension.

He tugs the strands—hard—pulling a soft gasp from my mouth.

"You don't want a gentleman, Elizabeth."

It's the smoothest I've ever heard his accent sound. Usually, the syllables are crisp and precise. But that sentence sounded like it was cushioned by velvet, sliding across my skin like decadent sin.

I'm so aroused I'm almost disoriented. My heartbeat is a wild echo in my ears. No matter how fast I inhale, I can't seem to pull in enough air. There's not a cell in my body that's currently unaffected.

Charlie's hand drops from my hair, his fingers prying my fist open and finding the metal that's now warm.

The lock clicks open, and then I'm being pulled into a dark room.

The first thing Charlie does is turn on the lights. Not a lamp. The overhead that illuminates every corner. His second move is to slip off his suit jacket, throw it onto the couch in the small seating area, and roll up the sleeves of his shirt. He tugs the white fabric from the waistband of his pants next, then begins unbuttoning.

His eyes don't leave mine the entire time.

And I stand there and stare at him like I've never seen a shirtless guy before. I've never seen *Charlie* shirtless before, which seems like the same thing.

I toss my purse onto the couch, then tuck a piece of hair—the same section he touched—behind my ear. I'm accustomed to being the initiator in these situations. To being treated like I'm delicate.

Charlie was right—I don't want a gentleman.

I think that's part of why I came so hard the last time, because he seduced me effortlessly. Because I never had to explain what I wanted. He pleasured me like he'd planned out every touch.

The conceit that's annoyed me at other times is an aphrodisiac right now. I'm a sure thing. Our interests are aligned, and I don't care if he's bossy about it.

I *want* him to be bossy about it.

He stalks toward me, looking every inch the god Chloe called him earlier. Imperious and unattainable. Too devastatingly attractive to be real flesh rather than chiseled marble.

Even in my high heels, Charlie towers over me. His fingers trail across my collarbone, leaving goose bumps in their wake, before stopping at the strap.

Rather than flick it off my left shoulder, he uses the thin strip of fabric to haul me closer. My hands land on his bare chest, encountering warm, firm skin. They spread, seeking more contact, my nails scoring crescent-shaped marks.

Charlie steps back so fast I stumble.

"Get naked and get on the bed," he demands roughly. "Unless you want that dress ruined."

I don't. It's one of my favorites.

But it might be worth it, to witness Charlie lose control. I'm heady with the power of affecting him, my gaze trailing from the half-moons indented on his chest to the carved topography of his stomach. Lower, to the growing bulge in his pants.

I knew hooking up with Charlie wouldn't be a fumbling encounter, but experiencing it is something different.

"*Lili.*"

My flower-painted Oscar de la Renta dress flutters to the floor a few seconds later, pooling in a satin puddle at my feet.

It's very satisfying, watching Charlie's hands still in the midst of unzipping his pants. He stares at me, standing in a strapless bra and matching thong. I step out of my red-bottomed stilettos like I don't notice or care about his reaction. I was tempted to leave the heels on, but my feet hurt. The silent pad of my bare feet takes a little away from the dramatic effect of strolling past Charlie like I'm a model on a catwalk, but not much. I can feel his eyes on my ass as I saunter toward the bed, the lacy underwear I'm wearing invisible from his angle.

He stalks toward me as soon as I'm perched on the edge of the mattress.

A couple of rejected dresses lie in a heap on the quilt beside me. My entire room's a mess. Charlie doesn't appear to notice. Or care.

My legs spread to accommodate him, the ironed fabric of his suit pants rasping against my bare skin.

I'd rather he was naked. But there's something insanely sexy about this view—the tease of seeing his sculpted abdomen and happy trail, but nothing more scandalous.

"You didn't follow directions." His hand slides up my ribs, making me shiver.

"Sorry. I assumed you knew how to take a bra off." The tremble in my voice when his palm cups my breast spoils the sarcasm that's supposed to be there. And the effect is totally ruined when his other hand strokes the damp lace of my thong.

"Are you always this wet, Kensington? Or is this just for me?"

I swallow the truth with the plea for more that wants to spill out. This is already the best sex I've ever had, and I'm not sure if that's pathetic or optimistic.

The thick ridge of his erection is right against the throbbing ache that's all I can focus on. I'm soaking another pair of his pants.

I'd rather be dripping on his cock.

Charlie yanks my thong to the left and circles my clit with his thumb. I moan—loudly—and his smile is smug.

Whatever. A nun would have filthy thoughts about him.

His thumb leaves my clit, and I open my mouth to protest. I'm falling backward before I can say a word, a light shove of his palm splaying me flat on my back. He unhooks my bra with an impatient flick and a pointed look. The lace joins one of the piles of clothes around my room. Then, his hands move lower, pulling my thong down and opening my thighs wide. I can feel the sting of the stretch in my hamstrings. So much for weekly Pilates making me more flexible.

Excitement reaches a fever pitch, overwhelming the vulnerability from being on display this way. I've never had a guy just *decide* to go down on me. There's always been some suggestive maneuvering or not-so-subtle request involved.

But there's no question about Charlie's intention. He props one of my legs over his shoulder and licks the length of my slit. Two of his fingers press inside of my opening while his tongue flicks my clit. Swirls and sucks. He's playing my body like a maestro, hitting each sensitive spot precisely.

The build is dizzying; it happens so quickly. A different form of the insane propulsion I experienced at the track earlier. Except now, the whole world is standing still. Nothing else is moving, but I'm flying.

There's finesse and skill—the perfect pressure in the perfect places—but I'm most focused on the speed. How I'm reaching the peak that's sometimes hard to climb impossibly fast.

I cry out his name when I come. Scream it really, the rush of euphoria washing away all my inhibitions. Decimating any awareness of what exists beyond this bed.

When Charlie's head lifts, his lips are glossy. His pupils are blown wide, the tendons in his neck raised in sharp definition.

He's made me orgasm twice, and I've yet to see his cock once.

I just came so hard that my toes are tingling and the edges of my vision are as fuzzy as an old photo. But all I can think is, *More*. Not only so I can experience the staggering satisfaction again. But so I can finally witness him lose complete control.

Charlie tugs the waistband of his suit pants down. His dick bobs free.

It's bigger than I thought it'd be—and I wasn't making small estimations. Long and thick. The flared tip flushed dark red and damp with pre-cum. He fishes a condom out of his pocket, then fists his massive erection to roll the prophylactic on.

There's something incredibly sexy about the sight. The consideration, for one, that he's not leaving the responsibility of protection up to me. But also the pause of preparation, intensifying the anticipation of contact even more.

The veins on his groin and cock are raised. Ropes of lean muscle twine down his arms.

The sight is incendiary, a signal of what's about to take place. There's no question about what's going to happen next. And I want it so, *so* badly, the pull of need dragging me under like a powerful undertow.

"Did I tongue-fuck the ability to speak out of you?" he asks conversationally, tossing the condom wrapper away. "You haven't said a word since you stopped shouting my name."

"Oh, you need me to talk you through it?"

The head of his cock probes my pussy, but he doesn't push inside. I can see the shininess of my arousal on the tip.

I don't know where to look. Anywhere but away.

His straight jaw clenches sharply, so rigid I'm concerned it might snap in half, as he stares down at me.

This is so *intimate*—and not in the obvious sense of us both being naked.

My lungs burn, reminding me inhales are important.

He still doesn't thrust.

"Are you going to fuck me or not?"

"Many times," he promises.

But there's still no stretch. He's dragging the flared head of his cock up and down along my swollen, sensitive flesh, the slickness creating a smooth glide. Taunting me with the thick length I'm desperate to have inside of me.

His hand is holding my thigh against the mattress, keeping me from moving very much. I try anyway, attempting to lift my hips and hurry things along.

The erotic torture finally ends.

I moan, watching him push inside of me. My feet flex, and my fingers fist the quilt I'm lying on, adjusting to the thick invasion. He inserts a few inches and then withdraws, less than half of the rubber coating his cock now shiny. His grip on my thigh tightens, bicep flexing, as twin lines wrinkle his forehead.

It's a delicious sort of pain, like massaging sore muscles. It hurts at first, but that only feeds the underlying pleasure.

"More," I beg, trying to lift my hips again. They don't move a centimeter.

I'm at his mercy, and it only amplifies my arousal.

A devilish smile spreads across Charlie's face. "More what?"

*Everything.* I need it faster and harder and deeper.

I need more of *him*, filling a place that's never felt so empty.

I clench my inner muscles. The tip of his dick is still lodged inside of me, so I manage to suck him in a tiny bit deeper.

Charlie grunts, no longer looking amused. His right hand slides higher up my leg, his thumb finding my clit and drawing circles that start slow, then quickly speed up.

I wasn't sure if I'd be able to come again. But he proves me wrong. The heat that pooled in my pelvis starts to simmer, tingles sparking up my spine. His dick slides deeper, the contrast of his lazy thrusts and rapid rubbing the most incredible sensation I've ever experienced.

My inner muscles tighten again, this time clenching around a hard cock.

I come, calling his name like a claim. Like a reminder of who's inside of me, even though it feels like I'll never forget.

# CHAPTER 16
## Charlie

Lili tangled up in a white sheet is a sight I could get used to waking up to.

The cotton fabric is draped artfully across her stomach. Wound around her hip. I watch each rise and fall of her chest, the slight motion making the fabric flutter. Her fingers twitch on the pillow, and her head turns in my direction. The sheet shifts lower, barely hanging on to the curve of her right breast.

Fuck, she's gorgeous. Classically beautiful and strikingly stunning.

I lied to her the first time we met. No horse has anything on Elizabeth Kensington. But I could tell, from the way her spine stiffened as soon as I spoke, that she'd heard a lot of superficial compliments. That they'd become more of a nuisance than a gift. She's entirely opposite of my mother in that way. In other ways too.

Talking to her that day was fun.

Fucking her last night was more fun.

I'm getting harder, the longer I stare at her. The sheet is still covering my favorite parts of her body, but I no longer need to use my imagination to picture Lili naked. I memorized every inch last night—before, during, and after the three rounds of sex.

My first thought fully registers. I *could* get used to this sight.

I'm not just attracted to Lili. I like her. I didn't even consider sneaking out last night before falling asleep. Partly because I was absolutely knackered. Partly because lying with her felt nice.

Now, it's sending a frisson of doubt through me. Waking up in bed together feels more intimate than what we did last night. The shades are drawn, but enough golden light is sneaking in around them to make it obvious it's no longer night. That we slept together—in both senses of the word.

Lili shifts again. So does the sheet, fully revealing her perky tits. The throbbing in my cock gets worse.

I start to stroke myself, lazy tugs that replace uneasiness with bolts of pleasure.

"You're insatiable." The rasp of her voice is sexy, the sandpaper texture not just from sleepiness, but also a reminder of how loudly she was screaming a few hours ago.

She might hate *me* half the time, but Lili loves my cock.

My head rolls to the left, my eyes meeting hers. Open now, the brilliant blue bright and amused.

"Are you complaining?"

"Yes." She glances at the clock, then right back at my dick. "I don't like to wake up this early."

"I didn't wake you up."

"You should've. Unless you'd rather fuck your hand than"—Lili pulls the sheet away, putting her lithe figure on full display, and her thighs part, pulling my gaze from her tits to her pussy—"me."

I shift so I'm above her, my mouth going straight to one of her tits and adding to the bites I already left on her breasts. She has a bikini tan line that I trace with my tongue before kissing a trail down the center of her stomach. Abdominal muscles contract in response to my touch, a gasp leaving her mouth when she realizes where I'm headed.

Her eyes flutter closed. The rises and falls of her chest are faster. When I press a kiss just inside the curve of her hip bone, then suck hard, she bites her bottom lip.

"Fuck," she gasps, the huskiness of her voice even rougher now.

She's so wet that I can smell it. See it, the pink flesh shiny and slick, even before I lick her slit. I part it with my tongue to circle the opening of her cunt.

Lili swears loudly as her entire body reacts, back bowing and fingers fisting. I press her thigh harder into the mattress as she grinds against my face, hoping she can feel my smirk.

She loves my mouth too.

And while I've never been selfish in bed, I've never experienced any satisfaction similar to watching Elizabeth Kensington come undone because of me. The first time it happened in that hallway at her grandparents' house, I told myself it was lingering relief she'd accepted my apology, but there's no excuse for it right now. I just … like seeing her this way. I've never seen a more beautiful sight than a naked Lili, covered in hickeys from my mouth. Gasping my name like it's her favorite word. Begging for more.

She's so bloody responsive, like she was made for my touch.

"Charlie … please … fuck … more …"

Lili can't even form a full sentence, and it has me satisfied as fuck as I suck on her clit, then flick it.

She's squirming in the messy sheets as much as I'll allow, tangling them even more, while I eat her out like she's my last meal. Fighting the urge to hump the mattress because the sound of her breathy begging has me so hard that I'm desperate for any friction. It seems impossible there's blood left anywhere else in my body.

Her breathing is getting faster. Her moans are getting louder. And then she's coming, her sweet taste flooding my mouth.

I sit up, already reaching for a condom. I always carry extras, but we've basically blown through my emergency stash. This is the last one.

Her pussy is still pulsing when I push inside, the clasp extra tight as she struggles to take me. I have to clench my ass to keep from coming right away, the sensation of tight, wet heat even better than I remember. It feels more incredible with her every damn time, despite experience telling me the opposite. Novelty has always held more appeal in the past.

"Fuck," I growl. "You feel so fucking good."

Her inner muscles spasm, sucking me even deeper into heaven. "It's too much," Lili pants. "I can't …"

"I didn't think you were a quitter, Kensington."

She's breathing hard, still trembling around me. I can't tell if she's still coming or already about to come again.

"I"—she gasps when I slam so deep that my balls bounce off her ass—"hate"—moans when I hook her knee over my hip—"you."

I chuckle. "Very convincing."

Her nails dig deep into my shoulders.

And I slow my thrusts, ignoring the need burning through me, hit by the unfamiliar urge to make this last. To savor the sight of Lili under me, breathless and basically speechless.

I want her to think about this long after we both leave this bed.

I want to leave some permanent mark on her, not just hickeys.

I want her to think about how much better it was with me the next time she's shagging someone else.

"*Charlie.*" Her voice is filled with annoyance now, mixing with lust.

I'm hardly pumping my hips, the slow drag against slick skin fucking excruciating. My balls are heavy and tight, my tensed muscles begging for relief.

"Why'd you stop?" she whines.

I dip my head, my mouth finding that sensitive spot where Lili's shoulder joins her neck. Right on top of her trapezius muscle. I trace the line of sinew with my tongue, then suck—hard enough to leave another bruise. Her pelvis bucks against mine.

"More, Marlborough."

I like how she calls me Charlie and by my last name. Lili might know I'm a duke, but she doesn't treat me like one. I doubt she even knows my formal title.

"Thought you said it was too much?"

I'm enjoying this in spite of the aching pressure in my groin. Lili is mesmerizing.

Her nails scratch down my back as she huffs with annoyance. "I can take it."

"Yeah, you can. Your cunt takes me so well."

I pull out, the latex shiny with her arousal. I swipe two fingers through the wetness, mesmerized by the feel of the slippery glide. She's *so* wet. Literally dripping. Swollen and needy and desperate for me.

Her pussy tightens as I circle it, like she's trying to pull my fingers inside. Frantic for something to fill her again.

Blood roars in my ears as my dick jerks, just as eager.

I shove two fingers inside of her. Lili chants my name as she writhes on the mattress, trying to force my fingers deeper. She moans when I curl them, hiking one leg higher.

"You want to come again?" I don't recognize the sound of my own voice, roughened and hardened by the basest of instincts.

"*Yes,*" she breathes, nodding wildly.

She's unraveling. Rather than victorious, I can feel the threads of my own control fraying like an invisible string is tying my arousal to hers. If she's falling, I want to jump too.

Holding off becomes physically impossible.

I replace my fingers with my cock, shoving into her with one harsh stroke. I revert to rough, deep thrusts, hammering into her with enough force that the bedsprings and the headboard both protest. It just fuels me to pump faster, stuffing her full with each shove, barely remembering to hold some of my weight off of her.

Lili comes with a loud cry, spasming around me in a tight fist that squeezes the cum right out of my balls. My cock swells as my climax goes on and on, the pleasure so intense that it's almost painful.

My breathing matches my racing heart when I withdraw, reaching for a tissue on the table next to the headboard and crumpling it around the used condom before collapsing back onto the bed. I can feel my pulse everywhere—the tips of my fingers and the tip of my dick—as the sweat on my skin starts to cool.

*Fuck,* that was good.

Lili looks as dazed as I feel. She hasn't moved since I pulled out, still sprawled in the same vulnerable position.

My head is blissfully empty, my body temporarily sated. I'm enveloped by a sensation of peace, the same escape I get from standing on the edge of a cliff or riding around Newcastle. I didn't know it was possible to find this feeling anywhere else. I've never associated it with the physical satisfaction of sex before.

Lili's head rolls my way a couple of minutes later. Or maybe it's been hours. Days. I'm not exactly counting seconds right now.

Her blue eyes appear amazed, which fuels the satisfied glow in my chest. Lili's looking at me like I'm a god, and I'll happily become her personal deity.

She says nothing. Neither do I. We just stare at each other, rapid pants transitioning to even inhales and exhales.

Then, her eyes look to the clock.

Lili's relaxed expression shifts to alert.

"Shit!" she exclaims, sitting up straight. "I'm supposed to be in Chloe's suite in five minutes."

I yawn. "For what? The wedding isn't until three."

"We're all getting our makeup done. And hair styled."

I glance at her. "You look good to me."

She looks freshly fucked actually. Swollen lips. Flushed cheeks. Tangled strands.

Makes me want to make a mess of her all over again.

But Lili's already out of bed, darting into the bathroom. When she reappears, it's to open the closet and yank a dress off of its hanger. Dunno why she didn't grab one of the dresses flung across every surface in her room.

I scrub a palm across my face. I should head back to the room

I've never even been to. The valet handed me the key when Lili and I got back from dinner … and I requested my luggage be unloaded and left at the front desk.

*Fuck.*

Last night, that sounded quicker and easier. This morning, the last thing I feel like doing is going down to the lobby just to get a clean pair of boxers.

A sigh heaves my chest when I realize I have no other option.

My hand drops at the sound of a loud thud.

Lili is scowling at one of her suitcases. She sighs, then starts to twist and shimmy, trying to reach the zipper of the dress she's half wearing, which is bloody entertaining to watch.

Finally, she abandons her efforts and pins me with a pleading glare. "A little help?"

I groan as I get up, but I don't really care. The sooner I go grab my stuff, the better. Then, I should shower. Maybe get a little more sleep.

The scent of her perfume hits, the closer I step. The same aroma my head is filled with, that the sheets I slept on smelled like.

It's Chanel. I saw the glass bottle in the bathroom when I got up to take a piss last night. An oddly intimate thing to know about someone, exactly how they smell.

My knuckles drag along Lili's spine as I slide the hidden zipper upward. I take my time, centimeter by centimeter, and I can tell Lili's fighting the urge to squirm.

Goosebumps rise in reaction to my touch, and I wish she were still naked so I could see how far they spread.

I lean forward and kiss the vertebra at the very top of her spine as soon as the zipper's set, swiping my tongue against her smooth skin. Some primitive part of me loves that she hasn't showered yet. She smells like her fancy perfume. She also smells like sex. Like *me*.

Lili's exhale is shaky as she reaches for her phone and room key. "Thanks."

"You're welcome." I cross my arms, not missing how her gaze darts down to my crotch for one last peek.

"I'll, uh … I'll see you at the wedding."

I nod.

She's gone a few seconds later, the door shutting with a soft click.

I find my clothes in the mess on the floor and pull them on, patting the pockets to make sure I still have my phone and wallet. I toss the collection of condom wrappers and make a decent attempt at straightening the sheets before leaving the room and heading down the hallway.

I decide to skip the elevator and take the stairs instead. They're just as fancy as the rest of this place—plush carpet and scrolling details on the handrail.

An older couple is standing at the front desk. I wait for them to wrap up their queries about what brand of soap the hotel uses, then inform the young man working that I'm here for my luggage.

He disappears into a back room, returning with my leather duffel bag, but not the canvas garment bag that contained my other suit.

I exhale, already having a frustrating feeling before he confirms that nothing else is stored back there but that he'll check with the rest of the front-desk staff to locate the garment bag.

I take the duffel and head toward the elevators, slowing when I see Lili's friend Tripp approaching from the opposite direction. He's dressed casually in athletic shorts and a faded T-shirt, his eyebrows rising slightly when he takes in my suit and bag.

"Hey, Charles."

"Morning."

"Big day."

I shift my weight between my feet, antsy to keep moving. "Yeah. I guess."

He's here because he cares about the couple getting married. I'm here because of my meddling grandmother.

"Wish we could head back to the track today. I'm on Theo about a trip to Monaco next week."

"Monaco?"

"Yeah. We're all headed to Saint-Tropez tomorrow. Weird idea to have a group honeymoon, if you ask me, but Chloe has always done things her own way. None of us have seen her much the past two years, so …"

*I'll* be in Saint-Tropez next week. Not for an extended vacation with my friends, but to sell the villa. But I don't mention that to Tripp.

"Nice," I say instead.

"How'd it go last night?" The question comes out rushed, like he's been holding it back.

"It was fine."

Fucking understatement, but I barely know this guy. I'm not going to go into detail. To mention that last night was full of firsts for me. First time I ate a meal with a woman, just the two of us. First time I woke up with someone else in the bed. First time I wasn't eager to get out of there. *She* left first, for Christ's sake.

"I'll see you at the wedding," I add, then continue walking.

I need some coffee before more conversation. Preferably a shower too.

"Charles."

I glance back. "Yeah?"

Tripp shoves his hands into his pockets. "I've been the guy who gives no fucks before, so I know this makes me a hypocrite. And Lili can make her own choices. But you hurt her, and I'll kick your ass. I won't be the only one taking a swing at you either."

My jaw works as I stare at him. "Who I fuck is none of your business."

Tripp stiffens. "*Lili*'s my business."

"Because she broke up with your buddy?"

I don't fully understand the dynamics among Lili's friends. I've never been part of a large group like that, bouncing between boarding schools.

Tripp's eyes flash. "Because *she* is my *buddy*."

"You meddle in all your buddies' lives or just hers?"

Tripp tenses even more. "All of them. It's called caring about someone, Marlborough. Maybe you should try it sometime."

My fingers curl tight around the handle of my duffel. "You don't know anything about me."

"Exactly. That's why—"

"Morning, guys." Cal Winston is walking this way, dressed similarly to Tripp.

Just makes my attire stand out more, and I watch a muscle in Cal's jaw jump as he puts together what me standing in the lobby in last night's clothes means. I feel smugger about that than I should. I've never given a flying shit about a woman's exes before. But I don't like that Lili dated him. That he ever let her feel like her money mattered to him.

I know what it's like for someone to look at you and only see one aspect of your identity—a piece you had no control over. It fucking sucks.

"Morning." I keep my greeting short, eager to get out of here before more of Lili's friends show up.

"Have you seen Fran?" Cal asks Tripp. "She was supposed to pick out a tie for me."

"She's probably in the bridal suite, getting her hair and makeup done," I say, then continue walking toward the elevator.

Jab the button twice, then release a long exhale as soon as the doors slide closed.

Undecided if I should have said more or less just now.

# CHAPTER 17

## *Lili*

Four pairs of curious eyes land on me as soon as I walk into Chloe's bridal suite. The only person who pays me no attention is the stranger I assume must be the makeup artist, who's busy spreading foundation on Gwen's face.

Chloe's sister gives me a jaunty wave. "Hey, Lili!"

Her chipper chirp is an assault on my eardrums. My whole head feels like it's vibrating.

I'm not hungover, just *extremely* sleep-deprived.

"Sorry I'm late," I announce, tucking a stray strand of hair behind one ear.

I finger-combed it the best I could in the reflective doors of the elevator on the ride up to the top floor, but I couldn't do much about the smears of last night's makeup still on my face. I had done a terrible job of washing it off before bed, half delirious from all the dopamine swimming through my system.

Self-conscious about my bedraggled appearance—I look walk-of-shame chic without the chic—I head toward the breakfast buffet that's set up by the windows. At least my dress covers the bites and bruises scattered across my breasts and marking my inner thighs.

Each step is a reminder of the burn between my thighs.

It's a good sore. A satisfied sore. A *noticeable* sore.

I'd thought I'd learned what sex was like a while ago. Mostly because that's *always* what it's been like. But what I'd thought was awesome, occasionally amazing, has now been relegated to a solid B. Not even a B-plus. A *B*.

And I'm a little mad at Charlie and his A game, honestly.

He set a new standard I'm not sure where to find again. Maybe it's British men? Aside from a fling in college with a French foreign exchange student, all the other guys have been American.

That's a better theory than it just being … him.

Chloe, Fran, and Bridget descend on me like vultures as soon as I take a seat on the couch with my full plate. The tug of lace against sensitive skin makes me squirm as I settle against the cushions.

"How was dinner?"

"Why didn't you answer any of my voice messages?"

"Holy shit, did you hook up with him?"

My best friends toss questions at me rapid-fire.

I take a long gulp of coffee, then answer, "Dinner was good. I overslept and haven't checked my phone yet. And … yeah, I did."

Fran squeals as soon as I answer her question.

"What's going on over there?" Gwen calls. "Are you guys gossiping without me?"

Chloe waves a hand in her sister's direction. "You don't know him, sis. Focus on your makeup."

"You mean, focus on just sitting here?" Gwen replies dryly.

"How was it?" Bridget asks, leaning closer.

"How big was it?" Fran has scooted so close she's practically in my lap.

I take a bite of cantaloupe. "It's Chloe's wedding day. I don't think she wants to hear about my sex life."

"Actually, I do," Chloe tells me. "I went to a dinner with Theo's work friends, and all the girlfriends-slash-wives got drinks after. A few shots later, one of them said she hooked up with Charles Marlborough a couple of years ago, and it was the best night of her life."

"Her poor boyfriend-slash-husband," I say.

Also, that's not encouraging to my preferred theory.

My friends all look at me expectantly, none of them indicating they'll let this go.

"There's a reason I'm sitting right now," I say. "Everything's sore. Pilates was *not* adequate preparation for some of the positions."

Fran's jaw practically unhinges. "*That* good?"

"You guys are definitely gossiping without me!" Gwen shouts.

Chloe shoots her sister a sweet smile. "Your makeup looks amazing!"

The three of them refocus on me, and now, I'm pretty sure Gwen and the makeup artist are listening as well.

"Yeah," I answer Fran. Charlie's not here to have his massive ego inflated even more. Not that he's under any illusions that I didn't enjoy it. My throat is as raw as my vagina. "It was that good."

"So, the date must have gone well too," Chloe says.

I nod. "It did."

*Best date I've ever been on.* That, I don't say aloud. Praising his bedroom skills was one thing, but I'm not going to admit how much I enjoyed the entire evening. I'm self-conscious, recalling how much I confided in him at the restaurant.

"Where did he take you?" Bridget asks, stealing a grape off my plate.

"To dinner. It was a restaurant called The Beach House."

Fran glances at Chloe. "Have you heard of it?"

"Yeah, I have," she replies. "It's supposed to be really nice."

I nod in agreement. "It was. You and Theo should go sometime. Make sure you get the pistachio tiramisu for dessert."

"Are you going out with him again?" Fran asks.

I shake my head. "Doubt it. We're leaving for Saint-Tropez first thing tomorrow, remember?"

Bridget smirks. "But we still have one more night here …"

I pop a piece of fruit in my mouth so I don't have to reply. Do I want to have sex with Charlie again? One thousand percent. But I'm rapidly realizing it's a dangerous idea. Not only will it further recalibrate my body to some impossible standards, but the sex wasn't just physical. There was some layer of trust and understanding that amplified everything. A connection I'd never experienced before, which appeared before any clothes came off.

I'd thought Chloe was being overprotective, cautioning me about getting attached. Turned out, she might have been right on the money. I'm best off preserving last night as a special, sexy memory.

"We'll see," I say. "I want to find out what the other options are first."

Fran groans. "You do *not* get to snap up another guy. You already got the duke who turned me down. My fragile ego is still recovering from that."

Bridget snorts. "Your fragile ego recovered when you met that wannabe actor at Proof. Is he still texting you?"

"Yes." Fran pouts. "But he's not *British*."

Chloe laughs. "You're welcome for getting married here."

There's a knock on the door.

"Fran? You in there?"

It sounds like Cal.

"Yeah," she calls back. "What's up?"

"You said you'd pick out my tie."

Fran rolls her eyes. "Did you bring options, Cal?"

"Four."

She stands and strides over to the door.

Cal's standing in the hallway, wearing navy slacks and a white button-down, four ties draped over one arm and a sheepish smile on his face.

"Sorry, I just—" He spots me sitting on the couch. Stares for a few seconds, smiles, then holds up his arm. "Which one?"

Fran surveys the options. One silver, one striped, one skinny, and a pink one with a subtle white pattern I can't see from here.

"Pink," she decides.

"Really?"

"Really. Real men wear pink. Now, go check on Tripp. He's never been on time for anything in his life, but today, that changes."

"Tripp is up. He's eating breakfast. We'll all be there on time."

It seems like Cal is careful not to look in my direction before Fran closes the door in his face, but it might be my imagination.

Aside from the elevator reflection, I haven't surveyed my appearance, but I'm pretty sure I currently look … like I was having sex all night.

I recall Bridget's words on the plane—*I think it would be good for Cal to see you with someone else*—and pray that she's right. I don't blame Cal—at all—for how our relationship ended. My own insecurities were at fault. He would have signed a prenup if I'd asked. He wasn't with me just for the money. In many ways, he was a safe bet, and that didn't change in one evening. It just made me realize I didn't *want* a safe bet. If no one could ignore my immense wealth, I wanted to experience what it was like to be with a guy who made me feel more than simply safe.

Cal never would have challenged me to race him. He fretted over me even stepping on the track when we went to Monaco for Jasper's twenty-first. And our relationship was more romantic than passionate or physical. I never once felt like I would *die* if he stopped touching me, which was the state I spent most of last night and the start of this morning in. I hadn't known that desperate level of desire existed.

I sink a little lower on the couch once it's all girls again, poking at the scone on my plate. "Do you think he knows?"

"That Britain's most eligible bachelor was in your bed last night? Definitely," Bridget says from my right, not looking up from the magazine she grabbed from somewhere and is now flipping through.

I scoff. "He's not Britain's most eligible bachelor." Then glance at Chloe, the resident expert on England. "Is he?"

Her shrug is not exactly comforting. "I mean …"

Bridget taps the magazine she's reading. "It says it right here. *Charles Marlborough, the eighth Duke of Manchester and Britain's most eligible bachelor, was seen leaving exclusive gentlemen's club The Ivy House with respected barrister Henry Sutherland.*"

"That's a tabloid."

"So? Do you think he's met the royal family?"

I roll my eyes. "Can we stop talking about Charlie, please? It was a fun night. It's over. It's Chloe's wedding day. We're leaving for Saint-Tropez tomorrow. After today, I'll probably never see him again."

That last sentence isn't as reassuring as I'd like it to be. More … melancholy.

Fran walks over to where Bridget and I are sitting. Flashes her phone screen at us. "Which hairstyle should I do? This one or"—she swipes to a new photo—"this one?"

Chloe's mom arrives right as Gwen's makeup gets finished. She starts crying as soon as she sees Chloe and again when the bridesmaid dresses my mom designed are revealed.

I've never really considered what my wedding day would look like. It's always felt far off, even when Cal mentioned marriage. But as I watch my best friend enjoy hers, it's easier to imagine than I thought it would be.

I can see Fran and Bridget fussing over me the same way they're doing with Chloe right now. Collins, my college roommate, would be here too. Wren and Rory. Aunt Hannah. Gigi. And I doubt my mom would be sobbing like Mrs. Beaumont, but I think she'd probably dab at her eyes when she saw me in my dress. I've always known I'd ask if I could wear hers. My dad would definitely cry before we started down the aisle, and I'd probably make a joke about how if anything went wrong, we would get it right at my second wedding.

The only part I can't picture clearly is the groom.

# Charlie

Weddings aren't my favorite. They're actually my *least* favorite type of societal event, typically filled with sentimentality and stiffness. I'd rather sit through multiple matches at Wimbledon in the baking sun than witness a ceremony in a cool church.

I fiddle with the thin edge of the paper program that was handed out to all the guests as they entered the stone chapel, attempting to hide my impatience even though no one's being subtle about staring at me.

It took me ten minutes to make it from the doors to a seat in one of the pews. Fig is serving as one of Theo's groomsmen, so I'm sitting alone.

I read through the program listing the order of the ceremony and the members of the wedding party for a tenth time—my eyes lingering on *Elizabeth Kensington* for a few seconds longer than the

other names.

"Hello, Charles."

I glance up, the collar of my shirt getting hot when I register who's standing at the end of the pew. Beatrice Campbell. Her best friend, Alexandra Green, is a step behind.

"Hello, Beatrice." I nod at her friend. "Alexandra."

Alexandra blushes furiously.

"Are these seats taken?" Bea asks, nodding to the empty wood beside me.

"No," I reply.

"Do you mind …"

"Of course not." I curl the program in my palm, wishing I'd shoved my way into a full pew instead.

I haven't seen Bea since … my father's funeral probably. I don't remember her being there, but I'm certain the Campbells were invited. The time before that was likely at one of Fig's parties. I'd attended them all back when I was in medical school.

She looks the same as she did then—proper and poised. I've never seen her upset or irritated, just a perpetual beam of placidity.

She looks beautiful, too, and I should tell her so. It's the expected compliment.

Before I can open my mouth, she speaks. "How … how have you been?"

The question is tentative, like I'm a wild animal she'll scare away if she talks too loudly.

"All right," I reply. It doesn't feel like as much of a lie as it used to. Despite a shitty night's sleep, I feel more energized than I have in a while. Not just from the marathon of sex, but the change of scenery. I needed it more than I'd realized. "How about you?"

"Good. I'm working as a clothing buyer for Harrods now. Is Blythe still interested in fashion?"

I tense a little when Bea brings up my sister. It's an innocent query—I think—but I don't appreciate the mention, like she's trying to fit herself into my family. "Yes."

She crosses her legs. "I wasn't sure if you'd be here."

That, I don't believe. If Fig heard I was coming, she did too. But I play along.

"Me neither. I've been … busy."

Her nod is understanding. "I'm sure it's been a big adjustment."

There's nothing except sympathy in her voice.

I clear my throat. "Yes, it has been."

I glance around, taking note of all the attention aimed this way, hoping the ceremony will start soon. But guests are still filing in, packing the pews to capacity.

My grandmother will hear about this before her morning tea, I'm sure. Bea knows exactly what she's doing, sitting with me. Knows me attending a wedding will fuel speculation about when—who—I'll marry and is purposefully including herself in the conversation.

The Campbells are one of the most affluent families in Britain. I've never even kissed her.

She's after a title, not money or love.

The transaction I've spent my entire life expecting feels emptier than I thought it would. I assumed marrying one of the well-mannered women my grandmother had spent years pushing me toward would be simple and straightforward. Like checking a box on my list of duties.

I'd choose someone I liked. Respected. But I wouldn't love her. I wouldn't repeat any of my father's mistakes. He married my mother because he wanted to, not because she was the best option. If he'd placed less of a premium on beauty and intrigue, Blythe and I would have grown up with a mother.

Marriage is a problem for my future self to figure out. I'm twenty-six. My father was thirty-three when he got married. That's still seven years of freedom.

Organ music begins to play, signaling the start of the wedding. My head turns with the rest of the assembly, and I smile when Fig saunters by, escorting Lili's friend who hit on me. Fran, I think.

Lili's the last bridesmaid to enter, her elbow hooked with Theo's younger brother's. Her hair has been curled and partially pulled back; her makeup flawless.

She's stunning, impossible to look away from.

So, I don't. I stare openly, tracking her progress down the aisle. When everyone stands to see the bride, I do too. But I'm not looking at the figure clad in white. My eyes refuse to leave Lili.

She doesn't look my way. Her focus is on her best friend who's about to get married.

Chloe reaches the altar. Her father lifts the veil, kisses her cheek, and then places her hand in Theo's. He shaved his beard for the big day, his face fully visible as he beams at his bride.

The bridesmaid next to Lili leans in to whisper something to her. She smiles in response. Nods.

Then, her eyes catch mine.

We stare at each other the same way we did in bed this morning. In a church packed with people, it feels like we're completely alone.

I can't tell what Lili is thinking. She's smiling, but it's still. Frozen in place. Expected rather than enthusiastic.

When the minister starts speaking, she breaks eye contact.

My attention wanders during the ceremony itself, my focus torn between stealing looks at Lili and fighting the urge to bounce my knee impatiently. It lasts about an hour, and then the procession happens in reverse, Theo and Chloe the last to leave.

I escort Beatrice and Alexandra outside. It's the polite thing to do, even if neither of them is my actual date. I engage Alexandra in conversation as we file out of the church, hoping that paying her attention will smother speculation that Bea and I are secretly engaged.

The reception is taking place in the nearby carriage house, guests milling around on the lawn and then gradually making their way over to the other building.

I spot my godfather a second before he calls me over. "Charles!"

Louis Haywood was one of my father's closest friends. The only true one he had possibly. Balding—although his top hat hides it—portly, and good-natured, he never let my father's sharp tongue cut too deep. Stuck around. I have memories of him scattered throughout my childhood, as if he were a permanent member of our small family.

I haven't seen him since the funeral.

I've dodged him since the funeral.

I say a quick farewell to Beatrice and Alexandra, then head in his direction.

"Good to see you, Louis," I say and mean it.

"Splendid to see you, my boy!" His smile is so wide that it squints his eyes to accommodate its size. He shakes my hand, then clasps my palm between both of his. "How've you been?"

"Better," I admit.

Louis's enthusiasm fizzles, his hands releasing mine and

reaching up to squeeze my shoulder.

I've wondered previously if he knew about my father's financial decline, and I wonder about it again now. But I didn't ask before, and I don't ask now.

This isn't the proper place, and the answer won't solve any of my current problems.

"I've got some time in my calendar next week," he tells me. "Would love to make a trip to Newcastle. It's been too long."

"I'll be out of town," I tell him. "Maybe the week after?"

Louis nods. "Out of town? A vacation?"

"Not exactly. I'm … selling the villa in Saint-Tropez."

He's silent for a moment, and I'm worried he'll ask why directly. He doesn't.

"How's Blythe?" he questions.

"She's"—I smile wryly—"Blythe."

Louis and I talk alone for a few more minutes before our conversation expands with more people, friends of the Hugheses who are of Louis's generation. I end up talking with a group of former schoolmates from Oxford.

No one is really sure how to act around me. By rank, I'm the most important person here. But the guys my age are ones I drunkenly played pool with. Me being the *future* Duke of Manchester mattered a lot less than me being *the* Duke of Manchester.

I'm suspended in the weird place of recalling those relaxed days during an *irresponsible* point in my life and now having to interact with the same people from a *responsible* position of esteem.

It's strange and slightly uncomfortable.

But I suck it up, same as I do with all my other duties.

# CHAPTER 19

## *Lili*

Chloe laughs as her dad dips her during their father-daughter dance.

I smile at the sentimental sight. Grab one of the disposable cameras off the table and snap a photo of the sweet moment.

Next to me, Bridget sniffs. I pat her thigh.

Today has been an emotional day for all of us.

"Come on, guys." Tripp appears, perching on the edge of the empty seat to my left. "We're almost up. Final rehearsal out on the terrace."

It was Fran's idea to perform a group dance at Chloe's wedding. My song suggestion. Hugo's job to choreograph it. Tripp was the organizer. Cal and Jasper were in charge of designing and printing the T-shirts.

The final result is … a spectacle.

"We've practiced twenty times," Bridget says, sipping more champagne.

"And you were late on the last clap on Thursday. Plus, we didn't get to practice last night because someone"—a pointed glance at me—"wasn't around."

I roll my eyes. "*My* clap was on cue."

"Fine." Tripp leans back in the chair. "If you want Chloe to remember our tribute to twenty years of friendship being an amateur performance—"

"For fuck's sake, Tripp." Bridget stands. "This is supposed to be *fun*." She stalks toward one of the doors that lead out to the terrace.

Tripp bounds up eagerly, leaving me sitting alone at our table.

I sneak one last glance at Chloe dancing with her dad, then grab my glass and follow them toward the exit.

The blister forming on my left pinkie toe throbs, and I deliberate if it's worth changing into less cute but more comfortable shoes for the dance. I'll see how much it bothers me during our final rehearsal, I guess.

I step onto the stone pavers, rushing to catch up with Tripp and Bridget. Jasper, Cal, Hugo, and Fran are already huddled up ahead, Jasper holding a bundle of white that must be the themed shirts.

I don't see it coming. One second, I'm vertical, running through the steps Hugo came up with in my head. And then I'm falling, my stomach lurching as I pitch forward. I toss the glass on instinct, lifting my arm to cushion the hit. One of my heels catches between the pavers. I'm kept airborne for an extra second, teetering, before gravity prevails. My hand, shoulder, and head collide with unforgiving stone.

"Lili!"

"Oh my God."

"Can you hear me, Lili?"

"*Fuck*. She's bleeding."

"Are you okay?"

A cacophony of concerned voices swirls around me as I absorb the fact that I'm now lying on the ground.

I inhale shakily. Exhale an "Ow."

It *hurts*—everywhere. And I can feel a stickiness on my hand. My stomach roils sickeningly, even though I'm lying still.

I blink a few times, then sit up, making sure to rest all my weight on my uninjured hand. My left is what hit the ground, my right's reflexes slower, thanks to the shattered glass lying a foot away. At least I didn't fall on the sharp splinters. I'm nauseous at the thought.

My friends are all clustered around, Bridget and Fran crouched on the ground beside me.

"I'm okay," I say. "I think."

"You're bleeding," Fran whispers.

"I know." I don't look, but I can feel it.

Not just my wet palm, but warmth trickling down my shoulder.

"Here. Apply some pressure." Jasper holds out one of the shirts.

I don't take it. "I'm not getting blood all over that. What about the dance?"

"You're bleeding, and you hit your head," Cal tells me. "You're not doing the dance, Lili."

I want to protest, but I know he's right. Based on everyone's worried expressions, I look as bad as I feel. The only upside to my injuries is that my blister isn't bothering me anymore.

"You guys can still do it," I say, taking the shirt from Jasper reluctantly.

Hugo scoffs. "Without you? No way. We'll perform it for Chloe some other time."

"You should go to a hospital, Lili," Fran says. "Get your head checked. And"—her eyes dart down to my arm—"you might need stitches."

Disappointment swamps me. It's bad enough I ruined the dance performance. I don't want to miss the rest of the reception. And I *definitely* don't feel like spending the rest of the night sitting in a hospital.

"She's right," Bridget agrees. "You should get looked at, just in case."

Murmured agreement from the guys.

I close my eyes. Blow out a long breath.

"Can one of you go get Charlie?"

Silence.

I crack one eye open, not a fan of the half-pitying, half-disbelieving look Fran and Jasper exchange.

Tripp sighs. "He doesn't really seem like the *hold your hand* type, Lili."

He's undoubtedly thinking that I fell for the Charles Marlborough charm after one night, but I don't feel like explaining the real reason to Tripp.

"I don't want him to hold my hand," I say through gritted teeth. My head is starting to throb worse now. And I'm trying not to cause a scene, but my scraped arm fucking *stings*. I close my eyes again since that helped a little. "I want him to take a look at me."

"You need a doctor, not a duke," Jasper says. "I'm no gynecologist, but I guess I can give it a go."

Someone muffles a laugh. Fran, I think. *Traitor.* There's also a grunt, like an elbow was thrown.

"My vagina is fine, asshole. Can someone just *get Charlie*?"

There's a dramatic sigh as one of my friends makes his or her disapproval known, but when I open my eyes again, Hugo is missing.

I exhale, too, then gingerly roll my shoulder. My fingers are starting to ache from gripping the shirt so tightly, and I feel foolish, sitting in the middle of the terrace.

But between the nausea and the throbbing in my temples, standing or moving sounds like a terrible idea. At least the curtains covering the doors mean I'm not on display for the whole reception to gawk at.

Bridget brings me a glass of cold water that I take tiny sips from while staring into space. Fran stays by my side while Jasper and Tripp stand like sentries. Cal kneels, picking up the larger pieces of the broken glass then tossing them into the garbage can next to one of the tall oaks.

"You guys don't have to stay out here."

Jasper snorts.

Cal gives me an incredulous look. "Of course we're staying with you."

Hugo returns, alone, a few minutes later.

I take another gulp of water before asking, "Did you find him?"

"Uh-huh. He said he needed to take care of something first."

*I told you so* is stamped all over his face, echoing in the silence surrounding me, and then it's interrupted by Tripp's muttered, "Dick."

I try to ignore the pang of disappointment that appears. I didn't ask for Charlie because I needed him to comfort me or because we went on a date that ended with lots of sex. I asked for him because he's the one person here who I know has some medical training and I'd like to avoid spending the remainder of my best friend's wedding in a British emergency room.

"Okay," I say, defeat saturating the two syllables. "I guess I should go to the hospital."

No matter how inconvenient a trip to the ER is, I'm not willing to risk a brain bleed or whatever else can result from a head slamming into concrete.

Cal nods in immediate agreement. "I'll drive you."

"In a strange city, on the wrong side of the road, after drinking?" Bridget shakes her head. "Call a driver."

"I'll ask Chloe what—"

"No," I rasp, interrupting Fran. The pounding in my head feels like it's worked its way into my throat. "Don't tell Chloe. Make up some excuse if she asks about me. I don't want to ruin her wedding. Someone at the front desk will know a car service. You guys stay here, and Cal will text you once we know more. Right?" I glance at Cal.

He nods again. "Right."

"All right." I blow out a breath. "Can you guys help me up?"

One of the terrace doors shuts, followed by the pound of confident footfalls.

"Don't bloody move, Lili."

I swallow—hard—as soon as I hear his voice. Slump with something that feels similar to relief and then try to sit up straighter. For the first time since I realized I was falling, I feel better.

Charlie crouches down next to me, then sets a first aid kit down on the pavers. "What happened?" he asks briskly.

Fran scrambles out of his way, leaving the two of us on the ground alone.

I have to clear my throat twice. "I fell. Tripped. Fucking heels."

His warm fingers cover mine, coaxing my tight grip on the shirt loose so he can inspect the scrapes on my palm. He frowns at what I hope are just shallow cuts.

"Can someone flash a light?"

I look away from the brightness when it appears, not wanting to see the blood.

I stare at Charlie's focused expression instead. Trace the line of his jaw and the angle of his nose and the slope of his forehead with my eyes. Features so perfect and proportional that they look like they belong to one of the Greek mythology sculptures in my favorite exhibit at the Met.

"Higher," he instructs.

The light moves, but my eyes don't. It feels like the pain is fading a little, but maybe I'm just getting used to it. Or more distracted than I was.

"She hit her head too," Jasper says, the closeness of his voice making me think he's the one holding the light. I don't look away from Charlie to confirm.

"Okay. You can turn off the light."

A soft rustle as Charlie rummages through the bag he brought. He glances up, catching me staring. "This is antiseptic," he tells me. "It's going to sting."

"It already stings."

But I understand what Charlie means as soon as he presses the damp gauze against my palm. A hiss escapes my mouth before I can stop it, the burn so intense it feels like my skin should be smoking. I bite down on my tongue until I taste copper as the gauze moves to my shoulder, the singe of invisible flames following right behind.

"Quietest you've ever been with my hands on you," he says, low enough so that only I can hear—I hope.

"Don't be a wanker."

Charlie chuckles under his breath. "Who taught you that one?"

"I searched some British insults earlier."

Another low laugh, and then he tosses the gauze to the ground. I make the mistake of following the motion, grimacing at the rusty stains.

"Where'd you hit your head?"

"By my left temple. I was holding a glass in my right hand, so I was trying to fall that way."

His fingers slip into my hair, running lightly across my scalp. I wince when he finds tender skin.

"There?"

I nod. "Yeah."

"Did you lose consciousness?"

"No."

"How much have you had to drink?"

My cheeks warm. It feels like a personal question, coming from him. Like he knows I ordered my second drink right after seeing him talking to several beautiful women, including the blonde he sat next to during the ceremony.

"Two," I answer.

"Was the flashlight bothering your eyes?"

I shake my head, then immediately regret it. "I just don't like looking at blood."

"You have a headache."

It's more of a statement than a question, but I answer anyway. "My head hurts, yeah. The concrete wasn't soft."

Charlie doesn't crack a smile. "Who got married today?"

"Chloe and Theo."

"Where did you start college?"

"Yale."

"What did you have for dinner last night?"

"Fish."

"What's your favorite color?"

"You don't know the answer to that."

He relaxes a little, making me realize how tense he was before. "I don't think you have a concussion."

I relax too, relieved. "Great. I really didn't want to go to—"

"We're going to the hospital, Lili."

"What? You *just* said I'm fine. Slap a couple of Band-Aids on my arm, and I'll change into another dress."

This one is ruined, ripped and stained, which makes me more emotional than it should. Shock maybe. Not only do I love this dress, but it's one my mom designed. One that matches two of my best friends' and will be in all the photos of Chloe's wedding.

"I said I *don't think* you have a concussion, not that you're fine, so we're going to find out for sure."

I groan. "Charlie ..."

"Are you walking, or do you need me to carry you?"

"You're overreacting." I stand slowly, ignoring the hand he offers, hiding the flinch of pain in the hopes that he'll change his mind.

"We'll see. Let's go."

He's planning to come with me, I realize. Which is not the

direction I saw this evening taking. I thought he'd walk out here and tell me some Tylenol and Neosporin should do the trick.

I can't decide if Charlie accompanying me is a good or bad idea. His presence is reassuring, and he'll know how to navigate a foreign health-care system I have no experience with.

But I'm … embarrassed that he's seeing me like this. I want him to see me as confident and sexy and capable. Not as a clumsy, foolish, tipsy mess.

"You don't need to come with me," I tell him.

Charlie doesn't bother replying. He's zipping up the first aid bag and tossing the gauze he used in the trash can.

"Here." Bridget hands me a pair of plastic flip-flops. "Chloe got those for anyone wanting to change out of heels."

I didn't even notice her duck inside.

"Thank you," I say, stepping out of my heels and slipping the flip-flops on instead. They're a little big, but not too bad. And a lot more comfortable than Louboutins.

Cal appears beside me. "Do you want him to take you?" he asks quietly.

I bite my lip. Nod.

He exhales. "Do you want me to come too?"

It's a genuine offer, and it means a lot. It's a caring gesture from my friend Cal, not my ex-boyfriend–slash–safe harbor.

"I'm good, Cal. Thanks." I squeeze his arm with my uninjured hand, trying to silently convey how much I appreciate the offer.

Tripp is sidling up to Charlie. "Lili doesn't need a chauffeur."

Charlie's jaw flexes as he hands the first aid kit to Fran. She offered to bring it back inside. "You want her to drive herself to the hospital?"

"No, of course not. But one of her *friends* will go with her."

Animosity is suddenly humming in the evening air. Mostly emanating from Tripp, who's normally one of the most easygoing people I know.

Charlie raises one eyebrow. "Know a lot about intracranial hematomas, do you?"

"Throw around as many medical terms as you want, man. But if you think I'm going to let Lili go off with you while she's injured and—"

"Stop making me sound like an invalid, Tripp," I say. "I'll go with Charlie. Then, none of you have to miss the rest of the reception."

Cal grunts. "Stop worrying about the damn reception, Lili."

"How much have you had to drink?" Tripp asks Charlie rudely.

"Tripp!" I chastise. "He's not—"

"Nothing." Charlie holds Tripp's gaze for a few seconds, then glances at me. "Sooner we leave, the sooner you can reunite with your *friends*."

I nod reluctantly, still not thrilled about having to go to the hospital.

"Are you sure you don't want us to come?" Bridget whispers to me.

"I'm good," I tell her.

"Call if you need anything." Fran squeezes my hand.

I walk toward Charlie, leveling Tripp with a half-pleading, half-annoyed look as I pass him.

"He's just worried about me," I tell Charlie as we start along the path that leads away from the carriage house and toward the hotel.

"I know. That's why I didn't punch him."

I snort, then shiver. It's chillier out than I would have thought possible, considering temperatures were in the eighties earlier.

The warm weight of Charlie's jacket settles over my shoulders a few seconds later. He's wearing the same suit from last night, the one that spent the night on my floor, but there's not a single wrinkle in the stiff fabric.

I startle, then begin to protest. "I'm going to get blood on it—"

"Don't care."

Arguing sounds exhausting. He's as stubborn as I am.

"Thanks."

A low hum is his only response.

There's no one standing at the valet stand when we reach it. It's only nine o'clock, earlier than they assumed any guests would be departing, I guess.

"Someone is probably at the front desk …" My voice trails off as Charlie leans down and opens the stand.

After surveying the interior for a few seconds, he stands with a pair of keys clutched in one hand.

"Stay here," he instructs, then jogs toward the parking area.

A slight breeze picks up, blowing hair away from my face. I tug Charlie's jacket tighter around my shoulders, inhaling his delicious scent deeply.

Something sharp pokes at my chest. After glancing at the darkness to ensure Charlie isn't in sight, I loosen my grip on the fabric and stick a hand into the inside pocket, my fingers brushing against something hard.

I stare at the rectangle. A matchbox. I squint at it until the scrambled letters make sense. *The Beach House*, it reads. The name of the restaurant where Charlie and I ate last night. I remember seeing a matchbox beside the lit candle on the table. I almost knocked it off with my wineglass at one point. But I don't know why it's in the pocket of Charlie's suit.

The crunch of gravel makes me jump. I quickly slip the matchbox back where I found it, focusing on the approaching car instead. Headlights sweep across the bushes beside me before the convertible rolls to a stop.

I rush toward the passenger side, the flipped interior layout automatic for the first time, not wanting Charlie to climb out and assist me. I have some dignity left, and I'd like to preserve it.

It looks like Charlie's forehead furrows, but he says nothing as I slam the door shut and click on my seat belt.

And all I say before he hits the gas is, "You would've been a really good doctor."

# CHAPTER 20
## *Charlie*

The last time I was in the A&E was fifteen months ago.

I had bad memories of hospitals before that. All the visits associated with my knee surgery. And even longer ago, a faint recollection of my grandfather, pale and surrounded by beeping machines.

Until my father died, I thought I'd spend a lot of time in hospitals. My intention was to become one of the scrub-clad figures rushing up and down the white hallways with an efficient urgency.

I didn't just drop out of medical school because of the responsibilities of becoming a duke or because of the financial mess. I left because that terrible night made me question if I *could* do it.

Could I be the one to tell someone their father was gone forever? Could I walk the hallways of a hospital without that memory rattling around in my skull?

I didn't know, and I was fucking scared to find out for sure.

Just like I'm scared now.

I shove a hand into my hair and release a long exhale, not making eye contact with anyone passing by. They're staring at my formalwear, I think, not because they know who I am. It's been more than a year since a tabloid ran photos of me leaving a pub or a club. I know because I haven't been to a pub or a club in more than a year.

I glance down the hallway, then return to studying the worn linoleum.

Lili said she was fine going back to an examination room alone, and I'm second-guessing whether I should have pushed harder to accompany her.

Also questioning if I should have come in the first place. She was surrounded by close friends who have known her for years. They would have looked after her. Taken care of her. Comforted her. Known what she needed a hell of a lot better than I do.

But she asked for *me*.

She was hurt, and she asked for me.

No one has ever done that before. No one has ever needed me before.

And I couldn't walk away from that. I didn't want to.

So, I'm stuck in the hallway with ghosts of the past, feeling sick to my stomach because of a *woman*.

I'm 90 percent certain that Lili is fine. The scrapes on her hand and shoulder were shallow. They'll start to scab by tomorrow. And she was alert and aware, not vomiting or confused or exhibiting any symptoms to suggest a serious brain trauma.

But none of my medical training is helpful right now. I'm suffocated by the same feeling of helplessness that drowned me when my dad died.

*There was nothing we could do.* That's what the surgeon told me.

"Charlie?"

My gaze snaps up, anxiously scanning Lili from head to toe as she stops in front of me. She looks the same as she did when a nurse escorted her back, except she's now carrying a folded piece of paper.

I stand. "That was fast."

Felt like days, but I don't think she was gone for more than an hour.

"Yeah." Lili nods. "We would've been at New York General until midnight."

"All set?"

"All set." Lili waves the paper at me. "Discharge paper. And I can take two"—she glances at the printed text—"paracetamol for pain. You know what that is?"

"Acetaminophen. Same thing as Tylenol. We can stop to pick some up."

"No need. I brought Tylenol with me."

Lili heads for the automatic doors. I follow, breathing a little easier once we're outside.

We walk toward the car park in silence. Lili seems lost in secret thoughts, and I'm focused on pulling in plenty of clean oxygen that's not tinged with the chemical taste of antiseptic.

Almost to my convertible, she abruptly asks, "Can I drive?"

I stare at Lili, contemplating hustling her back inside the hospital and demanding they take another look at her head. *What is she thinking?* "No bloody way."

"Why not?"

Her pout would be effective under any other circumstances.

"*Why not?*" I repeat in disbelief. "You're drunk, injured, in a foreign country, and—"

"My blood alcohol content is point-oh-four. They tested it. My head is fine, and the cuts are going to hurt regardless. I know which side of the road to drive on. Please?"

Her blue eyes are pleading. Hypnotizing.

But my, "No," is firm, and her face falls.

"Fine," Lili snips, pulling her phone out of the pocket of my jacket. "I'll just call a cab."

I blow out a long, irritated breath. "Why the fuck would you do that?"

"Because I don't want to ride in a car with you."

That stings, but I don't let it show. "But you want to *drive* a car with me in it?"

"Yes! Then, I'll have something to focus on as a distraction. I won't have to just sit there and think about how I missed most of my best friend's wedding reception and how—"

She stops talking suddenly.

"And how ..." I prompt.

Her lips stay stubbornly shut.

I sigh again. "Tell me, and I'll let you drive."

Her eyes widen. Then, she sucks her bottom lip into her mouth, and I have to focus on reminding my dick that now's not the time to get hard.

There's dried blood on her dress. Black smears beneath both eyes from her makeup running. Her lipstick is gone, and strands of hair are steadily escaping the fancy twist it's partially pulled back in.

But Lili's still the most beautiful woman I've ever seen, swimming in my jacket and wearing a pair of oversize flip-flops.

"I shouldn't have asked for someone to get you, but I was just hoping to avoid coming here. I didn't think you'd *insist* on a trip to the hospital, and I definitely didn't mean to force you to come here with me. I appreciate you driving me, but I can't handle another silent car ride back to Carys Park with you thinking how stupid I am to have tripped and ruined your whole night."

I stare at her for a few seconds, Lili's cheeks turning redder the entire time.

She thinks she ruined my night. Thinks I regret coming when she asked for me, that I wish I were somewhere else right now.

She couldn't be more wrong.

"You didn't ruin my night. And I don't think you're stupid. It could have happened to anyone."

"*Could have.* But it happened to me."

I release a long breath. "My dad died in a car accident, Lili. This is the hospital they brought him to. That's why I didn't say much, driving here—because of shit from the past. And because I was worried about you. You didn't force me to do anything, and I would've been bloody pissed if I'd found out you'd gotten hurt and no one told me. What side of the road should you drive on?"

Blue eyes blink at me, filled with shock. Sadness. Sympathy. And … a softness that makes the back of my neck itch.

There's a very short list of people I'd show up at a hospital for— let alone *this* hospital—and Lili looks as surprised as I am that she's included on that list.

She tugs my jacket closer around her slim frame. We're only a couple of miles from the coast, wind whipping through the car park.

"Left," she answers confidently.

I hold out my keys.

Lili takes them.

My stomach flips as I climb into the passenger side.

This is a larger sacrifice than she realizes. I didn't fuck up my knee playing rugby, the way I made it sound to her last night. I was in a car accident when I was seventeen. Three of the other guys walked away with minor injuries. Piers Colborn who was driving, broke his arm. But my leg took most of the impact. If I hadn't been wearing a seat belt, I probably would have died. And I haven't gotten into a vehicle someone else was driving since.

I've never been able to give up the control, and my dad's death only amplified that urgency.

Completely illogical, me handing the keys to an injured American after nine years of not even letting a professional driver pick me up somewhere.

This has nothing to do with her driving abilities and everything to do with me wanting to make Lili feel better.

I wipe my sweaty palms on my trousers as she turns the key in the ignition. The Aston Martin's engine rumbles to life. My dad owned three, but this '66 was his pride and joy. I wonder sometimes what him not driving it that last night means. If he'd had some premonition of when and how it would all end.

"Is this a bad time to tell you I've never driven stick before?"

I glance at her as the car rolls through the open spot in front of us. "Please tell me you're kidding."

She simply smiles. Turns the wheel toward the exit.

"Pull over."

"You said I could drive!"

"When I thought you knew *how* to drive."

"It can't be that hard to drive stick. Boys do it."

I shake my head. "I'm serious, Lili."

"And I'm kidding. I drove a race car yesterday; you think I can't handle this antique?"

"It's *vintage*, and I didn't get to see you drive. I was racing too, remember?"

Lili shifts, and it's not very smooth thanks to her injured hand.

But she glares when I try to help her, then smiles when we pick up speed.

And I care about catastrophic possibilities a hell of a lot less than I should, watching her drive my car.

Pembroke is a small coastal town. We bypass most of it since the hospital is on the outskirts, the road quickly becoming empty of other cars.

I move around in the passenger seat, trying to get comfortable on the unfamiliar side.

Despite the strangeness, there's a sudden lightness expanding in my chest, pushing away the worried weight that often rests there. Maybe because I survived some demons today, sitting in that waiting room again. Maybe it's the woman beside me.

I blame the ease for the next words out of my mouth. "You in a rush to get back?"

She glances over at me, the car swerving a little, and I swear.

Her lips purse as she deliberates. "No," Lili decides. "They probably already served the cake."

I roll my eyes but keep them aimed on the road in hopes that it'll encourage Lili to do the same. "Take a left up ahead then."

She listens, the convertible rolling down a road that turns to dirt. I can hear the ocean. Smell the brine in the air.

Lili parks, then asks, "Where are we?"

From this vantage point, it looks like the middle of nowhere.

I pop the door open. "Come look."

The moonlight is eerie. Romantic as we follow the path that's been worn in the grass to the edge of the cliff.

"Wow." Lili is staring straight ahead. Salty wind blows the loose strands of her hair straight back. Her dress swishes around in ripples of plum, revealing flashes of her legs.

I stuff my hands in my pockets. "You don't get this in New York."

"I never said I hated England, you know."

"You never said you liked it either."

"Maybe I haven't decided how I feel about it yet."

"Let me know when you do."

I'm not sure we're still talking about England. Not sure why I brought her here, to what looks like the end of the world. I always come to the cliffs alone.

Waves crash against the rocky shore a hundred feet below, white spray flying, the whipping wind carrying it even farther. The tall grass around us is mowed flat from its force. A full moon bathes everything in silvery light.

"Is Newcastle near the coast?" Lili asks.

"Not too far," I reply.

"With cliffs like this?"

"Yes."

"Do you go there a lot?"

"No," I lie.

I'm not sure why. Probably because this feels like a lot.

I'm suddenly worried every time I come to the cliffs, this is what I'll picture. Lili in her purple dress with wild hair, her skin glowing in the moonlight. She wasn't supposed to realize this was a special place to me rather than a random stop.

"You should."

I hum in response, but I doubt she hears it over the wind.

"We had a dance planned to perform for Chloe at the reception. Shirts printed and everything." She sighs. "Today was supposed to be perfect, and I ruined it."

"She'll understand, Lili."

"I know. I just wish she didn't have to."

"Do the dance in Saint-Tropez," I suggest.

"You heard about the trip, huh?"

"Tripp mentioned it."

She nods. "Who was the woman you were sitting with at the wedding? An ex?" Her tone is absent, her eyes still on the ocean.

I can't tell if she cares about what the answer is or if she's simply curious. Can't decide if I care if she cares.

"I don't have any exes."

"Right. *Prat.*"

I chuckle. "You were worried Cal saw your money first, you second? I *know* women look at me and see my title. Beatrice included."

Lili sighs. "I know you're going to make me regret saying this, but you have other redeeming qualities than some stuffy title."

A gust of wind blows my snort away. "Thanks."

"I don't get it. The whole title thing … what's the big deal?"

"Aristocracy is history. Tradition. Power. Prestige. Hierarchy. And you can't buy it or create it. You have to be born into it … or marry it. The harder it is to have something, the more people want it."

"I guess." Lili's still looking straight ahead, so I can't read her expression. "And you're okay with that? Some woman marrying you because of your title?"

"Wasn't your parents' marriage arranged?"

I know it was actually. Her brother Kit made a comment about it while I was hanging out with him and his friends at the Hamptons party I attended.

"My parents are in love," she informs me.

"I know."

That was obvious at that same party.

Twin lines appear between Lili's blue eyes as she studies me. "You're right; their relationship started as a … business merger, I guess. It changed."

"If I don't have a son, I'll be the last Marlborough to hold this title. It can be … simpler to both have clear expectations in a marriage."

"So, you'd be fine with it?"

I blow out a breath. "I don't know. I just always assumed that's what that part of my life would look like."

"I couldn't do it." Lili's voice is fierce. "Get married for any reason besides love."

Ironic, our different stances. Her parents married for business but stayed together for love. Mine married for love—allegedly—and that marriage imploded so catastrophically that my sister hasn't seen our mother since she was five. Different starts and different outcomes.

"I hope you find it, Lili."

I can feel her eyes on me. Mine stay straight ahead.

"Why don't you drink?" she asks abruptly.

"I do sometimes. Just not often."

"Why not?"

I rub the back of my neck. "You don't want to ask my favorite color first?"

Her laugh gets lost in the wind, and I wish I could have listened to it for longer. "You don't have to answer."

I pull in a deep breath of briny air. "My dad was pissed when he died. Drunk, I mean. Before then too. I'm like him in a lot of ways. I guess I was looking for one way to be different. And I like staying in control. Alcohol makes people unpredictable."

Lili nods, saying nothing.

And I need to say something. Because this moment isn't just uncomfortable. It's unbearable. The salt in the air is burning open wounds.

"What song were you going to dance to?"

She side-eyes me. "You won't know it."

"How do you know?"

Lili lifts an eyebrow. Pulls her mobile out of her pocket and tells it to play "Accidentally in Love" by Counting Crows.

I don't recognize the title or the band. When the song starts playing, the melody is unfamiliar too. But it does make me wish I'd gotten to see her dance to this.

"Show me your dance."

Lili laughs again. This one lingers for a few seconds. "Absolutely not."

"Why not?"

"Because it's meant to be a group dance, and it was *not* choreographed by a professional. It's embarrassing at best, mortifying at worst. No way am I doing it now, alone."

"Fine." I grab her uninjured hand, then tug her toward me

gently. I'm just looking for an excuse to hold her one last time, if I'm being honest. I like the way her body fits with mine, like she was always meant to be there.

The ground is uneven, the wind unforgiving. Light limited.

But we sway on the edge of a cliff, me in a suit and her in a dress and my jacket, to a silly song about falling in love accidentally. Much slower than the up-tempo beat suggests.

And I know it's a moment that will stay with me a lot longer than she will.

# CHAPTER 21
## Charlie

Cheerful chatter fills the lobby as I step out of the hotel's dining area with a paper Costa cup in hand. The sunny noise does nothing to improve my sour mood.

Lili's friends were waiting in here when we got back last night, including a worried-looking Theo and Chloe. They all thanked me for going with her—even Tripp—before escorting a yawning Lili upstairs. I'm positive at least one of them stayed with her all night.

There was absolutely no reason to think she wouldn't be fine, but I spent most of the night staring at the plaster ceiling, concerned anyway.

Lack of sleep, paired with irritation about *why* I couldn't sleep, has trimmed my temper down to a short fuse.

Theo is standing by the lifts, talking with a group of his family members. He grins and heads this way when he sees me.

"Good morning," he tells me.

Unlike me, Theo appears well rested, which is a surprise. Last night was his wedding night.

"Morning," I repeat, substantially less cheerful. "And congratulations."

I didn't have a chance to talk to him after the wedding or before leaving with Lili.

"Thanks. I'm really glad you could make it, Charles." Theo's smile dims a little. "Especially with Lili's accident. Taking her to the hospital and everything. That meant a lot. To me and to Chloe."

I shift uncomfortably. The praise is unwarranted. And unnecessary.

"Not a problem," I tell him.

Theo nods, his smile back in full force. "We're headed to Saint-Tropez later today. Chloe's family has a place down there, where we're spending the week. Jasper's talking about a trip to Monaco while we're in France. I know we sort of lost touch after university and after …" He clears his throat. "Would be nice to catch up, if you want to come along."

He's being generous. Fig basically foisted his friendship on me, and Theo would tag along occasionally. I'm not a friend he owes any obligation or outreach to.

"I appreciate the invitation," I reply. "But I can't."

This weekend was an escape from everything, but I can't keep running from my responsibilities. I have to make my next move with investors. Decide how much I'm going to share with Louis when he visits. Check in with Blythe.

And if I tell Theo I'll be in Saint-Tropez in a few days, he'll ask why, and I'll have to lie or draw attention to the truth.

"I get it," Theo says. "If you change your mind, it's an open invitation."

"Open invitation to what?"

I spin as soon as I hear her voice, ridiculously eager to see Lili.

Aside from the white bandage on her left hand, she looks like her usual self. By usual, I mean beautiful. Her silk blouse covers her shoulder, and her thick hair hides the lump on her head.

The rest of her friends are clustered by the reception desk, a huge pile of luggage beside them. They're checking out. Heading to France.

"I was seeing if Charles wanted to join us in Saint-Tropez," Theo answers. "Unfortunately, he can't make it."

Lili looks disappointed.

I hate that I notice. Care.

So, I speak without thinking. "Not all of us can take weeks off of work."

It's one of the—if not *the*—worst things I could have said. I know Lili is sensitive about her job and how people perceive it. And I basically just announced I consider my role more important than her career.

Theo chuckles, oblivious to the regret I'm swamped with. "No kidding. I had to work Saturdays for the past two months to get this time off."

He's a barrister at a high-powered firm.

"Good luck with your work, Charles." Lili smiles politely after using my full name—another sure sign she's pissed. "I'm sure there's a jousting tournament or two that requires a duke's attendance."

Theo says nothing this time, finally clueing in to the tension.

I swallow. "I didn't mean—"

"We're ready to go, Theo," Lili says, then turns away.

She's leaving. Leaving the lobby. Leaving England.

And I'm not planning to visit New York before next summer, if then. This could be the last time I see her for another year. For … *ever*.

Panic surges through me, the sudden force of it debilitating. "Lili—"

She turns quickly, like she was hoping I'd stop her, but her expression says *Fuck off.* "What?"

I run my tongue along the backs of my teeth, trying to come up with something to say. Stopping her was an impulse, not a well-thought-out decision. "You should put some ointment on the cuts once they start to scab. They'll heal faster. Itch less. And if you get a headache or—"

"If I need medical assistance, I'll call a *doctor.*"

I hide the flinch, but the verbal lash stings anyway.

This time, when Lili walks away, I don't try to stop her.

Theo punches my shoulder lightly. "Made a right mess there, mate," he says. "Take care."

I grind my molars, nod, then continue walking toward the lift to head upstairs and pack.

Thanks to traffic, the trip back to Newcastle Hall took close to two hours. I drop my duffel bag and my garment bag—of course my suit showed up this morning, after I no longer needed it—on the floor of my room unceremoniously, along with the laundry sack provided by the hotel. My suit jacket from last night is on the very top. Lili gave it back to me before she headed up to her room last night. I yank it out, studying it. It smells like Chanel perfume.

The matchbox I took from the restaurant is still in the pocket. I move it to the drawer of the small table beside my bed, still not sure why I grabbed it on our way out. I just wanted something I could look at and remember that night, I guess. Some memento that would last.

My suit jacket gets tossed on the armoire in the corner of the room.

There's a knock on the door as I'm unpacking clean clothes.

"Come in," I call out.

Conrad appears a few seconds later. Gray-haired and stoic, he's lived at Newcastle Hall longer than I have. Along with his wife, Martha, who's the cook. Two more people relying on me to keep everything afloat.

"Was it a good trip, sir?"

I gave up on getting Conrad to call me Charles years ago. It's Your Grace, Mr. Marlborough, or sir. He's known me my entire life. Even before we moved here full-time, we'd spend summers here.

I'm the third Duke of Manchester Conrad has served.

"It was fine," I answer.

Conrad nods briskly. "Do you need anything?"

"I'm all set. Is Blythe here?"

"Lady Marlborough is at the London residence, I believe."

"Did she say for how long?"

"She did not, sir."

Typical. Blythe is technically an adult, but she still feels like my responsibility. She was supposed to return from Saint-Tropez yesterday, but she rarely sticks to a predictable schedule.

Conrad picks up the laundry bag from the hotel. "I'll take this to be laundered."

"Thank you."

"This too?" He reaches for the jacket.

"No. Leave that."

It's another memento.

Conrad nods, then disappears back into the hallway, shutting the door with a soft *snick*.

After I finish unpacking, I change into riding clothes, then send a quick text to Blythe, checking in. There are several new messages from Ellis and a photo of him on a boat with a blonde woman, the Statue of Liberty visible in the background.

My leather boots thud as I descend the main staircase and cross the tiled floor of the front hall. It's overcast out, but warm, the air heavy and sticky.

I follow the left path, in the opposite direction of the gardens surrounding the right wing, toward the stables. It's a large stone structure, close to the pond Blythe and I used to swim in when we were younger. The entrance to the barn is curved brick, which echoes my steps louder than the stairs did. I stop to snap a photo, then send it to Ellis, along with a short response to his messages.

Only two stalls in the stable are occupied. I sold Churchill, my father's prized stallion, shortly after he died. The fox hunter was only three years old, too boisterous and virile for the limited attention I had to give him.

My black gelding is almost twenty, happy to graze all day and amenable to the occasional canter. He came with the name Kensington—after the palace in London, *not* the family—and this is the first time I wish I'd changed it. Reminders of Lili are not what I need right now.

Blythe's horse came with the name Windsor, but she changed it to Gilbert for some reason.

I feed Gilbert an apple, then start saddling Kensington. He bloats his belly when I tighten the girth—a trick he's done since my father bought him as a yearling. He's only fooled me twice—and not in more than a decade.

A flock of sparrows startles from the branches of the huge oak that shades half of the pond as we start off at a slow amble. Kensington snorts once, his gait remaining even and steady.

Churchill would have been halfway to the property line by now. Selling the stallion was in his best interest. But it was the first item on a long list of changes that followed my father's death. I keep losing more and more, it feels like. And that would be a lot easier to accept if I knew an end to it was approaching.

I let Kensington walk with little direction from me, content to inhale deep lungfuls of fresh air and enjoy the peaceful quiet. Watery sunshine peeks out occasionally, warming my face.

Eventually, the stone rectangle appears ahead. Most rides, I end up coming to the cemetery, so it's not surprising that this is the way Kensington went.

I slide off his back when we get close, leaving him to graze.

Grass has finally grown around my father's grave. It sat bare for most of last summer, and then winter killed any progress off.

My grandfather is buried here too. Same with my great-grandfather, all the way back to the second Duke of Manchester. One day, my bones will rest here too.

It's a depressing thought.

The graveyard is a depressing sight.

Not just morbid, although it's that too. There's little to it—a stone wall that stretches about four feet high, enclosing the plots of land, marked with heavy slabs of rock with neat letters hewn into the surface. The closest tree is a few dozen feet away.

My father's grave is the shiniest, my grandfather's—the second-newest addition—noticeably more weathered. I pause to grab a fistful of wild primroses before I open the wooden gate to enter through the narrow opening in the stone wall, letting them scatter like uneven drops of rain.

I used to come here just to glower and gripe, but I guess I've moved past—or through—the anger stage of grief.

I can't remember which step comes next, but I know I haven't reached acceptance yet. Not of my father's death exactly—that feels very real and very permanent—but of everything else that's changed since he died. The role that I knew I would step into since I was a kid, but assumed I wouldn't inherit until decades from now. The burden that's so much heavier than I expected.

My father always used to say that challenges reveal someone's true character.

If that's true, I'm not sure what the past year says about mine.

# CHAPTER 22

## *Lili*

Sunlight glints off the calm waves so brightly that my eyes burn despite the barrier of my sunglasses.

I stare toward the beach, a stretch of sand that appears to be nothing more than a thin tan strip from here. Bracketed by shades of blues. The vastness of the sky overhead and the spread of the sea surrounding me. The only dots of other colors are the boats around us and the striped umbrellas on the beach.

"You look serious."

I half smile at Bridget as she takes a seat beside me. "Not serious. Just appreciating the view."

"It is amazing, huh?" She swipes a hand across her forehead, catching the strands getting blown around by the breeze and tucking them behind one ear. "Doesn't make me miss New York—that's for sure."

"Poor Chase."

Bridget shifts beside me. "Actually, we broke up, so I doubt he'd care."

"You *did*? *When*? *Why*?" I fire the questions at her rapidly.

"On the Fourth of July. Fran knows because she and that actor she met at Proof were with us." She looks away, toward the horizon. "We fought all the time. He worked crazy hours at the restaurant. Anytime someone left a complaint, he'd be in a bad mood for a week. Plus, one of the waitresses had a huge crush on him, and I think something happened there." Bridget frowns, then glances back at me. "I wanted to tell you, but I also wanted to forget about it during this trip. Focus on Chloe. And I figured you had enough to think about with the whole, uh, Cal thing."

"I'm sorry, Bridge." I nudge her shoulder with mine. "You can *always* talk to me, no matter what else is going on."

"I know." She pauses. "You're handling it well, you know. Way better than I would have. You and he seem … good."

"We are," I reply. "It *is* good."

We've been in Saint-Tropez for four days. Spent most of that time on this sailboat, enjoying the summer weather and stunning scenery. Each evening, we've gone to a different nightclub in town to dance and drink. Cal, Bridget, and I are the only ones who've gone home alone every night. Cal and Bridget were expected, as the two in relationships. Me? I've tried to flirt but been tempted to claim a headache and leave early every night. The only thing stopping me was that I was worried it would set off a chain reaction of everyone fretting about my health again. It took a couple of days for them to stop asking about my previous injuries.

The best part of the trip has been that things with Cal feel the most normal they've been since before we started dating junior year.

It feels like a former version of our friendship, as relaxed as it is with Tripp and Jasper and Hugo.

I know I'm not the only one relieved about it.

"I heard Theo invited Charles."

The sound of his name is an unpleasant shock. I've been doing a decent—more like mediocre—job of pretending he doesn't exist.

I didn't expect to see him after Chloe's wedding. But the fact that he turned the invitation down is extremely irritating. And evidence that we're on different wavelengths. Because I—despite my convictions that we were a several-times-in-one-night kind of fling—would have happily spent this week leaving nightclubs with him. While he opted to stay in England and *work*.

It's the dismissal in my grandparents' hallway all over again, except worse.

Because now, I know what the full experience is like. And because he took care of me, then danced with me in the moonlight.

"I guess."

"You guess?"

"That whole thing with him was … nothing."

Bridget laughs. "Nothing? Lili, the guy begged you for a date. Drove you to the hospital. None of that's nothing."

"He did not *beg* me for a date. And a cab driver would have done the same thing."

"He made a bet he was sure he'd win. And unless you *paid* him to drive you, it's not the same thing."

I exhale. Denial hasn't done much for me. "Okay, it was something. It felt … different with him. That something that'd been missing before? It wasn't missing with him."

She nods. "So, call him."

"I don't have his number. And even if I did … I wouldn't know what to say to him. He lives in England. I live in New York. Even if he wanted anything, how would that work?"

"Your private jet would probably help."

I scoff. "I'm being serious, Bridget."

"So am I. You make it work if you want it to. Neither Chase nor I wanted to. Chloe and Theo did and look at them now." She shakes her head. "I can't believe *Chloe* is *married*. Makes me feel old."

"Me too. My mom got married when she was twenty-five."

"And your parents are still together. That's impressive."

Bridget's parents got divorced when we were in middle school. So did Jasper's and Fran's. It was a collective rough patch.

"Maybe we should take a trip to Vegas when we get back home," Bridget muses. "Or to Canada. Meet a hunky hockey player."

I roll my eyes. "I can't. I have interviews next week."

One could result in a trip to Canada, ironically, but I don't tell her that. She'd probably try to tag along.

She sighs. "Yeah. I should probably see if the gallery is still standing."

Bridget manages a modern art gallery in the West Village.

She taps her glass of iced tea against mine, then drains it. "I'm going to swim. You coming?"

"In a bit," I answer. "Just going to soak up a little more sun."

"'Kay." Bridget stands, stretches, then dashes to the back of the boat.

I finish off my glass, too, then lie back flat and focus on nothing but the sun's warmth.

# CHAPTER 23

## *Lili*

A shiny black car is parked in front of the Beaumonts' house when we return from a full day out on the water.

"Are you expecting someone?" Chloe asks Theo.

"Actually … Charles asked me for the address this morning." Theo glances in the rearview mirror. At me. Everyone else is looking at me too. "I wasn't sure if he was actually coming …"

I say nothing, staring at the car as I rein in the emotions ricocheting through me.

He changed his mind. He came. Mostly, I'm happy about it. But I'm also apprehensive. Not only because of the tense terms we parted on, but because those tense terms told me I was getting too attached.

"Is that a *Bugatti*?" Jasper asks.

"Looks like the Divo," Tripp responds.

Hugo whistles. "What are those? Three? Four?"

"Almost six," Tripp says.

"Six what?" Fran questions. Without waiting for an answer, she bangs against the back of Jasper's seat. "Can you get out, Jas?"

"Million," Hugo breathes. "Do you think he'll let me drive it?"

I climb out of the car, pulling the seat forward for Fran before continuing toward the front door. Everyone else seems to hang back.

The air-conditioning feels heavenly against my skin—coated with a combination of sweat, sunscreen, and salt water—as I walk through the entryway and toward the kitchen. The wall of glass doors shows off the dazzling view of the pool and the ocean past it.

Charlie is standing next to one of the loungers, scowling as he talks into the phone.

He runs a hand through his hair, then grips the back of his neck before turning around. I watch as my presence registers on his face. His attention stays on me as he continues talking on the phone.

A few seconds later, Charlie hangs up and heads toward me.

His attractiveness hits me all over again, like I'm seeing him for the first time.

The sound of the door sliding open and closed only amplifies the charged silence. No one else has come inside yet. They're all drooling over his car or gossiping about us probably.

He speaks first. "Lili."

"Charles." I keep my tone cool.

He doesn't leave a polite amount of distance between us, like I expected. He stops inches away, his hand reaching out and his fingers curling around my left wrist. Charlie lifts my arm to inspect my palm, then twists it to look at my shoulder.

The scabs have started to flake away, revealing the healed skin beneath.

"How'd you make time in your busy schedule for a trip to

France?" I ask.

One corner of his mouth kicks up before he drops his hold on my wrist. Hopefully, he couldn't feel how fast my pulse was fluttering. "I'm here for work."

Wrong answer.

I cross my arms. "What kind of work are you doing *here*?"

"None in this house. But since I was in Saint-Tropez, I thought I'd stop by."

"Lucky us," I drawl. "Getting a visit from a *duke*."

A muscle in Charlie's jaw jumps. I'm pleased—and a little nervous—about it. Poking bears comes with consequences.

"Cut the duke shit, Lili. I know I—"

"Acted like an uppity arsehole?"

He shakes his head. Smiles faintly. "I didn't mean it the way you thought I did. You have a *job*, a career that comes with vacation time. I have a *role*, duties that I can never separate from. That's all I meant."

I gnaw on my bottom lip, not missing the way Charlie's gaze narrows on my mouth. Heat unfurls in my stomach like plumes of smoke, my body reregistering that he's really here and all that could mean.

His explanation makes sense. More than that, it sounds genuine. Forcing me to face the fact that I was more disappointed he wasn't coming than angry about how he declined.

"Do you want me to go? I'll leave right now."

*Yes* should come out of my mouth. Not because I want him to go, but because it's alarming how easily my annoyance evaporated. How badly I want to kiss him. More than kiss him.

"Hello?" Chloe's voice calls out. "Any intruders?"

I glance over one shoulder to watch them all approach. "Way to hurry in with the backup, guys. If someone were here to rob the place, I'd be dead by now."

"I don't know any criminals who drive Bugattis," Hugo says. "Wicked car, Charles."

Cal scoffs. "Do you know *any* criminals?"

"Glad you could make it," Theo says, shaking Charlie's hand.

I don't know Chloe's husband that well since they live so far away. But it's cute how he acts around Charlie, like a younger brother looking up to an older one.

They talk back and forth for a bit; Charlie's attention divided the whole time. He's waiting for my decision, I realize.

"I'm going to take a shower," I announce. "Charlie's going to stay. He also *loves* it when other people drive his cars, if you guys want to try out the Bugatti."

I sashay out of the kitchen before anyone can say anything.

Washing off the day's stickiness is a relief. I empty both suitcases in my quest to find a cute outfit, settling on a Dior sundress. It's strapless, so it doesn't rub any healing scrapes. The scabs are itchy, just like Charlie said. I have been dabbing ointment on them, but I won't be telling him that.

Blow-drying my hair and applying a full face of makeup takes another thirty minutes. The plan is to stay here for dinner tonight since we've eaten out the past few evenings.

I'm overdressed for eating on the patio and then lounging on the couch, but it feels nice to dress up. A shot of confidence I need to face Charlie.

He's here for me.

He might be in Saint-Tropez on business, but Charlie's here—in

Chloe's family's house—because of me.

Because he feels bad about how our last conversation ended?

Because it happened to be a convenient stop?

Because he wanted to see me?

I shake my head as I spritz on some perfume. I don't know why I'm obsessing over this.

Everything I told Bridget earlier is still true.

Geographically, we're incompatible. There's long-distance, and then there's different continents. I'm happy for Chloe, but I've never understood how she was able to leave behind everything she knew to stay in London. She *loved* living in New York. And Charlie is tied to England in ways Theo isn't. The way people talk, he's practically part of the royal family. I can't picture him walking in Central Park or standing on the observation deck of the Empire State Building. He fit on the manicured grounds of Carys Park and at the edge of the cliff he brought me to.

Then, there's the other more important consideration—he's a heartbreaker. Chloe warned me, and he told me the same thing himself. Charlie doesn't have any interest in pursuing a relationship. A commitment I'm not sure I want either. We can't both have a foot out the door, or it'll go nowhere.

My phone buzzes with an incoming call from my mom while I'm slipping on shoes. I've sent her photos from the trip, but we haven't spoken since I left Grandfather and Gigi's house early on July 5.

I flop down on the bed to answer.

"Hey, Mom."

"Hey, honey. How's the trip?"

"It's great. Saint-Tropez is beautiful. You and Dad should get a place here."

Mom laughs. "We don't have time to visit all the homes we already have, honey."

"Where are you? It's loud."

"JFK. I'm supposed to speak at a Future CEO conference in Miami tomorrow morning. They just delayed the flight by an hour."

"How long are you staying in Miami for?" I ask.

"Hang on one second. Crew!"

A few seconds later, I hear my dad's muffled voice.

"That was a prime spot by the windows," he says.

"We're about to sit for the next three hours," Mom replies. "I wanted to walk around. I'm talking to Lili."

"Hi, sweetheart!" Dad's voice is louder now, like he's right by the speaker.

"Hi, Dad," I respond, smiling even though he can't see.

"Did you seriously buy a copy of *Haute*?" Mom asks, sounding amused.

"Of course. How else am I supposed to find out summer's top swimsuit styles, Red?"

"Go read it by the windows," she tells him. "I'll be over in a little bit."

"Okay," he says cheerfully. "Bye, Lili!"

"Bye, Dad."

"Sorry, sweetie. What were you—oh, right. We're only staying for two nights. I have the conference in the morning, and your dad is attending some meetings. Then, we're going to a fundraiser for the children's hospital."

"That sounds nice. Have you guys decided when you're heading back to LA yet?"

"Not yet. I'll keep you posted. I've been helping Hannah with the planning for the Kensington Consolidated gala, so we won't be missing that this year."

"Good. It was strange without you and Dad last year."

Neither of my parents works at Kensington Consolidated, but they're who most people associate the company with. The king and queen of New York society, even though they've primarily resided in Los Angeles for the past twenty-three years.

"What have you been doing in Saint-Tropez?" Mom asks.

I fill her in on the past few days—boating and swimming and eating, basically. She laughs when I tell her about the group dance we finally got to perform for Chloe and Theo last night. We say our goodbyes a few minutes later.

I hang up, check my appearance one last time in the mirror, then head down the hallway.

An open doorway makes me pause. Charlie's bag—the one he had at Chloe's wedding—is sitting on the floor just inside one of the empty guest rooms. Chloe or Theo must have shown him where to stay when I was in the shower.

His bag is unzipped, a familiar cover snagging my gaze.

After a furtive glance around, I tiptoe inside for a closer peek.

My breathing stalls as I focus on the letters on the cover, trying not to lose patience with myself as I squint at them, ascertaining if they say what I think they say.

They do.

It's *Middlemarch*.

My next inhale is a little unsteady. I continue staring for a few more seconds, and then head back into the hallway.

I was expecting lots of activity downstairs, but it's completely quiet.

When I walk into the living room area, Chloe, Fran, and Bridget are all lounging around, sipping from wineglasses.

"Where are the boys?" I ask.

Fran smirks. "You mean, where's Charlie?"

Heat in my cheeks tells me I'm blushing. That's *exactly* what I meant.

Bridget winks, then nods toward the glass windows that look out at the pool. I walk over and glance outside.

Theo, Hugo, Jasper, Cal, and Tripp are all seated on the line of lounge chairs, sipping on beers. Charlie is standing, leaning against the large teak table, talking to a rapt audience.

I still can't believe he's here. I'd convinced myself I'd never see Charlie again.

He points toward something past the pool. The guys all glance that way.

Me? I'm focused on the flex of his muscular forearm, on full display thanks to his rolled-up sleeves. The warmth in my face spreads, sliding down my spine and settling in my lower stomach.

It's strange, seeing him casually chatting with my closest friends. Looking like part of my world.

I continue into the kitchen, where appetizers have been spread out.

Louise, one of two maids the Beaumonts employ here, offers me a glass of Chevalier-Montrachet Chardonnay, which I gratefully accept. André, the chef, is busy preparing dinner—what looks like bouillabaisse. The scents of saffron and garlic swirl in the air as I sip on the crisp wine, then nibble on a slice of cheese from the plate.

Everyone else migrates to the kitchen gradually, including

Charlie. I avoid looking at him as I chat with Chloe about the play she's auditioning for once she and Theo are back in London. Overcompensating for the acute awareness buzzing in my bloodstream. His presence lingers like an unsolved mystery I can't forget about.

André serves the bouillabaisse out by the pool. We're a couple of miles from the coast of the French Riviera, but the nearness of the ocean is evident in the salty breeze. Leaves sway on the trellis that shades part of the table.

I don't sit by Charlie. I feel … shy around him. He's here for me, but we're not together. Outside of the bedroom, I'm unsure how to act. What the boundaries are. What the expectations are. My friends aren't subtle about glancing between us as we all take seats, which only adds to my uncertainty. If I didn't like him, if all I admired about Charlie was the size of his dick, I wouldn't care. I'd be relaxed, joking and laughing and looking forward to a night of incredible sex.

But I do like him. And I do care.

I end up next to Jasper, then try to eavesdrop on Charlie's conversation with Theo at the other end of the table between bites of savory stew.

We play cards after dinner. First euchre, then Texas Hold'em.

When Bridget starts yawning, I check the time on my phone, shocked to see it's nearly midnight.

Fran is first to stumble upstairs. The rest of us follow, the slow treads and shutting doors the same soundtrack as the past few nights.

I step into my room, releasing a long exhale once the door is closed.

It's a relief to no longer feel on display.

These are my best friends. They knew me in elementary school, when I first discovered crushes. They've met every guy I ever dated—with the exception of Lawrence because everything with Cal felt too fresh—and they teased me about breaking hearts long before any of us knew what that really felt like.

And it feels like they've all already realized that I *like* Charlie.

I thought we were done after he turned down Theo's invitation to come here and—unintentionally?—insulted me in the process. No part of me expected him to show up in France. He's *constantly* showing up when I least expect. Even when I think I'm prepared to see him, I'm not.

Charlie's like one of those jack-in-the-box toys. I think it's closed, tightly contained, and then he suddenly reappears. And instead of a disturbing clown, I'm faced with a gorgeous man.

I run through my evening skin care routine, change into a silk nightgown, then slip between sheets that smell like lavender. Stare at the strip of moonlight beaming across the hardwood floor.

It's completely silent in the house.

It'd be peaceful, if not for my erratic pulse and racing thoughts.

My fingers fiddle with smooth fabric, deliberating my next move. Do I sneak into his room? Do I wait until—

My bedroom door creaks slightly as it opens.

I rise up onto my elbows, squinting in the darkness at the shadowed figure approaching my bed. Swallow—hard—when he takes a seat on the edge of the bed. The mattress lowers a little bit with the added weight.

"Do you want me to leave?"

The same question he asked earlier.

The low rumble of his baritone raises bumps on my skin. My

heart is trying to beat out of my chest, and my breathing is uneven, and my skin is suddenly extra sensitive. When I lie back down, the rasp of the sheets is enough to make my nipples hard.

I recognize the feeling from the last time we were in a bedroom together.

The Charles Marlborough effect.

I tell him the same answer. The truth. "No."

He didn't turn on any lights this time. My eyes have adjusted to the dark, but I can't see well enough to tell exactly what he's doing.

I hear the rustle of fabric. The crinkle of foil.

My thighs clench together, trying to alleviate the ache that's appeared. My body is already conditioned to anticipate pleasure from his.

The mattress dips again, lower, and then there's a warm body lying beside mine.

I think the rustling meant he's naked, but I don't reach out to confirm.

This feels … deliberate. Not the frantic rush of our first night together. We didn't just happen to end up at the same wedding this time. He chased me. Maybe not to Saint-Tropez, since he said he had business here, but to this house. To this bed.

"We did the group dance for Chloe last night," I tell him, for some random reason.

Charlie tucks an arm behind his head, bicep bulging. "Yeah?"

My thighs are squeezed so tight I'm concerned I could be cutting off circulation down there.

"Yeah. She loved it."

"Not surprised. Wish I'd gotten to see it."

"Our dance was better," I say, then bite my bottom lip.

Reminiscing about a romantic waltz in the wilderness isn't typical pillow talk with a fling. "How's Blythe?"

Bringing up his sister isn't much better, but it's the first thing that pops into my head.

"I hadn't heard from her in three days, then she texted me ten times after dinner because she blew a fuse at the flat. So … her normal self."

"That's good."

"Mmhmm." He rolls toward me, left hand landing on my hip.

I pull in a quick breath, his touch spreading across my skin like ripples on the surface of a pond.

"You're good at cards," Charlie tells me.

"Don't sound so surprised."

He chuckles, skilled fingers finding the hem of my silk slip and sneaking under it. Teasing strokes brush back and forth across my leg, slowly moving higher.

I relax my thighs and spread my knees, battling the urge to grab his hand and shift it up to where I really want it.

Charlie makes a husky sound in the back of his throat. Then he's hovering over me, tossing the condom packet in his right hand onto the pillow beside mine before gathering most of my hair into his fist. His hips drop into mine, the firm ridge of his erection rubbing that needy spot.

"You're fucking soaked, Lili."

"I've been wet since you got here," I admit.

He growls, grabbing my right knee and hooking it over his hip as he grinds his erection against my clit. "You know what I think about all the time now?"

"Work?" I pant.

I catch the ghost of a smile before his mouth lands on my breast. He sucks the raised point of my nipple, then bites gently.

I try to contain the desperate whimper, I really do, but it bursts out anyway. If anyone else is still awake, they likely have an exact idea of what's happening in my room.

"I think about this tight cunt." He pushes two fingers into my pussy. "And I think about this sinful mouth." He kisses me, tugging my lower lip between his teeth. "And I think about these perky tits." He lets go of my hair to tweak my stinging nipple, the fingers of his other hand curling, making my inner muscles spasm. It's not his cock, which is what I really want, what I can feel—hot and hard—against my thigh. But it still feels *so* good—another hit of an addictive drug.

I'm soaking his hand. Probably soaking the sheets too.

I wiggle against him, trying to stimulate more friction. I love the way he touches me urgently, but doesn't rush, yet I hate it too. I want this to last forever, and I need it to happen now.

"I'm close."

"I know." He sounds deservedly smug. "Your cunt is squeezing the shit out of my fingers."

His hand shifts, hitting a different angle, and the burst of spectacular sensation almost sends me over the edge. My moan is loud. Desperate.

He's *way* too good at this.

His thumb rubs torturous circles around my clit. I bite my tongue so hard that I taste blood, trying to keep from shouting as pressure continues to build in my pelvis. As he coaxes me to the edge and keeps me there. My fingernails sink into his shoulders, scratching and scoring. Silently begging.

I beg out loud too.

I'm feverish with desire by the time he reaches for the condom.

I cry out in response to the sudden stretch.

My inner muscles contract around his erection, finally alleviating the empty ache.

It's better than I remember. I don't know how that's possible.

Charlie's hand slides down to my hip so he can adjust me exactly where he wants. His mouth moves to my neck. He bites gently enough not to break the skin. Hard enough to leave a mark.

I lift a hand and shove my fingers into his hair. His lips press against my collarbone, sucking, bruising more skin.

It's hot, him *branding* me almost. I shouldn't like it, but it's about to send me over the edge.

"I'm going to wear a bathing suit tomorrow," I say as his lips move to a new spot.

I'm not sure why that comes out. Some reminder, I guess, that we'll see each other in the morning, when these marks will be visible. He agreed to go sailing when Theo was talking about the boat earlier, so I know he's not intending to take off first thing.

There's a pause. Followed by a gruff "I don't give a fuck."

He's still pumping into me, but the pace is slow. And no matter how much I whine or wriggle or attack his back, he doesn't thrust any faster.

Finally, I lose patience. I maneuver away until his dick slips all the way out, then roll over to face him.

"Sit up," I tell Charlie, stripping the sheets down the bed and crawling toward him.

His abs bunch as he complies, leaning back on his palms with his thighs spread. His thick cock almost stretches to his belly button, the latex covering it glossy in the moonlight spilling through the curtains.

A midnight fantasy come to life.

I climb onto him, squeaking when he flicks one of my nipples with his tongue. I rub over his erection a couple of times, then reach down to guide him inside. My toes curl as I sink down slowly. He feels bigger from this angle. Hits deeper.

My entire being buzzes with impatience, but he's huge. I won't be able to *walk* tomorrow if I don't give my body time to adjust.

Charlie doesn't touch me. He lounges like a god on a throne, watching me straddle him. But I can feel the tension humming through him. The muscles of his thighs are bunched, the V between his hips flexed so sharply that it looks like an edge you could cut yourself on. And it feels like he's swelling inside of me, somehow becoming harder and thicker.

I finally manage to take him all, my ass brushing against his balls, so full that *stuffed* gains a fresh meaning.

He still doesn't touch me, watching me work myself up and down, fucking myself on his cock like it's my personal sex toy.

But the way he's watching me, like it's taking all of his restraint to cede control—to not flip me over and rut into me like an animal—makes me feel like the sexiest woman in the world.

That devilish gleam—that burning desire—is what sends me over the edge.

I can't think.

Can't talk.

Can't see.

I just *feel*.

And then I fall.

# CHAPTER 24

## *Charlie*

The view of Saint-Tropez from the water is stunning. It's a perfect portrait of summer—sunlight shimmering off the waves surrounding the bobbing boats. Blue skies and blue seas, and the color's brightness is so startling that I'm not sure why anyone associates it with melancholy.

I associate it with Elizabeth Kensington.

And she's where my gaze keeps catching, disregarding the rest of the stunning scenery.

Lili is seated at the very end of the diving board that sticks off the stern of the yacht we're on. Wearing a white one-piece, her dark hair blowing around in a wild halo.

She walked out there about ten minutes ago. Rather than jumping, she sat. And she's been perched at the end ever since, her head tilted back so her face is angled toward the sun.

If I still had a trust fund, I'd spend it all to find out what Lili's

thinking about right now.

"Lili! You scared?"

Tripp and Jasper dived into the ocean a few minutes ago. They're treading water beneath the diving board now.

"That might have worked when we were kids," she calls back to Tripp. "I'm sunbathing."

"Well, I'm jumping," Jasper announces. "So, get in or get off."

Lili waits until they climb the ladder to execute a perfect swan dive from the ten-foot drop.

She stays under for longer than I expect. I tense, only relaxing when her head breaks the surface. Right by the ladder, an impressive distance from where she entered the water.

"We get it, show-off," Hugo says as Lili climbs onto the boat. "You were swim team captain."

"Not my fault you're afraid of sharks."

"*Everyone's* afraid of sharks," Hugo replies. "Some people are just more aware of it."

Bridget snorts. She's sprawled out on the full length of the cushion next to mine, reading a book. So am I, one of two I brought.

Lili tosses a towel on the teak deck and lies down on it. I swallow, watching a drop of water roll into the hollow of her throat. As mesmerized by the sight of her now as I was when she was out on the diving board. As when I woke up in her bed.

"You see this, Charles?" Theo leans forward from his spot beside Chloe to show me his phone screen.

I squint at the headline. *Highland Promotes Piers Colborn to International COO*, it reads.

"You were at Eton together, right?"

I don't bother asking how he knows that. Theo didn't go to Eton, but I'm sure he's friendly with lots of our peers who did.

"Right," I reply.

And I haven't seen him since.

Trauma either binds people tighter together or separates them, in my experience. Piers and I were teammates more than anything. After the accident that robbed me of my ability to play rugby, it was easier for both of us to lose touch and try to forget what'd happened.

I'm glad to hear he's doing well though. Bloody impressive, COO at twenty-six.

I rub the faded scar on my knee involuntarily, then stand and shrug my shirt off. "Going to check on the local shark population for you, Hugo."

He doesn't reply. When I glance over, he's smirking at Lili.

I'm confused, until Jasper whistles. "Shit, man. Did you lose a fight with a grizzly bear?"

Flashes of last night fill my head.

"I won the fight," I tell him. "But it was one hell of a match."

One of the girls snickers. I'm not sure who because I'm focused on Lili's pink cheeks.

I didn't realize she'd left scratches on my back, but I'm not mad about it. Her suit hides most of the marks I left on her body last night, but there's a purplish hickey visible on her collarbone now that gravity has fanned her hair across the towel.

I take the stairs to the upper deck two at a time. Dive off the board into calm turquoise water and emerge with the taste of salt in my mouth.

The water is chilly, but not cold. Refreshing after sitting out in the sun for the past couple of hours.

Jasper jumps in next, followed by Cal. The rest of Lili's friends jump in soon after. Even Bridget, who announced earlier she was staying dry today.

It's hot out, and it's getting late in the afternoon. We'll head back to shore soon.

Lili is the only one who stays on board.

I tread water for a few minutes, listening to banter about the perils of sharks and stingrays and shipwrecks, then swim to the ladder.

Lili hasn't moved, so I grab a dry towel and sit down beside her. Deliberately flicking some water on her in the process.

She scowls, shading her eyes. "Do you mind?"

"Sorry." I grin.

Today has been fun. Even the thought of meeting with the real estate agent later today hasn't dampened my mood much.

The trip to Saint-Tropez has been an even better escape from the cycle of stress and worry and anger than Theo's wedding was. The rest of Lili's friends seem to care about my title as much as she does—not at all. Getting to know Theo better has been nice too.

It's a chance to experience what my life was like before my father died. Minimal obligations and responsibilities.

My life is still privileged in so many ways. But I started to view that privilege as a prison at some point, and that's a very isolating way to go through life.

"You come here a lot?" I ask Lili.

"No." She sits up, mirroring my posture. "Been a while actually. Since … high school?"

"Surprised your family doesn't have a place here."

"We have one on the Amalfi Coast," she tells me a little sheepishly.

"Do you go there a lot?"

"At least once a year usually. My dad owns part of AC Milan, so that's always where he wants to take our family trips."

I sort of … forgot how wealthy Lili is. And that she's from the kind of family that takes vacations together.

The reminder of how different our lives are dims my mood a little. All I have to offer her is a title—one she doesn't care about.

She glances at me when I say nothing. "You follow football, right?"

"Is the king English? Yes, I follow football."

She rolls her eyes. "I don't know much about the Premier League."

"It's where all the best teams are. That's all you need to know."

Lili scoffs. "Don't mention that to my dad." She reaches for the tube of sunscreen someone left on the deck. Holds it toward me. "Do you mind putting some on my back? I want to lie out for a while, but I don't want to get burned."

I take the bottle from her. "If you wanted me to touch you, you just had to ask."

She tries to grab it back from me. "Never mind. I'll ask—"

"You already asked me. Turn around."

She huffs but listens. I squeeze some of the white lotion into my palm, then start rubbing it over her right shoulder. She groans softly when my thumb digs into her deltoid, and the sound shoots straight to my dick.

If we were alone, I'd flip her over and fuck her right here.

"Are you okay?" she asks me quietly.

"Yeah. Why?"

"I don't know. You seemed … extra serious when Theo was

talking about that guy you went to school with."

I'm startled—pleasantly surprised—that she was paying close enough attention to me to notice.

I squirt more sunscreen out, then move to rub her other side, careful not to disturb the scab on her shoulder. It's almost gone, revealing the new, pinker skin beneath.

"I didn't injure my knee *playing* rugby," I confess. "I was in a car accident when I was seventeen. Piers Colborn, the guy Theo mentioned, was the one driving."

Lili's back expands with a sudden breath under my palm.

"It was an accident. The other driver wasn't paying attention. Ran a red. Piers and I just happened to be on the wrong side of the car. Hadn't heard his name in a while, is all. Took me by surprise."

"Were you friends?" she asks.

"Friendly. Teammates mostly. We were on our way to practice when it happened. My father was furious. He'd never wanted me to play rugby in the first place. Tried to sue the Colborns and everything." I shake my head.

"I'm sure he was worried about you."

"Worried about not having an heir. With good reason, as it turned out."

"I'm sorry that happened to you, Charlie."

"I'm fine," I tell her, attempting to ignore the expanding pressure in my chest.

I've never *told* anyone about that accident before, and something about the soft sympathy in Lili's voice has my heart going haywire.

This version of Lili is very different from the woman who left scratches all over my back and then climbed onto my lap because I wasn't fucking her fast enough.

And the one who haughtily forgot my name—multiple times.

I like all three versions.

More than I should probably since she'll be headed back to New York in a couple of days.

With that *temporary* thought in my mind, I write *MINE* on her back in sunscreen, right between her shoulder blades.

I can't see any of the hickeys I left on her from this angle, but I know they're there. Know she's probably sore, too, from riding my dick the way she did.

"What—are you writing something?" she asks.

Smart.

In addition to being fiery and impatient and occasionally sweet, Lili is smart. She notices things I don't even register myself, like the way the mention of Piers affected me.

"Nope."

I smear the sunscreen around, making sure her whole back is covered, then lie down on my towel and close my eyes.

After a few seconds of hesitation, Lili lies back down too.

Her hand brushes against mine in the few inches between our bodies. Without opening my eyes, I link our pinkies together.

She doesn't pull away. She curls hers around mine too, covering the metal of my signet ring.

When I glance over a couple of minutes later, she's smiling up at the clear sky.

# CHAPTER 25
## Charlie

Tripp and Hugo cheer loudly when the waitress brings another bottle of tequila over. I've lost track of how many shots they've done. Pretty sure they have too.

We're in one of the circular leather booths nestled in the corner of the VIP section. The song changes to one I recognize, but can't name, the heavy bass beat making the entire building vibrate. If I had to guess, I'd say this is a spot Blythe frequents when she stays at the villa.

It's clearly the most popular nightclub in town, based on the long line outside that Tripp bypassed with a few words and a wad of cash.

He nudges a full shot toward me with a questioning tilt of one eyebrow.

I shake my head, shouting, "I'm good," over the commotion around us.

After my meeting with the real estate agent this afternoon, I

drove to dinner at a local restaurant and then came here.

"It's good shit, man," Hugo tells me. "Might lighten you up a little."

Jasper grins to my left. "He's got to stay in fighting shape for Lili."

At first, I think he's talking about the scratches on my back. Then, I follow his gaze to the bar that stretches the length of the building, on the opposite side of the dance floor.

"You've got some competition, man," Tripp says.

The girls left to dance a few songs ago, Chloe dragging Theo along with her to a chorus of whip sounds from Hugo and Jasper.

But Lili's not on the dance floor with her friends any longer. She's perched on a stool, smiling at the three guys surrounding her.

"Lili can take care of herself," Cal comments.

I slide a glance at him. He seems like a decent guy. The top three reasons I dislike him is that he dated Lili. And the distant fourth is that he didn't fight for her. What kind of fool would let her go?

Me, I guess.

I let her walk away from me at Carys Park. And I've held back some since I arrived in Saint-Tropez, disturbed by the urge to see her again in the first place. I easily could have made this trip *without* seeing her, and I rearranged my plans to ensure that I did. I've never done that before—chased a woman. *Craved* anyone the way I want to be around her.

"Oh, I know," Hugo says.

"They're all goners," Tripp concurs. "Look at that. Free drink number five. She's got a real collection going."

If this is what it's like to have a group of male friends, I don't want it. They're purposefully needling me—even Tripp, who I thought wanted me far away from Lili. He seems to have resolved his concerns about me taking advantage of her. And honestly? I think that means I'm being more obvious about my feelings than I should.

"Damn, she did the hair flip," Cal comments. "That move always worked on me."

Even her *ex* is trying to make me jealous. I can't decide if that makes me like Cal more or less.

After a few torturous seconds, I look at Lili again. Five guys are gathered around her now. One touches her arm. She reaches for one of the glasses in front of her—Tripp was right about the collection—effectively shaking him off.

My jaw is so tight that it's starting to ache. I don't get jealous. Women pay me attention, and I choose whether or not to indulge it.

That relaxed indifference is splintering apart, leaving a dark, ugly coil of jealousy behind.

*Mine.*

I wish I'd left those four letters written on her back. Then, maybe men wouldn't be swarming her.

She's *not* mine though. She's free to talk to and flirt with whoever she wants, and I'm not going to be the arsehole who pisses all over that simply because the sight of her with other men feels like a serrated knife is sawing into my chest.

I try not to notice. Attempt not to care.

But it's a fight I'm fucking losing.

Three women stop by our booth. I barely spare them a glance, letting the other guys entertain them.

The next time I look at Lili, she's staring this way. Our gazes collide across the crowded expanse of the club, all the external noise surrounding us fading away.

And she winks. Fucking *winks*, like she can tell how irritated I am and finds it amusing.

One of the men steps closer and says something that has Lili shaking her head. I catch the clear outline of *no* in her response, but the wanker doesn't step away.

And I stand, knowing I've been waiting for an excuse to. Push through the crowd, hoping I'm imagining the whip sounds behind me.

She watches me walk toward her.

I don't pay any notice to her crowd of admirers. I shove through, ignoring one's protest, until I'm standing right in front of her.

Lili smirks. Swipes her tongue along her lower lip. "Couldn't stay away, huh?"

"Time to go."

She tilts her head. "Why? I'm having fun."

I lean into her, not missing the way her breath catches, and her pupils dilate. If I slipped a hand under her dress, I'd find her panties wet.

"You wanted my attention, Lili? You fucking have it. Time. To. Go."

She reaches into one of her many beverages, plucking a cherry out and setting it on her tongue. Her cheeks hollow as she sucks it off the stem, blue eyes overflowing with mirth.

"Nah, I'm not tired," she drawls, tossing the stem away. "And I like this song," she adds, tilting her head back. She curled the strands so they fall in silky waves that I'm dying to shove my hands into. "It makes me want to dance."

I step closer, so I'm wedged between her long legs. My right hand slides up her thigh until I reach the bunched hem of the minidress she's wearing.

Her lips part, but nothing comes out.

"If you wanted to dance, you should have danced sooner."

Lili's chin lifts stubbornly. "I'll dance whenever I want."

"You don't want to dance. You want me to fuck you." I glance over one shoulder, pleased to see her prospects have all disappeared. "Did you think they'd be able to make you come like I can? Or were you just trying to make me jealous?"

In the dim light of the club, her eyes are all I can see. They beam bright, like my personal North Star.

A shade of blue I've never seen before. One that seems to change based on where we are. What she's looking at. Focused on me, they're fucking brilliant.

If she asked me what my favorite color was, the honest answer would be whatever mysterious pigment her eyes are.

Lili swallows. I watch the delicate muscles of her throat contract.

She wets her lips before replying, "I was just being friendly."

She reaches for one of her drinks. I slide my palm higher, higher, *higher*, until my fingertips are brushing wet lace.

*Knew it.*

Pink streaks across her cheeks, knuckles turning white on the glass she's holding.

I ghost my fingers back and forth, smirking as Lili fights the urge to squirm. "I could make you come right here. Remember how fast you came, rubbing that tight cunt all over me? I wasn't even touching you that night. You want me to touch you tonight, Lili?"

Her eyes darken, turning hazy with heat.

And she's not the only one affected.

I can feel my hold on control slipping.

It's not scary. It's not the fog of alcohol or the velocity of a vehicle. I'm purposefully loosening my grip so I can experience the high of letting go.

This trip isn't a vacation for me. Or an exciting investment opportunity, like I told Theo when he asked what business I was here on.

It's an ending. The close of a final chapter. The start of me going to extremes to salvage what I can.

For a little longer, I want to forget about it all. And Lili's the only person who can make that happen.

I *need* her.

My patience has burned down to nothing.

"You have three seconds, Kensington."

She sets her drink down and leans closer. Our breaths mingle. Hers smells like cherry.

"Three seconds or *what*, Marlborough?"

The countdown in my head has already expired.

Elizabeth Kensington wants to battle? I'll give her a bloody war.

And this time, the Brit won't lose.

I tug her off the barstool and hoist her over one shoulder in one smooth motion, palming Lili's ass to ensure her short dress doesn't ride up even higher. Smirk at the sound of her shocked gasp as I grab her purse off the counter and head straight for the exit.

Once we're outside, I set her down.

The valet gapes at me as I hand him my ticket. Lili huffs as she adjusts her dress, but I catch her grin before her hair swings forward to partially cover her face.

She loves to compete as much as I do.

My car revs up less than a minute later, the valet casting an admiring look at the vehicle before handing me the keys. I slip him a bill, then attempt to help Lili into the car. She swats my hand away, and I grin as soon as the door's shut.

It takes me five minutes to decide where I'm going. Or to come to terms with it rather.

I wasn't planning to come here at all. Even before I decided to go see Lili and Theo offered me a place to sleep, I planned to stay at a hotel instead of the villa.

But leaving without coming here feels wrong all of a sudden.

And some part of me wants Lili to see it, for her to hopefully be impressed while I still have something to show off.

For my last memory here to be with her.

She frowns, confused, as I turn down the lane. Lights line the driveway every dozen feet.

Before the final curve, I veer right onto the grass. Hit the brakes and shut off the car. Climb out.

Another door slams as Lili does the same.

"Where the hell are we?" she asks. "This isn't—"

I cut her off with a firm kiss, bracketing her face between my hands and backing her against the front fender of the car. I've been hard for her all day, watching her strut around the boat in a swimsuit. It feels like my balls must be navy by now.

She kisses me back with the same intensity, lifting one leg and wrapping it around my waist. Mewling eagerly into my mouth as she rocks her pelvis against mine. I grip her hips, letting her gyrate against me, but not touching her anywhere else.

"More," she pants, breaking our kiss and sucking in greedy gulps of oxygen. "I need more."

I drop my hands and step back. She teeters in her heels, gravity nearly replacing my hold on her.

Lili huffs. "Tosser."

I almost smile, catching myself just in time.

"This isn't all about you, Lili. You got my attention. You got me hard. What are you going to do about it?"

I'm not a fan of the wicked smile Lili gives me. Or rather, I love it too much.

It's dangerous. Reeks of ruin. The smirk of a seductress.

A grunted "Fuck" spills out when she sinks down to her knees in the grass.

I have to rest a hand on the warm hood of the car when she palms my erection through the stiff material of my trousers. Grit my teeth when she slowly starts working the button and zipper, my weaker knee threatening to buckle the entire time.

I figured she was going to tug her dress up and demand I fuck her. Not get on the ground.

"Take off your shirt," she tells me, reaching to tug my pants and boxers down.

My fingers curl into a fist as hers wrap around my throbbing dick. They look so delicate, the nails painted a light shade of pink, against the raised veins and flushed skin.

I grunt as her hold tightens, battling the urge to thrust. The teasing is torture, and she fucking knows it, staring up at me with wide, satisfied eyes as I struggle to retain some control.

I unbutton my shirt and toss it away, not caring where it lands on the grass.

Her palm presses against my stomach, and then her nails rake down my abs. Red lines linger over the ridges, like marks from skiers on freshly fallen snow.

I swear again, the sting barely registering through the haze of arousal as I grip the base of my erection and smear the pre-cum that's collected at the tip across her full lips.

"*Lili.*" That's all I can manage, two syllables that are soaked with urgency.

She blows on the tip, then takes me into her mouth like she's ravenous for a taste. She sucks me deep, her cheeks hollowing and her eyes watering when I hit the back of her throat.

Her hand squeezes, then pumps the inches she can't swallow. Releases me from the warm wetness of her mouth and flicks the sensitive slit at the end with her tongue before circling the flared head. Her lips close around the tip, a seal of suction that has my balls drawing up tight.

I grunt, my awareness of the entire world narrowing to nothing except this. All the medical terms I memorized, all the ancestral history my father ensured I learned, all the rugby plays I mastered … there's nothing but blank space in my brain. Right now, I couldn't even come up with my own damn title.

Some of Lili's hair falls forward. I collect as much of it as I can and fist it so my view of her face is unobstructed.

Her hands explore as her mouth continues to suck my cock, nails scraping and fingers tugging. Her left hand plays with my testicles, and then her right hand slides down my leg.

At first, I think she's just bracing herself. But when I feel her palm rub against the puckered scar on my knee, I decide the position is deliberate.

A harsh grunt leaves my mouth. That skin is not normally

sensitive, the injury long healed and the scar itself a thin white line, but something about her touching me there—about her choosing to touch me there, like some silent message she's glad I didn't die in that accident, heightens everything else I'm experiencing.

Hot pressure builds deep and low in my groin, my balls high and heavy. I barely have the presence of mind to choke out a warning to Lili before the pressure snaps, the first wave of my release hitting like a tsunami as my dick pulses in her mouth. Filling it with so much cum that white liquid spills down her chin, even as her throat shudders with rapid swallows.

I pull her up and turn her around, pressing the small of her back so she's bent over and lying flat on the car's hood, yanking her dress up and her panties down.

The headlights flickered out at some point, but the driveway lights are bright enough for me to see how swollen and wet her cunt is. How much blowing me turned her on.

My dick is already inflating again, satisfied but not sated. I can't fucking get enough of her. I always want more—want everything.

"Was it that good, Charlie? You came kinda fast. I bet those guys at the club would have lasted longer."

She's teasing me. But I'm seeing red at the thought of her touching anyone else.

I smack her ass, watching pink bloom across her pale skin. "Is that what you want, Lili? You want a different cock right now?"

She gasps, and I watch her exposed pussy pulse.

I might as well have not come at all; my dick is so hard. Makes rolling the condom on easy.

I pump my dick between her trembling thighs, but I don't give her a single inch.

"Answer me."

Her frustrated groan makes me smile. Her nails scrabble against the hood of the car, trying to find purchase on something but only finding smooth metal. This car is supposed to sell with the house, which is probably for the best. I'm never going to be able to drive it again without picturing her spread out on it.

I spank her other ass cheek, so she's sporting matching handprints.

"Wanker!"

"*Answer me*, Lili, or you don't get to come. Whose cock do you want?"

"I can't—" She pants, her breathing rapid and irregular. Her hair's a wild array across the shiny metal. "I can't think of a worse British insult right now, but just know I'm thinking it."

I'm glad she can't see my face because I can't hold back the smile this time.

Am I genuinely pissed she was flirting with other men in front of me? Yeah.

But I'm also getting off on this fight, of forcing her to admit what she wants from me. She knew exactly what she was doing, which tells me she's getting off on it too.

I slap her ass a third time. Lili bucks back against me, shouting my name, mixed with lots of swears.

"Do you want to go back to the club?" I suggest innocently. "Maybe you can find—"

"Fuck you, Charlie."

"You want to," I tease.

Lili turns her head so she's lying on the opposite cheek. "I want it, okay?"

"Want what?"

She glares at me, but the effect is ruined by her swollen lips and flushed cheeks. "I want *your* cock, Charlie. Now, *fuck me* with it or else I'll hitchhike back to that club. Alone."

Good enough for me.

I thrust into her. She's soaking wet but so tight that I have to work to get inside of her.

I can barely hear the wet slap of our bodies colliding over the sounds Lili is making. It's the most vocal she's ever been during sex—I guess because we're out in the middle of nowhere, it seems like—and it urges something primal in me. I pound into her hard and fast and rough, taking my pleasure but feral for the sound of hers.

I fuck her over and over again, unable to look away from the sight. I'm not going to last long, and I want to memorize this moment.

How she looks with me inside of her.

How it feels like her cunt was made for me to fill it.

I don't know how near the closest neighbors are, but I'm sure they hear her shout when she comes all over my dick.

# CHAPTER 26

## *Lili*

I never imagined what the aftermath of hot sex on the hood of a car would be. I never imagined *I* would have hot sex on the hood of a car.

But if I'd guessed, the follow-up wouldn't have included wandering around the grounds of a gorgeous villa.

"This place is incredible," I tell Charlie.

Steps descend from the patio surrounding the pool, leading down to a dock that calm water laps against.

Charlie walks past me, toward the detached structure designed in the same style as the gigantic main building. It's a pool house or a guesthouse, it looks like.

"You know the owners?" I call after him.

A question I should have asked when we first got here, but I was … distracted. Charlie has this unique ability to wipe logical reasoning from my brain, which is incredible and inconvenient.

I follow him into the guesthouse. It's an open floor plan, one wall the kitchen with an eating nook against the opposite wall. A cozy seating area is past it with two open doorways revealing the bathroom and bedroom.

It's beautiful. Also messy.

And I say this as someone who currently has clothes draped over every surface of the room she's staying in.

"Um, wow."

Dirty dishes are stacked in the sink. Beach towels are draped over the backs of chairs. Books lie open on the couch, partially played board games on the floor. Pillows are lopsided. Even the paintings hang crooked.

Charlie is scowling, turning around in a slow circle in the center of the room.

"Blythe," he mutters darkly.

"Your sister?"

"Yes. I knew she was upset, but I didn't think she'd …" He shakes his head.

I pull the pink elastic off my wrist, twist my hair into a bun, and secure it the best I can without looking in a mirror. Hopefully, there's not a chunk I missed.

There's no dishwasher, which isn't ideal. No dish gloves either. But it's a small miracle the manicure I had done for Chloe's wedding has lasted this long. It had to start chipping sometime.

"What are you doing?" Charlie asks as I flick the faucet on and rummage under the sink for a sponge and some soap.

"Washing the dishes." I let an unspoken *duh* dangle.

"Leave it, Lili. I'll deal with this."

I don't reply, just continue scrubbing.

*"Lili."*

"Those books aren't going to put themselves away."

Charlie heaves a sigh before walking over to the couch. I set the first plate in the drain rack, then pick up a second one. It's kind of cathartic, sudsing and rinsing. Satisfying to set the sparkling, dripping dish down.

This is not my first time washing dishes. But as much as it makes me sound like a spoiled rich girl, it's not a frequent occurrence.

We clean in companionable silence.

It's weird.

Not the quiet. That's comfortable—the rustle of couch cushions and trickle of running water from the tap.

The domesticity is strange. From the club to cleaning.

Every time I think I have Charlie figured out, he surprises me.

He went from barely looking at me on the boat to confiding about the accident that made him decide to pursue a medical degree.

Fucking me on the hood of his car to fluffing pillows.

He acts like a duke—distant, dignified, reserved—one minute, then tosses me over a shoulder the next.

That contrast does something dangerous to me, especially since I've only seen that shift take place around me.

I set the last clean dish down, then dry my hands on the towel hanging from the fridge door.

Charlie's tidied everywhere else. Everything's tucked or fixed or straightened. He's in the bedroom now, stripping sheets, so I duck into the bathroom to pee and wash my hands. Wipe the counter and hang up the towels while I'm in there.

When I walk out of the bathroom, Charlie is leaning against the kitchen counter, talking on the phone. I have no idea who he's talking to or what he's saying because the conversation is taking place in French.

I had no idea Charlie spoke French. Another hidden facet to this man.

I wander past him and back out to the pool. More exterior lights flicker on, activated by the movement.

The light doesn't extend far enough for me to see the ocean, but I can hear the muffled crash of water against the shore. I take a seat at the top of the pool steps, swishing my feet in the cool water. It's lagoon-like, appearing carved into the stone ground like it sprang into a natural existence.

A few minutes later, I hear Charlie's footsteps approaching.

"Sorry," he says, sitting down beside me. "Just taking care of a couple of things."

His arm brushes mine as he slips off his leather loafers and dips his feet in the water too. The hems of his pants dampen in the water, but Charlie doesn't seem to notice. He stares straight ahead at the main house, seeming lost in thought.

"So … you own this place?"

That's the only reasonable explanation I can come up with for why his sister would have been here and his apparent unconcern about trespassing.

"Yes."

"It's nice."

A conspicuous understatement. I thought the Beaumonts' place was big. This villa makes their house look like a fisherman's cottage. Not to mention its jaw-dropping location, right on the coast with private water access.

"Yeah." He exhales.

I bump his knee with mine. "If this whole duke thing doesn't work out, you could start a cleaning company."

Charlie huffs a laugh under his breath. Glances around, like he's registering where we are for the first time. "I haven't been here in years."

"I love the cypress trees. And I'm pretty sure that's a fig." I point it out.

"Do you work on projects like this?" Charlie asks. "Design gardens at private houses?"

"I have, yeah. Last spring, I worked on Christian Davis's house."

Charlie's expression is blank.

"The actor?" I prompt.

He shrugs. "I don't watch a lot of movies."

"Okay, well, he's pretty famous in the US."

"Did you date him?"

He sounds jealous, and it's more thrilling than him stalking across the club was. Because I wasn't trying to make him jealous this time, but I think he still is.

"No. His *wife* hired me for the project. They'd just gotten married and bought their first house together. She wanted the yard to feel like home."

Charlie's nod is slow. "This villa was my dad's wedding gift to my mom."

"Oh."

I can see the resentment in his expression now, like he gave me permission to view it by uttering those words.

"I don't know why he didn't sell it after they got divorced. But he didn't, so now, I have to."

I don't fully understand what he means by that. Why he feels like he *has* to sell it. Because of the memories, I guess? It would be hard to look at a physical symbol of your parents' relationship, knowing the relationship itself is permanently wrecked.

His parents didn't just get divorced; his dad died. They'll never be a complete family again, and that would be hard enough to accept without additional reminders.

Asking more questions doesn't feel like my place, so I just whisper, "I'm sorry, Charlie."

"It's fine," he says quickly. Then, softer, "*I'm* sorry. I'm dropping a lot on you today."

"I don't mind."

More than that, I like it. I'm not sure who else he confides in. *If* there's anyone else he confides in. He reminds me of an ancient god, some iteration of Zeus, ruling the sky, or Poseidon, the sea. Powerful. Unique. *Alone.*

I flick some water with my toes. "What was your dad like?"

"He was …" Charlie exhales. "He was a hard person to describe."

"Oh." I focus on the ripples disturbing the surface of the water, giving him the out.

"He blamed me."

I glance over, the glimpse of his profile reminding me of the man I met in Atlantic Crest's polo stable what feels like forever ago.

It's so bizarre how life unfolds sometimes. A little less than a year, and it feels like decades since we first met.

Most of my life, I didn't know Charles Marlborough existed. And now, it's hard to remember a time when he didn't cross my mind hourly.

"Blamed you for what?" I ask.

"For everything. Nothing I ever did was good enough. At some point, I stopped trying to live up to his expectations. But I still wanted his approval. He'd take me for these long rides around the fields at Newcastle, and whenever he said something to annoy me, I'd get Kensington to gallop. Papa would get annoyed, but he'd also be proud. He wanted to control me. He also wanted a son who was strong enough to stand up to him. I realized I couldn't be both. I don't think he ever did."

My chest aches. I assumed Charlie was still grieving his father. But I didn't realize how … unresolved things had been between them. That their relationship had been complicated in addition to getting cut short.

Something else occurs to me.

I quirk a brow at him. "Kensington?"

It's hard to tell for sure, but Charlie's cheeks look a little ruddier than they did a second ago. "He's named after the palace."

"Uh-huh. It's a good name."

"Yeah, it is." He pauses. "Hell of a lot better than Lexington."

I smile, experiencing a sudden burst of nostalgia at the memory of our first meeting. Would we still be sitting here if I'd introduced myself as Elizabeth Kensington from the start?

"You're a good polo player," he adds. "Not sure I ever told you that."

"I was going to be an equine vet. Back when I was going to be a vet, I mean. After that changed … I kept riding for a while. Polo was more fun than just cantering around in circles." I slide a glance his way. "You're good too."

He's better than me, but that's as magnanimous as I'm going to be. I can still picture his smug smile when he accepted that trophy.

"Maybe we'll have a rematch."

"Does that mean you'll be visiting New York soon?"

I sound hopeful. I'm not sure if he can hear the hope. If I want him to hear it.

Charlie runs a hand through his hair. His elbow grazes my shoulder. "Probably not. I, uh … things with my mom have never been great. She left when I was ten. Blythe was only five. I've tried to see it from her perspective. Tried to move past it. But this last trip, I spent more quality time with Ellis, my cousin. Don't see myself showing up for another visit anytime soon."

"She's not the only person who lives in New York."

*Subtle, Lili.* I might as well hand him a key to my penthouse.

"I have a lot going on here," he says. "In Britain, I mean."

It's a gentle letdown, but it still prickles unpleasantly. "Right. Balls to attend and carriage rides to go on."

He shakes his head, chuckling under his breath. "What about you? Do you know what project you're working on next?"

"Not yet. I have some interviews next week."

"All in the States?"

"The interviews are over the phone. If they make an offer, I'll go visit the sites in person before accepting. Two are in the US. One's in Canada. And one's in Ireland."

"Ireland?"

I think there's more than polite interest in his voice as he mentions the location closest to England, but I could be imagining it.

I kick the water again, sending more ripples across the surface. "Yeah. There's a university in Dublin that's expanding its campus. They need a landscape architect for the exterior space."

"Have you worked on a campus project before?"

I shake my head. "But the Canada job would be as part of the design committee for the Toronto Olympics. I want that one more."

"Wow, Lili."

"It's not that big of a deal. It's just an interview. I haven't gotten it, and even if I do, I'd just be—"

"It's a big deal, Kensington. Whether or not you get it, you should be proud."

I swallow. "Thanks."

His praise does something strange to me. It's overwhelming, a sensation I want to savor yet also run from.

I stand on the stairs, my fingers finding the hidden snap beneath the tied back of my silk Prada minidress and tossing it toward one of the terra-cotta lounge chairs. My bra flies through the air next. My thong got left by the car.

I stroll around the perimeter of the pool, adding an extra sway to my hips because I can feel his eyes on me. As soon as I reach the deep end, I leap, cool water closing over my head. I sink until my toes brush the slick tiled floor, then kick back to the surface.

Charlie hasn't moved.

I start to float on my back, staring up at the starry sky. My thighs drift open gradually. I'm not sure how much Charlie can see, between the water and the limited light. If he can see anything, he's getting one hell of a view. Not that he hasn't seen it all before.

"Wanna race?" I call out without looking his way.

About a minute later, I hear a loud splash. I let my legs sink until I'm treading water again, staring straight at Charlie's smirk. His hazel eyes are focused on the swell of my breasts.

"And add to my perfect record of beating you? Sure."

"I'm an *excellent* swimmer," I inform him.

Five of my six records at Dalton Academy are still unbroken, seven years after I graduated. I decided not to swim in college.

"I heard. Team captain."

My eyes narrow at his nonchalance. "Did you swim at Oxford?"

"No." He pauses. "They tried to recruit me though." His smirk grows. "Never told you where I went to university."

I duck under the water to avoid responding, swimming to the far end of the pool as fast as I can. My lungs are burning by the time I emerge.

I've never swum naked before. It feels strange in a scintillating way, the smooth glide of cool, chlorinated water refreshing and arousing as it drips off my face and rolls down my neck.

Charlie surfaces next to me, and I shout, "Go!"

I have a bad feeling that he's as good at swimming as he is at polo and driving. And sex. I'll take whatever slim competitive edge I can get.

I breathe away from him and toward the wall on the lap down, smiling underwater when I execute a perfect flip turn. *Still got it.*

When I breathe for the first time on the return trip, he's even with me. I dig deeper, muscles burning as I propel myself through the water as fast as possible. I screw my eyes closed, pretending he's ahead because that's a very real possibility.

My hand hits concrete, and I bob upright, glancing to the right. He's there.

*Damn it.*

"Did you win?"

Charlie shrugs, his broad shoulders glistening with water. "I just got here."

"You did?"

"We'll call it a tie."

"Does that mean you really won?"

He swipes a hand across his forehead, clearing the water dripping from his hair. "Dunno. Honestly."

A smile spreads slowly. "Your poor perfect record," I tease.

He moves so fast that I don't see it coming, arm wrapping around my waist and tugging me down. I barely have time to close off my airway and shut my eyes before I'm submerged, my hair floating around me.

It's a few feet here, shallow enough to stand but deep enough to plunge if you want to. We wrestle underwater, Charlie fighting his way to the surface first. I bob up a few seconds later, gasping for air and reaching for his shoulders. He evades me, and I end up grabbing his forearm instead. I think he lets me drag him toward me because he's got at least a hundred pounds and six inches on me.

We're both laughing, the sound mixing with the splashing water and buzz of the cicadas.

The shift from playful to charged is gradual. Hands linger. Caress. We stop breaking eye contact.

And then he's kissing me, his lips bruising as he hungrily demands entrance to my mouth. I wrap my arms around his neck and my legs around his waist, forgetting we're both naked until the rough hairs of his happy trail tickle sensitive flesh, still tender from our last round of sex.

I only have one day left in Saint-Tropez. We're flying straight back to New York while Chloe and Theo return to London separately.

I have no idea when I'll see Charlie again after this trip, and that sends a spiral of panic spinning through me. A stab wound couldn't keep me from fucking him, let alone a sore vagina.

He's hoisting me out of the water, forearms flexing before my ass lands on the hard tiles decorating the perimeter of the pool.

"Lie back," Charlie says huskily.

I do, the rough stone of the patio scraping my back. Charlie kisses a line upward, starting at my knee, teeth sinking gently into the soft flesh of my inner thigh before moving even higher.

This isn't the wild, untamed sex we had earlier. It's tender and intimate, his tongue licking and swirling and teasing until my insides liquefy. I slip back into the water, he climbs out to grab another condom from his pants, and then he fucks me against the slick wall.

Another first for me—sex in a pool.

Charlie carries me into the outdoor shower after I admit I'm not sure I can walk. Least he can do in exchange for that ego boost.

I smile dreamily the entire short trip, my system still swimming with endorphins.

There aren't any walls to the shower, just a circular wire frame that's covered by climbing greenery. It makes me feel like I'm standing in the middle of a rainforest.

"I like this," I murmur, gesturing to all the plants.

"Yeah, I thought you might." Charlie sets me down to turn on the water. It's warmer than the pool was, the spray like a heavy mist falling around us.

"Maybe you shouldn't sell this place." The words come out easily, my tongue loosened by the dopamine hit and the way it feels like we're the only two people in the world right now.

Charlie tenses next to me, and I wish I'd kept my mouth shut. He's clearly sensitive about the topic of this place.

"It's already done," is all he says, turning the faucet to the right.

The water cools a little. Or maybe that's just the effects of my orgasm continuing to fade.

We finish rinsing. Charlie grabs two towels from the guesthouse for us to dry off with.

I comb the tangles in my hair out the best I can with my fingers, then ask, "Will you braid my hair?"

He clears his throat before replying, "Sure."

While he does, I ask a question I've wondered about for a while. It feels like we're in a bubble right now, both drunk on sex, secret thoughts slipping out more easily in the late-night air.

"Why'd you walk away in the hallway at my grandparents'?"

"Because I was losing control."

I smirk as his talented fingers sift through my hair. "I had all my clothes on."

"You wreck my control just by existing, Elizabeth Kensington."

My smile freezes on my face, those words suspended in the air between us like some shimmering force.

I swallow hard. "That's either the nicest or the meanest thing anyone has ever said to me."

He kisses the top of my spine, then lets my braided hair drop. "You're welcome."

# CHAPTER 27
## Charlie

For the second time in two weeks, I rush into a hospital. Wind my way around patients and doctors and other frazzled family members until I reach a desk.

"Grace Marlborough." I slap a hand on the counter. "What room is she in?"

I suck in an impatient breath as the nurse tells me to wait a moment, otherwise still for the first time since my mobile buzzed in the middle of the night with a call from Elsie.

Since I answered, it's been nonstop motion. Slipping out of Lili's bed. Packing my stuff. Driving to the airport. Flying back to London. Driving here. The short wait is excruciating by comparison.

"She's in 386," the nurse tells me. "But, sir—"

I'm already jogging down the hall, the rest of the nurse's words lost in the blood rushing in my ears.

I reach room 386 and discover what the nurse was trying to

tell me. Granny is fast asleep, the monitors beside her bed beeping evenly. I exhale for what feels like the first time in hours.

"Charlie."

I turn to see Blythe standing in the hallway, holding a bag of crisps in one hand. Her tan skin is pale, the usual flippancy on her face replaced by stark fear. I'm to her in three strides, pulling her tight into my arms.

"Elsie called you?" I was waiting until I got here so I could see what the situation was like first.

Blythe nods against my chest. "Elsie called me."

"Is she still here?"

I need to thank her. For calling me and for getting Gran help so quickly. For going above and beyond the role of an employee once again.

"No," Blythe answers. "She headed home to get some rest. Granny's sedated. She won't wake up for hours. That's all I understood from what the doctor said—"

"Shh," I say, pulling her tighter against me. "Don't worry. We'll straighten it all out."

"She's all we have left, Charlie."

My throat feels too thick to swallow as my heart constricts. "She's still here."

A gurney gets pushed down the hallway, and we have to move to one side. Rather than return to a waiting room, we end up in the hospital's cafeteria.

It's just past noon. Fairly crowded with hospital staff and other visitors and patients who are mobile enough to leave their rooms.

My appetite is nonexistent, but I buy a sandwich anyway. I haven't eaten since last night. Blythe picks up a yogurt.

We find an open table and sit in green plastic chairs.

"Did the villa sell?" Blythe asks dully, ripping the top off her yogurt.

The fist around my heart squeezes tighter. "It's getting listed tomorrow."

The agent thinks it's going to sell for more than I thought, which is a good thing. But I can't help but feel like a failure, staring at my sister's blank expression. I can't even bring myself to chastise her for the disaster she and her friends left behind. I'll lecture her later, when we're not sitting in a hospital, and she doesn't look so defeated.

"Do we need money?"

I'm too surprised to say anything except, "What?"

"You heard me." Blythe's tone is sharper now, cutting to the truth like a predator closing in on a kill. "Are you selling the villa because we need the money?"

"I …" All the times I considered telling her, it never occurred to me Blythe might be the one to ask me. That I'd have to lie to her, or else tell her the ugly truth.

"It's an easy question, Charles. Yes or no?"

It's not an easy question.

It's the hardest thing I've ever had to say to my sister. Because she's going to want a full explanation of how this happened, which will mean altering her memory of our father forever. Letting her learn he wasn't the successful, cunning man we both thought he was.

My knee begins bouncing. "I'm handling it, Blythe. Okay? I'm sorry about the villa, but I—"

"How bad is it?"

Sweat pricks under the collar of my shirt. "It's not … good."

"Do I need to leave school? Are we going to lose Newcastle?

Will Granny—"

"No. I—we'll be fine. Things are tight now, but I have a plan. Just trust me."

Blythe doesn't look reassured.

Honestly, I don't blame her. It took me weeks—months—to wrap my head around this reality. I'm not sure it's fully sunk in yet actually.

There are still moments when I forget, when I drive up to Newcastle and imagine walking inside to find my dad sitting by the fire, reading a leather-bound book. Ready to chastise me for staying out late or for not receiving first-class honors. When I wake up and there's no weight yet. When I'm around Lili.

"How long have you known?" she asks me.

I avert my eyes. "Since Papa died."

"Does Granny know?" Her voice is higher again.

"Yes."

"Why didn't you tell me?"

"You know why, Blythe."

She sighs. "It was Papa's fault."

"He made mistakes," I acknowledge.

"How could he?"

A question I've asked myself a thousand times. "People make mistakes. I'm sure he didn't mean to—"

"Ruin our lives?" Blythe finishes bitterly.

My chest heaves with a long sigh. "I felt the same way when I found out. Pissed and angry and resentful. It changed nothing. He loved you, Blythe. Loved you so much. I'm sure he thought he could fix everything before it affected us. Just because he was wrong …"

I shrug helplessly.

Comforting other people has never been my strong suit. I was raised to never show weakness, so I never had much exposure to sentimentality.

I probably would have made a terrible doctor.

*You would've been a really good doctor.* Lili's voice sneaks into my head without warning, a tumble of memories from the past couple of days following close behind.

She's probably pissed at me, as she should be.

Sneaking out of her bed in the middle of the night to answer Elsie's call, then leaving a note that I had to return to London because of business for everyone to find—both decisions I could categorize as mistakes.

I was overwhelmed. With worry about Gran—and panic about Lili.

She was supposed to be sex. A beautiful distraction from the fifty-pound weight stuck on my shoulders.

I didn't want to care about her. Didn't think I was capable of it, honestly. My father might have loved Blythe unreservedly—and shown affection toward me in certain ways—yet I never witnessed him express warmth toward anyone who wasn't a blood relation. If he ever loved my mother, it didn't last long.

But the weight on my shoulders has been joined by a brick in my stomach as I think about how I left Lili lying in bed. Left a hastily scribbled note on the counter that didn't even address her directly.

Does she hate me for it?

Worse, does she not care at all?

I'm exhausted. Physically since Lili and I didn't get back to Chloe's until almost two a.m. and Elsie called around four. Mentally and emotionally, too, as I worry about Granny's health and everything else challenging my family right now.

Blythe and I finish picking at our lunch, then head back upstairs. Granny still isn't awake, but Blythe sits with her while I receive an update from one of her doctors.

They've determined Granny had an ischemic stroke. They did a CT scan when she arrived and have administered medication to restore circulation, which she seems to be responding to, but they're continuing to monitor her while awaiting test results.

If Elsie hadn't checked on her in the middle of the night, she'd probably be gone.

I thank the doctor, then return to Granny's room.

She's awake now.

"The nurse said her vitals look good," Blythe tells me. Her face is still drawn, but there's a spark of life there. A little color. "She said Granny should try to get more rest."

I squeeze Blythe's shoulder, then lean down to kiss Granny's wrinkled forehead. I'm so used to seeing her with curled hair and a matching skirt and jacket. Linen this time of year. She looks so tiny in the standard-issued gown and mechanized bed.

"It's good to see you, Granny."

"I don't need to rest, Charles," she says, impertinent as ever. "I need you to get me out of here."

"Try to close your eyes for a little bit," I reply. "Relaxing will get you out of here sooner. We'll wait out—"

"There's no reason to sit somewhere else when there's plenty of space in here."

*She's scared*, I realize. She's scared, and she wants us to stay with her.

"All right." I pull up a chair alongside the hospital bed, opposite

Blythe.

"I'm going to use the loo," she tells me and Gran, then disappears into the hallway.

"Probably off to plan her next trip now that she knows there's no funeral to attend."

I sigh. "Gran …"

I deliberate on telling her that Blythe knows the truth and is dealing with that, but decide now isn't the moment. It'll upset her, knowing Blythe sees Papa differently, and that's not what she needs right now.

"How did it go in Saint-Tropez?" Granny asks.

"Fine. The house is listing on tomorrow. Realtor expects it will move fast."

"Good. And the investors?"

"Nothing solid," I admit.

I narrowed the options down to three before leaving for France. Before making a final decision, I'd like to get Louis Haywood's opinion. I know he's familiar with at least one of the companies.

Gran sniffs. "You need to start considering alternatives, Charles."

"*What* alternatives?"

"You're the Duke of Manchester. There isn't a woman in the country who would turn down a proposal. Find a wealthy one, and this unfortunate situation will be a worry of the past."

I exhale, studying my clasped palms.

Her suggestion isn't a surprise. Even forgetting the urgency of the financial situation, I've always known I'd need to have kids to pass the title to. Something I don't really care about, honestly, but Gran sure does. My dad did too. And no matter how mad I am at my father—about a long list of things—I've never been able to fully shake the compulsion to take his opinion into consideration.

"I'm not ready to get married."

*Seven years.* I was supposed to have seven years of freedom left, same as my father.

"Are you ready to declare bankruptcy? To lose *everything?*"

I flinch, but they're fair shots.

In the fifteen months since my father died, I've failed to find any lasting solution. I'm not a businessman who understands strategy and investments and market shares. I was supposed to be a doctor.

"Charlie, the doctor's here."

Blythe walks into the room, a white coat–clad man right behind her. He introduces himself as Dr. Wallace, then tells Gran they'd like to take her down for an electrocardiogram to assess any heart problems that might have led to her stroke.

She's wheeled out a few minutes later, leaving me and Blythe alone in the sterile room that smells like antiseptic.

"You okay?" Blythe tilts her head as she studies me.

For the first time, it feels like my little sister is older than me. She looks poised while I feel like I'm falling apart.

"Yeah. Just tired."

She nods, and we sit in silence, waiting for Gran to come back.

# CHAPTER 28

## *Lili*

"There's my girl!" Dad exclaims as soon as the door swings open.

"Hey, Dad." My voice comes out muffled since he's already pulled me into a tight hug and my face is now smooshed against his chest.

I got lunch with my mom two days ago, but this is the first time I've seen my dad since I got back to New York. Based on his reaction, you'd think we'd been separated for months.

He kisses the top of my head and then releases me. "How are you? Mom said you had a good trip?"

"I'm good. And, yeah, the trip was great. Did she show you the photos I sent?"

"She sure did," Dad confirms. "Made me miss Europe. We've been talking about taking a trip to Italy. This fall, once football season has started? Will you be around?"

"I'm not sure yet," I reply. "I'm still figuring out my next project."

Dad nods. "Well, keep it in mind. Your mom is in the living room."

"Kit and Bash here?"

He shakes his head. "They're running late."

Typical.

I kick off my shoes and pad down the hallway toward the living room. Mom's sitting on the sectional couch with her legs curled under her, flipping through the glossy pages of a magazine between sips of wine.

I glance around the room. Mom redecorated recently. My parents own this building, but this isn't the penthouse I lived in growing up. It's where Dad resided before they got married, which they've downsized to now that none of us are living at home. I have my own place a few blocks away, and Bash has chosen to crash at Kit's new place, now that he's graduated and is living in New York permanently.

"Hey, Mom." I flop down beside her.

The silk of her blouse brushes my cheek as she leans over to kiss my head, just like Dad did.

Bash might be the baby of our family, but since he sprouted to six-five, I'm the one who gets treated like it.

"How was your day, honey?"

"Fine," I reply, rubbing the arch of my foot. It's still suffering from all the days I've worn heels lately. "I got brunch with Fran, Bridget, and Jasper. Then had the Dublin interview this afternoon."

Mom closes the magazine and tosses it onto the coffee table. "How did the interview go?"

"It went well. I liked the team a lot. They're supposed to get back to me next week."

"That's exciting." Mom takes a sip of wine. "I've never been to Ireland. Your dad and I will have to come visit."

"Visit where?" Dad walks into the living room, a bottle of wine in one hand and two more glasses dangled in the other.

"Ireland," Mom replies. "Lili might be working on a project there."

"That's close to Italy," Dad says, winking.

"Dad, our last vacation got moved three times because of your and Mom's schedules. I'm not planning my job around it."

They exchange one of those looks where they have an entire conversation without saying a single word.

"Fair enough," he tells me, filling a wineglass and handing it to me. "Congratulations, sweetie."

"Thanks. But I haven't actually gotten the job yet."

"They'd be fools not to hire you," Mom tells me, smiling at Dad as he tops off her glass with another splash of wine. "Such service."

"Anything for my girls," he replies, kissing her soundly on the mouth.

"Gross," I mutter into my wine.

They both laugh as the doorbell rings.

"I'll get it," I volunteer, padding back into the entryway to answer it.

When I open the front door, my brothers are both standing in the hallway. Bash with a hand planted beside the doorway with a wrinkled button-down on. Kit is slouched against the opposite wall, wearing a faded Rangers T-shirt. The brim of a baseball cap is pulled low over his eyes.

"Seriously, you two?" I prop a hand on my hip. "Would a little effort kill you?"

I'm wearing a pink maxi dress with a flower pattern on it.

"Maybe." Bash gives me a lopsided grin and a one-armed hug before passing me and heading into the penthouse. "Welcome home, sis."

I knock Kit's cap off as he follows, and he scowls. "Thought you were still shopping your way across Europe."

"I was at Chloe's *wedding*, Christopher. Not on a global shopping spree."

His scowl deepens. Mom only calls us by our full names— Elizabeth, Christopher, and Sebastian—when we're in trouble. And she can be mildly terrifying, so those aren't positive memories.

I *did* go shopping in Saint-Tropez, but I don't mention that to my brother.

"And you could use some new clothes. You can't possibly show up in that"—I give his basketball shorts a pointed look—"at the office."

"I know how to dress for work, *Elizabeth*. Just didn't feel like dressing up to eat dinner with you."

I stick my tongue out at him as I close the door. "You're starting soon, right? End of August?"

"Yeah." There's an edge to the word, one I'm surprised to hear.

"Are you …"

"Everyone's in the living room?"

Kit walks off before I can answer. I trail behind him, feeling the lines form on my forehead.

I always assumed Kit was excited about working at Kensington Consolidated. It's our family's company. If my dyslexia hadn't made an office job like that sound miserable, I know it's where I would have ended up. But he sounds decidedly *unenthused* about it, and I'm now realizing he hasn't mentioned it once this entire summer. I'm not even sure if he's been to see his fancy corner office yet.

When I return to the living room, Bash's sprawled on the rug, and Kit has stolen my seat next to Mom on the couch.

I end up in one of the armchairs, Dad in the other. He's having another silent conversation with Mom, head tilts and eyebrow lifts and forehead wrinkling substitutes for syllables.

It adds to the mystery of tonight. We don't have dinners, all five of us, with any regularity. Barring a special occasion—I can't come up with any—my brothers and I getting summoned for a Wednesday night meal is random.

"Is something wrong?" I blurt out.

Bash and Kit both glance up from the tray of appetizers they were demolishing.

"Nothing's wrong," Dad says carefully. "But we do have some news to share with you."

"*Please* let it be another jet," Kit says around a mouthful of cheese. "Lili hogs it."

"Like you'd be using it for business." Bash scoffs.

"Well, your mother and I will be using the jet to move back to New York," Dad says. "Permanently."

We all stare at him.

Kit speaks first. "What?"

"Your mother and I have decided to move back to New York. For good. We're selling the house in LA. No more split schedules between coasts."

"But … what about your work?" Bash asks.

The whole reason our parents left New York in the first place was for Dad's job.

Dad glances at Mom, then exhales. "I've decided to return to Kensington Consolidated. Your uncle Oliver is announcing me as COO at the company gala this weekend."

We all stare at him in shock, Kit looking the most stunned.

Dad worked at Kensington Consolidated before my brothers were born. But he has never—not once—mentioned returning to work there. I didn't consider it as a possibility. I assumed my parents would continue jetting between coasts until they retired.

"This is a good thing," Mom says, glancing around at all of us.

Dad nods in agreement. "It's a change we've talked about for a few years. But it took a while to find the right person to take over the production company. I made Raymond a promise. But Kensington Consolidated—New York—has always been our home. You kids have all ended up on the East Coast, and it feels like the right time for us too."

"Wow," I say. "Congrats, Dad."

Bash and Kit chime in, echoing the sentiment.

It's not until I'm in the kitchen after dinner, pulling ice cream out of the freezer, that I have the chance to ask Kit, "You good?"

He was quiet during dinner, barely chiming in as I relayed a—selective—retelling of my trip to Wales and Saint-Tropez. No mention of Charlie or my trip to a British emergency room. Bash talked about his summer internship and upcoming fishing trip to Alaska with some college buddies. Nothing from Kit.

"Yeah," he replies, grabbing the carton from me and a spoon from the drawer and stealing a bite of mint chip.

I glance toward the doorway, making sure we're still alone, then lower my voice. "You sure? You seem … off."

"I'm just adjusting to being back in the city, getting resettled."

"Is this about Dad working at Kensington Consolidated?"

Kit blows out a long breath, then drops his spoon in the sink. "You were smart to choose something different," he tells me.

"No. I was too dumb to have a Kensington Consolidated–worthy GPA." I take a big bite of ice cream.

Kit frowns, then flicks my shoulder. "Don't talk about yourself like that. The only person allowed to call you dumb is me—when you buy shoes that look the same as the five million other pairs you already own."

I roll my eyes, but I'm smiling. "You're going to kick ass at the company, Kit. All that's changed is, Dad will be there to see it in person."

"Thanks, Lili."

We smile at each other, and then Kit ruins the sweet moment by informing me I have chocolate on my chin.

I clean it off, scoop most of the container into a bowl, and then head back out onto the private patio. Mom is lying on one of the reclining lounge chairs, scrolling on her phone.

I assume it's work, until she flashes me a photo of a yellow Lab.

"What do you think?" she asks. "He's adorable, right?"

"You're getting a dog?"

Ever since Teddy, our family's golden retriever, died, Mom has insisted no dog could ever replace him.

"Your father and I have talked about it."

Mom smiles suddenly.

"What?" I ask.

"Nothing. I just … didn't really ask him about Teddy before I adopted him. Funny to think about how things change, is all."

"Are you getting a dog because you're moving back to New York?"

Mom sets down her phone and reaches for the bowl of ice cream I brought out. "That's part of it, I suppose. This feels like a new chapter, being back in New York full-time. The last time we lived here permanently, we were just starting our family. I want to put down some more roots. And … I'm planning to step down as editor in chief at *Haute* next year."

"You are?"

She nods. "It's time."

"Wow. That's big."

My mom bought her fashion magazine when she was younger than me. She's worked there for longer than I've been alive.

"It is," she agrees. "It's been an amazing experience, but it has to end sometime. I want to focus on new adventures. Take a vacation without rescheduling multiple times. Get a dog. Do you think they'll have room for him or her as a patient at Hallsen Veterinary Clinic?"

I roll my eyes when she mentions my make-believe veterinary clinic. "Mom, you *have* to stop bringing that up."

She laughs. "Fine."

I steal the ice cream back, take a bite, and then lie back to stare up at the sky. You can't really see the stars here—the city lights are too bright.

"Why did you marry Dad?" I ask.

There's a noticeable pause as my question registers.

Mom rubs a finger against the side of her wineglass, creating a soft singing sound. "The easy answer is that your grandfather made an arrangement when I was sixteen."

"But you wouldn't have married him if you didn't want to."

Mom's smile is proud. "No, I wouldn't have."

"What's the hard answer?"

Something I've always wondered, honestly.

My parents don't have a perfect relationship, but they're perfect for each other. They have the sort of synergy that seems fated, not something you could manufacture with a fixed arrangement.

"I married him because he felt safe," Mom tells me. "Because we were equals in money and ambition. I'd seen Gigi stand in Grandfather's shadow my whole life, knowing that could never be me. It works for your grandparents, but I … I needed more. Not to be happy, just to make that part of my life bearable. That's what I thought then at least."

"And now?"

Mom studies me for a few seconds, and I know she's dying to ask why I'm asking. "Now, there's nothing scarier than the thought of losing him. This whole life I have? You and your brothers? It's all because of him. Nothing—not *Haute* or rouge or anything else—is more important than that. Me stepping back at *Haute* and your dad returning to Kensington Consolidated is because we want to spend more time with each other and you kids. We've both reached points in our careers where it makes sense to cut back."

I smother a smile. Only my parents would consider being COO of a multibillion-dollar company and running a luxury fashion house "cutting back."

Mom reaches for my left hand and turns it toward her.

I yank it away, blushing. "Mom!"

"Just checking. I didn't think you'd get engaged without telling me, but just in case."

"I *would* tell you if I was getting engaged. I'm *not* engaged.

I'm not even dating anyone. Partly because …" I contemplate how much to say. "It's hard, you know. Whenever I meet a guy, I have to wonder what he sees. Me or money. Your relationship with Dad always looks so easy. You make it look easy. Work too. All of it. So, so easy."

"Oh, honey." Mom's eyes fill with sympathy. "*None* of it is easy. It took me a long time to come to terms with my relationship with your father. If he'd been a little less stubborn, our marriage—your childhood—would have looked very different. And juggling work with being a mom and a wife? Finally dropping one of those balls feels like the biggest relief. But I've never been comfortable with sharing my struggles or insecurities. And I never wanted you or Kit or Bash to worry about anything you shouldn't be concerned with."

"I didn't get the project in Canada," I admit. "The job I really wanted. I found out yesterday."

"You're just starting your career, sweetheart. You have years—decades—to accomplish everything you want to."

Kit's getting a corner office and an assistant."

"That was your uncle Oliver's decision. He would have offered the same to you if you'd decided to work at the company."

I stare into my glass. "Do you think Dad's disappointed I didn't?"

"No, I don't."

My gaze lifts to look at my mom. "Are you disappointed I didn't want to work in fashion?"

"No, I'm not."

I nod once, the certainty in her voice quieting some of the doubt in my head.

"You want to know why?"

I nod again.

"Because there's nothing you could have done to make us prouder than to forge your own path, Lili. Everyone expected me to work at Ellsworth Enterprises, if I worked at all. Just like everyone thought your dad would spend his whole career at Kensington Consolidated. I didn't buy *Haute* because I'd always wanted to own a fashion magazine. I did it to prove to myself that I could. Just like your dad wanted to show that he could succeed in a building that didn't have his last name plastered on the side."

I smile. "The letters are too big, aren't they?"

Mom matches it. "Obnoxious really."

We sit in companionable silence for a few minutes, staring at the twinkling lights of the city.

"Did something happen with Cal on your trip?" she finally asks.

"We're not back together, if that's what you mean. He … he made me feel safe, but I was never scared to lose him."

Mom nods, letting the topic drop. She always offers advice when I ask for it, but never pushes me to talk. When I told her I broke up with Cal, she didn't ask if I was sure or what happened. She made frozen margaritas, French-braided my hair, and painted my nails.

"I met someone else," I admit.

A pause.

"Do I know him?"

I gnaw on my lower lip. "You've met him. Charles Marlborough. He was meeting with Asher when you and Dad first got back."

"The *duke*?"

I sigh. "He's more than that. It's just a … title."

"I didn't mean it like that, sweetheart. I'm just … surprised. You've never mentioned him before. I didn't realize you two knew each other."

Because I pretended not to know him. I almost smile at the memory of Charlie's annoyed expression.

"He was at Chloe's wedding. He went to college with her husband."

"Are you two dating?"

"*No.* No, we're not dating. I don't even—he's exasperating. Superior and opinionated and pompous and—" I stop talking when I see Mom smile. Clear my throat. "But he's the first guy who doesn't seem to care that I'm a Kensington. Even Cal … I think Cal cared; he just pretended not to. Charlie scares me. Scares me in a good way, I mean. Or maybe it's bad. Losing him … scares me."

I never really had him though.

He left me in Saint-Tropez with a hastily scribbled note. Walked away for a third time, and it's a pattern I can't keep repeating. Each time, it breaks my heart a little more. *He* breaks my heart a little more.

"I'd like to meet him. Again, I mean."

I eat more ice cream before telling her, "That probably won't happen. It's not going to work out."

"Why not?"

"I'm not … I don't see how it would. It's too complicated."

*He doesn't care enough.*

I'm too embarrassed to say it. I thought we were turning into something real that last night at his villa. But then he took off like he had always planned to, with the most basic of explanations, and now, it feels like I just saw what I wanted to.

"People say complicated like it's a bad thing," Mom muses. "But it just means more effort is required. And there's nothing worth having, Lili, that doesn't require some effort."

I nod.

I don't ask her what it means if I'm the only one willing to make an effort. I already know the answer.

# CHAPTER 29
## *Charlie*

Gran gets released from the hospital four days after she was admitted, refusing my suggestion she come stay at Newcastle Hall while she recovers and insisting her staff in London is capable of caring for her. Dr. Wallace clears the choice, and Elsie tells me privately that Gran already has a full slate of visitors lined up.

Blythe leaves for Florence a day later, informing me on her way out the door that Zara's family has a flat in the city so the trip will be "basically free." It's the first time she's acknowledged our conversation in the hospital cafeteria, and as irritating as I found her reckless spending before, I hate her worrying about money even more.

I meet with four investors in two days, none of them offering the magic number I'm looking for. The one that will wipe my debts

clean.

They know I need the money—there's no other reason I'd be shopping around—and they're preying on my position of weakness. But if I can't clear the debt, there's no point in selling.

I ride Kensington early each morning—the most exercise he's gotten in months—hoping I'll come up with some magical solution trotting through the moors. Mulling over Gran's suggested fix.

I was supposed to have more time. But so was my dad.

I'll need to get married eventually—unless I *really* want to disappoint the past seven Dukes of Manchester—and I need money now. Marrying an heiress would be a loan I wouldn't have to pay back. A safety net for Gran and Blythe.

And I thought I'd made peace with marrying for convenience. Thought I fully understood what my life would look like. But I'm learning there's a lot more to this role than I realized. I'm so sick of being stuck. Of there being an endless list of tasks, but never feeling any sense of accomplishment.

I also miss Lili.

She's the main reason I'm balking at the idea of marriage, if I'm being honest.

Getting married to a woman who wanted a title wasn't just a hypothetical before. It's what I fully expected to take place eventually.

But now, I've experienced what it's like to be with a woman who couldn't care less about my title. Who *knows* me in ways I've never let anyone else in.

I could call her. I don't have her number, but I could get it from Theo. Reach out, apologize for how I left, and then …

And then I don't know what.

I've been so consumed by figuring out how to get through this financial mess that I haven't considered what I'll do if I *do* manage to resolve everything. That feels too preemptive since nothing is.

Mid-week, an invitation to Kensington Consolidated's annual gala arrives. I spend an afternoon sitting in my father's—*my*—office, staring at it.

I don't think it's from Lili. Asher Cotes added me to the list, I'm guessing. But there's a high chance Lili will be there. It's an excuse to see her. To talk to her, in person, and at least leave things more resolved than they currently are.

After a moderately productive day of paperwork and a meeting with one of my father's barristers, I drive to the local village pub for dinner.

It's close to Newcastle, the trip taking less than ten minutes, but I haven't been here since becoming the duke.

The sight of it feels like stepping back in time a few centuries. A former coaching inn, the building has been lovingly preserved, original floors and beams intact, rather than renovated, like most of downtown Buckleby.

My arrival causes quite the stir—I figured it probably would, and it's one of the reasons I've avoided this place. I get recognized in London sometimes, but not like here. Here, *everyone* knows who I am.

A pretty blonde is drying glasses when I take a seat on one of the stools. She glances at me, does a double take, and then nearly drops the pint.

I groan internally, wishing it weren't too late to turn around and leave. But it is. Everyone who watched me arrive will also watch me leave.

"Hello, Your Grace." The blonde's tone is flirty as she rests her elbows on the counter right in front of me.

She leans forward, her full breasts nearly spilling out of her low-cut top. I look because it's that view or crane my neck back to stare at the ceiling, then immediately feel guilty.

Next, I think, *What the fuck?* because interest and appreciation are what I *should* be experiencing when looking at a woman's tits. Not the niggling sensation of doing something wrong.

"Good evening." I sound stiff, confusion and compunction holding me captive as I try to figure out when talking to—looking at—a woman who's clearly interested in me started to feel like a crime instead of a good time.

"Was wondering when you were going to stop by again, Charlie," she says when I add nothing else.

We've met before, apparently.

I can't remember if I've shagged her or not. Fig and I used to frequent this place whenever he came to visit over breaks and such, and plenty of those nights ended with us so pissed that we'd have to stumble home through the fields.

Can't remember her name either.

"Been busy," I tell her, giving my standard response to just about anything these days.

"I'm sure." She reaches for the empty glass abandoned by my elbow, her fingers lightly brushing my forearm in a touch that could be considered unintentional, but I doubt is.

The glass gets added to the rack of dirty dishes, and then her attention is back on me. "You ready to order?"

I pick the first dish I see on the menu—wood-fried chicken— and after a moment of deliberation, I add on an ale. She serves it to me immediately. It's a local one, brewed in town, the hoppy, fruity flavor one of the best things I've tasted in a while.

"Thanks …"

"Ada," the bartender supplies with a smile. "Let me know if you need anything else."

I nod, then take another sip.

A few minutes later, I hear my name.

I suppress a sigh, deciding I'll be eating whatever Martha cooks from now on, before I turn around.

Dr. Evans's wide smile creases the corners of his eyes. "It *is* you."

"Dr. Evans." I cough, some beer going down the wrong pipe. "What are you doing here?"

We're not that far from London, but farther than most people in the city would venture for a dinner.

My former surgeon glances toward one of the back booths, where a red-haired woman is sitting. "Getaway with the missus. She's a Galway girl, so London gets to be a little much for her at times." His gaze returns to me, peering closely enough to notice the dark circles under my eyes and the day of scruff that's grown. "How are you, Charles?"

I roll the pint glass in one palm. "All right. Knee is holding up."

He glances down at the leg he operated on. Smiles again. "Glad to hear it."

"I went to medical school." I blurt the sentence, not really meaning to say it. "Started medical school," I amend. "Only made it halfway through."

Dr. Evans's expression is sympathetic. I'm not sure if it's because he heard about my father's death and surmised that was the detour or because I sound as pathetic as I feel. "Halfway is still an accomplishment," he tells me.

I shrug, not wanting to be rude and disagree with him outright. It doesn't feel like much of one.

I miss that purpose. The ability to make a difference. Going to medical school wasn't an impulsive decision I hadn't thought through. It was an achievement I wanted, until my life fell apart.

"Are you considering finishing?" he asks me.

*Am I?*

I didn't know I was, until he asked. If I knew Blythe and my grandmother and all the staff employed by the dukedom were taken care of, it would be a serious thought.

"I don't know," I answer. "Maybe."

"It's a hard profession, Charles. I haven't met a single colleague who didn't consider an alternate path."

"It's more than that. Leaving medical school … it didn't have much to do with medical school."

Dr. Evans nods. "I heard about your father's passing. My condolences."

"Thank you." I hesitate before adding, "He died on the way into surgery." Something the obituary didn't mention. The collision had knocked him out cold, but he was still breathing when he arrived at the hospital.

The sympathy on his face shifts to understanding. "We can't save everyone, Charles. But we wouldn't save *anyone* if we didn't try."

That sentiment does nothing to improve my financial predicament. But it does make me feel a little better—for the first time in days. It might not be with medicine, but there's a lot I'm trying to save.

Ada delivers a steaming plate of chicken in front of me, and I twist around to thank her.

She gives me a flirty smile in response that, once again, prompts no reaction from me.

"I'll let you enjoy that," Dr. Evans says, clapping a hand on my shoulder. "Just wanted to say a quick hello. It was good to see you, Charles."

"You too, Dr. Evans," I tell him.

He reaches into his trouser pocket, retrieving a business card that he hands to me. "My friends call me Devon. And they *call*, if they ever want to talk."

I nod, taking the card. "Thanks Dr.—I mean, Devon."

"For whatever it's worth, Charles, I think you'd make an excellent doctor." He smiles, then heads back toward his wife.

He's only the second person to say that to me, and it means almost as much as it did the first time.

# CHAPTER 30

## *Lili*

Kensington Consolidated's annual gala is being held at one of the fancy hotels downtown. The venue and date change from year to year, ensuring there's plenty of speculation about both in New York society, along with who will score a coveted invitation.

I'd rather be somewhere else.

Outdoors at the very least. It's stuffy inside, even with the air-conditioning blasting, and already crowded, with more people continuing to pour through the ballroom doors. They look around the decorated space with wide eyes and awed expressions.

Mom and Aunt Hannah took charge of selecting the location and coordinating decor. Their combined tastes are evident in the elegant floral arrangements and the patterns of lights projected on the walls. String lights hang in loose drapes from the ceiling, creating a soft ambiance.

I smooth the front of my black silk dress, ensuring it's falling flat over the lace-edged slip underneath. I bought it for this event, and I knew it was perfect as soon as I saw it. It's decorated by a painted skyline of the city, the Statue of Liberty standing proud in the center. It feels like I'm wearing a literal work of art.

A uniformed waiter offers me one of the evening's custom cocktails—a Kensington Sour.

I take one, gulping half before I hear my name.

Asher's wife, Sophie, is winding her way through the crowd toward me. She's my godmother. She and Mom have been friends since meeting in business school.

I hug Sophie back tightly when she reaches me, then answer all of her excited questions about how my summer has been so far. She demands to see photos of Claremont Park and Chloe's wedding, *ooh*ing and *aah*ing over the few I have on my phone.

We get interrupted after about ten minutes. The woman wants to talk to me, not Sophie. She smiles good-naturedly as I make polite inquiries about the woman's kids and recent trip to Bern, well acquainted with the snobbery at these types of events.

I don't work at Kensington Consolidated, but this event isn't about the company. Not really. It's about the brand—the interest in my family that I can't escape. I know it's about to expand since Uncle Oliver is announcing my dad's new role tonight. More eyes will be on us than ever before, and it makes me want to leave for my next project as soon as possible. Flee the noise and find some quiet away from the Kensington legacy.

I talk to seven more people before spotting Bridget standing by one of the columns and excusing myself to rush over to her.

She giggles as I squeeze her tight. "A moment with New York's princess? Lucky me."

I roll my eyes as I release her. "Your dress is super cute."

"Thanks. I love yours too."

"Have you seen Fran or Tripp?" I ask.

Cal and Hugo arrived around the same time I did, but I haven't seen our other friends. Jasper is in Atlanta on a work trip.

"Not yet." Bridget sips her Kensington Sour. "You didn't tell me Charlie was coming."

My body freezes as my gaze darts around, scanning faces, until I find him. Talking to Tripp's dad, John, near the French doors that lead out onto the balcony.

Wearing a tuxedo, looking every inch the dignified aristocrat, is Charlie. In New York.

"You didn't *know* Charlie was coming," Bridget realizes.

I gnaw on my lower lip, likely ruining my lipstick. "No."

I was considering telling him about my trip to Dublin next week. Not in a *hey, can I come visit you* way, but more of a *I got the job I told you about* way. If he'd said *Hey, why don't you come visit?* I probably would've said yes, but I wasn't expecting it. I didn't think we'd be in the same place anytime soon—possibly ever again.

I'm mad—hurt—about how he left France. But I also miss him.

He didn't make then break any promises. I was too cowardly to tell him how I was feeling; that the time we'd spent together felt suspiciously like falling in love.

"Have you talked to him since …" Her voice trails off. She's probably unsure how to state the truth in delicate terms.

"No."

I haven't talked to Charlie since he left Saint-Tropez. And he decided to come to an event plastered with *Kensington*—literally, it's displayed everywhere—after telling me he wouldn't be coming to New York anytime soon.

After leaving my bed in the middle of the night without even bothering to wake me up. What the hell kind of "urgent business matter" happens at four a.m.?

"Maybe he wanted it to be a surprise?" Bridget suggests in a blatant attempt to make me feel better.

"Maybe," I mutter, glancing at the lectern on the stage before tossing back the rest of my cocktail.

I'm supposed to go up there when Oliver gives his speech about Dad returning to Kensington Consolidated.

I'm happy for Dad. Happy for him *and* Mom, embarking on this new, slightly simpler chapter of their busy lives. But I don't love the attention it'll draw to my family. The scrutiny that will inevitably extend to me with fresh speculation about who I'm dating and what restaurant I'll be spotted at next.

"Why didn't you mention you'd invited Charlie?" Hugo asks, appearing with a glass of scotch in one hand and a small plate of appetizers in the other.

I have no idea how he's planning to eat anything with no free hand. Everyone's still standing and mingling, the place settings at all the tables pristine.

Bridget's *shut up* motion is quick, but I catch it.

"It's fine, Bridge," I say. "Yes, Charlie is here. No, I did not invite him, nor did I know he'd be attending."

"Oh." Hugo hurriedly takes a sip of scotch.

I go to drink more, then frown when I find my glass empty. "I'll be back," I tell my friends, then weave through the crowd toward the bar. The *opposite* direction of where Charlie is standing.

Four people stop me on the way. The first three are virtual strangers I exchange more obligatory, polite small talk with. The fourth causes a wide smile to break out across my face.

"Grandpa!"

My grandfather has smelled like tobacco and old paper and leather for as long as I can remember. The same aroma that fills the study he seems to spend most of his time in despite the size of the massive mansion my dad grew up in.

I inhale the comforting scent deeply as he hugs me, kissing the top of my head. I'm almost as tall as him in my heels.

His smile is fond as he squeezes my shoulder. "How are you, Lili?"

"I'm good," I tell him.

I've always been closer with my dad's father than my mom's. The photo album of my early years, which Mom pulls out annually on my birthday, is filled with photos of me with Grandpa. Me asleep in his arms. Me perched on his lap behind his desk. Me playing with the blocks he set up in one corner of his study.

My brothers have always insisted that I'm his favorite, and I don't think they're wrong.

Maybe it's because I was his first grandchild. Maybe it's because I'm named after his late wife. Maybe it's because I buy him a birthday gift each year, and Bash and Kit usually forget.

Maybe it's because of that day at the cemetery.

Whatever the exact reason, we're close.

Two men pass by, one of them calling out, "Wonderful party, Arthur." Grandpa nods in acknowledgment, but his attention remains on me.

"How was Chloe's wedding?" Grandpa asks.

"It was good."

He raises both eyebrows. "An awful lot of *good* going around."

"It was incredible," I amend. "Wales was beautiful, and the venue Chloe picked looked like something out of a fairy tale. It was just … strange. I've known her since we were four. She was the first of my friends to get married."

Grandpa nods. "Don't be growing up too fast, Lili. You have plenty of time to accomplish anything you want to."

"So do you."

He smiles. "I'm glad you had a good trip. Even happier you're back in New York. You'll be at dinner next week?"

I shake my head. "Unfortunately not. I got an interview for the Dublin project. I'm flying there for a few days."

"Congratulations. That's fantastic news."

I nod. "I hope so." Glance at the stage again. "It's a big night."

"It is." Grandpa nods, his expression now neutral.

My dad and Uncle Oliver have a very different relationship with Grandpa than I do. One I've only deciphered bits and pieces of, mostly from whispered conversations between Mom and Aunt Hannah about Arthur *this* and Arthur *that*. Enough to tell me that Grandpa might be a doting grandfather, but he wasn't a doting father. Around me, Dad and Grandpa are always civil, often friendly, and occasionally strained.

For some reason, my dad deciding to return to Kensington Consolidated seems to be a strain.

"You wanted Dad to keep working in LA?" I ask.

Grandpa studies me, visibly weighing what to say. We usually confine our conversations to lighter topics. He's started gardening since he retired, so we talk about the outdoors a lot. Or books he's read and I've listened to. He's the one who recommended *Middlemarch* to me.

"I wish your father had never moved to LA," he finally replies.

"Then … aren't you glad he and Mom are moving back?"

"I am." Grandpa nods. "But I convinced myself leaving was what your father truly wanted. If that was the case, he wouldn't be coming back."

I think back to what Mom said, about her and Dad forging their own paths.

"Maybe he had to leave to know he wanted to come back."

Grandpa studies me, the corners of his eyes crinkling. "You're very wise, Lili."

I shrug modestly. "I *am* Arthur Kensington's granddaughter."

He chuckles.

"Hi, Dad."

"Crew."

I turn from Grandpa to smile at my father.

His eyes soften when he looks at me, and then his jaw tightens when he glances back at Grandpa. "Oliver is looking for you. He has some business associates who would like to meet you."

Grandpa kisses the top of my head again. "We'll talk later, Lili. I want to hear more details about your trip. And that Irish project."

"You know where to find me," I tell him.

He chuckles again before disappearing into the crowd.

Dad kisses my cheek. "You look beautiful, honey. Speech starts in a few minutes, okay?"

"Okay," I reply before he disappears back into the crowd.

I continue toward the bar that was my original destination, playing with the diamond bracelet on my wrist that belonged to

Dad's mom.

Cal is leaning one elbow beside the display of wines for guests to choose from, waiting for the bartender to finish mixing his drink. I order, then stop beside him.

He smirks. "Having fun?"

"Sort of. You?"

"This is the highlight of my summer, Kensington."

I roll my eyes. "How sad for you."

"Tripp said you got an exciting offer in Ireland. Congrats."

"They haven't formally offered me the position yet. But thanks." It'll be embarrassing if I don't get it, considering the number of people already congratulating me on it. I take my drink from the bartender. "How've you been?"

He slides a glance my way, like he's checking to see if I'm asking about what he thinks I'm asking about. Nods. "I broke up with Violet."

"Yeah. I … heard."

Fran told me when we had brunch a few days ago.

Cal nods. "I figured you had."

"Do you … want to talk about it?"

He exhales. "I liked Violet. But I started dating her to make myself move on from you. And turns out … that isn't exactly the most solid basis for a relationship, so …"

"Sorry," I say. Not sure exactly what I'm apologizing for but feeling like I owe him one anyway.

"Don't be. You were right about us. Right that we weren't right for each other, I mean. Seeing you with Charlie … you never acted that way with me."

My stomach roils at the sound of his name. I chug a healthy

amount of my drink to force it to settle.

Cal lifts both eyebrows, silently questioning my sanity.

"He's here," I explain. "For some fucking reason."

"Uh, for you?"

I scoff. "Not bloody likely."

"You sound British," Cal comments.

I glare at him. "Whose friend *are* you?"

He lifts both hands in a peace-making gesture. "Yours. Just saying … that's my guess. Why else would he come all this way?"

"Work?" I suggest.

I'm still not clear what the job description for a duke is, but it seems to take up a lot of his time. And Charlie had a meeting at Kensington Consolidated the last time he was in New York. He's somewhat connected to this business world.

I swallow another sip of Kensington Sour, avoiding looking toward the doors.

"If he's *not* here for you, he's a fucking fool, Lili."

I reach over and squeeze his forearm. "You're a good guy, Cal Winston."

"I know. It's exhausting."

My laugh is a soft huff as I watch my parents walk toward the stage with Oliver and Hannah. Grandpa follows with Bash. No sign of Kit yet.

Showtime.

"I'll see you later," I tell Cal, catching his nod before heading for my family.

# CHAPTER 31
## *Charlie*

A hush falls over the room as soon as Oliver Kensington appears onstage.

Everyone's taken their assigned seats, the classical music playing as ambient noise lowering to an inaudible level.

"Good evening, everyone," Oliver tells the attentive crowd. "On behalf of the board and my family, I'd like to welcome you to Kensington Consolidated's annual gala. As many of you know, we hold this event every year. Not only to celebrate our achievements as a company, but to also give back to the community. This year, all proceeds will go to Habitat for Humanity, a nonprofit that works tirelessly to build affordable housing. We're fortunate to have their CEO, Linda Wilson, with us tonight. I am sure she would be happy to answer any questions for anyone looking to become involved in the organization. And if you'd like to make a financial donation, please see Martin at the back table. Martin, wave a hand."

A middle-aged man standing to the left of the stage waves one hand.

"I'm proud to kick off the contributions with this commitment from Kensington Consolidated. We'll be donating a hundred million dollars toward this incredible cause."

Loud claps fill the room as the CEO covers her shocked face with her hands.

"Now, as many of you know, Kensington Consolidated is a family company. My earliest memories are visiting my father at the office. For as long as I can remember, I wanted to contribute to that incredible legacy. Serving as Kensington Consolidated's CEO for the past twenty-three years has been an immense honor. And in that official capacity, I have an announcement to make."

Whispers start to ripple through the room as Oliver pauses. Crew Kensington steps onstage, followed by a white-haired man I assume is Arthur Kensington. Lili appears next, followed by her mother and brothers. She's smiling, but it looks a little forced. Not the carefree one I got used to seeing.

"Come over here, Crew." Oliver claps his brother on the shoulder when he joins him at the lectern. "I'm thrilled to announce that, effective immediately, Crew will be rejoining Kensington Consolidated's board and serving as the company's COO. Hollywood's loss, our gain. You had a longer career out there than most, little brother."

Lili's father rolls his eyes good-naturedly as laughter echoes through the room. He says a few words to his brother, shakes his dad's hand, kisses his wife, then hugs his kids. They look like a whole happy family up there, loving and supportive.

I realize this was one of the "internal changes" Asher referred to during our phone call.

After the Kensingtons leave the stage and take seats at the head table, dinner gets served. The starter is a cantaloupe and cucumber soup, followed by a plate of salmon, served with asparagus, radish, and pickled strawberries.

Dessert is a buffet.

I walk out onto the huge balcony rather than wait in line, pausing when I spot the figure standing and staring at one of the marble sculptures.

Hands in pockets, I head for Lili, only stopping when I'm a couple of feet from her. "They need some plants out here."

It's all stone—the floor, the railings, the sculptures.

She stiffens, recognizing my voice, but doesn't look away from the work of art. I study it too. A man, draped in a toga and holding three arrows. "Ares?"

"Apollo. He was the god of archery."

"People used arrows in war," I say, feeling the need to defend my guess for some reason.

Perhaps the naked disdain in her voice.

I have my answer as to whether Lili is angry about the way I left Saint-Tropez. The realization isn't entirely depressing. She cares if she's mad. If she were indifferent—or worse, over it—it wouldn't have mattered when or how I left.

"Did you bring a date?" Lili asks, sounding bored.

My head rears back with shock. *The fuck?* She thinks I'd bring another woman to her family's event?

My tone is deceptively calm as I answer, "No."

Lili clicks her tongue. "I'm sure Beatrice would have loved a trip to New York."

My confusion—and irritation—grows. "I wouldn't know. Since I didn't ask her."

She hums, then drains the glass she's holding, her hand falling back to her side.

The dress she's wearing is black with a white cityscape that's unmistakably New York. I'm not sure if she meant it as a reminder, but it serves as one. This is her home. And her parents are moving here, only strengthening her ties to it.

I came all this way to chase after a woman who will always live on this side of the Atlantic and who—if her annoyance is anything to go by—doesn't even *want* to see me.

"What are you doing here?" Lili asks, echoing my thoughts.

She finally turns to face me, the force of her beauty hitting me full-on. Blue eyes. Dark hair. Full lips.

It's the same thrill as jumping off a cliff—an adrenaline rush, followed by a hard landing.

I've seen her naked. Seen her laugh. Seen her dance. Seen her swim. Seen her scowl.

But I've never seen her cry before.

I think I imagined it at first. But then another droplet of water streaks down her cheek, hesitating, then falling to the brick patio.

Lili sniffs. Blinks rapidly before handing her empty glass off to a passing waiter.

It feels like I'm talking around a mouthful of gravel as I ask her what's wrong. Is she upset about … us? Is something else going on? I'm completely confused, but I don't think admitting that is going to help anything.

She repeats, "What are you doing here, Charlie?" rather than answering my question.

I opt for the simplest answer. "I got an invitation."

Lili mutters, "Asher," under her breath, confirming my suspicions about who sent it. Her eyes narrow. "Why didn't you tell me you were coming?"

I stare at her. "What are you talking about? I texted you."

She didn't answer, so I assumed she was mad at me. That only strengthened my resolve to see her in person. I never assumed she didn't receive it.

Pink streaks her cheeks. "I-I didn't get it. I delete texts from numbers I don't have saved."

For some reason, I think she's lying. Not about not getting my text, but something else. She's fiddling with her bracelets, the way she does when she's nervous or unsure.

"Theo sent it to me," I tell her, like that's necessary information.

It should be. My conversation with him went something like this:

> **ME:** I need a favor.
>
> **THEO:** Hey! Sure. What is it?
>
> **ME:** Don't ask any questions, please.
>
> **THEO:** Got it.
>
> **ME:** Can you send me Lili's phone number?
>
> **THEO:** I don't have her number.
>
> **ME:** Your wife does.
>
> **THEO:** You want me to steal it from Chloe's phone?
>
> **THEO:** Have you talked to Lili since you left France?
>
> **THEO:** Is everything all right?
>
> **ME:** Do you know what a question is, Hughes?
>
> **THEO:** 212-535-1012
>
> **ME:** Thanks.
>
> **THEO:** Don't cock up again!

Bloody embarrassing.

"If you wanted my number, you should have asked *me* for it before you snuck out in the middle of the night."

I wince, rubbing the back of my neck. "There was an—"

"'Urgent business matter.' Yeah. Got it."

Even without the air quotes she uses, I'd have gotten her doubt, thanks to the heavy emphasis she places on the excuse.

"I didn't want to leave, Lili," I say softly.

"Well, we were both going to. Right?"

*Right* is a rhetorical question. We both know the answer. I knew how different our lives looked when this thing between us started. I just never expected it to matter this much.

"Lili!" A teenage girl skips toward us. "Your grandmother is looking for you. She wants to introduce you to some friends, and *please* don't make me go back in there without you because she sort of scares me." She shoots Lili a pleading smile, then glances at me. "Hi! I'm Wren."

"I'm Charlie," I tell her.

Wren gasps dramatically. "The duke? My mom and Aunt Scarlett were just talking—"

"Where's Gigi?" Lili asks quickly.

"This way," Wren replies.

Lili glances at me. "Have a safe trip home, Charlie."

Then, she heads inside.

A chill creeps across my skin that has nothing to do with the blast of air-conditioning as she and Wren enter the building through the nearest door.

A sense of loss. It feels like watching a boat sail away that I really, really wanted to be aboard.

I walk past the statue of Apollo and continue to the railing.

We're only up one story, so there's not much of a view. A small, walled garden juts off from the hotel's lobby. Around and above, towering skyscrapers. I feel like I'm standing in front of Kensington Consolidated's headquarters again, dwarfed by their staggering height.

I prefer looking around and seeing stone walls. Grassy hills. Rugged moors. Wooden gates. That scenery will always be home to me. Even busy London feels different to this, where it seems the entire city could collapse around you like a tower of blocks.

"Lot quieter out here, isn't it?"

I glance to the left, my spine straightening and my stomach tumbling as Crew Kensington approaches me.

We met—very briefly—at the Red, White, and Blue party his mother-in-law threw.

"Warmer too," I reply. The heavy layers of my suit have trapped a lot of humidity inside.

Lili's father nods, stopping beside me to take in the same limited view. "I'm looking forward to winter. Been a little while since I experienced one here." He glances at me. "You look familiar. Have we met?"

"I'm Charles Marlborough. We met at the Fourth of July party in the Hamptons."

"That's it." Crew snaps his fingers. "Nice to see you again. Had to be a bit awkward for you."

I stare at him, totally taken aback. If Lili told her father what I said about her, there's no way he'd be aiming a friendly smile toward me right now.

"Because you're British," Crew clarifies.

I must look confused.

"Oh," I realize.

"Sorry. Dad joke." He sips from the glass tumbler he's holding. "What do you do, Charles?"

I decide to be honest. "Right now, I'm trying to figure out how much I care about doing exactly what my father wanted me to do."

"Ah, parental expectations." Crew smiles. "Been there. Your old man used to pulling all the strings?"

"He was."

"Was? Is he …"

I nod. "He died last year."

"Very sorry to hear that. Sounds like he left you with a lot."

"In some senses."

A lot of stress? Guilt? Uncertainty? Expectations? All yeses. Money? Advice? Support? Love? Not really on any of that.

"My father manipulated me and my brother for years. Pitted us against each other. Made everything a competition and changed the rules whenever he felt like it. At one point, I left. Turned my back on most of what he'd wanted for me and walked away, just to prove I could."

"Do you regret it?"

"No. But I'm not sure I'd do it the same way all over again." He looks down, swishing amber liquid around in his glass. The huge cube of ice clinks against the side. "Leaving didn't make me care any less about what he thought. Didn't make us any closer or me any freer from his expectations. Or keep my father from making his opinions about my choices known."

"At least I don't have to worry about that last part," I say.

Crew chuckles. "True."

"Charles! You made it!" Asher Cotes is strolling toward us, the wide smile on his face evidence of the perpetual cheer I've come to associate with him. "And good, you've met Crew."

"We've met before," Crew says. "At Josephine's celebration of his countrymen no longer running this place."

I smile wryly.

Lili might look like her mother, but she shares her dad's sense of humor.

"Way to be a terrible host, Crew," Asher says. "Ask about soc—I mean, football instead."

"You follow football?" Crew asks me.

"Only Premier League," I tell him. "You should have bought part of Man U rather than AC Milan."

Crew smiles. "Who told you I own part of AC Milan?"

Another voice joins our conversation before I have to answer. I assumed his ownership was common knowledge, but I guess not.

"Why am I not surprised you two are hiding out here?" Oliver Kensington approaches, yanking his tie so it loosens a little.

"Relaxing," Crew corrects. "Not hiding."

"Stargazing really," Asher adds.

They knock fists.

Oliver rolls his eyes, then turns to me and sticks out a hand. "Oliver Kensington."

"Charles Marlborough," I reply.

"Nice to meet you, Charles."

We shake hands.

Oliver bears a striking resemblance to Crew—strong genes in this family—but his demeanor couldn't be more different. His mannerisms remind me of my father actually. Nonplussed and assured, but a little uptight.

"Charles?"

I glance to the left, my jaw tightening when I see my mother standing a few feet away.

"Excuse me," I say to Oliver.

He nods, then turns to talk with Crew and Asher.

I walk toward Georgia, who's wearing a floor-length gown and a diamond necklace. Her hand is looped in Derek's elbow.

"Hello … Mum."

I'm never sure what to call her to her face. Mum seems too warm. Georgia too cold.

"Charles," she repeats. "What are you doing here?"

"I was invited." I give her the same answer I offered Lili and hate the comparison.

One woman means a lot more to me than the other, and it isn't the one standing in front of me.

"Oh. You—I didn't know you were in town."

"It was last minute," I answer.

I wait for her to ask more questions. But she doesn't. She doesn't bring up Blythe either.

Georgia simply stares, like she doesn't know what else to say to me.

Maybe she doesn't. We're so far from a traditional mother-son relationship; it's almost laughable.

"All's well in England?" Derek, surprisingly, is the one who speaks next.

"It's fine," I tell him. "Enjoy the rest of your evening," I say to them both.

Then, I head for the doors, having had my fill of the balcony.

My mom doesn't try to stop me, and I resolve to stop trying with her.

# CHAPTER 32
## *Lili*

"Let's go," I suggest impulsively, slipping my heels back on under the table.

Hugo swallows the last bite of his mini éclair. Raises both eyebrows. Glances around the crowded ballroom. "It's only eleven."

"We've eaten, socialized … I'm over it. Let's go to a club."

Hugo glances at Fran like, *You wanna take this one?*

She clears her throat. "I saw you talking to Charlie out on the balcony. Did it go …" Her voice trails off as she waits for me to supply the rest of the sentence.

"I don't want to talk about it."

Immature maybe, but accurate.

I don't want to think about it either. And I want to *not think* about it while dancing at a club with my best friends because we're young and fun and *single*, and now seems like the perfect time to

celebrate that.

"Oh-kay." Fran manages to make that syllable last forever, then looks at Hugo like, *You're up.*

I huff, exasperated by their silent—and audible—conversation.

"Looks like we've got a runner," Hugo comments.

We've all been runners at one point or another. It's a shorthand Bridget came up with in high school, when we first started going out in the city. Speed—jogger, runner, sprinter—conveys urgency. You say you're going for a jog in the morning if a drunk guy asks for your number a third time. Your cousin is a future Olympic sprinter if he moves your drink for you so it "doesn't get knocked over." That was a line Fran used one night out in Saint-Tropez.

"I'm a jogger. *At most.*"

And I'm not fleeing from Charlie because anything he said made me feel uncomfortable. I'm desperate to be anywhere else— anywhere he's not—because he's going to come back in from the balcony at some point, and it'll feel like my heart was shoved into a blender all over again.

"I'll be in the limo," I announce, standing. "Leaving in five minutes."

I head for the exit without waiting for any responses, snagging a bottle of Dom Pérignon out of one of the boxes stacked behind the bar on my way out. The busy bartenders don't even notice.

Deep lungfuls of night air help clear my head a little as I descend the steps. It feels as hot out as it did when I arrived three hours ago, which is awfully annoying.

Halfway down, I pause to pop the bottle. The cork flies … somewhere, bubbles fizzing over my hand and dripping down onto the worn stone stairs. Some specks of foam land on my dress too.

"Lili?"

Cal is standing with two guys leaning against the railing. Both look vaguely familiar, but I'm not able to come up with names. One of them is smoking, the lit cigarette dangling lazily between two fingers.

"Hey." I wave, then hiccup, giggling as I cover my mouth with one hand.

Cal peels away from the other guys, missing the amused look they exchange. The smoking one winks at me, and I flip him off.

*That*, Cal sees.

"You okay?" he asks cautiously, stopping at the same stair level.

"Fabulous," I answer. "When did you start smoking?"

"I don't smoke," Cal tells me. "I was just talking to Levi and Damian."

Yes, those are their names. I feel triumphant, like I was the one who just solved the mystery of their anonymity. Take another sip of champagne, to celebrate.

"We're going clubbing. Are you coming?"

He glances behind me. "We?"

I swig more champagne. The glass bottle feels extra slippery, more condensation appearing in the humid air. "Everyone."

Cal stares at me. He looks as dignified as when he first arrived. Tie straight. Cuff links intact. His blue twill shirt is perfectly smooth, not a wrinkle in sight.

I, on the other hand, look nothing like when I showed up. My hair is frizzing. My lipstick gone. My dress is creased and sprinkled with droplets of champagne.

I swallow more. Probably best to climb into the limo with an empty bottle.

"Where's Charlie?" Cal asks.

His name burns my throat worse than the bubbles.

"Charlie lives in England. Probably in a castle because he's a duke." I swing the bottle of champagne, spilling more. "Did you know that he's a duke? He doesn't like to talk about it, but he is. And dukes marry British girls who care about titles. They know nothing about Greek mythology though. Did *you* know Apollo is the god of archery?"

Cal drags a palm down his face. Mutters something that sounds a lot like, *Fuck my life*.

"You're drunk, Lili," he informs me.

"Not yet." I take another sip of champagne. More of it spills onto my dress. "Planning to get there soon though."

"Yeah … I think you're already there."

"Nope." I pop the *P*, then take another step down the stairs.

Cal grabs my arm, making me stumble. Or maybe I was already unsteady. "Let's go inside. Eat some dessert. Drink some water."

"*No*. I'm leaving."

"Yeah, that's probably better," he agrees. "Go home and get some rest—"

"I'm going *clubbing*, Callahan. You can come with me, but you can't stop me."

I take another step. *Try* to take another step rather. It moves right before my foot lands. We were due for another major earthquake in New York City, I guess. It's been centuries.

Except I'm not falling. And the world isn't shaking.

Cal is carrying me, bridal-style, down the rest of the stairs.

One of the guys he was with—Levi or Damian—wolf-whistles.

I flip them off again. "I don't like those guys."

Cal half smiles. "They like you."

My nose wrinkles. "No, they don't."

"Yeah, they do. Levi was in the middle of asking me if you were single when you came out here."

"I'm sorry."

"Don't be. I just … wasn't sure what to tell him."

I deliberate, then decide. "I am. Single. We didn't get this far, remember?" I kick my feet, the way I imagine a bride doing.

"I wasn't wondering about me, Lili."

People *really* want to talk about Charlie tonight.

It feels easier, discussing it with Cal, than it did inside with Fran and Hugo.

Must be the night air. Nothing to do with the near empty bottle of champagne.

"It didn't hurt this bad when we broke up. I think … I think because Charlie brought the book."

"What book?" Cal sounds confused.

"*Middlemarch.* I gave you a copy." After a moment of deliberation, I add, "It was a bad gift. You should have hated it."

"I didn't hate it."

"Yeah, you did. And you should've. And I should've wanted to give you something different."

Cal sets me down carefully next to the limo. I lean against it heavily as he pulls the door open.

"Where did he bring it?"

I exhale. "It was in his bag. In France. I was … snooping, and I saw it."

I crawl into the limo, kick off my heels, and sip more champagne.

Cal eyes the bottle like he's contemplating wrestling it away from me. I'd like to see him try.

"Maybe you two should start a book club," he suggests.

I snort. "I'm done with that … *cad*."

"Okay, Lili."

He doesn't believe me.

I slump down on the cool leather, staring blankly ahead at the black privacy divider and trying to remember the name of the nightclub in Brooklyn where we went for Hugo's birthday two years ago. That place was fun.

And then I'm flying forward, a panicked shout of my name the last sound I register before everything goes black.

# CHAPTER 33

## *Lili*

The buzz of fluorescent lights is obnoxious. And blinding. The brightness sears into my eyeballs, making spots dance across my vision. And the humming is endless, burrowing into my brain like a drill.

A woman with curly black hair, wearing a white coat, appears around the curtain, distracting me from the irritating beam. The drone I can still hear.

"Hi, Elizabeth. I'm Dr. Moore. How are you feeling?"

"My head hurts. Otherwise, I feel fine." Same thing I told the EMTs and the other two doctors who checked me over since I arrived at the hospital.

"Do you remember what happened?" she asks.

"A car swerved to avoid a biker and hit the back of the limo I was in."

Dr. Moore nods. "Very good. There doesn't appear to be any

issues with your memory."

"So, I'm … fine?" I ask.

"You likely have a grade 2 concussion. Your CT scan didn't show any bleeding or skull fractures. We still need to get your forehead stitched, but you should be feeling back to normal in a few days."

I lift one hand, tentatively touching the gauze taped there.

Since I wasn't wearing a seat belt, my head slammed into the counter above the minibar in the limo. I haven't asked to see the cut, but one of the EMTs assured me it would only require a couple of stitches and I'd barely have a scar.

Considering the hysterical scene surrounding me, I'm not sure I can trust he wasn't just trying to keep everyone calm.

"You're still not experiencing any nausea? Double vision? Dizziness?"

All I can think about is Charlie crouched beside me at Chloe's wedding, asking similar questions. No offense to Dr. Moore, but I preferred him as my physician.

"No."

My stomach's a little queasy, but I think that's mostly due to the amount of champagne in my system.

"Excellent." She scribbles something on my chart, then hangs it back off the end of the bed. "You have quite a … concerned cohort out in the hallway. I can update them, or I can let them in for a few minutes. Your call."

"They can come in," I say.

My parents must be frantic. My friends worried. Technically, the accident wasn't my fault, but it feels like it was. And it happened at a very public event, attended by my entire family and almost everyone they know …

My stomach heaves. I'm tempted to call out to Dr. Moore—tell her I changed my mind—but the door is already opening.

Mom rushes in first. Followed by Dad, Kit, Bash, Grandpa, Aunt Hannah, Uncle Oliver, and my cousins, Rory and Wren. Behind them, Fran, Hugo, Bridget, Tripp, and Cal enter.

No Charlie, and I don't realize I was looking for him until the disappointment of his absence settles in my stomach.

*It's a good thing*, I try to convince myself. Means the accident must not have been the spectacle I was worried about.

Because I think he'd be here if he knew about it.

"I'm fine," I repeat over and over again as they all fawn over me.

Feeling stupid and selfish for wishing someone else were here when they all showed up for me.

"All right—whoa!" Another doctor in navy scrubs enters my room. Tries to enter my room rather. He doesn't make it past the threshold because there's nowhere for him to go. "I'm going to …"

I miss whatever else he says because he's still holding the door open.

And standing in the hallway, talking to Asher, is Charlie.

He looks terrible. His usual level of hotness, I mean, but with haunted eyes and messy hair and a missing suit jacket.

I stare until he catches me, his features freezing with surprise, then softening slightly into concern. His eyes dip down to look me over—so briefly, like the day we met—and then are back on mine.

Someone's talking to me. Squeezing my hand.

"Lili! Lili!"

I hum, forcing myself to focus on Mom's face.

"Do you want me to stay with you, honey? While you get your stitches?"

My family's oblivious, but my friends have figured out my distraction, glancing between me and the hallway.

I clear my throat. "Could I get a minute first? Just a minute alone?"

I aim the question at the doctor. He looks relieved, honestly, to have a reason to back out of the crowded space.

"I'll check on another patient and be back shortly," he tells me.

Then, he leaves, the door shutting before I have the chance to look at Charlie again.

"Are you feeling worse?" Mom asks.

"She looks paler," Wren remarks.

"We should get a second opinion," Grandpa suggests, pulling out his phone. "I know the chief of neurology at—"

"*I'm fine*," I announce. Louder than I mean to talk.

Everyone's silent now, staring at me.

My eyes are fixed on the ceiling. "Can someone get Charlie?" I ask the plaster.

More silence.

"The duke?" Bash whispers to Kit.

At least, I think he means to whisper. It's normal volume in the quiet room.

"I will!" Fran chirps.

No one moves.

"Uh, you all"—Fran gestures toward my family—"are blocking the door."

My mom squeezes my hand one final time. "We'll be right out in the hallway, honey."

I nod. "Thanks."

They file out one by one, until the room is empty, except for the buzzing that won't quit.

I stare at the ceiling until the door reopens, and Charlie steps inside.

His throat works a couple of times as he walks toward me, crossing the small room in a couple of strides.

"Hey." His voice is rough around the edges, the raspy way it sounds first thing in the morning.

I struggle to sit up straighter. "Hi."

I can't do anything about the ugly gown or the gauze on my forehead, but I can at least have decent posture.

Charlie's mouth opens. Closes. Opens. Closes.

Obviously, he has no idea what to say to me. I was extra cold to him at the gala, mostly because the shock of seeing him from afar was nothing compared to the torture of talking to him.

He came because of business. Because Asher had invited him.

I've never wished it were possible to undelete a text more because I'm dying to know what he sent to me. Was that the only reason he gave?

"Wanna sit?" I pat the pale green hospital blanket.

He swallows again before he perches on the edge of the mattress, resting both elbows on his thighs. "I, um … I …" His voice trails off.

"You didn't have to come, you know."

*But I'm glad you did*, gets caught in my throat. His smell is familiar, and the scent sets off fireworks in my stomach.

I'm still a little tipsy. Reeling from the collision and the commotion that took place in the past hour. And suddenly, unexpectedly shy, like a teenager meeting her boy-band crush after a concert.

"I wanted to," he tells me.

I raise an eyebrow.

"Well, not *wanted* to," he amends. "I hate that you're here. But I … needed to see that you were okay."

"I'm okay. Might have an ugly Frankenstein scar on my face, but I'll survive."

Charlie leans forward and kisses my forehead, right next to the gauze. So softly that it's lighter than the brush of a feather. A tickle almost. But heat spirals through my chest and pools in my belly, like he touched me much more intimately and much less politely.

"You'll always be beautiful, Lili."

*Beautiful.*

The first word he ever said to me.

Unshed tears burn my eyes, like I'm staring into the overhead lights again.

"Did you, uh, have fun at the gala?" I ask, fighting through the wave of emotion.

Charlie chuckles, but it's a hollow laugh, lacking any real amusement. "No. If you could stop ending up in the hospital during every formal event we attend, that would be bloody wonderful."

He says it like we'll attend more events together, which won't be the case. Because we live in different places and want different things. And what was supposed to be a fun anecdote about a summer fling somehow turned into a tragedy.

*I love him.*

The thought appears in my mind. It's not a question or a consideration. It's already happened, like a true fall. One you hardly notice, and then you've landed.

It's terrifying. So much scarier than any other I've ever

experienced. It feels like I'm standing on a spinning merry-go-round with nothing to hold on to.

Hugo was right; I'm running.

When I've run before, it was always easy. A relief even. Decision made—on to someone new. It's how I knew breaking up with Cal was the right decision. Because I was sad, in the aftermath, but I also felt better. I'd stopped forcing something simply because he was an old friend and my family approved of him, and it was the right decision.

And I knew, maybe the same second that Charlie approached me in that stable, that this would be different. I didn't want him to leave. I was disappointed when Chloe called and our first conversation ended. Since he departed France—essentially doing the running for me—I haven't felt relieved once.

He's going to leave again. He's only here for—I don't even know how long he's staying. I was too busy reeling from his proximity to ask. But I know it won't be for long.

My next project's location hasn't been decided. There are multiple opportunities to consider, and I refuse to be the girl who reshapes her identity for a guy. I'm not going to relocate to England and *hope* that he's ready for a relationship sometime soon.

I pick up a corner of the blanket and twist it around my thumb. "Thank you for coming. It means a lot. But … you should go, Charlie."

He has family here too. Maybe he can see them while he's in town.

He's silent for a few seconds.

"You want me to go?" Charlie doesn't sound offended. More … resigned. Like he knew the request was coming.

"You should, yeah. I promise I'll avoid limos for a while." I keep my tone light, already close to losing it.

My eyes feel hot, tears on the horizon again. I wanted to talk to him, but now, I'm not sure what to say.

I'm embarrassed he's seeing me like this. That I got drunk and tried to go clubbing because I couldn't stand to stay in the same room as him. Mortified I keep playing the part of a damsel in distress when I want him to see me as strong and capable. Humiliated I can't admit to him how I really feel because I'm terrified he doesn't feel the same.

*Weak.*

I feel weak, and I've never felt weak before. I've felt stupid, struggling to read simple sentences. I've felt defeated, seeing people's faces change when they hear my last name.

But there's always been strength beneath. I might get sick of some of the attention, but I'm proud of my family. I'm proud to be a Kensington, and I've always felt like one.

Brave. Bold. Capable.

I don't feel brave or bold or capable right now.

"Okay," he says. Charlie's expression is impassive. I can't tell what he's thinking. "And avoid wearing heels."

I manage a smile. "No promises, but I'll walk carefully."

"Okay." He weaves our fingers together for a few tantalizing seconds, squeezing twice. I stare at the gold signet ring on his pinky. It's stamped with what I assume is his family crest. But I don't know for sure—I never asked. "Take care, Elizabeth Kensington."

I swallow. "You too, Charles Marlborough."

He nods, stands, then … leaves. Again.

I turn my head to the right, facing the solitary window, letting the cotton pillowcase catch my tears.

The door opens again a minute later.

I don't look. I just sent away the one person I want it to be, so it doesn't really matter. I'm too drained to care who else is seeing me like this.

"Oh, Lili." Bridget's voice is tender as she takes the spot Charlie just vacated.

I say nothing.

She exhales. "The doctor's wondering about your stitches."

I swipe at my cheeks. "Send him in."

The sooner I get stitches, the sooner I can get out of here.

"He's still in the hallway."

We're not talking about the doctor anymore, I know.

"Doesn't matter."

"What are you doing, Lili?" she asks softly.

I'm running. Because it feels like if I stay in this place, I'll shatter.

# CHAPTER 34
## *Charlie*

hen I walk out of Lili's hospital room, everyone's staring at me.

Her parents. Her brothers. Her uncle. Her grandfather. Her godfather.

Her friends, at least, know who I am. Have some sense of our relationship.

But Lili's family members all look significantly less friendly than they did the previous times I met them. They're all worried about Lili, and none of them have any clue why I'm here.

I couldn't *not* come. I overheard a couple at the gala say that there had been a car accident involving Elizabeth Kensington, and I arrived outside right as the ambulance was pulling away from the curb. Cal told me which hospital they were taking her to. Even offered me a ride, but I'd rented a car at the airport when I arrived this morning that I drove here.

She asked for me, same as she had the last time she got injured. This time, it wasn't for my medical opinion.

And I … froze. Everything I came here to tell her—apologies about how I'd left France, explanations about why I'm so consumed by my family and my role—got sidetracked during her chilly greeting. It felt like the return of the Elizabeth who purposefully pretended not to know me on multiple occasions. Like the past few weeks had been wiped away and we were back in the same place where we'd started.

In her hospital room just now, she was different. Softer. But still withdrawn. And clearly shaken from the accident that had ended with her in the hospital … again.

Maybe it's fate—that, as an aspiring doctor, I'd end up with the most accident-prone woman on the planet.

Except I'm *not* a doctor. I gave up that dream to deal with all the problems plaguing me. Problems I was planning to share with Lili. Problems that sound like excuses now.

And I'm not *with* her. I lost any chance with her. Bungled this from the beginning because I was so arrogantly certain that I'd never fall. That emotional distance was one way in which my father and I *are* similar.

Tripp, surprisingly, is the first person who approaches me. "Good to see you, man," he tells me, clasping my hand and giving me a hard pound on the back.

Cal does the same gesture.

"Thanks again for …" I clear my throat.

Cal nods. "I knew she'd want you here."

That makes one of us. I'm not sure if I made anything better by showing up.

There's no sign of Jasper, but Fran gives me a hug. Bridget disappeared into Lili's room after I left it.

"I've got to … head out." It's a pathetic farewell, but I'm not currently in the best shape.

My red-eye landed in New York at nine a.m. I checked into my hotel as early as I could, passed out for several hours, then put on this tux. This evening didn't play out the way I'd hoped it would, and I've spent too much time in hospitals recently.

I'm expecting expressions to harden when I announce I'm leaving, but they all still look sympathetic. Makes me wonder what the hell Lili told them about us.

I stop to say goodbye to Asher, avoiding meeting Lili's family's eyes. Her mom and aunt are whispering, and her brothers are both frowning.

"Thank you for the invitation."

Asher nods. Then lifts an eyebrow. "I didn't realize how well you knew the family."

"I don't really. Just … her."

He opens his mouth like he wants to say something, then thinks better of it and shuts it. "Been keeping an eye out for any investment news with your hotels …"

I avert eye contact. "I haven't sold."

"If you're still wanting to, I have some contacts in Europe who I think would be interested. They haven't done much in hospitality, but they prioritize quality over quantity. Might be a good fit. I can get you their contact information, if you'd like?"

"I'd appreciate it," I tell him.

I trust Asher's judgment. And I'm so sick of treading water. If it's a deal that involves a fair price—the amount the shares are actually worth—I'd seize it like a life preserver.

"Great. I'll get it to you on Monday."

"Thank you."

We shake hands before I continue down the hallway. As soon as I'm around the corner and out of sight, I let my shoulders slump. Press the button for the lift and lean against the wall, covering my yawn with one hand.

Everything feels raw after my conversation with Lili. I'm still sorting through the panic she was injured, the relief that's she okay. The uncertainty of not knowing what to say.

"Charles."

I turn at the sound of my name, then stiffen.

Crew Kensington is walking toward me. There's no sign of the friendliness that was on his face when we spoke at the gala as he looks me up and down before stopping a couple of feet away. His eyes—the same blue as Lili's—search my face.

The lift arrives, doors opening with a ding.

I don't move.

"When we spoke earlier, I wasn't aware you were on the sort of terms with my daughter that merited a trip to the hospital."

He pins me with an intense stare, broad shoulders squared. I have maybe an inch on him, but I don't feel very tall right now.

Crew Kensington is an intimidating man. I've been told I'm one, too, but I don't feel very powerful right now, either.

"I just wanted to make sure she was okay."

He cocks his head, considering that. "I don't have an issue with you coming here, Charles. I'm wondering why you're leaving."

"She ... asked me to."

Crew doesn't appear surprised by the revelation. "Lili has always been independent. Creative. A little unpredictable. In twenty-five years, I've never been sure what she'll say or do next. Her asking for you … that tells me you're important to my daughter. Very important. And my daughter is very important to me, Charles."

I swallow at the subtle threat in that last sentence. The tone of a billionaire accustomed to deference. "She's very important to me too."

His stern expression softens a fraction. "Then, as someone who fell in love with the woman who raised Lili, I'll offer you a little free advice: It's not going to be easy. That's not a reason to give up. That's a reason to fight harder. She's stubborn. You want a chance? Be stubborner."

"So … I should stay?"

Crew shakes his head. "Listen to her, Charles, but stand up to her too. I doubt you came all this way to hear my brother give a bad speech."

"I didn't."

This time, he cracks a small smile. "You showing up here said a lot. Give her some time to realize it. Sometimes, we have to let things go to realize they're what we really want. If your father was anything like mine, he told you love was the least important thing in life. Don't believe him. Decide your own priorities."

I nod.

"She told you I own part of AC Milan, huh?"

"She did," I confirm.

"My boys barely give a shit." Crew sighs, like that's been a long-term source of disappointment for him. "If you ever want to go to a game, let me know. I don't make it to as many as I'd like, and it would be nice to witness one with a real fan who's not more interested in the snack bar."

I haven't been to a football match since my dad died. We used to go to a lot of games together. He was an avid Aston Villa fan. His life priorities went something like the dukedom, his kids, gambling, and football. The order changed.

And Crew is right; I don't think love was anywhere on the list. Certainly not the romantic kind. He never remarried or even introduced me and Blythe to a woman.

"I will," I say, my throat suspiciously thick.

"Crew, where …" Scarlett Kensington's voice trails off when she sees I'm the one talking to her husband.

She continues approaching us, tucking a piece of her long, dark hair behind one ear. Lili does the same thing.

"Hello, Charles."

"Hello, Mrs. Kensington."

"Scarlett, please," she corrects, holding out a hand that I shake. "It's nice to see you again."

"You too," I reply, hiding my surprise. I wasn't expecting her to remember our brief interaction weeks ago.

Scarlett smiles, then glances at her husband. "The doctor wants to talk to us." She catches Crew's concerned expression. And mine. "Just to discuss discharge procedure."

I relax. Discharge is good. Means she's headed home shortly.

"I'll be right there," Crew tells his wife.

She nods, smiles at me again, then heads back down the hallway.

Lili's father sticks a palm out. I grasp it, giving him my firmest shake.

Crew doesn't let go right away. "If you treat my little girl with anything less than the utmost respect, I want to make it clear, we're going to have a massive fucking issue, Marlborough. I don't give a shit about your title. I have a fuck ton of money and very few hobbies. If you hurt Lili, I'll bury you. Got it?"

He's dead serious, but I want to smile. Not because I don't believe him—I do—but because I'm glad he's Lili's father. Happy she has a family who would go to war for her.

"Got it, sir."

His eyes narrow, like he's trying to decide if I'm being glib.

I'm not. It's a sign of respect—respect he just earned.

Finally, Crew nods. "Next time we see each other, I promise I'll remember you."

"Glad I finally made an impression."

One corner of his mouth curves up a tiny bit. "Can sort of see why she likes you."

Following that small endorsement, Crew turns and walks away.

I hit the button for the lift again. It's late—past midnight—but I no longer feel that tired. Residual adrenaline is coursing through me.

When I reach the lobby, I pull out my mobile and call my cousin.

Ellis answers on the second ring. "Wassup, Duke?"

"You busy?" I ask.

"Nah, just playing video games."

"Want to meet me for a drink?"

"Meet you for a drink … you're in New York?"

"Yes."

A pause.

"Is everything okay? Did something happen with your mom?"

Ellis witnessed most of my last visit. The distance between me and my mother, which only expanded tonight.

"Georgia's fine. I came for a work thing."

"You sure do work a lot," he comments.

"Drink, Ellis. Are you in or not?"

"Are you going to sip water this time?"

"I'll be at the same place we met last time in ten minutes," I tell him, then hang up.

He arrives shortly after I do, a bike helmet tucked beneath one arm.

This bar isn't any nicer than I remember it being, but it's significantly busier than it was during my last visit. More popular with the weekend crowd, I guess.

Ellis's smile is wide as he approaches the booth. I snagged the last open one.

"Duke! You're really here."

"You can call me Charlie, you know," I tell him.

He shakes his head. "How will everyone know you're a duke then?"

"I'm fine with everyone not knowing I'm a duke," I inform him.

"What's this?" He picks up the scotch I ordered for him when I arrived.

"Decent liquor," I reply.

I know he's had it before—at Derek's fancy country club.

Ellis grins. Lifts the glass. "Cheers!"

I lift mine, too, and tap it against his, echoing the exclamation. We both sip.

"So, what was your work trip?" he asks.

I swish the scotch around in my glass, watching the brown liquid splash up the sides and then drip down. "I went to the Kensington Consolidated gala earlier."

"Why?"

I give him the answer I should have told Lili. "Because of Elizabeth Kensington."

Ellis chokes mid-swallow. Swigs some more scotch, coughs, then blinks rapidly at me. "What?"

He heard me or else it wouldn't have just sounded like he needed the Heimlich maneuver.

But I repeat myself. "I went to the Kensington Consolidated gala to see Elizabeth Kensington."

After over a year of my telling mostly lies and half-truths, it feels good to be totally honest.

"*Dude.*" His voice lowers, like we're swapping secrets. "You've … slept with her?"

"Yes."

"How was it?" he asks eagerly.

I reach for my glass. "None of your goddamn business."

I've never discussed those details about a woman before. Men who go into specifics about their sex life usually seem to be compensating for something.

With Lili, it's more than that. There's also blinding possessiveness involved. Those intimate moments are ours alone.

"Okay, okay." Ellis leans back in his seat. "So, are you, like, dating her?"

"No."

"Why not?"

"I-I don't know."

There are too many reasons—all of which I don't feel like discussing—and not a single one that seems sufficient.

I'm currently confused about everything. *I don't know* has

become my standard response instead of *I've been busy*, and I don't think it's much of an improvement. Might be a downgrade actually.

"So … bad night?"

"Could have been better." I drink more scotch. "Tell me about you. What's new?"

Ellis launches into a long response, like no one has asked him that recently. We've exchanged sporadic texts over the past few weeks, but none of his messages were that detailed. He's seeing the woman in the photo he sent from the Statue of Liberty. She's an aspiring nature photographer, and they're planning a trip so he can surf and she can take pictures. His birthday is in a few weeks, he reminds me, and I make a mental note to remember to text him on the date.

I listen, asking questions occasionally, but the buzzing that used to be in the back of my head? It's still there, and it's not stress about potential bankruptcy.

It's a long list of all the things I should have said to Lili.

And it's almost as distracting as the woman herself.

# CHAPTER 35

## *Charlie*

There's a knock on the door of my study. Rather than accomplish anything productive, I'm striking matches on the box I took from the restaurant I brought Lili to on our first—and really only—date. I moved it from the drawer next to my bed to my office when I got back from New York, wanting some reminder of her to stare at.

"Come in," I call out.

Conrad appears a few seconds later. His nose wrinkles, smelling the smoke lingering in the air. "I'm sorry to disturb you, sir."

"What is it?"

"We appear to have a trespasser," Conrad replies.

"A trespasser?" That catches my attention.

Conrad nods gravely. But there's a glimmer of something in his expression that's different from his typical stoicism.

"On the property?" I prompt. "Are you sure they're not just …

lost?"

Buckleby is a small town. Hardly a crime hotspot. And Newcastle Hall sits on twenty thousand acres. You could be wandering on the surrounding property without realizing so for a while.

"She's standing in the gardens, sir."

I spin in my chair and glance out the window.

For a few shocked seconds, I can't move. Then, I stand so fast I nearly knock over my chair. "I'll take care of it, Conrad."

I make it downstairs and into the gardens in record time.

She hasn't moved, still staring up at the cherry tree. Most of the stone fruit is gone, thanks to the thieving birds.

My heart is pounding so fast that it feels like it's trying to beat out of my chest.

"You could have called," I say.

Lili doesn't turn around, continuing to look up at the leaves instead. "I don't have your number. I deleted it, remember?"

She could have easily gotten my number the same way I did. I don't say that.

"But you had my address?"

"I asked the car service to bring me to Newcastle Hall. Saw your convertible and knew I was in the right place."

Lili spins to face me, wearing a navy blazer and a neutral expression. Her hair is perfectly straight, strands of it almost copper in the sunlight.

My gaze goes to her forehead first. There's a pink line that's about a half-inch long above her left eyebrow. The only evidence of how the gala two weeks ago ended.

"What are you doing here, Lili?" I ask softly.

She glances away at a starling that's landed on a nearby bench. "I was in the neighborhood."

"Buckleby?"

"Fine, vicinity. Ireland."

"You got the job," I infer. "Congratulations."

"Yeah. They offered it to me while I was there. I haven't accepted the position yet. They gave me a few days to decide, even though I had to push the second interview because of—" She clears her throat delicately, gesturing toward the thin scar. "Well, you remember. And since I was on this side of the Atlantic, I thought … I wanted to see you."

She practically whispers those last five words.

"It didn't seem like you wanted to see me in New York."

"I *did*," she insists. "You just—I mean, *I* just—you caught me off guard."

"Good thing I've had months to prepare for your arrival."

She blushes. "You're right; I should have called. If you want me to go, I will. I didn't mean to intrude or—"

"I don't want you to go."

That's the one thing I'm certain of. Everything else is murky.

It's bizarre that she's here, standing in the sprawling gardens of my childhood home. A backdrop to her beauty I didn't think I'd ever witness.

Elizabeth Kensington has an exhilarating, exasperating habit of stripping me down to the most basic of impulses. Of removing all the layers of my careful control.

She never reached out to me after the gala. And I've been especially busy negotiating a deal with the company Asher put me in touch with. Between that, checking in with Blythe, visiting with my grandmother, and overseeing everything else I'm responsible for, I didn't even realize two weeks had passed. Doesn't mean I haven't thought about her—a lot—as the matchbox in my office could attest to.

I thought her silence meant we were done.

But now, she's here, smiling tentatively like she's not sure what to say either, and I'm confused again.

"Do you want a tour?" I ask.

Lili glances—very deliberately—at the moors that stretch until they meet the horizon. Grass interrupted by the occasional stretch of stone wall or shadow of an oak and nothing else.

"Of what?" she asks.

I snort. "Stable's this way."

Lili follows me out of the garden and around the front of the house. She gazes up at the strands of ivy clinging to the crumbling brick as we pass the exterior, her expression unreadable.

I have no idea what her childhood home looks like, but I could make a good guess. In California, probably one of those fancy, modern, minimalistic white mansions right on the beach with lots of glass. In New York, probably the top floor of one of the coveted buildings overlooking Central Park.

Newcastle Hall is stately and majestic, but it isn't new or expensive. It has creaks and aches. Locks that stick. Stairs that squeak. The upstairs taps take a full minute to start running hot water.

I'm not embarrassed of this place, but I've never been more aware of its flaws than I am right now. My entire life, I've assumed I'd marry a woman who saw my title as a selling point. I didn't have the same fear as Lili—that it's all someone would see—but I assumed it would be a factor. A *positive* factor.

And I developed feelings for the one woman I've met who sees my title as a disadvantage.

So, the fact that she's here, seeing all this from a perspective and a background so different from mine, is strange. Makes this part of my life seem like a larger section of who I am.

Kensington sticks his head out as soon as we enter the horse barn. Gilbert ignores us, chomping on some hay.

"This is the famous Kensington?" Lili asks, coming up beside me.

"I never called you famous," I tell the horse.

"He's *beautiful*," she says, rubbing his nose.

I smile. Kensington bobs his head.

"See? He likes it."

"Uh-huh."

I glance across the aisle. "And that's Gilbert. Blythe named him."

Lili nods. "Like *Anne of Green Gables*."

"Like what?"

She rolls her eyes. "Never mind."

"Do you want to go for a ride?"

Lili's face immediately lights up. "Yeah."

I show her into the tack room, pointing to a pair of Blythe's boots she can borrow.

Ten minutes later, we're riding side by side, away from Newcastle Hall's looming shadow.

I'm shocked by how comfortable it is. How it feels like this was a planned visit, not a total surprise. How easily we talk as the horses trot along.

"What's that over there?" Lili asks once we're about a mile from the manor.

I follow her gaze to the stone wall that encircles the graveyard filled with my ancestors. "The cemetery."

I wasn't intending to bring her here as part of the tour, but it's the route I'm accustomed to taking. And there's not much else to see, as she already pointed out. Past the next few fields, the forest starts.

Lili urges Gilbert ahead rather than guiding him away.

We dismount in tandem, like we've come here a thousand times together.

The horses grasp on to the opportunity to graze on the lush grass as I follow Lili toward the wooden gate that leads inside. A distant grumble sounds, so I cast a concerned look up at the sky. It's gloomy now, not just overcast, dimming like a dying light bulb.

"Is it okay to go in?"

"Sure. Not much to see though."

I hold the gate open for her, then follow her inside. The gardeners maintain this place the same way they mow and maintain around the main buildings on the estate. The grass around the graves has been trimmed short, stone slabs the only interruption in the stretch of space. No flowers or benches or mausoleum.

Lili walks toward my father's headstone first. The last in line with the shiniest surface.

The flowers I scattered last time I was here are gone. Decayed, same as the bodies buried in the earth.

"Do you come here a lot?" She has to ask because there's no evidence I come at all.

"Define *a lot*."

She smiles, but it's a sad one.

Sympathy from Lili feels different. Makes me feel safe and supported rather than pitiable and alone.

She revises her question to, "Do you come here?"

"Yeah." I nod once. "My father had a low tolerance for others' input. There's a lot I never said to his face … things I say to this stone now."

"Do you think he can hear you?" There's no judgment in her voice, only curiosity.

"No," I answer. "But I'm not really talking to him. I'm letting it out of me, if that makes any sense."

"It does."

There's another rumble in the sky. Louder … closer.

But I don't move or suggest we leave. I come here alone, always. To vent and curse and rage. To expel some of the stress sitting on my shoulders. It's my shooting range, not a sanctuary.

Standing here with Lili is unexpectedly peaceful.

"I'm named after my grandmother," she tells me. "The original Elizabeth Kensington. I never knew her. She died when my dad was really young, so he never really did either. He doesn't talk about her very often, and neither does my uncle Oliver. And my grandfather *never* talks about her. Grandpa and I are really close, but I don't dare ask him. I can just … tell it's off-limits.

"When I transferred to Cornell to finish my degree, I had to do a site analysis project in one of my classes. I chose the cemetery where my grandmother was buried. It had been designed by a French landscape architect. There are sculptures and ponds and bridges … it's a beautiful place. The first time I visited, there was a man already standing at my grandmother's grave. I wasn't sure what to do, and then he looked in my direction, and I realized it was my grandfather.

He didn't say anything. He set down the flowers he'd brought, kissed my cheek, and left. We've never talked about it. I never told my dad.

"But I've gone back to her grave a few times, and there are always fresh peonies on it. She's been gone for forty-five years, and he brings fresh flowers to her every week. My grandfather isn't a religious man. Not sentimental either.

"My point is … there's no right or wrong way to grieve. You don't have to come here because you feel like you should. You don't have to think he can't hear you because that's the logical assumption."

I don't come here to grieve my father. I'm still too angry to grieve him the way a son should mourn his father.

And right as I open my mouth to tell Lili that—to tell her why—the sky splits with a jagged flash of lightning. The deafening crash is followed by an immediate downpour, like the crack fractured the bottom of a full bucket.

I grab Lili's hand and pull her toward the gate.

Another deafening crack of lightning reverberates across the open earth surrounding the cemetery, followed by the sound of thunder.

Kensington and Gilbert have huddled under a nearby tree. I'm grateful they didn't bolt. It was stupid not to turn back as soon as the clouds thickened.

We're not that far from the barn, but the ride back is going to feel like an eternity in this weather.

Lili drops my hand when we reach the horses, grabbing Gilbert's reins and patting his neck. He prances in place, tossing his head anxiously. Kensington is calmer, but still uneasy.

Dripping branches sway overhead. They're not providing much

shelter, but better than nothing.

It's a temporary respite though. We have to move. This is the stupidest possible place to be standing during a thunderstorm.

"Are you okay to ride in this?" I call out to her.

"I can handle myself, Charlie," Lili tells me, then hoists herself into the saddle without bothering to find a makeshift mounting block. Not that there are many options out here.

"I know you can," I respond, vaulting onto Kensington's back. "But I'm still going to bloody worry about you. Ready?"

Gilbert takes off, and I urge Kensington after him.

The rain hasn't lightened at all. If anything, it's falling faster. I'm soaked in seconds, squinting through the sheets at the horse and rider ahead.

I can feel the ground rumbling beneath the horses' thundering hooves as another roar of thunder rolls overhead.

Lili is crouched low over Gilbert's neck, her seat steady as she steers him toward the barn. She reaches the stable first. The deluge of rain is enough to keep Kensington moving faster than his normal pace, but he refuses to accelerate into a full gallop.

By the time we reach the main doors, Lili's out of the saddle, slicking her soaked hair out of her face. She shouts something at me as I dismount.

"What?" I yell back, pulling the reins over Kensington's head.

"I said, *I beat you!*"

I roll my eyes, but I'm grinning as we lead the horses inside. A loud crack of lightning splits the sky, the sound making Gilbert shy to the left.

"You got him okay?" I ask.

"I'm good," Lili responds, leading Gilbert straight into his stall and starting to strip his tack off.

I do the same with Kensington as the rain continues to assault the roof. It sounds like standing inside a drum during a rock concert.

The storm is still raging by the time the horses are untacked, groomed, and happily munching on hay.

Lili walks into the feed room right as another round of thunder shakes the foundation. She tosses the dandy brush she used on Gilbert into the plastic grooming bin. "Are you sure this building is safe?"

"It's stayed up for three hundred years." I finish wiping the bridle, then toss the towel away.

Lili's perched on the table mostly used for mixing grains, studying the row of polo trophies on the shelf. She leans over and picks up the one I won in the Hamptons, shaking her head once before setting it back.

"You can have it."

"I don't want your pity prize." She rolls her eyes, then wraps her arms around herself.

"You cold?"

The fans are spinning at full speed overhead, and her clothes are so saturated with water that they're dripping.

"A little."

I reach for one of the Barbour jackets on the row of hooks. When I look back at Lili, she's in the midst of taking off her top.

"I don't think that's going to warm you up much," I say, shocked that my voice sounds normal.

She's wearing a black lace bra—so sheer that it's see-through. Her borrowed boots get kicked off next, and then she's peeling down her pants. Her underwear matches the gauzy material of her bra.

I toss the jacket on the table and step toward her in a trance, the sudden need to touch her skin my singular focus. My hands land on her hips, sliding over her stomach and then down to cup her ass.

Lili shivers, pressing closer against me. Her hands slip into my hair, shaking errant drops free.

I groan.

Because it feels good, but mostly because it's *Lili* touching me. I'm so hard that it's physically painful, my wet trousers tighter than a straitjacket, but I'm also experiencing a sweet sense of relief.

*I missed you*, I think.

Her hands slide down my chest, settling on the waistband of my pants.

"I don't have a condom," I say. Lust has spread to my vocal cords, my tone a similar consistency to gravel.

Lili says nothing. She doesn't pull away either.

For a few seconds, all I can hear is the rapid drumming of rain on the roof and the frantic pulse of my heart thumping in my chest.

"Do you … need one?"

I tense.

James mostly stayed out of my romantic life. My *sex* life really, considering my intention has always been to fuck around until I was forced to get married. But one of my most vivid memories of my father was the evening he called me into his office and hammered the importance of using protection into my brain. Told me women would try to trap and manipulate me, that an "illegitimate" child would ruin the Marlborough bloodline. An archaic view I disagreed with, but I wasn't interested in a baby, so it was easy enough to nod along. Whenever this suggestion has come up before, it's been easy to turn down. They were flings with women who were essentially strangers. I barely knew them, much less trusted them.

I trust Lili. I know she's asking because she wants *me*.

My entire life, I've looked ahead to the day I'd get married and have kids with the enthusiasm of a prisoner headed to his execution. An unpleasant inevitability. A stressful obligation.

Having a kid with Lili doesn't freak me out.

Is it something I'm ready for now? No.

Is it something I want—with her—someday? Yes.

And the thought of filling her with my cum? It's even more arousing than leaving marks on her with my mouth.

"Guess so." Lili's hands drop, and she jerks free from my grip.

Once again, I waited too long to say what I was thinking. What I *want*.

"Lili …" I reach for her.

She takes another step back, grabbing the jacket I tossed away and pulling it on. It's a men's size, so it hangs to her mid-thigh.

Lili zips the jacket up as high as it'll go, then crosses her arms. Her hair is wet, and her mascara is smudged beneath her eyes. She's as beautiful as ever, standing barefoot in a barn jacket.

Her gaze holds mine defiantly, and I can see the hurt swimming in the blue.

My chest aches so strongly that I'm tempted to rub at it.

"I just needed a minute to …" I'm not sure how to explain that my father conditioned me into believing all women were trying to trap me into marriage without sounding like a paranoid prick.

"Forget it, Charlie."

"I'm not—"

"Your Grace?" Conrad's voice cuts me off. "Mr. Marlborough?"

I head into the aisle because his second call was closer, and there's no way he's going to see Lili half naked.

Conrad is standing in the overhang, shaking rain off his umbrella. Relief washes over his expression when he sees me striding toward him. "I was worried you'd gotten caught out in the storm."

"We did. But we made it back fine." I frown. "You shouldn't be out in this weather."

"Neither should you," he retorts.

"We were just waiting for the rain to ease off."

Water is still dripping off the edge of the roof, but the lashing sheets are no longer falling.

"Very well. I'll see you back at the house."

"I'll walk back with you, Conrad."

I turn toward Lili's voice. She's changed back into her wet clothes and pulled her damp hair back into a neat bun. She doesn't even glance at me as she walks past, and my stomach sinks to the concrete floor.

Conrad gives me a questioning glance.

I nod. She wants space, and maybe some distance will help me figure out how to fix this. "I'm going to give the horses their evening grain, and then I'll be behind you."

"Very good, Mr. Marlborough."

"I'm Lili." She introduces herself as soon as she reaches Conrad. "We met earlier."

Conrad smiles. "I remember, Miss Kensington."

"Just call me Lili."

"He won't—"

Conrad cuts me off. "Might I escort you back to the Hall, Lili?"

I glower at my traitorous butler. The only person I've heard Conrad call by their first name is his wife. He's unfailingly formal most of the time. He likes Lili, and he wants me to know it.

"That would be lovely, Conrad."

Conrad offers her his elbow, lifting the umbrella so it's mostly covering Lili before they step outside.

"My apologies Newcastle has given you such a gloomy greeting. The estate is quite beautiful on sunny days."

"It's quite beautiful on rainy days too," Lili replies. "Do you get many storms like this?"

"Eh, one or two a summer. This is the worst one since …" Conrad's voice fades as they walk farther away, swallowed up by the remnants of the storm.

I lean against the open doorway until I can't see them anymore.

# CHAPTER 36

## *Lili*

Entering Newcastle Hall is like traveling back in time. The interior is as palatial as the exterior. Carys Park was renovated and updated, but Charlie's home has been perfectly preserved.

The soles of the riding boots I borrowed squelch against the tiled floor of the entryway. A sweeping staircase is straight ahead, the wall behind it covered with painted portraits. There's a shiny Steinway standing in one corner, an impressive set of antlers mounted above it.

"Shall I show you upstairs to get changed?" Conrad asks, pulling my attention from one of the marble busts displayed around the room. "I had your luggage placed in the Crimson Room."

"Oh." I waver on what to tell Conrad's expectant expression.

I brought suitcases here because I came straight from the airport, not because I was intending to spend the night. Because how our last conversation had ended wouldn't stop bothering me and I had given

in to the urge to see him.

Conrad lifts a thick eyebrow as the pause lingers.

"I'll, um … I'm just going to wait for Charlie," I tell him.

Conrad casts my wet clothes a disbelieving look, but he's too polite to comment on my bedraggled appearance. "Follow me," he says.

He leads me into an opulent sitting room. A massive stone fireplace takes up most of one wall, matching upholstered armchairs angled on each side of the hearth. Another wall overlooks the gardens I walked around earlier. It's made from a mosaic of glass, framed by ornately carved wood—a dazzling design that reminds me of an ancient church.

Conrad picks up a striped blanket from the back of the overstuffed sofa and hands it to me. "I'll be back with some tea."

"You don't have to—"

He's already hurried off.

The blanket is wool but surprisingly soft. I wrap it around my shoulders. I'm not that cold anymore, but it's cool inside. An earthy dampness similar to being in a basement, like the thick brick walls are entirely insulated from the outside. I haven't heard any thunder or lightning in the past ten minutes, which hopefully means the storm is dying down. The patter of rain isn't audible on the roof or windows.

I wander over to one of the paintings on the wall. It's a young boy on horseback. He's unsmiling, expression so serious that it's almost severe.

Footsteps sound.

I glance over, expecting Conrad. Charlie's approaching instead.

My cheeks warm as soon as I see him, an immediate flush I

wish I had more control over. Remnants of embarrassment and lust buzz in my blood, paired with a heavy dose of uncertainty. In the barn, it felt like we were the only two people in the world. We're still isolated, but it's no longer as easy to pretend we're entirely alone.

"Is this you?" My eyes return to the painting I was looking at before.

"Yes."

"You look"—*unhappy*—"serious."

"My mom had just left. My father wanted new portraits to hang."

Something in my chest splinters. Most people assume I had a happy childhood because I'm rich. That money buys happiness. Charlie's proof that's not always the case.

"Here's the tea, Lili." Conrad appears with a tray that he sets on one of the tables scattered throughout the room. "Can I get you anything, Your Grace?"

"I'm all set, Conrad. Thanks."

Conrad nods, then disappears again.

I decide to pour myself a cup of tea. Not my typical drink of choice, but Conrad went through the effort of making it for me. And it also gives me an excuse to avoid looking at Charlie.

"How long can you stay for?" he asks.

I continue stirring a cube of sugar into the flavored water, watching it dissolve while analyzing the sentence structure. It feels like an intentional phrasing. An indication he wants me to stay. But maybe he's just being polite because it's obvious how far out of my way I came to see him. Subtle—casual—isn't showing up at a guy's house with two oversize suitcases.

"I have a flight out of Heathrow on Thursday morning."

Today's Tuesday. I *could* stay two nights.

"Are you planning to see Chloe while you're here?"

I swallow, glance at him, then admit, "I don't know. I didn't tell her I was coming."

Surprise flashes across Charlie's face. He doesn't ask why, which I'm grateful for.

Instead, he says, "I have a meeting in London tomorrow morning. And then a garden party I'm supposed to attend in the afternoon. You could go see Chloe in the morning and then come to the event with me?"

"I don't want to … impose."

I'm expecting a tease about me showing up, bags in hand.

But his earnest response is, "You're not."

My inhale is unsteady. Part of me was hoping he'd push me away. Make me feel crazy for coming here even. *Anything* to make my departure on Thursday easier. To convince myself this visit was a mistake.

"I doubt getting caught in a thunderstorm was on your daily agenda until I showed up." I take a sip of tea. It's too sweet—I added too much sugar—but the warmth is pleasant.

"I hate my daily agenda," Charlie tells me. His tone is somber, his expression as stoic as the one immortalized on the wall.

"Then, change it," I suggest. "Don't dukes do *whatever they bloody hell want?*"

He cracks a smile at my poor imitation of his voice but doesn't comment. "Come on."

I set down my empty teacup, abandon my blanket, and follow him back into the grand hall I entered earlier. Charlie heads straight for the stairs.

I run my hand along the varnished banister as I ascend, my gaze trailing over the portraits on the wall.

On the landing, I stop. "Is this your dad?"

I'm certain it is. There's a striking similarity between the two men. They have the same nose, a similar jawline. Identical thick, dark hair.

The main difference in their appearances—aside from a few decades—is the harshness the artist managed to capture. It's like a painting of a sculpture rather than a living, breathing being. A stiffness that's uncomfortable to look at, let alone be around.

"Yes." Charlie only glances at the portrait for a few seconds before continuing upstairs.

In the brief time I've been here, I've realized that Charlie's feelings toward his father are much more complex than I initially realized. That there's a lot more than grief there. There's resentment. Maybe even bitterness.

A long hallway stretches from the top of the stairs.

"Nice house," I comment as I head toward the rounded opening Charlie is walking under.

An end table with an expensive-looking vase sits to the left. I feel like I'm observing a museum.

He glances to the left, so I can see the corner of his mouth quirk up. "You miss the skyscrapers."

It's a statement, but I answer it like a question. "No, I don't."

New York is home. It's familiar. It's filled with family and memories with my closest friends.

But it's also the city where my last name means the most. Where the spotlight is brightest and the whispers the loudest. Where I have to walk past the office I could have inherited instead of Kit.

Escaping all that—just being Lili—is really nice.

Charlie stops at a doorway halfway down the hallway. "Conrad had your *suitcases* put in here."

I roll my eyes at the emphasis he places on my multiple pieces of luggage. But all I say is, "Thanks."

The same shyness from earlier is making its return.

I feel like I'm back in Saint-Tropez, sitting at the very edge of the diving board. I've put myself out there, and crawling back to solid ground will be uncomfortable and cowardly. At some point— soon—I'll have to jump.

"I'm just a couple of doors down." He nods to the right.

"How many bedrooms does this place have?"

"Fourteen."

"That's it?" I tease.

He shakes his head once before reaching out and twisting the doorknob open.

The Crimson Room is not the overload of red I was expecting based on the name. The draperies around the four-poster bed are maroon, but the rest of the room is shades of cream and more dark wood. My two suitcases are stacked neatly next to the armoire in the corner. Past it, another doorway leads into an attached bathroom.

"Meet me downstairs when you're ready," Charlie tells me. "We'll grab dinner at the pub."

"Okay." My voice comes out quiet, so I clear my throat once. Bob a nod before he turns back toward the hall, then start toward my suitcases.

"Lili?"

I glance over my shoulder.

Charlie has paused in the hallway. The rakish grin he's wearing has my heart rate accelerating.

"Make yourself comfortable. But don't plan on sleeping in here."

He's gone before I can do more than blink.

An hour later, Charlie drives us into town.

I took pub to mean casual—I'm wearing linen pants and a fitted T-shirt—but Charlie wears his typical slacks and a blue-and-white-striped oxford.

My hair is already pulled back in a ponytail, but I glance down at the pink elastic on my wrist as the wind whips through my hair. I'm not sure he's ever noticed I still wear it, and I feel a little silly for doing so. Not enough to take it off though.

Buckleby looks like something out of a fairy tale. I don't think I drove through the town on my way to Newcastle Hall, but I might have just been too nervous about my destination to notice.

*Quaint* is the word that keeps coming to mind.

Everything's quaint. The honey-hued stone houses we pass look straight out of a storybook. The main street that's constructed from cobblestones, lined with clusters of flowers spilling out of wooden boxes.

I wanted to know what was so special about this place. Why Charlie chooses to live *here* rather than London or New York or any of the other hundreds of places where he could.

I know it's his childhood home, but that doesn't mean he has to live here full-time. Based on the conflicted way he talks about his father and the concerned way he mentions his sister and the way he hardly mentions his mom at all, I have a feeling Newcastle Hall isn't overflowing with fond family memories.

Charlie parks by one of the few wooden buildings, a red sign pronouncing it the practically named *Buckleby Inn*.

Streaks of brilliant color are beginning to spread against the sky that's now completely clear, signaling the start of sunset, as we head inside.

It's noisy in the pub, jubilant cheers and joyful noise, which only grow louder with Charlie's appearance. They eye him appreciatively and me curiously as Charlie guides me to one of the booths along the far wall.

"I'll be right back," he tells me, then heads for the bar top that stretches the length of the pub.

I track his progress—stopping to talk to an older man for a minute, then continuing to where a blonde woman is polishing glasses.

She beams at him, nodding as Charlie says something.

It becomes very obvious, very quickly that the pretty blonde bartender is very interested in Charlie.

He doesn't encourage her, simply smiling politely, but I'm jealous anyway. And wondering exactly how he's spent his nights since leaving Saint-Tropez. I haven't been with anyone else, and I assumed the same was true for him. Maybe he has. Maybe that's why he hesitated in the barn earlier.

The thought leaves a sour taste in my mouth.

Charlie returns with two full pint glasses in his hands and two menus tucked under one arm. He sets the beers down first, nudging one toward me, then drops the menus.

"What if I wanted champagne?" I ask.

I don't. I'm off sparkling wine for at least a year. But I'm irritated about the pretty bartender who was flirting with him and in the mood to argue.

"Try it. It's good." He takes a sip from his glass.

I try a tentative amount from mine. It's mostly foam, but I get a strong hit of the malty taste of hops. Run my tongue along my bottom lip.

His eyes are on my mouth now.

"Tastes like … beer," I announce.

"It *is* beer." Charlie drops his gaze and flips open one menu. Pushes the other toward me without glancing up.

My stomach does a mini acrobatic routine. I still haven't told him about my dyslexia, and I don't really want to bring it up here. Neither do I feel like squinting at squiggly letters.

"What do you get here?" I ask.

He glances up, twin lines appearing between his eyes. One eyebrow lifts. "You wanted to order your own drink, but not your own food?"

"I was just looking for a recommendation. Sheesh. I've never had … pub food before."

Charlie shakes his head, but I catch the curiosity in his expression. He's contemplating something. Contemplating me.

I hold my breath, waiting.

"The fish and chips are popular," he finally says.

"Great." I suck down more beer. "I'll get that. Does the flirty bartender take food orders, or do we have to wait for a waitress?"

One corner of his mouth curls up. "You sound jealous, Kensington."

He sounds happy about it, which I think is a good thing. I was thrilled when he finally stalked across that club in Saint-Tropez.

"I'm not." I am. "It's just … unprofessional."

Charlie makes an annoying humming sound. "A waitress will come over."

"Great."

"I haven't shagged anyone since you, if that's what you're wondering."

"I wasn't," I lie.

"Right." He smiles—that annoyingly condescending one that I used to want to slap off his face, but now kind of makes me want to kiss him. "So … how was Dublin?"

We haven't discussed my trip to Ireland—my supposed reason for stopping by here—and I wasn't expecting for it to come up at all.

"It was good. I tried Guinness." I point toward the beer he brought me. "This is better."

"High praise."

"The campus is so green. So different from Cornell. And the new buildings they built are really cool. Newer, obviously, than most of the campus, but they were so beautifully constructed. I sent a bunch of photos to my aunt Hannah. She's an architect. Anyway, they have all these sustainability initiatives they're wanting to implement, like rainwater capture and filtration. They also want to do a green roof and—"

"Do you know what you'd like to order?" A woman—not the blonde from the bar—appears next to our table.

Charlie nods to me, indicating I should go first.

"I'd like the fish and chips, please," I say.

She nods, then glances at Charlie.

"Two of those."

"Got it." The waitress ambles away.

Charlie's staring at me, like he's waiting for me to continue, but

I'm feeling self-conscious.

"It was a good trip," I conclude lamely.

"I've never been."

"To Ireland?"

He nods. "Fig—you met him at the wedding—and I have talked about a trip, but it's never happened."

*You could come visit me.* I think the words, but I don't say them because it feels like I'm treading a very fine line here and those would fall to one side.

"How long is the project?" Charlie asks me.

"Three to four months probably." Not my longest project, but my longest one outside the States. I tilt my head. "Can I ask you a question?"

"Of course."

"What do *you* do? I mean, I know you're a duke. But I don't really get what that means as far as a job description. Or is there not one? Do you really just get to do whatever you want?"

Charlie cups his glass of beer, and I get the distinct impression that this is a subject he doesn't really want to discuss. But I'm so *curious.* Not only to know more about his life, but to also find out what all is holding him here.

"It varies a little," he tells me. "The Duke of Manchester—that's me—owns properties throughout England. Some for personal use, like Newcastle Hall or the villa in Saint-Tropez. Others are commercial. Hotels, apartment buildings, office buildings, commercial storefronts. Some of the spaces are leased. Some, like the hotels, are businesses I also own. There are employees in place who manage day-to-day operations for almost everything. But it all runs up through me. I have to sign off on staff changes or building repairs or lease renewals or tenant changes or press features. It's a huge mountain of paperwork basically."

"Could someone else do all that for you? If you wanted to do something else, I mean?" *Like be a doctor?*

"I'm not sure, honestly," he answers. "That's never been done before." His expression twists. "My father would have …"

"Maybe he shouldn't have a say."

His nod is slow. Like he wants to agree but isn't sure he really can.

Our dinner arrives a few minutes later. Crispy cod and greasy fries taste a lot better than I thought they would.

Maybe it's the company. Or the beer I wash down each bite with, which tastes better with each sip.

By the time we leave the pub, it's pitch-black out. We walk to an adorable ice cream shop down the street.

I order the chocolate-whiskey flavor. Charlie chooses sea salt, which I tease him mercilessly about until I sample it and discover it's actually delicious.

He paid even though I tried to.

I've never dated a guy who had more money than I do. That would be a very limited list of eligible bachelors. And men have always seemed aware of it, which has made me self-conscious.

With Charlie, I just steal most of his ice cream.

It feels a little like Charlie is trying to show Buckleby off. He points out some of the storefronts as we sit at one of the picnic tables outside the ice cream shop while I contemplate ordering a second ice cream.

"What have you done in New York?" I ask him as we're throwing our empty containers away.

I'm too full to eat another bite, I decide.

"What do you mean?" he responds as we start back toward the car. It's still parked at the inn.

"Well, I know you've been there. What did you do there, aside from play polo?"

"You mean, *win* at polo?" he says, sounding like the imperious jerk who flashed his trophy at me.

I roll my eyes, not deigning that with a response.

"Not much. It was partially a work trip."

"That's why you were at Kensington Consolidated?"

"Yeah."

He says nothing else, glancing away, and I get the distinct impression that he doesn't want to talk about it.

I'm not sure why—because it's my family's company maybe?—but I let the topic drop.

Lights are on in all the houses we already drove past once, cozy squares that add to their charm. They fade to darkness quickly, the car's headlights the only illumination. We don't pass a single vehicle on our way back to Newcastle Hall.

It's so different from what I'm used to. You can't venture out in New York at any hour and have the roads be empty.

Charlie grabs my hand as we walk from the convertible to the house, our fingers entwining naturally. This is our second date, technically, but it feels like our hundredth. Like this is just an average Tuesday night.

I can't decide if I love or hate that.

We've barely walked inside when a woman's voice calls out, "That you, Charlie?"

"Yes," he calls back.

I glance at him, unsure. She sounds younger than most of the staff I've seen.

"I went to see Granny earlier, and—" A young woman appears. Then stops—moving and talking—as soon as she spots me and Charlie. Focuses on our clasped hands. Frowns. "You have a *girlfriend?*"

I wave at her with my free hand. "You must be Blythe. I'm Lili."

She and Charlie look a lot alike. She's a shorter, leaner, even more scowly version of him.

Blythe studies me like she's not sure if she wants to be best friends or mortal enemies. "Where is your shirt from?" she asks abruptly.

I glance down to remind myself what I'm wearing. "Uh, I think it's—"

Charlie cuts me off. "You're not buying any more clothes, Blythe."

Blythe glares at him. "Well, not *now* since I found out we're—" She quits talking abruptly. "I like your shirt."

"You can have it," I say impulsively.

I'm a few inches taller than her, but I think it'll fit her. Or she can tuck it in.

One less thing for me to bring back.

And … I want Charlie's sister to like me. I'm not above bribery.

"*Really?*" She appears stunned, all the snark suddenly absent.

"Really."

"Cool, thanks," Blythe says, then disappears down the hallway.

"That was a really warm welcome—for her," Charlie tells me. We're still holding hands.

I laugh as he tugs me upstairs. "I'm honored."

A few minutes later, he leads me into his bedroom.

An ornate fireplace takes up most of one wall. A green velvet chaise lounge is angled in one corner. A four-poster bed with a massive matching chest of drawers takes up most of the rest of the space.

It's cozier than the rest of the house. It smells like him. A pair of running shoes is tossed in the corner. The bag he brought to Wales and France hangs off the closet's doorknob. *Middlemarch* sits on a side table, beside a clock, a bookmark stuck about halfway through.

I stare at it. Then walk over and pick the book up. "You're reading it?"

I didn't feel like I could ask him about it after snooping around. But it's sitting out in plain sight.

"Yeah. It's good."

"Would you tell me if you hated it?"

"Yes."

"Because you only care about two opinions?"

"No. Because I wouldn't lie to you."

I swallow, flipping through the first few pages. The lines blur, and it's not only because of my dyslexia.

"It's really long though. Been reading it for weeks, and I'm not even halfway done."

"The audiobook was thirty-five hours." I keep flipping pages, deliberating. "I listen to a lot of audiobooks ... because I have dyslexia."

I hear his steps as he approaches me, but I keep my eyes on the book.

"Lili."

"Huh?"

"Lili." He grasps my chin, tilting my face toward his. "I've heard of it. What exactly does it mean?"

"It's a reading disability. I have a bad case of it. Writing and spelling can be challenging, but reading is the worst. Sometimes, it looks like the words are swimming off the page. Or scrambled, so I have to look for a long time for anything to rearrange and make sense. I got diagnosed when I was pretty young and had special accommodations in school. But it was still … hard. I'd feel stupid that my brain worked differently. Kit did well in school, even though he fucked around most of the time, and Bash got straight A's so easily. My parents probably paid my way into college—both of them. And I've figured out ways to deal with it the best I can. But there are still times when … it's why I wanted you to tell me what to order. Why I didn't read your text. Most people who know call or send me voice messages." I exhale. "You don't have to say anything. I just … I wanted to tell you."

His thumb moves back and forth against my chin. "I'm glad you did. You are the smartest, most driven, most creative, most passionate person I've ever met, Elizabeth Kensington. And knowing everything you've overcome … it just impresses me more."

If I wasn't already in love with him, I'm pretty sure that earnest response would have done the trick.

"Not compared to—"

"Compared to anyone," he says fiercely. "Everyone. I believe that. But you have to too."

"I'm trying to."

Trying to stop ranking my accomplishments along my family members'. Trying to stop assuming the opportunities I get are because of my last name. Trying to stop searching for the project that will make me feel like I contributed something important to the world.

"I'll remind you anytime you want."

I resist the urge to rub my chest to check on the pang that appeared. Attempt some levity. "That's going to be hard since you still haven't asked for my number."

"You mean, 212-535-1012?" he says, without missing a beat.

I gape at him. "You *memorized* my phone number?"

"Yes."

I rise up on my tiptoes to kiss him. Charlie responds instantly, his hands squeezing my hips and then sneaking underneath the hem of my shirt.

I focus on his top lip, sucking it into my mouth. He groans, palms spreading until they cover my entire lower back, then teases the seam of my lips open with his tongue. My breathing has turned rapid and uneven. I can feel my heartbeat between my thighs.

He's taking control of the kiss, but I'm not ready to cede the power.

I push him toward the bed. He backs up the few steps to the edge of the mattress while managing to keep our mouths fused together, pulling me so close that there's no space between our bodies at all. I can feel the firm lines of his chest through the fabric of our shirts. The thick bulge of his erection is pressed against my stomach.

Charlie's hands move higher, lifting my shirt. I rest my palms against his abs, then shove.

He lands on the edge of the mattress. More out of surprise than any superior strength on my part.

"What are you ... *fuck.*"

I sink to my knees between his spread thighs, answering his question.

After that, neither of us does much talking.

# CHAPTER 37
## Charlie

I should tell her.

I was *going* to tell her. At dinner. And then after dinner. And then when we got home.

But she was so excited, talking about Dublin. And then she brought up New York while we were eating ice cream, like she was trying to ask if I would ever consider living there. And then, in my bedroom, she shared something I doubt she'd told many people. That led to several rounds of sex.

Nowhere between any of those moments could I find a good moment to tell Lili that my dad lost all his money and left me with a title, property, and debt.

She's leaving tomorrow, and I have no idea when I'll see her again.

How do people *do* this?

My entire life, my relationships with women have been easy.

Straightforward. I've known exactly what I wanted from them, and I knew exactly what they wanted from me.

Then, I met Lili, and there was no playbook.

It took three introductions for her to even acknowledge we'd met. I'm rarely prepared around her, usually impulsive, and it's all with the intended outcome of just spending more time around her. Because no matter how long, it never feels like long enough.

I'm not sure what she wants from me. *If* she wants anything from me.

No matter how much she opens up, it always feels like she's holding back. She could have just asked me last night if I'd ever consider moving to New York. Then, we could have had the conversation we'd both been avoiding.

"Why didn't you tell me you were dating Elizabeth Kensington?"

Blythe flounces into the dining room, fully dressed. I check the time on my watch, shocked she's up this early.

"I'm not."

She rolls her eyes before taking the seat two down from the head of the table. "Ada texted Zara, saying you had dinner with a woman at Buckleby Inn last night. Then, you showed up here with her— *holding hands*—and she spent the night in your room. I doubt you two were discussing Parliament reforms. That all sounds like dating to me."

Blythe grabs a scone off the table, slathers it with raspberry jam, then stares at me expectantly.

"I'm not dating her," I repeat.

"You should," Blythe tells me. "I mean, get in line because she's basically New York's It girl, but she must like you a little if she came all the way to *Buckleby*."

"Drop it, Blythe. I don't ask about your … blokes."

My sister smirks. "Do you want to hear about my Spanish lover? I met him in—"

"I *don't*," I say hastily.

"She's a billionaire. If you married her, we'd have plenty of money."

My throat draws tight, like an invisible fist is squeezing it, as Blythe casually mentions my biggest fear.

Lili ended things with her last boyfriend—a guy she'd known for decades and was with for two years—because she thought he'd never be able to see past her money.

And here I am, in desperate need of it.

That's why I haven't told her the entire truth about the dukedom. Not just because it's embarrassing or because I haven't settled on a solution.

Because I'm worried she'll second-guess my feelings for her. Especially if she finds out I was at Kensington Consolidated, looking for an investment they didn't make. If you focus on the facts, it doesn't look great, more like I'm scrounging around. I already told her I'd anticipated having an arranged marriage, likely with a woman who coveted a title. I just left out what *I* needed to gain from it.

"I told you, I'm taking care of it, Blythe."

She nods, not asking more questions for once. Or pointing out that I told her I'd take care of it, but I haven't *actually* taken care of it.

My meeting in London is with Louis Haywood. He visited Newcastle last week to discuss the deal on the table with the company Asher had put me in touch with. I finally told someone the truth about why I needed to sell.

Louis was surprised, but not shocked.

He had known my father well. As well as anyone could. He admitted to knowing about some of the problems, but he had no idea the extent. He agreed this deal was the best solution, which was reassuring.

Not that I have another option.

It's a best-case scenario in so many ways, but I can't shake the feeling of failure. Auctioning off pieces of businesses that have been fully owned by my family for generations isn't a success to celebrate.

"Good morning!" Lili appears, entering the dining room, wearing a sundress and a wide smile.

"Morning," Blythe chirps.

"For you." Lili sets some folded fabric down in front of my sister. "My shirt from last night. Conrad already had it washed. And I added a dress I thought might look cute on you. If you don't like it, just—*oof.*"

Blythe has catapulted out of her seat to hug Lili.

"Thank you!"

"You're welcome," Lili replies.

She looks surprised when Blythe lets go, and I get a glimpse of her expression.

Not what I expected to see. Lili comes from an affectionate, loving family and has a close friend group that bickers like siblings.

Blythe's reaction is less surprising to me. Not only does she adore anything related to fashion, but she's lacking any female role models. No mom, no aunts, no sisters. She has her friends—and Gran, I suppose—but that's it.

Still, I'm taken aback when Blythe sits back down. She's already finished everything on her plate, which is usually when she takes off from the few meals we eat together.

I usually eat breakfast alone—looking out at the gardens—before eventually heading up to my study to start on the day's pile of paperwork.

"Your mom founded rouge, right?" Blythe asks eagerly as Lili heads for the chair opposite her.

I stand to pull it out for her. Lili curtsies when she reaches it, and I roll my eyes. Blythe's eyes bounce between us, as if she's making more assumptions.

"Yeah, she did," Lili answers, reaching for one of the scones set on the table.

Martha, our cook and Conrad's wife, bakes them fresh most mornings.

"That is *so* cool." Blythe is basically vibrating in her chair. "Do you get to wear any of the clothes you want? Do you get to see all the designs in advance?"

"I can make requests," Lili says. "There are usually extra samples. And Mom had sketches all over the house when I was living at home. So, yeah, I see them. Unless it's for something special. My best friend, Chloe, got married in July, and my mom designed the bridesmaid dresses. She and Chloe were the only ones who saw it ahead of time. That one I tried *really* hard to sneak a look at."

"Does she design anything *you* want her to? Like, when *you* get married, are you going to have her design your wedding dress?"

I cut a sharp glance at Blythe, but she's not looking at me. She's not thinking about *me* marrying Lili, and it causes this sharp pinch in my chest as I picture Lili walking down the aisle in a white gown toward some faceless man.

"Oh. Uh …" Lili's cheeks flush. "I always thought I'd wear my mom's dress actually. Not that I'm, uh, getting married anytime soon. Plenty of time to decide."

"Vintage can be really chic," Blythe says. She's trying to act nonchalant, but there's a noticeable lack of bubbliness all of a sudden.

I don't know what happened to our mom's wedding dress, and I'm certain Blythe wouldn't want to wear it even if it were located. The rest of her life will be filled with these little realizations—reminders of what a mother-daughter relationship should look like—and I wish I had said some things to Georgia last time I saw her rather than walking away with my mouth shut.

"Are you studying fashion in college?" Lili asks, and it seems like she's steering the conversation away from moms on purpose. Like she's realized what dimmed Blythe's enthusiasm.

Another pinch.

"Yeah. I just have one year left. Then, I'm hoping to work as a buyer. Or maybe intern at a fashion house."

"I know rouge has an internship program. If you're interested, I can have someone there send you more information about it. My friend Celine worked there for a year after we graduated. I'm sure she'd love to talk to you about it."

"Really?" Blythe looks thrilled. "That would be *amazing*. I've never been to New York. Working there would be a dream."

Lili smiles. Glances at me. "Are you sure you two are related?"

"Funny," I tell her, reaching for another scone.

"We look exactly alike," Blythe says, taking Lili's comment literally. "Everyone says so."

Lili laughs. "Yeah, you do. I just meant … because Charlie hates

New York."

"I don't *hate* New York," I argue.

"Dislike then. It's fine. You're a country boy at heart."

Blythe snorts. "Charlie likes London. He'd go out all the time there. He's just staying here because he thinks it's what Papa would have wanted."

I exhale as I heap clotted cream on my scone, avoiding looking at Lili. "It's more complicated than that, Blythe."

"I know."

She's not placating me—for once. Ever since she discovered the details about what Papa left us with, she's been more subdued. Stopped teasing me about hardly ever leaving this place. She hasn't come home with armfuls of shopping bags.

I'm conflicted on how to feel about it. I'm grateful that she's becoming more responsible. But it also breaks my heart a little bit— because I wasn't able to protect her from it. To fix things before they affected her.

Blythe pelts Lili with more questions about New York while I sip on coffee and finish my scone, letting Blythe monopolize Lili's attention.

This is the smallest this huge room has ever felt.

When Blythe darts upstairs to get something, Lili glances at me. "What time do you have to leave for your meeting?"

I glance at the clock. "In about an hour."

"I called Chloe. I'm meeting her for brunch."

"Sounds good," I say. "I can drop you off on the way."

Blythe rushes back into the dining room, breathing heavily. "Which bag?" she asks.

I don't glance over; certain the question isn't meant for me.

Lili tilts her head, deliberating. "Left one," she says. "I have the same one in black."

"Charlie brought it back from New York for me."

At that, I look over. Blythe is holding up two purses. And one *is* the bag I brought back. The one I wasn't sure Blythe ever opened, let alone used.

"Lucky you," Lili comments. "My brother Kit gave me a *candle* last Christmas."

I smile. "The bag was from Georgia, Blythe."

"That'd be more convincing if all of 'her' gifts weren't hand-delivered by you."

I have no response to that.

But I don't need one. My sister is too busy talking to her new best friend.

# CHAPTER 38
## *Lili*

Chloe squeals as soon as she sees me. The elderly man seated one table over sends a disgruntled glance in our direction before returning his attention to the newspaper spread across the table.

"You're *here*!" Chloe flings her arms around me as soon as I'm within hugging distance, squeezing me so tightly that I'm concerned my ribs could crack.

"I'm here," I say into her hair. She's cut it since I saw her last, the ends barely brushing her shoulders.

Chloe returns to her seat, literally bouncing in place as I sink down opposite her. "The waiter recommended it," she says, nodding to the two bowls of green soup on the table.

I lean forward and sniff. "What is it?"

"Cucumber gazpacho with honeydew melon and lemon verbena."

"Hmm." I swallow a spoonful. "It's really good."

"Right?" Chloe scoops some up too. "*So?* Are you moving to Ireland?"

"I haven't decided," I tell her.

"When is the interview in DC?"

"Friday."

"Wait. Does that mean that you'll be here another day?"

"I, uh …" I swish my spoon back and forth in my soup, creating tiny waves. "I haven't decided yet."

"Did he ask you to stay?"

My gaze snaps up, eyes absorbing Chloe's knowing expression. "What?"

She rolls her eyes, then reaches for her water glass. "You just happened to end up in *England* as part of your work trip to Dublin? Come on, Lili. If you want, I'll pretend to be oblivious. But we both know why you're here, and it's not to have lunch with me."

I exhale. "I wanted … closure."

"And? Have you gotten any?"

"No." I glance at the old man absorbed in his newspaper, then back at Chloe's knowing expression. "Every time I think it's the end, it somehow turns into another beginning. He's … it was supposed to be a fun fling this summer after the Claremont Park stress. I feel like I need to land this big, important project to prove that—to keep proving myself. I've been worried about what to tackle next for weeks, and Charlie made me forget about that. It's not fun anymore. I mean, parts of it are fun, but the rest is confusing and overwhelming and scary. He listens to me, and he pays attention, and then there are also moments where he just knows what I need. I thought I'd come here, and it would be weird and uncomfortable and … *over*, and it isn't."

"You're in love with him."

I drop the spoon. Rest my face in my hands. "I know," I groan toward the tablecloth.

"Fran told me he came to the hospital."

I lift my face enough to see her again. "You guys were gossiping about me?"

Chloe smirks. "We've been gossiping about you since he dared you to go on a date with him, Lili."

I roll my eyes. "That's not exactly what happened."

"That's exactly what happened. And don't think we didn't all notice that was the slowest you've ever driven. When we raced in Monaco for Jasper's twenty-first, Tripp was the only one who beat you."

"So? I was a little rusty."

Chloe's eyes dance as she leans forward. "Don't lie to me. I'm not saying you could have beaten him—"

"Rude," I interject.

"But you sure didn't try very hard. Because he fought for you. Look, I love Cal—I do—but he took you for granted. He assumed years of friendship equaled a perfect relationship with minimal effort. Charles wanted you, and he made sure everyone knew it. There's a big difference."

"I don't know *what* he wants," I admit. "He's never been in a relationship. He's planning to marry a woman dying to be a duchess. He just *left* in Saint-Tropez, like I was a hotel reservation with an enforced checkout time."

Chloe's forehead wrinkles. "He didn't tell you why?"

"Tell me why? What are you talking about?"

She sighs. "One of the partners at Theo's firm told him that

Grace Marlborough had a stroke a couple of weeks ago. She spent a few days in the hospital."

"Grace?"

"His grandmother."

"Oh."

His grandmother had a stroke.

That explains why Charlie left France so suddenly. It doesn't explain why I'm just hearing about it now.

*Why didn't he tell me?*

The simplest explanation is that he didn't consider me important enough to confide in. But then why did he fly to New York a week later? Why has he made me feel like a welcome visitor ever since I showed up on Newcastle Hall's massive doorstep?

None of it makes sense, and I haven't pushed for answers because I know it will pop this pleasant bubble I've been existing in since I arrived in England.

But I refuse to leave without getting them. I won't get on the plane tomorrow without knowing exactly where we stand.

Chloe seems to sense I need a break from discussing Charlie and pelts me with questions about New York.

I fill her in on some of the antics of our friends—Bridget is now dating a guy in a band, and Jasper might move to Miami permanently—and about Mom and Dad's return to New York. Dad started back at Kensington Consolidated a week ago. Kit's first day is on Monday.

Chloe tells me about the solo honeymoon she and Theo are planning—they've narrowed destinations down between Paris and Santorini—and the part in the play she just got.

By the time we finish brunch, my cheeks hurt from smiling so much. It's been too long since Chloe and I got to visit together like this, just the two of us.

I'm taken off guard by how natural it all feels. Waking up in Charlie's king-sized bed, eating breakfast with him and Blythe, driving into London together. How easily I can picture it as my everyday life.

Chloe gives me a long hug, then rushes off to a rehearsal after making me promise to keep her updated.

I don't need to clarify what she wants updates on.

It's still fifteen minutes from when Charlie said he'd pick me up, so I walk to a nearby park. I'm not sure if it's the same one Charlie was talking about at The Beach House, but it looks awfully similar. There's a fountain and lots of walking paths.

Unlike yesterday, it's clear and sunny out. I stroll slowly in my heels—Charlie would never let me live it down if I tripped and landed in the hospital a *third* time this summer—enjoying the soundtrack of voices and birds chirping.

I take a seat on one of the metal benches right as my phone begins buzzing in my pocket. I pull it out, expecting to see Charlie's name—telling me he's running early or running late—but it's not.

It's my dad.

I answer immediately, worried something is wrong. It's six a.m. in New York.

"Hi, Dad."

"Hey, honey." His voice is even and calm, which slows my racing heart some. But I ask, "Is everything okay?" just to be sure.

"Everything's fine. Your mom went to Boston with Hannah for a fundraiser, so I've got the penthouse to myself. I thought I'd try you since your brothers won't be up for several hours."

"So, I was your third choice?" I tease.

Dad chuckles. "Never. You're all tied for first place."

"Uh-huh. That's realistic."

"How's Dublin?"

I adjust the folds of my dress. It's one of my favorites—green and pink silk with a flared hem and a bow in the front. We're headed to what Charlie called a garden party next, so I dressed up a little extra before brunch.

"I'm in London actually."

A pause.

"For work?"

"Nope."

Another longer pause.

"I like him."

"Like who?"

"Charles."

I fumble for words. "What do you—how did you …"

I've never mentioned Charlie to my dad. And I haven't discussed him with Mom since that one night after dinner.

"I know it's probably not cool to get your father's approval. But he has mine, if it matters."

"Of course it matters, Dad."

My throat is thick with emotion, and he has to clear his before saying, "It's been a good trip?"

"Yeah. I'm only here for one more day. My last interview is in DC on Friday. For the museum project. Then, I'll have to make a decision."

And not just about my job.

"I had a meeting with Curtis Brentwood the other day. He lives in Chicago and was raving about Claremont Park."

"He was not."

"I swear. Said he takes his son there all the time. And either he should be an actor instead of an investment banker or he had no idea you'd designed it because he seemed shocked when I told him."

"That's nice."

"Yeah, I thought so too." I can hear the smile in his voice. "Also, your mom and I are going to an animal shelter when she gets back."

"You're really getting another dog?" I figured it would fall by the wayside with my parents' busy schedules.

"That's the plan," he tells me. "We spent so long getting you kids self-sufficient, but turns out, we kind of miss having someone to take care of."

"I'm glad for you guys," I say. "This new phase, it seems good."

"I agree. And I'll let you get back to your trip. I just wanted to check in."

"Thanks, Dad."

"I'll see you when you get back to New York?"

"Yeah, you will. I want to meet my new sibling."

He laughs. "Is Hallsen Vet accepting new cli—"

"*Dad.* Mom already asked, and it's *not* funny."

"Sorry." He doesn't sound the least bit sorry. "Have a good rest of your trip, honey. Love you."

"Love you too," I reply, then hang up.

I enjoy the sun's warmth for a few more minutes.

Then, I stand and head toward the corner where I'm supposed to meet Charlie.

# Charlie

Louis Haywood is alternating between puffing a cigar and sipping scotch when I walk into the private room he reserved at The Ivy House. It's not even noon.

I take the rounded leather seat opposite him, fighting the urge to cough as smoke swirls around.

The Ivy House is one of the oldest gentlemen's clubs in London. It has an exclusive membership list that's historically included prime ministers and members of Parliament and the royal family.

My father spent a lot of time here, but I've never seen much of the appeal. I'd rather relax in a pub or canter across the countryside. But it's where Louis suggested meeting, and I'm grateful to him for being one of the few people who's bothered to really see how I am rather than just offering condolences.

"Morning, Louis."

He smiles, appraising my appearance. "You're looking well,

Charles."

I'm in a suit because of the garden party I promised Gran I would attend later.

But I think he means something else. At this point, I'm just waiting on the final paperwork for the deal. Once that's signed by both parties, funds will be released. I'm close—so close—to everything getting resolved.

It's more than that though. I'm finally looking ahead. Weighing possibilities. Considering options. *Dreaming*, and it feels damn good.

An invisible weight that's gradually lifting, and maybe it's visible to others too.

"You too," I tell him.

Louis sighs. "Poppy has banned all my favorite things from the house. Says they're bad for my health."

That explains the cigars *and* the scotch. He's taking full advantage of his time here.

"Aren't they?"

Louis frowns, then snuffs out the cigar. "Spoken like a future doctor."

I think of the business card tucked in my wallet. I haven't called Dr. Evans since I ran into him at Buckleby Inn, but I've considered it.

I'm not even sure if returning to school is an option after taking more than a year off. But I want to find out.

"I was never a doctor."

"You could be. What's stopping you?"

"I'm considering it," I admit.

Louis leans back in his chair, more focused on me than his vices. "Good."

"My father wouldn't approve."

He heaves out a sigh. "James was a complicated man, Charles. You don't need me to tell you that. But he loved you and your sister. You were a lot more than a legacy to him. He might have had a hard time expressing that, but it was still true. And he left you with a heavier burden than any son should have to bear. Now that you've got everything sorted, I think he'd tell you to be selfish for a bit."

I can't picture my father ever saying those words. His whole identity was built around duty and responsibility. And just because he failed in some respects, I've never felt like that gave me the freedom to do the same.

"Maybe."

He half smiles, like he realizes I'm unconvinced. Like he knows that coming to terms with my father's expectations and plans—and loss—is something I have to accept myself, same as I've realized. That was easier to push to the side when I was focused on simply getting through the immediate issues, not having to map out a long-term plan. I'm scared to jinx the solution, but assuming the deal goes through as expected, I'm going to have less to manage and a giant source of stress alleviated.

"You knew my father before he got married."

Louis nods, even though I wasn't really asking. I know he and James graduated from Cambridge together over a decade before my parents met. "I did indeed."

"Do you know why he married her?"

A question I was never brave enough to ask my father. We didn't discuss the topic of my mother. She was taboo to talk about from the moment any painting with her in it came down from the walls. The one time I discussed her with my father in the past sixteen years was when her wedding invitation came and I informed him I was attending.

"Only the most obvious reasons. Georgia was beautiful and charming. She also appeared to care little about the title—at least at first—and I know that appealed to James."

"What do you mean?"

"You would understand better than me. Your father might have been a dutiful duke, but that doesn't mean he didn't struggle with the role. He found different ways to deal with it. Marrying your mother was one example—choosing a woman who was somewhat unexpected. The gambling is another. Men who are content in their lives don't take the sort of risks that—" He stops speaking abruptly, then reaches for his scotch. "I didn't mean to imply ..."

"It's fine, Louis. I'm trying to understand why he did what he did. What he would have expected from me if he'd ..." I shake my head.

"He never would have seen you become duke, Charles. No matter how long he lived. That's the downside of titles."

"Not the only one."

He sighs. "I'm sure. But comparing yourself to your father isn't going to make the role any easier. You're dealing with challenges he never did—with problems he created. Your loyalty to your family is admirable. But don't let it overtake your own ambitions. Your own happiness. You can be a doctor *and* a duke, if you so choose. Focus on the options you have, not the limitations."

I rub my fingers along the beaded edge of the leather armrest. "I met a woman. She's American."

"Ah. You're worried you're repeating your father's mistakes?"

"Not exactly. Lili's nothing like my mother. Our relationship is completely different from my parents'. But I do … I don't think I can be the son my father raised and the person I want to be around her. It feels like I have to decide between them."

Louis leans forward. "James raised a son who makes his own choices, not a man who always does what others expect. By choosing your own path, you're honoring that. I know you're angry about the burden he left you with, and you have every right to be. But don't let that convince you he didn't love you or wasn't proud of you." He pushes his glass away, closer to me, then reaches down and returns with a rectangular black box. "I was waiting to give this to you, but now feels like the appropriate moment."

I reach for it, opening the zipper that runs the perimeter and flipping the lid off.

It's a stethoscope. Black rubber and shiny silver aluminum.

I lift it out of the box.

"Your father ordered that three years ago, when you told him you were enrolling in medical school."

There's engraving around the curve of the diaphragm. *Dr. Charles Marlborough*, it reads.

"I knew where he'd kept it, so I grabbed it when I was at Newcastle last week. I had a feeling, after our conversation then, that there were a few things you were struggling with."

"Thank you," I say, still staring at it.

My father didn't raise any objections about my choice of career path, but I never got the impression he was particularly pleased with it. He would rather I went into banking or law. Some more distinguished profession.

I didn't realize how much that bothered me until now, as I'm faced with some proof of his support. Medicine wasn't what he would have chosen for me, but he was planning to give this to me at my graduation. He intended to support my choice.

"Thank you," I repeat. It comes out as more of a croak.

"He didn't want you to be the same as him, Charles. He wanted you to be better."

I nod, not able to come up with any words of response. I'm swamped with emotion, and it's not all negative. None of it is actually.

For the first time since he died, I'm grieving my father without any animosity.

I've been so furious with him. For driving recklessly. For his careless financial choices. Even for marrying Georgia and for letting their relationship fall entirely apart so that Blythe and I had no contact with our mother. Divorcing her didn't have to result in a total estrangement.

Right now, all that anger is absent. I'm remembering the happy moments. The rides across the moor and the trips to Villa Park for football matches and the talks in his study when he'd ask about my life and not just my grades.

I *miss* my father—and not just because of what his death left me with.

Louis seems to sense I'm overwhelmed. He pats my hand, then changes the subject to an upcoming trip to Edinburgh he and his wife are planning. Asks about Blythe. Inquires about Gran's health. And, with a cheeky smile, requests I tell him more about Lili.

I've avoided my godfather since Papa's death because I was worried about what I would say. Business strategy aside, I was concerned what Louis would think about my father after learning the truth.

But Louis doesn't seem to see him any differently. He was already acquainted with my father's flaws.

And talking with someone who knew my father—really knew him—is the closest I've felt to Papa since I got the call about the accident.

When I leave The Ivy House an hour later to pick up Lili, I feel a lot lighter than when I arrived.

# CHAPTER 40

## *Lili*

The lawn party is held at an estate outside of London. It's similar to events I've attended before—beautiful floral arrangements, uniformed staff, polite conversation—but feels distinctly British. The food being passed around on silver trays are finger sandwiches, filled with different combinations of sliced cucumber, cream cheese, and smoked salmon. Most guests are sipping on Pimm's, a fizzy cocktail that tastes like ginger and lemon. Suits are paired with top hats, dresses matched with fascinators. The other big difference is … Charlie.

Because he's not *Charlie* here. He's the Duke of Manchester, and he's treated like it. From the moment we arrived, he's been fawned over. Deferred to.

Men give him respectful nods. Women give him admiring glances.

He's the main attraction. The guest of honor.

I've experienced attention by proxy before.

But at least around my family, I know what my role is. My connection to them is clear. Everyone here is wondering what my relationship to Charlie is … and I don't know the answer any more than they do.

He introduces me to everyone who approaches him. Some people seem to recognize my last name. Many don't. Or if they do, any interest dims in comparison to the opportunity to talk to Charlie. I'm relegated to the side of conversations, not knowing the places they're discussing or the people they're talking about, and I no longer feel like I fit here.

A white-haired woman, wearing a yellow dress with a matching lightweight coat, approaches about ten minutes after we arrive. Her hair is carefully curled, and she's wearing block heels while carrying a small handbag. Her focus is all on Charlie at first, then slides to me.

A noticeable frown forms on her face, and a trickle of dread chills my chest.

I know who this is, even before Charlie excuses himself from the current conversation and bends down to greet the older woman, pressing a kiss to her wrinkled cheek.

"Hello, Granny."

I also know his grandmother does not like me.

"Charles," she acknowledges. "Who's this?"

I hold a hand out before he can reply, refusing to appear outwardly rattled even though my stomach is churning.

Her opinion is one of two Charlie cares about. I might have won Blythe over, but something tells me his grandmother won't be as interested in my clothes or my hometown.

"I'm Elizabeth Kensington."

Her expression doesn't so much as twitch. I can't tell if she recognizes my last name or if Charlie has ever mentioned me to her, but my instinct is, the answer to both is no.

"How lovely to meet you." She makes the simple sentence sound demeaning, her accent turning the words crisp and cool.

"This is my grandmother, Grace Marlborough," Charlie says.

There's an undercurrent of warning to his words, and it's not aimed at me. Grace sniffs, then purses her lips.

"What a beautiful day," I say, the weather the best—and safest— subject I can come up with.

"We get a lot of rain in England," Grace informs me.

"Well, it's not raining today," I point out.

"How astute, my dear." The endearment is condescending, not affectionate.

Charlie's grandmother doesn't just dislike me. I'm pretty sure she actively hates me.

"That's enough, Gran," Charlie snaps.

At least her obvious disdain isn't in my head. He sees it too.

The thought isn't very comforting.

"Beatrice!"

I stiffen as soon as I hear the name. Of course the woman who wants Charlie's title is here. And of course his grandmother greets her like a long-lost friend.

I saw Beatrice at Chloe's wedding, but only from a distance. She's even more stunning up close. Her dress swishes around her calves as she approaches—the same appropriate length as all the women here are wearing. My minidress ends just above my knees, and it feels like another strike against me.

"Grace. So nice to see you." Beatrice bends to kiss her cheek the same way Charlie did.

"You as well, dear. Is your mother around?"

"Yes. Somewhere." Beatrice smiles at Charlie's grandmother, then glances at me. Her warmth dims, barely but visibly, before her gaze continues on to Charlie. "Hello, Charles."

"Hello, Beatrice," he replies, then rests a hand on my lower back. Both Beatrice and Grace track the movement. "Elizabeth, this is Beatrice Campbell."

I start when he calls me by my full name. He hasn't done so in weeks. But it fits better in this formal, awkward atmosphere, like a part I have to play.

"It's nice to meet you, Beatrice."

"You as well," she responds before taking a careful sip from her glass. Even the way she swallows screams elegance. "You were at the Hughes wedding, weren't you?"

"Yes. The bride is my best friend."

"The actress, right?"

Chloe would be thrilled about being referred to as an actress. I'm peeved by Beatrice's airy tone. "She attended London Academy of Music and Dramatic Art, yes."

"Oh, I see the Burtons," Grace says. "Come, Elizabeth, I'll introduce you. You must not know many people here."

It's an obvious ploy to separate me and Charlie. To leave him alone with Beatrice.

But I can't come up with any refusal that doesn't sound rude, so I nod and say, "That would be wonderful, Grace. Very thoughtful of you."

Charlie's hand slides to my left hip, squeezing once before

dropping.

I follow Grace over to a couple who appears to be in their sixties. She asks about their trip to Paris, then their grandchildren, before remembering to introduce me. I accept a glass of champagne from a waiter while I wait.

"This is Elizabeth Kensington. A guest of Charles's."

I'm surprised she added that second sentence. I wouldn't have put it past her to imply I bribed my way onto the guest list.

"Nice to meet you, Elizabeth," the woman says.

"Any relation to Oliver Kensington?" the man asks.

I nod. "He's my uncle."

"Well, I'll be. I don't know anyone who isn't looking to make a deal with Kensington Consolidated these days."

I smile, then sip some champagne.

"I love your dress," the woman tells me. "What brand is it?"

"Rouge," I reply.

She nods enthusiastically. "I thought so. I saw their show at Paris Fashion Week last fall and loved everything. Henry"—she elbows the man next to her—"was supposed to buy me some of their dresses."

"They were sold out, Rosie," Henry responds.

Rosie raises an eyebrow at me, as if she's expecting me to fact-check that claim.

I shrug. "It's my mom's label, so I've never tried to buy anything from them."

Rosie gasps dramatically. "My goodness."

Grace looks like she's sucked on a lemon. She obviously didn't anticipate my *American* family would be of any interest to the Burtons, and pathetically, this is the proudest I've ever been to brag about my family's accomplishments.

This is also the most inferior I've ever felt. As vain and spoiled as it sounds, I'm accustomed to being looked up to, not down upon.

I excuse myself a few minutes later, sneaking a glance at Charlie before heading inside. Beatrice is still standing by him, but they're not alone. An older couple—her parents maybe—are there too.

The residence isn't as large as Newcastle Hall, but it has a more complex layout with lots of narrow corridors. I have to ask two staff members in order to find a bathroom. I pee, wash my hands, then admire the wallpaper.

It's a soft green, depicting a peaceful oasis of snaking rivers and blooming trees, pink peacocks and prancing horses and proud lions.

I study it closely, the colorful, slightly ridiculous drawings oddly soothing.

There's a knock on the door.

"One minute!" I call out, then sip some champagne.

*Damn it.* I was hoping for longer solitude.

"Can I come in?"

Charlie.

I choke a little, bubbles burning my throat. I don't want him to think I'm hiding in here—even though that's pretty much exactly what I'm doing—so I step forward and flick the lock open.

He enters a second later, lifting one eyebrow when he spots me standing with a glass of champagne, staring at the wall. I didn't have enough time to look busy doing anything else, not that there are many options. I could have pretended to wash my hands, I guess.

I hear the lock click back into place before he walks toward me, and my pulse stutters like a pair of paddles just shocked my chest.

"Are you okay?" he asks, stopping a couple of feet away.

"Yep. I just needed a minute."

"Nine."

"What?"

One corner of his mouth curls up in the suggestion of a smile that I used to find infuriating and now consider charming. "You've been gone for nine minutes."

"That's … specific." I keep my tone light, but there's a fresh heaviness in my heart.

He didn't just notice I was gone. *He counted the minutes I was missing.*

I swallow, forcibly clearing the lump that's formed in my throat. "I thought you were exaggerating … about the whole duke thing."

"I know." Charlie shoves his hands into his pockets. "It's hard to … explain."

"Especially to an American, right?"

He frowns. "I don't care what color your passport is, Lili."

I glance at the wallpaper again, tracing the curve of the river with my pointer finger. "Your grandmother is feisty. Especially for a woman who just got out of the hospital."

Charlie sighs. "She told you?"

"Chloe did actually. But the better question is, why didn't you?"

"I don't know." He rubs the back of his neck. "I don't know. Things between us were getting …"

"Stale?" I supply. "Predictable? Passé?"

I'm proud of how steady my voice sounds.

I have a hundred percent survival rate in life so far. I'll make it through this too.

"No. *No*, Lili. It was … intense, and I didn't know how to deal with it. I had to leave, and I used it as a solution. Or an excuse. I'm used to dealing with things on my own. I'm sorry. I should have told you the truth."

"It's fine. It doesn't matter. You don't owe me explanations."

Rather than relieved, he looks angry. "The fuck I don't."

"You *don't*. I'm leaving tomorrow, remember?"

"I remember. And I don't see what your departure date has to do with anything."

"Never seeing each other again seems relevant."

His anger fades, amusement appearing instead. "I have no intention of never seeing you again, Lili."

I take another sip of champagne to avoid responding. I knew we'd do this before I left. I wasn't planning on doing it *here*.

"You're upset," he states.

"No," I lie, then take another sip.

He grabs the glass out of my hand and sets it on the marble counter so hard that I'm surprised it doesn't shatter. "Don't lie to me, Lili. Your honesty is one of my favorite things about you."

"One of your favorite things, huh? What else is on the list?"

A shameless fish for compliments. Because it's a nice distraction and because I genuinely want to know.

I'm expecting a crass answer. My mouth or my tits or my ass. Because our relationship has often been centered around sex or attraction, and it's easiest to keep it there.

Charlie doesn't reply right away. He crosses his arms and leans against the wall I was just admiring. But I'm no longer paying any attention to the wallpaper. It's all on him.

"Well, there's your eyes. My favorite color—Lili blue."

I try to swallow, but it's hard.

"There's also your tenacity. Your stubbornness. Your confidence.

Your kindness. Your loyalty."

He lists each trait as if I invented it. Like it's mine alone and some incredible accomplishment.

And it makes me want to cry. In a good way … and in a devastated way.

I suck my bottom lip into my mouth. "I don't belong here, Charlie."

"Bullshit." His response is swift. Unequivocal.

"They all want you to marry Beatrice."

"If by *they all*, you mean my grandmother, then you're correct. But I have no intention of letting my grandmother choose my wife. Or any plans to get married soon."

"We're … complicated."

"I'm not scared of complicated, Lili."

"I don't know where I'll end up working next."

"Pick the project you want, and we'll figure it out."

He's making it sound so simple. And then he's shoving away from the wall, coming closer, and I'm no longer feeling like an outsider.

That attention that everyone outside has been chasing after? It's wholly mine, the intensity the brightest, warmest spotlight I've ever been under.

"Turn around."

It's a command, not a request. I comply, mostly out of curiosity. He was quiet during the drive here, and since we arrived, he's been the proper, dignified duke I met at Atlantic Crest Country Club. Fully in control.

But now, as I face the mirror and stare at him, he's *my* Charlie. The man who challenges me at every opportunity yet also takes care of me like it's his job.

The man who's smirking as he undoes his belt and unzips his slacks.

My heart rate accelerates even more, my inner walls clenching around nothing as I grasp at the marble counter. "This doesn't seem like very duke-ly behavior, Your Grace."

"It is if I say so. And I can't watch you drink champagne without getting hard, thinking about that mouth around my cock, so I say it is."

He bunches my dress up and yanks my underwear to the side, letting out a rough, approving groan when he feels how wet I already am. I moan when he reaches my clit, my grip on the marble tightening and my hips bucking back.

"Do I need a condom, Lili?"

My eyes snap up to meet his in the mirror. "What?"

He hasn't brought up what happened in the barn yesterday. I haven't either. It was an impulsive, lust-soaked suggestion with a humiliating conclusion. Whatever his reason for hesitating, it clearly wasn't a step he was willing to take. We used them last night.

"Do I need a condom, Lili?" He repeats the question a little more urgently.

I can feel his erection pressed against my ass.

"No. I'm on—"

I can't finish the sentence because all I'm aware of is the stretch as he fills that empty ache.

I'm expecting a quick, fast fuck. None of the guests will miss me, but I'm positive everyone outside is wondering where Charlie is.

His thrust is swift, but the slide out is leisurely. A slow drag, during which I can feel every ridge and vein on his cock. It's an entirely new experience.

He keeps that pace—rapid, then relaxed—and it's driving me insane. I hold his gaze in the mirror, the expression on his face impossible to look away from.

Charlie's fucking me like he owns me. Like I'm his.

It's intoxicating and overwhelming. Completely consuming. I feel like I'm floating, no longer anchored to any reality.

Until he comes inside of me.

We lock eyes in the mirror as his dick jerks inside my spasming pussy, filling it with spurts of cum. It's the first time I've ever had sex without a condom, and I wasn't expecting it to feel any different. Just messier.

But the sensation of warmth? The extra slickness as he keeps pumping into me, prolonging the high? The severe possessiveness on his face?

It all feels different.

It all feels right.

It all feels real.

# CHAPTER 41
## *Lili*

Charlie insists on driving me to the airport the following morning, even though I offer to use the car service that brought me to Buckleby. We leave extra early so we can detour in London and visit some of the landmarks. I caught a quick glimpse of the London Eye when we were in the city yesterday, but that was it for sightseeing.

We roll along the long, straight street that ends at Buckingham Palace, pass the fountain in Trafalgar Square, spot the Tower of London's four peaks, cross the Tower Bridge, and then end up on Westminster Bridge to look at Parliament, Big Ben, and Westminster Abbey.

Charlie manages to find a parking spot near the cathedral, so we climb out to explore the area on foot. I'm acting like a tourist, asking questions and snapping photos, but he doesn't seem impatient. He indulges me. Reads the plaques aloud so I don't have to squint at

them. Laughs, when I start talking in my best imitation of his accent to better blend in with the locals.

British will always be *his* accent, in my mind. Just like London isn't the place where Chloe lives or where Cal goes to school anymore. It's the city nearest to Charlie.

My favorite photo from the brief stop is a picture in Big Ben's massive shadow. The background is mostly the massive clock, the foreground our faces. Charlie's kissing my cheek, which is creased because I'm smiling so wide.

I'm staring at the snapshot of our happiness when a car gets cut off one lane over from us on the highway. A flurry of honking follows the near collision.

When I glance at Charlie, his jaw is clenched tight.

"I don't like being a passenger since my accident," he confides, a couple of minutes later. "It's … I feel more in control. I don't get into a car unless I'm the one driving it."

"That's understandable. It makes sense, I mean."

And then something else occurs to me as he takes the next exit.

"I … you let *me* drive you."

More than a little reluctantly, but I attributed that resistance to my injury and his fancy car.

"I know."

He doesn't say anything else. Doesn't tell me not to read into it or that it meant nothing.

"I'm … honored, I guess."

The corner of his mouth I can see curves up. "You should be."

Signs for the airport appear ahead. I remind Charlie of my terminal number.

Each second that passes, it feels like my heart is pounding faster.

I don't know how to say goodbye to him. It's never *been* a goodbye. He walked away in the Hamptons. He just left Saint-Tropez, me waking up alone with his side of the bed cold. Assuming he'd just woken up early and was already downstairs, until Chloe handed me a scrawled note with a concerned expression. And I all but shoved him out the door in New York, essentially to avoid this exact situation.

Every time, it's worse.

There are more memories. More feelings. I keep waiting for those to reach a point where they'll stop, too, but it hasn't happened yet.

Missing people isn't a novelty for me. Growing up, we split time between New York and LA. An accommodation my parents made for me because the New York school had better resources for my reading disability. As a trade-off, we spent school breaks and summers in California. With the exception of Gigi's Red, White, and Blue party, of course. I'd miss people in New York when I was in LA. People in LA when I was in New York. My family, when I left for college. Chloe, then Cal, when they moved to London.

But missing has never been this physical ache before. This hollow sensation in my stomach, like a part of myself has been carved out and is being left behind.

Charlie pulls along the curb outside the *Departures* entrance and turns off the car.

It's overcast out, so he put the convertible's cover up before we left. I almost asked him to braid my hair anyway, but I got distracted by saying bye to Blythe.

He looks serious, spinning the keys around his thumb—*so* serious—and all the lighthearted farewells I spent the drive here brainstorming fly right out of my head.

Charlie blows out a long breath. "I need to tell you something. Several things actually."

"Okay." My palms are starting to sweat, so I discreetly rub them against the joggers I wore for the flight. I'm flying straight to DC, but my meeting there isn't until tomorrow, so I dressed casual today.

"I should have told you sooner. I meant to tell you sooner. I just didn't know how to. Didn't want you to think …" He stares out the windshield. A few water droplets fall on it. "I found out, after he died, that my father had lost our entire fortune. Gambling, bad investments, huge donations, unnecessary renovations. I don't know the extent of it all, honestly. He was … he always acted larger than life. Maybe he was just too proud to admit he had made mistakes. I inherited all of his debt, along with the title. For the past year, I've been doing everything I can to avoid bankruptcy. To get investors and sell off enough to keep everything else afloat. To keep up appearances. If I declare bankruptcy, they'll take everything. If it were just me, it'd be one thing. But Blythe? My grandmother? All the staff? There's a deal on the table, one that will wipe out the debts in full. Save as much as possible. But I'll lose control of businesses and buildings that have been in my family for generations in the process, and that's …" He swallows. "That's been hard to accept."

It takes me about twenty seconds to process everything he just told me. "I'm so sorry, Charlie."

Pieces that didn't make sense before start to click into place. Why he was selling the French villa, his vagueness about work, the resentment toward his father.

"You're doing what you have to do."

He nods. "I know I am. Hasn't made it any easier, but I'm

accepting it. It's been impossible to move past while I was still worried about losing everything. As soon as I sign the deal, I think it'll be easier."

I swallow. "Charlie, I could …"

"No." His answer is immediate, before I've even gotten the offer out. "I'm not taking money from you. And it's part of why I didn't tell you sooner. I don't want you to ever think that I would, that your wealth has anything to do with us."

"It could just be a loan."

"I'm not taking money from you," he repeats. "But I want everything else. I want *you*, Lili. I just … I need a little time to sort things out. This deal is going to eliminate some of my responsibilities, and I'm-I'm considering going back to medical school. Reclaiming a little of what my life looked like before my father died."

"Really?" I'm thrilled for him.

"Really," he confirms. "I don't know if it'll be possible, with the time I took off. They'll be more lenient because of the circumstances and because …"

"Because of your title," I supply.

He nods. "Yes. I don't know how an … American school would compare, but I'm planning to look into it."

"Please don't."

Hurt flashes across his face before he works to erase it.

I undo my seat belt and lean closer. "That's not—I didn't mean it that way. I mean, I don't know if I'll be in New York. In the US even. If you want to go back to medical school, you should do it here. Blythe is here, and your grandmother is here, and I … I could be here. I don't want to give up my job, and I want to keep choosing projects that excite me. Not all of those will be in England. But … some could be."

He appears stunned. Apparently, the possibility I'd alter my life around him never occurred to Charlie. He was planning to be the one making the geographic concessions. "You would do that?"

I nod. "Yeah, I would."

"I love you, Lili."

Those four words upend my world. Everything that makes me, *me*, is tossed up and forced to resettle. My racing heart slows, and so do my surroundings. The world is a blur of light and color and noise, but I can't see or hear any of it. It's like I'm trapped underwater, with nothing but that sentence echoing in my ears.

"What?" I croak out.

I wasn't expecting him to say it. I didn't even think he felt it.

His smile is tender as he reaches out and tucks a wayward strand of hair behind one ear. "I love you, Elizabeth Kensington. I've loved you for a long time, maybe from that first moment I saw you standing in a stable. I saw you, and it was like the entire world stopped. What you overheard me say to Ellis? That wasn't just because I was sad about my father or stressed about money. It was because I'd been looking for you inside, because I wanted to talk to you again, and you were nowhere to be found. I was disappointed that none of the women who kept trying to talk to me were you."

For the second time, I start crying in front of him.

I held it together in the hospital until he left the room. I don't hold it together now. I fall apart, knowing he'll catch the pieces.

Charlie brushes the tears away with his thumbs. "I almost told you last night, but I didn't want you to think … I want you to feel safe with me, Lili. But I don't want to hold you back. If living here, even part-time, isn't what you want—if I'm not who you want—that's okay. I just needed to tell you. Life is fucking short, and I wanted you to hear it."

He glances at the clock on the dashboard, and I do too. If I don't hurry, I'm going to miss my plane.

"I'll get your bags out of the boot."

His thumb brushes my cheek one last time, and then Charlie opens his door and climbs out.

I sniff, the shock starting to fade.

When I step out of the car, an airplane attendant is already wheeling my luggage away.

Charlie gathers me into his arms, then brushes a light kiss over my lips. "Let me know when you land, okay?"

He seriously thinks I'm going to just walk away after what he just told me.

Truly thinks there's a world in which I'm not devastatingly in love with him.

When he tries to pull away, I don't let him. I fist the fabric of his shirt so tightly that my knuckles protest.

"I love you, Charlie. So fucking much. It absolutely terrifies me how much I love you. How my life felt perfectly full until you walked off when Chloe called me and how I've thought about you ever since. How you're the person I want when I'm happy or hurt or scared or … always. I want you always. And I'll wait, however long it takes for you to sort things out, because I don't want anyone else."

I kiss him hard, then hurry toward the automatic doors.

# CHAPTER 42
## Charlie

**M**y mother looks shocked to discover me standing on her doorstep.

"Hi," I greet, grip temporarily tightening on the cup of coffee I'm holding. It was the only stop I made on my way here from the airport, wanting to get this conversation out of the way before surprising Lili.

I wasn't supposed to arrive until tomorrow. But I signed the last of the deal papers a day early, then got on the first plane to New York.

"*Charles*. I—" She glances past me. "What are you doing here?"

No *nice to see you*. No *what a wonderful surprise*.

*What are you doing here?*

"I'll explain," I say tersely. "Can I come in?"

"Oh! Uh, yes. Of course."

It's not really an *of course* though. She looks uncertain and

uncomfortable, fiddling with a pearl earring as she leads me into the sitting area located off the entryway.

It's never been an *of course* with my mother. *Maybe, possibly, we'll see, one day, perhaps.* Those are her most common responses when I ask her about calling Blythe or visiting England.

And I'm done capitulating to her. She made her decisions, and it's not my responsibility to make her reconsider walking away from us. It felt more important to maintain some connection with my lone living parent after my father died. Less so now.

He made lots of mistakes, but he didn't choose to leave us. She did. She *keeps* choosing to leave us, and I'm finished acting like that's acceptable.

"Derek's out at a breakfast meeting. Had I known you were coming, I would have—"

"I'm here to see you, Georgia. Not Derek."

My mother nods once, hands falling into her lap and folding. Posture perfect. She looks regal.

I have a flash of memory. Her seated in the upholstered dining chair at the opposite end of the table from my father. Ten chairs running the length between them. Blythe and I always had to choose ends. Sides.

"Granny had a stroke."

She pales. "Is Grace all right?"

"She's fine. She spent several days in the hospital and has been at home resting ever since."

More like entertaining. Last time I checked in with Elsie, she told me Gran has been hosting a revolving door of well-wishers. I haven't visited Gran in several weeks. I told her she needed to apologize to Lili for her cold treatment at the garden party before I returned for tea.

I'd never given Gran an ultimatum before, and I don't think she believed me at the time. I'm certain she does now.

"The doctors have her on blood thinners that should prevent it from happening again," I add.

Georgia nods. "She's tough."

My jaw flexes. "Blythe is too. But do you know what she said to me when I got to the hospital? 'She's all we have left, Charlie.'"

"Aging is just as difficult for family members as—"

"That's not the bloody point! The point is, she needed you. She needs you, and you've never been there. Not once!"

"She's welcome to visit anytime—"

I interrupt her again. "Blythe's never going to visit you, Georgia. *Never*. You're a stranger who abandoned her."

My mother flushes. "It was a … complicated situation, Charles."

"You think I don't know what Papa was like? You think Blythe doesn't? We know because we lived with him for *sixteen years* after you left! You think I couldn't tell that you were miserable, even when I was a kid? I could. Divorcing Papa was one thing. But abandoning me and Blythe was another."

She starts fiddling with her earring again. "He'd only give me the divorce if I gave up my parental rights. Your father didn't want you seeing me or visiting here, so he made sure I had no custody claim. My options were to leave alone or not at all."

I stare at her, wanting to dispute it. Tell her that she must have misunderstood, that my father would never do that.

Problem is, he would.

I'm not even surprised to hear that he did. My mom leaving was a betrayal. Even before she did, he controlled everything.

The schools Blythe and I attended, who we socialized with, what activities we participated in. I can't imagine him relinquishing any of that control for us to go on a vacation with the woman who chose to leave him.

But …

"Parental rights wouldn't have mattered once I turned eighteen. Where have you been for the past *eight years*, Georgia? Did you forget how old I was after missing all those birthdays? Blythe is twenty-one!"

Her hands drop to twist in her lap, no longer neatly folded. "I'm sorry, Charles. I didn't—I wasn't sure if you'd even want to hear from me after—"

"It's not about me *wanting* to hear from you. It's about you *choosing* to have no contact with us."

"I sent the invitation," she nearly whispers.

And that's the only reason we've talked since she left. She mailed a wedding invitation to Newcastle.

Blythe refused to attend. My father told me going was a mistake. But I couldn't shake the certainty that I'd regret missing it—for a wide range of reasons. Wanting to see what my mother was like, wanting to see if she was happy, wanting to be the bigger person. Then, my dad died, family was suddenly in shorter supply, and I agreed to visit her and her new husband the following summer. I kept indulging her, but it ends now.

Maybe that's obvious on my face because she says, "I made a lot of mistakes, Charles."

"Yeah, you did. Papa too. All he left me, aside from a title I don't want, was a mountain of debt."

It's a relief to say that. Say it to my mother, in particular. Despite her many shortcomings in the role, she knew my father. Knows what the role of duke is like. This news means more to her than most people and like something she should know.

For the first time since she opened the door, my mom looks truly shocked. "What? I don't understand what—"

"There's nothing to understand. His barristers sat me down after the funeral to tell me it was all gone, plus a lot of overdue payments. That's one of the main reasons I came to New York the past two summers. To talk to American investors, try to salvage what I could."

My mom tucks a piece of blonde hair behind one ear. "I'll talk to Derek, see what he—"

"No. I didn't come here for your help. It's been taken care of."

"Taken care of? What are you—"

I cut her off. "I came to tell you that I'll probably be in New York a lot more often. We'll likely run into each other at other events. But this is my last visit here. The last time I'm going to make an effort. Please give Derek my best."

She scrambles to her feet when I stand, confusion written all over her face. "I-I don't understand. What happened? Your other visits have been perfectly pleasant."

We have different definitions of *perfectly pleasant*, I guess.

"What happened? You decided you didn't want kids, Georgia, after you already had them. I'm just respecting that decision, the way I should have done all along."

"Charles …"

"I have to go."

I head for the door.

"It's Ellis's birthday tomorrow."

I don't turn around, but my steps stop. "I know it's his birthday tomorrow. I'm going to get dinner with him, his girlfriend, and the woman I'm going to marry. Because an inability to show up—to fucking care—isn't a family trait, apparently. Papa wasn't perfect, but he was there. He came to my rugby matches, and he bought Blythe gifts without me having to suggest it ten times. I used to worry I was too like him. Now, I'm just grateful I'm nothing like *you*."

I walk out the door without saying anything else, accepting it might be the last time I see my mother.

# CHAPTER 43

## *Lili*

My heels echo loudly on the marble floor as I walk into the entryway of my grandfather's mansion, Charlie's hand clasped between mine in the tightest grip possible. He shocked me, showing up in New York a day earlier than he was supposed to.

I shouldn't have been that surprised though. For someone who's never been in a relationship, he's as naturally good at it as he seems to be at everything else.

Since I left London two weeks ago, he called me every evening to ask about my day despite the time difference. He showed up on my doorstep with flowers because it's "tradition." And he didn't act the least bit bored when we spent hours this afternoon wandering through the botanical garden in Brooklyn despite undoubtedly being exhausted from an overnight flight and the several rounds of sex that followed his arrival at my apartment.

I glance at the portrait that hangs in the center of the marble staircase, just above the split in the steps, as I lead Charlie toward the sitting room. It's a painting of the original Kensington family—my grandfather, my grandmother, Oliver, and my dad. My grandfather has never taken it down, the way Charlie's father removed his mother's portraits. The diamond ring on my grandmother's hand is the same one Mom wears now, the diamond bracelet on her wrist the same one I'm wearing right now.

We're the last to arrive. In a remarkable show of self-restraint, Charlie only complained about the traffic twice on the drive here.

At least this is the last time he'll be visiting me in New York for a while. I accepted the job offer in Dublin and will be relocating to Ireland at the end of next week for several months. During that stretch, I'm anticipating most of my weekends will be spent in London. Charlie is moving back into a flat he owns there since he reenrolled in Oxford's medical school and it's a much more reasonable commute than living at Newcastle. It's unlikely I'll be back in New York until the holidays.

Ben and Jerry, the beagles my parents adopted, are first to greet us. They're not related, but they were found together. The shelter suggested they go to the same home, and Dad told me—with an eye roll—Mom demanded the same.

Unsurprisingly, he's now the one who insists they come everywhere with my parents.

I squat to pet Ben, who happily flops on his back for a belly rub. Jerry is more reserved, sniffing at Charlie's shoes.

"You're late," Kit drawls.

I give Ben one final pat, then straighten. "Did Mom tell you six thirty instead of seven thirty? That's the only explanation for why you're here on time."

Bash laughs, slouched in the armchair next to the fireplace.

"We're just glad you made it," Mom says, playing the role of peacemaker as she approaches. "It's so good to see you, Charlie."

"You too, Scarlett."

He gives my mom a hug, and then she squeezes me.

"I told Kit seven," she whispers to me.

My dad walks toward us next, both beagles racing toward him. Most people who know my father would probably assume it's because he's the pack leader, but I'm certain it's because he feeds them more treats than my mom does.

He smiles down at the dogs before offering a hand to Charlie. "Welcome back to New York."

"Thank you. It's nice to be back."

They share a long look that I hold my breath during.

I know Charlie has met my father before—I know Dad likes him because he told me so—but this is the first time my family is meeting Charlie as my boyfriend. The only other guy they've met in that capacity was Cal, and that was under very different circumstances. My parents knew his parents. My grandfather knew his grandparents. He'd spent years around my family as my friend, so the transition to more—while not entirely smooth—was fairly easy.

Charlie's different in every way.

My brothers stand to greet us next, and my grandfather is the last.

Grandpa gives me a hug while Bash tells Charlie about the grizzly bear he saw in Alaska, pulling out his phone to share photos.

"You look happy, Lili," he tells me after dropping a kiss to the top of my head.

"I am," I reply.

I sneak a glance at Charlie, who's asking Kit about work. Kit's now an official employee at Kensington Consolidated and seems more enthused about the job since he's actually started there. I suspect his assistant has something to do with it.

"Excited about your trip to Ireland?" Grandpa asks.

"Very," I tell him. "You should come visit with Mom and Dad."

They're planning to visit Dublin in October.

"I would like that," he responds, which is a surprise.

I was expecting a kind but firm *no*. He and Dad don't really spend extended time together, alone.

I glance at Charlie, talking with my brothers again, and this time, Grandpa follows my gaze.

My parents are busy trying to keep their spoiled dogs off the furniture.

"I had the chef prepare all your favorites tonight. Seems like this will be our last family dinner for a while."

"It's only three months, Grandpa."

He smiles, and it's a bittersweet one. "I wasn't talking about your time in Ireland. Even after that project ends, it seems like you'll have a new home."

I blush. "I know it's not—we haven't been dating for very long, so …"

I'm expecting some caution. A reminder to not grow up too fast or not to get too attached to a new relationship.

Grandpa's smile is sentimental. "I knew your grandmother was *the one* the day I met her. Based on how many times you've looked at that boy in the last minute, you feel the same way."

I peek at Charlie again, catching him staring at me this time.

He winks when our eyes make contact, and it sets off a flurry of butterflies in my stomach.

I know him.

I love him.

But I still get giddy when he looks at me.

"Yeah," I tell Grandpa, "I do."

# EPILOGUE
## Charlie

Lili's wide awake, staring at the ceiling with headphones on, when my eyes open.

She smiles when she sees I'm conscious, slipping the headphones off. I catch the distant drone of the narrator's voice before she tosses the headphones away. "Morning."

"Morning." I roll so I'm hovering over her, planting a kiss on the hollow of her throat. "You're up early."

Lili moans softly as my mouth moves lower, her chest lifting and her hands sliding into my hair.

"What were you listening to?" I ask, playing with the strap of the nightgown she's wearing. I swear she buys these just to drive me insane. They don't really cover anything, and they definitely don't keep her warm.

My hand slides lower, cupping the heavy weight of her breast.

Lili gasps. "Honestly? Can't remember."

I chuckle. "Sounds riveting."

"*Charlie.*"

"Yeah?" I'm distracted, more focused on sliding my hand down her side and then bunching up her lacy slip.

"My parents." Gasp. "Your grandmother." Sigh. "Chloe and Theo." Groan. "My brothers." Pant. "Your sister."

I'm already sinking inside of her. "Can't you be quiet, love?"

Lili glowers at my smirk. Because we both know she's never ever quiet. Very vocal about her love of my cock actually.

She stayed up later than I did last night, visiting with her best friend and her mom, so I didn't get to do this before bed. I'm surprised I managed to fall asleep without my favorite evening ritual.

I fuck her slow, kissing her in an attempt to swallow the needy moans filling our bedroom and trying to remember what room Conrad put her parents in. I should have suggested they stay in the other wing. I think Crew likes me—at least, he gave me permission to offer Lili the engagement ring hidden in the one corner of my closet her clothes haven't overtaken—and I'd like it to stay that way.

Lili arches her back, breaking our kiss as her nails dig hard into my back. Her pussy clenches around me, trying to hold my cock inside of her. Trying to pull it deeper.

"*So good,*" she breathes, hips rocking against mine.

I lace our fingers together and hold our joined hands above her head. Heat is licking up my spine, and I'm rapidly reaching the point where I don't care who is listening or how they're related to her.

Our lips brush together again, and then I bite her lower one.

She whimpers, fighting my hold on her hands. "I want to touch you."

I pound into her harder, the mattress sinking under our

combined weight. "Just take it, baby. You take me so fucking well."

I lost track of the times we've had sex a long time ago. But it's still as addictive as the first hit of her was.

Lili relaxes her arms, her cheek rolling against the pillow and her lips parting as her wet cunt flutters around me.

"More," she demands, bucking up against me. Her pebbled nipples rub against my chest.

"I'm not bloody stopping," I assure her, reaching between our bodies and finding the place where she's stretched around me. Trace the taut, slick skin and then find the swollen bud of her clit. Pinch it.

Lili comes with a cry I'm slow to smother, her grip on my fingers so tight that she's cutting off circulation at the same time her tight pussy strangles my cock.

My climax goes on and on. My breathing is still heavy when I pull out and lie down beside her.

Lili doesn't move. I tug her hand down with mine, our connected fingers draped against the rapid rise and fall of her chest. Brush a kiss against her temple.

She sighs contentedly, then glances at me. Her cheeks burn. "We were *really* loud."

"We can work on being quieter tonight," I suggest.

She shoves me. "You're not getting laid until everyone leaves."

"Sure," I say, unconcerned, as I climb out of bed.

"I mean it, Charlie."

"Fine. Then, I'll kick everyone out after the party."

Lili throws a pillow at me. It bounces harmlessly off the armchair ten feet away from the bathroom door.

"You missed," I say cheerfully before shutting the door behind me.

It doesn't block the sound of her huff.

Chloe and Theo are the only ones downstairs when I enter the dining room.

My graduation from medical school was yesterday afternoon. All of our American visitors flew in yesterday morning, and I'm sure they're all fighting a serious case of jet lag this morning.

I should have mentioned that to Lili. Maybe I could have talked her into a second round in the shower.

"Morning," I say, grabbing a scone and taking my usual seat at the head of the table.

Theo looks up from the newspaper he's reading. "Good morning."

"No one else is up yet?"

"Just us," Chloe replies. "We *tried* to sleep in, but the walls in this place are kind of thin."

Lili chooses this moment to walk into the dining room. Shoots me a dirty look.

Theo fails at hiding his smile behind his paper.

"I'm going to take a quick ride," I say, then swallow a bite of scone.

It's been more than a week since I last rode Kensington. Over a month since I last visited my father's grave. Life has been extra hectic lately. I was studying for and then taking my final examinations. Lili was working on a project in Scotland. Blythe spent a few days here before traveling to London to see her friends. She lives in New York now, working as a fashion blogger for *Haute*.

Lili nods. I give her a kiss, wave at Theo and Chloe, then head for the stables.

Kensington greets me with a soft nicker. Blows out his belly when I tighten his girth. Ambles good-naturedly toward the mounting block.

I don't press the pace, enjoying the blue skies and the familiar scenery. It's a beautiful day.

Ten minutes later, I reach the cemetery.

Except … it looks nothing like it.

I dismount from Kensington. He yanks the reins from my limp hand, stealing a chance for unrestricted grass access.

And just … stare.

Until I hear the sound of approaching hoofbeats.

"I figured this was where you were heading." Lili swings down from Gilbert's saddle, letting him join a grazing Kensington.

She walks over, grabbing my left hand with both of hers and resting her cheek against my bicep.

I swallow thickly. "I can't believe you did this."

"Do you like it?"

There's hesitancy in her voice I'm surprised to hear, unsure how she could think I wouldn't.

"I love it. I love *you*." I kiss the top of her head, then look straight back at the graveyard to admire it again.

The stone wall is still here, but it's unrecognizable. There's a wooden archway over the opening in the piled rocks, blooming greenery beginning to climb over it. I spot the familiar shape of ivy. Smell the fragrance of the wild roses.

Purple bushes stand on either side of the archway while a mix of red, pink, and yellow tulips runs the entire length of the wall in both directions.

It's beautiful. All of it.

The grayness of graves and rocks doesn't look depressing amid the brilliant spray of color.

It's the kind of final resting place I wanted to give my father but was too overwhelmed and confused and *angry* to pursue it three years ago.

"It won't look like this in the winter," Lili tells me. "I can plant some evergreens and put in a box hedge. But all the flowers are perennials, so they should—"

I cut her off with a kiss, crushing her against me so quickly that she stumbles.

"Marry me."

Lili blanches, then releases a surprised huff. "Most clients just offer me a bonus if they're really happy with a project."

I smile. She does too.

And then our mutual amusement fades as we stare at each other, the moment gaining a new weight.

This isn't how I intended to ask her, right by a cemetery with the ring I bought her back at the house. Just like I hadn't planned to tell Lili I loved her right outside an airport.

But maybe that's how you know you found the right person. When it doesn't really matter where you are, and the words just won't stay inside any longer.

I was waiting to propose until I was finished with medical school, until our busy lives felt a little more settled.

I suddenly want—need—her to know I want to marry her, even if she doesn't walk down the aisle toward me for another fifty years.

"You're … serious?"

I nod. "So serious that I asked your dad." A conversation I stressed over for weeks. I even called Ellis and had him pretend to be Crew so I could run through what I planned to say. "And there's a ring hidden in the little bit of the closet I have left."

She rolls her eyes. "You *told* me to move all my clothes here."

"I know."

She didn't move them all *here* though. She still has her penthouse in New York, which I know for a fact has full closets. She's also left plenty of clothes at the London flat, where I've lived for most of the past two years. Honestly, I couldn't care less, but it's fun to tease Lili about her clothing collection. Kit does the same thing.

I tighten my grip on her hips, looking straight into her eyes. More red rushes to her cheeks, the longer I stare, but she doesn't break eye contact.

"This wasn't where I was planning to ask you. But I've been planning to ask you—knowing I would ask you—for a long time." I ghost my lips along hers, and Lili shivers. "Marry me, Elizabeth Josephine Kensington."

Lili bites her bottom lip before she nods. "Yes," she tells me. "Yes, I'll marry you."

I can't talk right away. This moment—this massive moment, where the person I want to spend the rest of my life with has agreed to spend the rest of her life with me—feels like it's expanded around me, blocking any words from coming out. Nothing seems like enough.

For the third time, I witness Lili cry.

"I love you so much," she sobs, burying her face in my chest.

I wrap my arms around her, holding her as tight as I can. Kiss the top of her head and murmur, "I love you," into her hair.

For a few blissful minutes, it feels like we're the only two people in the world, savoring the perfect bubble around us.

I only let go of her to walk over to my father's grave. Crouch down and brush a stray leaf off the top of the thick stone.

I wish he had been there yesterday to see me graduate. I wore the stethoscope he never got to give me, and I'd like to think he knows that.

I wish he could be at my wedding.

But today would look very different if he were still alive. Maybe things happen for a reason, as bloody awful as they are to accept at the time.

"Happy birthday, Papa."

I stand, then walk back toward Lili. She squeezes my hand before mounting Gilbert.

We ride back toward Newcastle Hall in sweet silence, stealing glances at each other like love-drunk teenagers.

Figures are visible out in the gardens as we ride nearer. Martha's been cooking for days in preparation of today's party.

After I graduated from Oxford with my undergraduate degree, Papa, Blythe, Granny, and I all went to Le Cinq, one of London's fanciest restaurants.

If you'd asked me then, I'd have said that my future graduation from medical school would look the same. The four of us and a four-course meal.

Six years later, I've lost a lot.

My father.

Large chunks of the legacy I thought I'd inherit.

But there's a growing crowd in the gardens—we were gone for longer than I'd realized—all of them here to celebrate this accomplishment with me.

The Kensington family, who flew all the way from New York

to be here. Chloe and Theo drove up from London. Fig's arrived, standing *right* next to Blythe, which makes me frown and decide to have a talk with him later. Gran is sitting at the metal table, sipping on tea as she talks to a beaming Elsie. My mom sent a card, which arrived two days ago.

And then there's Lili, looking at the gardens, not noticing my attention has drifted to her.

Dark hair blowing wild around her flushed face as she rides alongside me, following the same path that my father and I often went on. Where he'd lecture about duty and reputation and respectability, preparing me for the role I'd inherit.

It all felt false after he died. Maybe before then too. Arbitrary and meaningless.

I continue to stare at Lili, and nothing about my life feels false.

"I was talking about you," I tell her.

She glances my way, fighting with the wind for control of her hair. "What?"

"When I said 'Beautiful,' I was talking about you."

Her smile expands when she realizes exactly what I'm talking about, her blue eyes as captivating as they were the first time I saw her. I'll always consider her the most beautiful woman in the world.

But when I look at her now, *beautiful* is no longer the first word that comes to mind.

She looks like the one word I wrote on her once, back when I thought she never would be.

*Mine.*

## The End

# Acknowledgments

As soon as I finished the scene in *Fake Empire* where Crew meets his daughter, I knew that I would write Elizabeth Kensington a book. I wasn't sure when, or what the plot would be, but I was certain there was a compelling story to be told. Not only because I adore crafting strong female characters (and Lili is undoubtedly Scarlett's daughter) but because it felt like the perfect way to revisit the glamorous, glitzy Kensington world from a fresh perspective. Oliver and Hannah get their happy ending in *Real Regrets*, but it didn't strike me as a full-circle moment for the entire family, particularly Arthur. His dynamic with Lili influenced some of my favorite scenes. You'll see more of the Kensington patriarch, and many more familiar faces, in Kit, Bash, Rory, and Wren's books!

Mel, I was so nervous to share my first second-generation book with someone. It was incredibly important to me to do Lili's story justice, and I couldn't have passed it off into better hands. This book is infinitely better for your feedback and suggestions. Thank you for being such a bright spot during the most stressful stage of the writing process.

Jovana, it is always a relief to send you a manuscript knowing it will come back polished and refined. You go above and beyond with your attention to detail and accuracy. I am so grateful for your expertise. Your edits not only improve my books, they also make me a better writer.

Britt, I am never more excited to open a manuscript than when you send it back. You are every author's dream to work with—detailed input mixed with hilarious commentary. My cheeks hurt from smiling after reviewing this one.

Alison, thank you for such a thorough final pass. You can never have too many sets of eyes on a manuscript, and I'm so appreciative of your careful review. It's always a pleasure to work with you.

The team at Books and Moods, thank you for this gorgeous cover. It's everything I was hoping for and more, and captures Lili's and Charlie's story so perfectly.

Valentine, Tiffany, Kim, Christine, Ratula, and the entire team at Valentine PR, thank you for taking care of so much behind the scenes and allowing me to focus on writing.

Shane East and Mackenzie Cartwright, thank you for bringing Charlie and Lili to life. Katie Robinson and the whole team at Lyric Audiobooks, you could not make the production process any smoother. Thank you for all of your hard work.

All the bookstagrammers, bloggers, booktubers, and booktokers who take the time to read, review, and share my stories, thank you. I am so honored and appreciative of your support.

My family and friends, thank you for your endless love and encouragement. It took more than a few missed events and several all-nighters to finish this on time. Thank you for your patience and understanding about my very unorthodox work hours.

Last but certainly not least, my readers. You are the only reason I wake up each morning and get to write. That is a gift I will never take for granted. Thank you for reading.

# About the Author

C.W. Farnsworth is the author of numerous adult and young adult romance novels featuring sports, strong female leads, and happy endings.

Charlotte lives in Rhode Island and when she isn't writing spends her free time reading, at the beach, or snuggling with her Australian Shepherd.

Find her on Facebook (@cwfarnsworth), TikTok (@authorcwfarnsworth), Instagram (@authorcwfarnsworth) and check out her website www.authorcwfarnsworth.com for news about upcoming releases!

# Also by C.W. Farnsworth

**Standalones**

*Four Months, Three Words*

*Come Break My Heart Again*

*Winning Mr. Wrong*

*Back Where We Began*

*Like I Never Said*

*Fly Bye*

*Serve*

*Heartbreak for Two*

*Pretty Ugly Promises*

*Six Summers to Fall*

*King of Country*


**Rival Love**

*Kiss Now, Lie Later*

*For Now, Not Forever*


**The Kensingtons**

*Fake Empire*

*Real Regrets*

*False God*


**Truth & Lies**

*Friday Night Lies*

*Tuesday Night Truths*

**Kluvberg**
*First Flight, Final Fall*
*All The Wrong Plays*

**Holt Hockey**
*Famous Last Words*
*Against All Odds*
*From Now On*